D0053087

Angela Thirkell

Angela Thirkell, granddaughter of Edward Burne-Jones, was born in London in 1890. At the age of twenty-eight she moved to Melbourne, Australia where she became involved in broadcasting and was a frequent contributor to the British periodicals. Mrs. Thirkell did not begin writing novels until her return to Britain in 1930; then, for the rest of her life, she produced a new book almost every year. Her stylish prose and deft portrayal of the human comedy in the imaginary county of Barsetshire have amused readers for decades. She died in 1961, just before her seventy-first birthday.

"[Thirkell's] satire is always just, apt, kindly, and pleasantly rambly. Blended in with the satire, too, are all the pleasures of an escapist romance."
— *New York Herald Tribune*

"The happy outcome of her tale is secondary to the crisp, often quaint amusement one derives from discovering how deftly Angela Thirkell makes the most unexciting incident appear important."
— *Saturday Review of Literature*

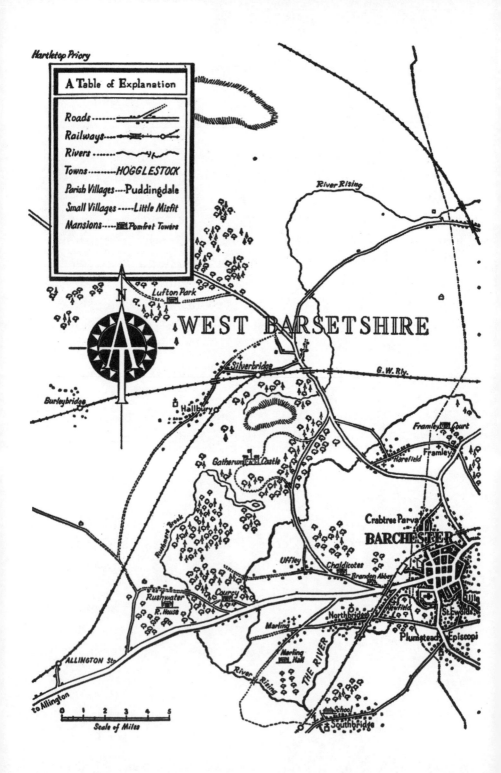

Hartletop Priory

A Table of Explanation

Roads	
Railways	
Rivers	
Towns	HOGGLESTOCK
Parish Villages	Puddingdale
Small Villages	Little Misfit
Mansions	Pomfret Towers

N

WEST BARSETSHIRE

Lufton Park

Silverbridge

G.W. Rly.

Burleybridge

Hallbury

Gatherum Castle

Framley Court

Harefield

Framley

Crabtree Parva

BARCHESTER

Rushmere Brook

Uffley

Chaldicotes

Brandon Abbey

Rushwater

R. House

Courcy

Northbridge

Harefield

St. Ewolds

Plumstead Episcopi

Marling

ALLINGTON St.

Marling Hall

to Allington

River Rising

THE RIVER

School

Southbridge

0 1 2 3 4 5

Scale of Miles

River Rising

A Map of the County of

BARSETSHIRE

Shewing the Situations of the
various great Estates and Seats

Other books by Angela Thirkell

A Double Affair

A Novel by

Angela Thirkell

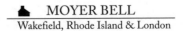

MOYER BELL

Wakefield, Rhode Island & London

Published by Moyer Bell
This Edition 2000

Copyright © 1957 by Angela Thirkell
Published by arrangement with Hamish Hamilton, Ltd.

All rights reserved. No part of this publication may be repro-
duced or transmitted in any form or by any means, electronic or
mechanical, including photocopying, recording or any information retrieval system, without permission in writing from
Moyer Bell, Kymbolde Way, Wakefield, Rhode Island 02879
or 112 Sydney Road, Muswell Hill, London N10 2RN.

LIBRARY OF CONGRESS
CATALOGING-IN-PUBLICATION DATA

Thirkell, Angela Mackail, 1890–1961.
    A Double Affair : a novel by
Angela Thirkell. — 1st ed.
        p.   cm.
    ISBN 1-55921-249-7
    I. Title.
    PR6039.H43043
    823'.912—dc21   97-3797
                                              CIP

Cover illustration:
Marguerite Moreno
by Joseph Granié

Printed in the United States of America
Distributed in North America by Publishers Group West, 1700 Fourth
Street, Berkeley, CA 94710, 800-788-3123 (in California 510-528-1444).

A DOUBLE AFFAIR

CHAPTER I

Unpleasant, not to say ominous, news from every part of the world was for a time almost entirely forgotten, or ignored, by much of Barsetshire, owing to the overriding interest in a marriage arranged, as *The Thunderer* puts it (though who arranges the marriages we do not know), between the Reverend Herbert Choyce, M.A., Vicar of Hatch End, and Dorothea Frances Merriman, whose Christian names had long been almost forgotten, buried in the affectionate "Merry" which all her friends and employers used. Miss Merriman had for a long time been secretary and friend to Lady Emily Leslie at Rushwater and had then been with her all through the war, in the house of her daughter Lady Graham. After her death she had presently gone to be friend and helper to Lord and Lady Pomfret at the Towers, which was in a way a home to her, for there she had formerly been secretary and friend to old Lady Pomfret for some years. Sometimes she felt a wish for an abiding place of her own, but she put her duty first and in any case had nowhere particular to go, as her parents were long since dead and her married and only sister though friendly was not interested. Then, while she was on a visit to Lady Graham, she and Mr. Choyce had become quietly and happily engaged. It was agreed by both of them that the marriage should not be hurried. Mr. Choyce had arranged a temporary exchange of pulpits with an old friend and did not wish to disturb this arrangement. The vicarage was in need of some repairing and redecorating. The one serious difficulty was Miss Merriman's strong feeling that the Pomfrets must not be left without a good secretary, and we think the marriage might almost have fallen through had it not been for Mrs. Belton at Harefield, a connection of the Pomfrets through the old Barsetshire family of Thorne. The Harefield solicitor, Mr. Updike, had a daughter with a first-class war record, used to posts of responsibility and at the moment out of a job. Mrs. Belton had told Lady Pomfret about her. She had gone to the Towers for an interview; both sides were pleased and within a few weeks she was established almost as an old retainer.

Miss Merriman found herself absorbed again in the routine at Holdings and it seemed to the county that things might go on like this forever. But the calm was broken by *The Thunderer*'s paragraph in the Court Circular Column, put in and paid for by Lady Graham, who had constituted herself a Matron or Duenna of Honour while Miss Merriman, in a kind of enjoyable delirium and a feeling of "Lawk-a-mercy-on-me, This is none of I," was carried along on the tide. The whole of Barsetshire, or at any rate West Barsetshire, was agog, and so many wedding presents were sent that Lady Graham saw she would have to turn her large drawing-room, known as The Saloon, into a show room: which, we may say, she was delighted to do.

"Now, Merry dear," said Lady Graham, "you want a *real* rest. If you will unpack the wedding presents, I will arrange them. I shall have those collapsible tables put up and some of the stands from the potting sheds on them—the ones like steps."

Miss Merriman asked why the stands.

"Because you are bound to have an enormous number of presents, Merry dear," said her ladyship. "All your friends and all my friends and darling Mamma's old friends and the Pomfrets' friends and everyone in the village and a lot of the Close—oh! and the Dean wants to marry you and I thought I would ask Canon Bostock from Rushwater to be the other clergyman, because he knew darling Mamma. And of course the wedding reception will be here. How Mamma would have loved it all and how she would have interfered," and Miss Merriman thought how Lady Graham was becoming more and more like, in many ways, her beloved mother, Lady Emily Leslie, Miss Merriman's friend and employer for so many years.

So Miss Merriman unpacked the wedding presents and carefully kept the cards that came with them so that (a) she could write thank you letters for them all and (b) could put each card with its affectionate or friendly message on the present for exhibition. Lady Graham, whose calm was seldom ruffled, became almost excited at the number and quality of the gifts, which varied from a complete dinner set (Lord and Lady Pomfret) to an original and extremely bad drawing of Holdings by the village artist, Mr. Scatcherd, and included other gifts mostly of a high level. Sir Robert Graham had given Miss Merriman a munificent cheque for clothes, which agitated her a good deal, for she liked to dress in her own quiet (and becoming) way. He also expressed a wish, tantamount to a command, to give the bride away and, much to the joy of Hatch End, Mr. Gresham from East Barsetshire announced that he would like to be best man. No one knew why and we doubt if Mr. Gresham did, but there was a strong suspicion that Lord Crosse at Crosse Hall had something to do with it.

The universally disliked Sir Ogilvy Hibberd, now disguised as Lord Aberfordbury, a name which no one could ever remember, was luckily abroad on a mission to Mixo-Lydia and could therefore safely be invited. And as the mission was to promote good feeling between Mixo-Lydia and Slavo-Lydia, it would have taken someone far better informed than Lord Aberfordbury to disentangle the secular ill-feeling of those revolting nations, besides the fact that both countries liked nothing better than to maim each other's cattle and burn each other's villages and were likely to resent deeply any attempt at interference with their ancestral customs and probably would have summoned the intervening powers before one of those well-meaning bodies of irresponsible meddlers who are only known by their initials, whereas the words which the initials represent are entirely unidentified by the general public.

The wedding date was fixed for the week after Easter at the village church. Sir Robert Graham, who had come to consider himself (on no grounds at all except non-interference) as the fountain and source of the whole affair, had, as vicar's church-warden and even more as himself, arranged the ordering of the service with the Dean of Barchester, who had expressed his desire to perform the ceremony and was to be assisted by Canon Bostock, Vicar of Rushwater in the later years of Miss Merri-man's loved employer Lady Emily Leslie.

"Robert thought," said Lady Graham to Miss Merriman while they were having lunch together alone, "that you would like Canon Bostock to be there because of darling Mamma. Why it takes two clergymen to make a marriage I don't know. Robert and I had three, but that was in London because Papa had taken a house for the season, so he said we might as well have the reception there. And we *must* have a little talk about your wedding dress, Merry."

This was the moment Miss Merriman had dreaded. She could not bear to seem ungrateful to Lady Graham—it would be almost like insulting the memory of Lady Emily Leslie—but to go up the aisle (and even worse down it again) dressed in white, would be more than she could bear. Indeed the thought of white sat as a spectre before her a great deal. But before she could say anything, Lady Graham went smoothly on, "I didn't want to bother you, Merry dear, so when I was in town, I went to Madame Sartoria."

"But she is your London dressmaker, Lady Graham," said Miss Merriman, feeling like the hare who hears the voices of the hounds from his (or her) lair.

"She dressed Emmy and Clarissa so beautifully for Lucy Marling's wedding to Mr. Adams," said Lady Graham, "that I knew she would understand. I want you to give your opinion."

While Lady Graham spoke, Miss Merriman's heart had been sinking steadily. She was going to be dressed as a bride for her own wedding and would not only look like mutton dressed as lamb, but most certainly also feel like it. As Lady Graham had left the room on her charitable errand, Miss Merriman had a full five minutes in which to make up her mind to tell her that she could not marry under such circumstances, to tell Mr. Choyce that she loved him devotedly but could not possibly be his bride in public, and to retire to live with her sister who didn't want her to come any more than she wanted to go. And all this depressed her so much that she hardly noticed Lady Graham's return with an armful of something wrapped in a white sheet.

"And I hope you will like it, Merry dear," said Lady Graham.

Much as Miss Merriman would have liked to shut her eyes, she was obliged in common courtesy to look. On her arm Lady Graham held a grey dress of most delicate material, soft yet strong, falling in lovely folds, inclining more to a pinky grey than a slaty grey, long sleeves, a high neck with a very slight V in front, and a full skirt neither too short nor too long.

"I thought you would like it," said Lady Graham, deliberately not noticing Miss Merriman's trembling lips. "The silk belonged to darling Mamma. She meant to wear it but never had it made up and it has been at Madame Sartoria's all these years. She remembered it and brought it out when I went to see her. She said you wouldn't need a fitting because you had so often come to her shop with one of the girls and I am sure you can trust her. She said: '*Je connais par coeur le corps de Mademoiselle Mérimanne.*' It is a present to you from darling Mamma."

At these words Miss Merriman began to cry quite openly.

"You will look delightful in it," her ladyship went on, ignoring Miss Merriman's tears, "and it will do beautifully for a dinner dress afterwards. There is a grey tulle veil with a little band of dull silver, and grey nylon gloves. I thought they would be better than grey suede. And the bag is grey satin, very soft, and I got you some silver shoes—*not* sandals."

At these thoughtful words Miss Merriman cried again.

"Mamma would have loved to give them to you. Don't cry," said Lady Graham. "You must cheer up and have a drink of water."

She was longing to suggest champagne but felt it might somehow disagree with Miss Merriman's principles at so early an hour when, to her eternal surprise, Miss Merriman lifted a tear-blotched face and asked if she could have some brandy. This Lady Graham was delighted to supply, and after a small wineglass of the refreshing fluid Miss Merriman was herself again.

"Father didn't like us to drink anything," said Miss Merriman, "but I did have brandy when I was ill and I liked it. Mr. Choyce always has a bottle in the dining-room. He says he learnt to have it handy in the blitz."

"Quite right," said Lady Graham. "And now there is just one more thing," and she laid a rather shabby blue velvet case on the table and opened it.

"But those are—I mean were—Lady Emily's pearls," said Miss Merriman. "Not her pearls for big parties. She wore them when we went abroad and her other jewels had gone to the bank. I haven't seen them for a long time."

"Because they were at the bank," said Lady Graham. "They were left to me and I want to give them to you because you loved darling Mamma," at which point both the ladies cried, most enjoyably.

"Will you put them in your room," said Lady Graham, "for your wedding day. I have had forty acceptances so far. Of course only a small wedding."

Miss Merriman looked puzzled. Then she realized that as Lady Graham was arranging the wedding she was, not unnaturally, asking many of her own friends. But if she, Miss Merriman, had been left to herself, how many friends of her own would she have asked? And the answer was easy: hardly any at all, for almost all the friends had come to her through the Leslies and the Grahams.

"We can manage the wedding party in the Saloon if it is wet," said Lady Graham. "Robert likes it to be used. And while we are about it, where are you spending your honeymoon, Merry?" at which Miss Merriman had to confess that beyond a visit to Liverpool to see her husband's former parish they had no ideas at all.

"Mrs. Morland rang me up this morning," said Lady Graham. "She is going on a visit to Crosse Hall straight from the wedding reception and begs that you will use her house at High Rising if it suits you. Ask Mr. Choyce and let me know."

Then, feeling that she had done quite enough for the present, she sent Miss Merriman away to rest, rang up Mr. Choyce, and told him that Miss Merriman would be dining alone that evening and it would do her good if Mr. Choyce could join her, as she was rather tired by the wedding preparations. Also that Mrs. Morland had offered the house at High Rising with her excellent cook-housekeeper and hoped that Mr. Choyce and Miss Merriman would use it for a few days' rest before going to Liverpool. For all of which Mr. Choyce expressed his gratitude to Lady Graham and asked after his affianced. Lady Graham said As well as could be expected and was rewarded by a laugh at the other end. A very happy laugh.

There was, from Lady Graham's point of view, only one drawback to the wedding. Her difficult Edith, who had gone on a long visit to her Pomfret cousins at the Towers, with the avowed object of attending daily an estate management college in Barchester so that she could help her father with his place, had been invited by her uncle David Leslie and his wife to visit them in America after Christmas. The Pomfrets, though quite fond of her, seemed perfectly resigned to losing her, so off she had gone by air at her Uncle David's expense and was apparently enjoying herself enormously. Lady Graham, who still considered that no girl's education was complete without a London

Season, was rather against it, but Sir Robert said if the girl couldn't stick to the job she had chosen she might as well go where she wished. There is no doubt that both her parents would have preferred her to go through with the course she had begun, but the youngest of a family is apt to get its way. Youth must be served: and now if it is not served it slams the door and serves itself.

An early date was fixed for Miss Merriman's farewell visit to the Towers. Lady Pomfret would send for her and return her and Miss Merriman would also be able to give—or refrain from giving, whichever seemed the more useful—some help to the secretary, Miss Updike, about the work she was doing. The car from the Towers came punctually after lunch, and Miss Merriman was carried away.

Anyone driving up to the Towers, the hideous mid-Victorian seat of the Pomfrets, would have been pleasantly struck by the prosperous appearance of the park, and though one might deprecate the New Look of the drive, which always used to be gravelled and kept one or two men at work on the surface and the wide smooth-shaven verges throughout the year and was now covered with some sort of concrete from end to end, it was delightful to see that the trees in the park were being tactfully looked after and a number of cheerful young saplings planted and tied to sticks to replace the giants that had decayed till they had to be felled, so dangerous had they become. The large basin which traffic had to circle had been lately cleaned. The stone was white, and several of the rather uninteresting anonymous stone deities who pretended to support the great central urn from which water poured ceaselessly into the pond had new noses and fingers—still rather too clean to match their weather-beaten complexions, but time would cure that. Only one thing was missing. The jet which used to rise high from a conch, precariously supported by a poor relation of the Triton family, was not sending its silvery column aloft.

Much as Miss Merriman always missed in her mind her daily

meeting with Mr. Choyce, she could not help feeling pleasure as the car stopped at the side door (for the front entrance with the great double ramp leading up to it was not used now) and there was Lady Pomfret waiting to receive her. On the previous evening Lady Pomfret, speaking with her husband about Miss Merriman's coming visit, had said that as far as she knew no one had ever kissed Miss Merriman, although she was such an old and valued friend of the family. Not even the children, she added, though they were all very fond of her.

"One just didn't kiss her," said Lord Pomfret thoughtfully. "When I told her you had said you would marry me, Sally, she was so pleased that I thought she was going to kiss me. But she didn't. Too much kissing now, don't you think, Sally?"

Lady Pomfret was inclined to agree with him, but said that as all Ludo's and Emily's young friends seemed to kiss people without noticing that they were doing it, she didn't think it would do any harm, and would probably vanish, as all fashions do. Lord Pomfret, amused, said what about Giles.

"Do you *never* notice your own children, darling?" said Lady Pomfret, a little reproachfully, yet with a kind of pride in everything her husband did. "He kisses all the old women in the village and they adore it, but he is terrified of girls. He'll get over it."

"Yes, I suppose so," said Lord Pomfret. "Though I admit I did not kiss old women in cottages, or young women either. In fact no one till I met you, Sally. I don't count Rosina."

"And who on earth is Rosina?" said his countess, curious but quite unmoved by his confession.

"One of my best friends," said Lord Pomfret. "She was cook and everything else in the house my father had in Italy and she looked after it when he was in England. She was rather kind to me when I was a boy. I think she was sorry for me not having a mother. She married the inn-keeper's son and has twelve children. I believe I'm godfather to one of them, but I couldn't get out to the christening, so the Sindaco, a sort of Mayor, took my place. I rather think he was the baby's father."

"Gillie! you never told me that before," said his wife indignantly. "Did they call the baby Gillie? Or I suppose it would be Giglio."

"Certainly not," said Lord Pomfret. "They called it Antonio after the local poacher. I daresay he was its father too. You never know. It's time to go to bed."

Now Miss Merriman's suitcase had been taken upstairs and there was Miss Merriman in the Countess's sitting-room, looking just like herself and somehow bringing into the room a safe, comfortable ordinariness. Rosina, the Sindaco, and the local poacher were all far away while the Pomfrets asked about the preparations for the wedding and Miss Merriman asked for news of the Pomfrets' children and whether the fox that ran to earth in Hamaker Spinney had been found, for his fame had spread as far as Holdings.

Lord Pomfret said there was no news of him, but rumour had it that he had gone over to East Barsetshire where Mr. Gresham was M.F.H. and was considered in the fox world to give a fellow a better run for his money than the West Barsetshire Hunt.

While Lord Pomfret was speaking Miss Merriman had a curious impression that he had at last grown up. Not that he had ever been a very young Young Man, for responsibilities had come to him early, but he was now speaking as a peer who was respected in the House of Lords and as a landowner who knew and accepted responsibility. In earlier days it had grieved Miss Merriman to see how his strength was always being used up to the last ounce by his zeal in everything he did. Now he was firmly in the saddle and if spared would be able to carry on the landowner's tradition of doing the best you can for your own land and your own people and so for the county and therefore, also, for England.

Miss Merriman asked after the children, but they were all

away: Lord Mellings doing well at Sandhurst, Lady Emily still at school, and the Honourable Giles Foster preparing to spend the Easter holidays at a kind of Super-Scout-Camp where his loving parents hoped he would meet his match and come home slightly less pleased with himself. And so the talk continued, about families and the estate.

"There is one thing I would like to ask," said Miss Merriman. "Would Miss Updike like any help or suggestions from me? Is she here, by the way? And I forgot to ask about Edith. I do hope she is being good."

Lady Pomfret said Miss Updike had gone to Barchester for the day and was looking forward to seeing Miss Merriman very much.

"I think it was tact," said Lady Pomfret. "Miss Updike thought you might like to be alone with us for a bit as it is only for one night. She is fitting in very well," which last words she said as carelessly as possible, lest Miss Merriman should feel a little sad that her place was so soon and competently filled. But when she heard Miss Merriman's true and heartfelt pleasure that her successor was giving satisfaction, she felt comfortable again.

"We were sorry that Edith gave up her estate management course and went off to America," said Lord Pomfret impartially. "What she needs is a husband who will beat her. She is pure Pomfret."

"Which is more than you are, darling," said his wife. "You must be what is called a sport—something the Pomfrets haven't thrown up before."

She may have said this in jest, but Miss Merriman wondered for a moment if it was meant for praise or blame. Then she saw the look of trustful love that passed between husband and wife and her fears vanished.

"You remember Macfadyen, Merry, the big market gardener who is one of the syndicate who have, thank God, taken the Towers off my hands," Lord Pomfret went on, for some time previously Mr. Macfadyen, together with Mr. Adams the big iron-master and Mr. Pilward the wealthy brewer whose son had married Mr. Adams's daughter, had formed a syndicate to take over most of the Towers and a good deal of the land, partly for office and partly for Mr. Macfadyen's experimental work in fruit and vegetables. "You must visit them before you go, Merry. They all want to congratulate you" and Miss Merriman said quietly that she would be delighted to see them.

"When I asked just now about whether there was any way in which I could help Miss Updike, I hope that I didn't sound intrusive," said Miss Merriman. "But if there is anything perhaps that I left unfinished, or that needs explaining, I should be so glad to do what I can. Otherwise I certainly won't interfere."

"Well, there is one thing that I do feel a little diffident about," said Lady Pomfret. "It is Nurse. Merry, you could always handle Nurse. I can't always. Of course we shan't have a nursery much longer now."

Lord Pomfret said Why. They had always had nurseries at the Towers, he added indignantly.

"Yes, darling," said his wife, "but there was more room then and certainly more rooms. We have hardly got enough rooms here, Merry, as you know. It was all very well when the children were small, but now they aren't. We can't make poor Ludo go on sharing with Giles in the old night-nursery forever. What we really want is to find a place for Nurse where she can have young children with someone under her. Then Ludo could have her room and Giles could have the old night nursery to himself and keep his trains there and nail the rails to the floor which he is always wanting to do. Miss Updike has the blue room. Gillie and I have our bathroom, thank goodness, but there is rather a scramble for the other one."

Miss Merriman said she thought she remembered there were two doors to that bathroom, which always led to trouble.

Lady Pomfret said the only way would be to put those things with Engaged on them that you could turn to Disengaged.

"If I know your children, Sally," said Lord Pomfret, rather unfairly we think, "either they will never use that gadget, or they will play with it all the time. Certainly Giles and his friends will. And what is more, they will never remember, or deliberately forget, which comes to much the same, to turn off the Engaged thing at one door if they go out of the other. I really wish we hadn't turned that room into a bathroom now. It is simply waste of space."

Miss Merriman then asked what was being done with the two rooms they used to call the sewing-rooms where, in old Lord Pomfret's time, the household linen used to be looked through and mended every week.

"And before it went to the wash as well as after," said Lord Pomfret. "I remember Uncle Giles's housekeeper telling me that. She said The Wash couldn't do half as much harm if the linen was in good condition when it went there. And she was right. You know, Merry, I am pretty busy one way and another and so is Sally, and Nurse isn't as young as she was. Let's go and look at it."

So they all went to the old sewing-room and Lord Pomfret opened the shutters, showing it as a pleasant room with one window onto the garden and one onto the stable-yard—now deserted except for the children's ponies and a couple of cars since Lady Pomfret had given up hunting.

"I'm going to have the rooms over the stable repaired and water laid on," said Lord Pomfret. "Those people who play polo at Greshamsbury need more stabling. They'll pay anything and they want rooms for two grooms to sleep."

"If I were a boy I would love to have a room of my own there," said Miss Merriman, looking thoughtfully across the yard. "And what a delightful bed-sitting-room this would be if one could put a bath into that sticking-out bit at the end. I think when I was here they called it the Powdering-Room."

"They would," said Lady Pomfret. "People never remember that The Towers wasn't built till about the middle of last century. More likely it was a sort of dressing-room. There seems to have been a basin, so I suppose there is water—or was!"

"Good Lord! I'd forgotten," said Lord Pomfret. "I'll get Roddy to look at that," for to his brother-in-law, Roddy Wicklow, he delegated any work about the house as well as an estate agent's out-of-door business. "We might put a bath in there and make a bed-sitting-room for Emily. The room is big enough for two beds if she has a friend to stay. Then the room where she is now would be free."

"What a good idea, darling," said Lady Pomfret, not daring to look at Miss Merriman. "It is quite extraordinary how one doesn't think of things."

"But Merry does," said Lord Pomfret, generously acknowledging her original suggestion. "I never knew her *not* thinking of things for other people. I hope you are going to be selfish for the rest of your life, Merry."

Miss Merriman, more touched than she liked to show, said anyone who married Mr. Choyce would have to be selfish, because he was so unselfish, and then Lord Pomfret closed the shutters and the ladies went back to Lady Pomfret's sitting room, Lord Pomfret saying not to wait tea for him.

"Miss Updike ought to be back soon," Lady Pomfret said when she had poured out tea. "She went to Barchester by the bus to do some shopping."

And sure enough, hardly had they begun their tea when Miss Updike came in.

"I don't think you and Miss Updike have met," said Lady Pomfret as the two ladies shook hands. Miss Updike, like the rest of her family, was tall and good-looking and had a very pleasant competent manner.

"I did meet your mother during the war," said Miss Merriman. "I was over in Harefield one day and went into the chemist's shop for something and your mother came in to have her arm bandaged. I think something had upset in the kitchen. She was so pretty."

"That's mother all right," said Miss Updike. "Father says if he had five shillings for every time mother does something to herself he would be a rich man. She is really wonderful at it," and Miss Merriman thought very well of Miss Updike's pleasant and loving attitude to her ill-starred parent. "Last week she upset a whole saucepan of boiling fat over the stove. It took me about an hour to clear up and it was lucky I was at home. She was hardly scalded at all," which last words she said with a pride that rather touched her hearers.

Then in came the tea, brought by a middle-aged woman whom Miss Merriman immediately recognized as Bertha, sister of the former boot-and-knife boy at the Towers. For there were still on the estate people misguided enough to believe that service at the Towers was better than serving behind the counter at Sheepshanks, or in the medicine and toilet preparations department of Gaiter's Circulating Library.

When they had all made a good tea Lady Pomfret let Miss Updike talk and Miss Merriman listened. It is just possible that Miss Updike, who had seen a good deal of the world during the war and was far from unintelligent, realized that she was, as it were, being put through her paces and was not unwilling to show them in a quiet way. Presently Lord Pomfret joined them and there was much talk about old days at the Towers, during which Miss Updike quietly went away.

Lady Pomfret asked Miss Merriman if she would like to rest or to walk round the garden. Miss Merriman chose the garden and they walked slowly up the green river of close-mown grass that meandered among the wilder part, along the stream that fed the fountains and so to the place where the water bubbled up from no one quite knew where in a kind of grotto. And if Miss Merriman's thoughts went back to happy and unhappy far-off days and things that were no more, her companion did not know it.

"And now I must go and see Nurse," said Miss Merriman, as they went into the house.

So up to the nursery she went and found Nurse engaged, as when was she not, in mending some of her ex-nurselings' clothes.

"May I come in, Nurse?" said Miss Merriman, as a Throne speaking to a Throne.

"Well, now, miss, this *is* a pleasure," said Nurse. "Come and sit down. When her ladyship told me the news I said 'And a good thing too. It's time Miss Merriman had a home of her own and Mr. Choyce is a very nice gentleman.'" And having uttered these congratulatory words she took up her work again, rather to the relief of Miss Merriman who was quite prepared for Nurse to enquire how many children she intended to have; perhaps on the precedent of Sarah, though we have always imagined that there must be some mistake in arithmetic in her case—or perhaps a year was a good deal shorter then.

So Nurse and Miss Merriman exchanged news of families; and here intelligent people will know that we mean by this of the families connected with the Grahams and Pomfrets, which by now included a quite creditable number of the generation younger than Edith, who was herself the youngest of a large family. Miss Merriman expressed her pleasure that Lady Pomfret had Miss Updike to help her. Nurse gave a grim and qualified approval which Miss Merriman quite understood as meaning that Miss Updike came, on the whole, up to her, Nurse's, standards and had better not deviate from them.

"As for Ludo," said Nurse, licking a piece of sewing cotton, sharpening it with her fingers and skillfully pushing it through the eye of her needle, "he's as nice a young gentleman as you could wish and always asks me to come and tuck him up at night when he's here, just like when he was a little boy. And Giles is just as much of a Rory-Tory boy as ever. Mad about horses he is. Emily's a good girl but she's a handful. She'll be leaving school before long. Dear, dear, they do grow up. If you'll wait a moment, miss, I've something for you."

She went to a chest of drawers and took out a fat parcel

wrapped in tissue paper and tied with a glittering tinsel ribbon.

"With best wishes for all happiness, miss," she said.

"Oh, *thank* you, Nurse," said Miss Merriman.

"You can open it now if you like, miss," said Nurse graciously, so Miss Merriman opened the parcel and found a mauve sateen nightgown-case embroidered with forget-me-nots.

"Oh, Nurse, *how* kind of you. You really shouldn't have given me such a lovely present," said Miss Merriman, comforting herself for her noble lie with the thought that Nurse would not be likely to see her bedroom at the vicarage. "And it's not only the present. It's the kind thought that counts," at which Nurse assumed an expression that can only be described as self-satisfied bridling, and after a little more talk Miss Merriman went back to the sitting-room where to her great pleasure she found Lord Pomfret with his wife, for once quietly doing nothing and pleased to have her company.

"I was talking to the Dean today," said Lord Pomfret. "He thinks very highly of Mr. Choyce and says he hopes they will get him in the Close sometime."

Miss Merriman said there was only one thing that could please her more than the Dean thinking well of Mr. Choyce, namely that the Bishop should think poorly of him, which piece of bravado made Lord Pomfret laugh and his wife looked gratefully at Miss Merriman.

"Sally and I have a small present for you, Merry," said Lord Pomfret. "She can tell you her half first."

"But you gave me a dinner service," said Miss Merriman.

"Oh, that was for show," said Lady Pomfret. "We want you to have something to remind you of the Towers. It's two dozen best linen sheets and pillow slips. We found a lot of linen put away when we were giving up the other end of The Towers, in perfectly good condition. I have had it all re-marked by a woman who understands white embroidery. It was what was kept for old Lady Pomfret's bed only. You must remember it."

"Yes. Lady Pomfret, my Lady Pomfret, had bought a good

deal not long before she died," said Miss Merriman. "How *kind* of you to think of me."

"I'll have them sent over to the vicarage later," said Lady Pomfret. "But we want to give you something that will impress people as well, so we hope you will like this. It was Gillie's idea," and she handed to Miss Merriman a green morocco case with D.F.C. stamped on it in gold. Miss Merriman opened it, almost nervously. Inside lay a spray of jewelled flowers in all colours, each blossom and leaf trembling on a thin coil of gold wire.

"Lady Pomfret's brooch!" said Miss Merriman, touching it gently. "I have seen her wear it so often. Her father gave it to her when she was married. It makes me remember—" and then she had to stop.

"I am quite sure she would like you to have it, Merry," said Lord Pomfret, almost in his Lord Lieutenant's voice. "And we shall like to think of you wearing it."

"Thank you both. Oh, *thank* you," said Miss Merriman. "I did love and admire her. I shall leave it to your Emily," at which excursion into the future loud protests were made by the Pomfrets, till everyone laughed and the point of emotion was safely past.

Then in came Lady Pomfret's brother Roddy Wicklow, the estate manager, with his pretty gentle wife, daughter of Mr. Barton the architect and his wife who wrote learned, well-documented, and slightly dull novels about the more obscure bastards of Popes and Cardinals. With them they had brought Mrs. Barton's last book bound in blue morocco with Miss Merriman's new initials tooled on it. Roddy, after the fashion of men, having greeted Miss Merriman at once fell into estate talk with his employer while his wife, rather shyly, asked Miss Merriman if she remembered the winter at the Towers when she, then Alice Barton, had experienced her first house-party and seen life.

"It makes me feel frightfully old," said Mrs. Wicklow, "to remember the Towers then. It was all so different."

"Well, that visit of yours was—let me think—nearly twenty years ago, Mrs. Wicklow," said Miss Merriman, who had always stuck to her own unwritten rule of addressing the friends and relations of her various employers by the more formal modes. "We are all getting on."

"I suppose we are," said Mrs. Wicklow. "Even Roddy is getting bald on the top, but he is so tall that people don't much notice it. I wonder why men go bald on the top and women don't as a rule."

Miss Merriman said she had wondered that herself and used to think it was because they wore hats that kept the air from their heads. But as the fashion of hats had almost gone out, except for occasions, it couldn't be that.

"Oh, Miss Merriman," said Mrs. Wicklow. "I wanted awfully to give you a wedding present and so does Roddy, but we didn't know what you would like. You know Sally used to breed dogs before she married Lord Pomfret and I've got some of her Airedales. Would you like a puppy? The last litter was lovely and I've just one left."

Now if there was one thing Miss Merriman did not want, it was a dog. Not but what she had always taken care of her Lady Pomfret's King Charles Spaniels, but it was from love of her mistress, not at all as a dog-lover. She knew that to people who liked dogs they were almost sacred, but the vicarage would, she felt, never feel like home if she had to share it with a dog. Besides which there was Mr. Choyce's cat to consider, who was almost one of the family and had a special little flap-door that he could push open when he came in late from the club.

"She's the best of the litter," said Mrs. Wicklow and her gentle dark eyes clouded—almost, Miss Merriman thought, a suspicion of tears. "But I'd love you to have her if you'd like it."

Miss Merriman thought quickly. The happiness of two people was at stake; Mrs. Wicklow's and her own. It was obvious that if Mrs. Wicklow gave her the dog—for bitch she did not say—it would leave an aching gap in her doggery—or whatever one called it. This was one of the rare cases when truth was not only right but agreeable.

"That is *most* kind of you," she said, "but Mr. Choyce doesn't really care about dogs. I think he had a dog that died—you will understand."

"Oh, I *do*," said Mrs. Wicklow, her large brown eyes growing dark with feeling. "When Giulia—that was one of old Lady Pomfret's spaniels—died, it was *dreadful*."

"I remember Giulia," said Miss Merriman, grateful for this escape. "Lady Pomfret had a stone put on her grave. But I believe all that part of the garden is vegetables now, for Mr. Macfadyen's Amalgamated Vedge Company."

So that danger was past and if Mr. Choyce's dog that died was an improvisation of Miss Merriman's we can only say that it did her credit and she was very lucky that it came off. She was delighted to have Mrs. Barton's book and asked both the Wicklows to write their names in it, which they willingly did and then went away.

Dinner was quiet and pleasant. When it was over Lord Pomfret went to the Estate Room with Miss Merriman and Miss Updike and it became abundantly clear to Miss Merriman, listening to the talk of the two others, that Miss Updike was going to be exactly what Lord Pomfret needed. A lady, very competent, obviously strong and bursting with health, with a good minor county background. If only she didn't go and get married at once, all would be perfect. Then she reflected that she would be getting married and deserting Lady Graham herself and had to laugh at it. But there were also the many years of devotion to her own old mistress at the Towers and she felt she had done all she could do. They all went to bed early and Miss Merriman hoped that she and Mr. Choyce were saying their prayers at the same moment, but remembering that he was dining with the Carters at the Old Manor House that evening, she laughed at herself and went comfortably to sleep.

On the following morning Lady Pomfret sent a note to Miss Merriman's room to say that she had to go to Barchester early but would be back before lunch and would Miss Merriman do whatever she liked and she thought Mr. Adams, who was at the Towers for a couple of days, would very much like to see her.

So when she had had a very comfortable late breakfast in her room and written some letters Miss Merriman went out of the Pomfrets' wing and walked along the front of the great house till she came to a door with a large brass plate on it, announcing the names of the various companies who now had their offices there. She pressed the bell and the door was opened by a commission-aire, who grinned.

"Nice to see you back, miss," he said, saluting. "Had a good time?"

"A very nice time, thank you, Pollett," said Miss Merriman, who had an almost royal memory for names and faces. "I daresay you have heard that I am going to marry Mr. Choyce, the vicar at Hatch End."

"Well, I did hear something of the sort, miss," said the commissionaire cautiously, "but people do say things you wouldn't hardly credit unless you was to see them. But I'm sure I wish you all the best, miss, and the Reverend too. I had a cousin of my father's was a verger. Funny thing, his name was Sexton. Was you wanting to see anyone in particular, miss?"

Miss Merriman said she had only come back for a night and would very much like to say good-bye to some of her friends in the office, shook hands with the commissinaire, went on to a door marked Private, knocked at it and went in.

Here lived Miss Cowshay, a very efficient secretary of the Hogglestock Rolling Mills, foundation of the wealthy ironmas-ter Mr. Adams's fortunes.

"Well, Miss Merriman, this *is* my lucky day," said Miss Cowshay. "I didn't know you were here. Do sit down and we'll have some coffee," and she pressed a buzzer on her desk and

ordered two coffees. "We were all ever so sorry you hadn't been
well and I hope your visit to Lady Graham has done you good.
But I needn't ask that. I saw the notice about your engagement
in *The Thunderer*. Mr. Adams likes me to go through the social
columns for him every day. My cousin that's on the Barchester
Chronicle wrote an ever so nice piece about Mr. Choyce. I'll
send it to you. I was passing the remark to Miss Carton of the
Costing Department at lunch only last week it did seem a shame
you hadn't a home of your own. Oh, I'm *ever* so glad. But we'll
miss you here, you know. Really, with Mr. Adams and Mr.
Macfadyen and Mr. Pilward it all seems like one large family,
and we'd got quite used to you being with Lady Pomfret and we
shall miss you quite a lot."

These words quite overwhelmed Miss Merriman, who had
never considered herself as a person who would be missed and
she said, quite truthfully, that she would miss all the people at
the Towers very much.

"I'm having a very quiet wedding," she said, suddenly thinking of the possibility of the whole staff turning up at Hatch End
in charabancs. "It seemed more suitable, as Mr. Choyce and I
aren't so young as we were," and then was smitten with com-
punction, thinking how much the Miss Cowshays do enjoy a
wedding. So she was relieved when Miss Cowshay said if she got
married she would have a quiet wedding and then throw a really
good party when she got back from the honeymoon, adding,
"Did you want to see Mr. Adams? I'll phone through to him."

Miss Cowshay then spoke on the inter-office telephone and
said Mr. Adams was just come in and would like to see Miss
Merriman in half an hour if she could spare the time.

"I daresay you'd like a look at the house, Miss Merriman," she
said. "We've got the scaffolding down in the big hall now."

So they went up to the piano nobile, which it is difficult to
describe in an English word as although it was, so to speak, the
ground floor, it was really on what would be the first floor in any
normal house, with a great double ramp up to the front door

outside. Here the hand of Big Business had made a good many changes since last we saw Pomfret Towers. The Great Hall, as it used to be called, was divided into offices by wooden partitions. The big fireplace was blocked with plywood, and radiators were placed at intervals along the walls. As for the ceiling, it was so high that no one ever looked at it and it had been left in its pristine horror of pseudo Gothic, colonized by large spiders and their friends.

"It does look different from what it was when I first came here," said Miss Merriman. "But that was more than twenty years ago, when old Lord Pomfret, and my Lady Pomfret were alive and the house was full of people."

"I daresay it quite gets you down," said Miss Cowshay sympathetically. "Mr. Macfadyen did want to leave the big fireplace, but Mr. Adams said it would mean draughts, so he had it covered up. What's behind that wood I couldn't say."

"I should think," said Miss Merriman, recalling memories of the Towers in old Lord Pomfret's time, "that by now it is quite full of birds' nests and twigs and a lot of loose bricks and some broken slates and possibly a bat that fell down and couldn't get up and a few dead sparrows."

Miss Cowshay said, with a ladylike shudder, that bats were nasty things.

"But I'm awfully glad you think it's all right," she added. "I mean I thought you might think it was a bit out of order to cover up an old medeeval chimney like that."

"I don't think it was really mediaeval," said Miss Merriman, trying hard not to sound affected in her pronunciation of the word. "It was built about a hundred years ago."

"Oh, well, they all say it's medeeval," said Miss Cowshay, on whom Miss Merriman's gentle correction had fallen unheeded. Miss Merriman wisely gave it up.

They then visited the great yellow drawing-room, the green brocade drawing-room, the library, Lady Pomfret's boudoir, and the small blue room, all of which Miss Merriman remembered as they once had been. But only for a moment. For there is something in us that wipes out a memory of the past, even as we look at what has replaced the past we knew. Only of our childhood do we keep a visual memory clear and strong enough to re-create the actual image of what things were, while what has replaced them seems but a shadow. When shades of the prison house of growing older begin to close about us, things of recent date are often blurred, while the forgotten past is crystal-clear. So, for Miss Merriman, it would be more difficult from now onwards to re-create the Towers as it was, for she had only known it in later years. But that did not matter. The rooms were not the rooms she knew. They were now partitioned into smaller rooms, with white paint, or plaster, or plastic every-where, and in them people were working for enterprises which were certainly useful and would probably make life easier and more pleasant for Lord and Lady Pomfret in their endless self-imposed task of work for others.

Miss Merriman said it was all most interesting and she was sure it was being a great success. A rather vague statement, but it was the best she could do, as she had little or no idea what exactly it was that the busy staffs of the various businesses were doing.

"Do you remember the chapel?" said Miss Cowshay. "It's kept locked and Lord Pomfret has one key and the office has one. But Mr. Adams is very particular about letting anyone use it."

"Do you mean that no one can go in?" said Miss Merriman.

"Oh, no!" said Miss Cowshay, with great refinement of vowels. "But Mr. Adams used to be chapel and though he goes to church now he doesn't want anyone to go in the chapel who wouldn't appreciate it and reely, Miss Merriman, though our staff are a very nice set you couldn't trust them."

"Do you mean they would—" Miss Merriman began, when it occurred to her that the word brawl, which she was about to use, would probably mean nothing to Miss Cowshay, or else be taken as meaning, darkly, something much worse.

"Oh, nothing of *that* sort," said Miss Cowshay in a shocked voice which made Miss Merriman want to know exactly what—if anything—Miss Cowshay had thought she meant. "But there's some of them you can't stop them writing their names on things. And we have to treat them all alike. I'll get the key, Miss Merriman. Oh, and excuse me, but when I saw the advert of your engagement in Mr. Adams's paper, I said to myself, 'Well, the *Daily Runner* for little me, but *The Thunderer* does get the posh engagements and no mistake.' I shan't *be* a moment."

She was as good as her word, came swiftly back with the chapel key and opened the door. Here all was peace. The patterned floor of lapis lazuli and white marble, the tall light windows, the marble columns, the seats of some light-coloured wood with their carved ends gradually acquiring the patina of age, looked as they had looked for the last hundred years, or thereabouts. Miss Merriman thought of her countess and said a silent prayer for her. Then she turned to the door. Lord and Lady Pomfret had asked if she would like to have the chapel for her wedding, but her allegiance was now to Hatch End and Mr. Choyce's church.

"That was *most* kind of you, Miss Cowshay," she said. "And when I am being married I shall think of the chapel. Now I must go back to Lady Pomfret."

So they went into the hall, where a quietly dressed man who was waiting for them introduced himself as Mr. Adams's private secretary and said if Miss Merriman weren't in a hurry Mr. Adams would be very glad to see her in his office.

"Well, I'll hie me back to my room," said Miss Cowshay. "I've all those reports to get out. Well, all good wishes, Miss Merriman," and she went back to her office while the secretary led Miss Merriman to the far end of the building, knocked at the door with a ground-glass top, and held it open for her to go in.

"Well, Miss Merriman, this *is* an unexpected pleasure," said Mr. Adams, coming forward. "If I'd known you were coming we'd have had the flags out. I haven't been so pleased since I don't know when. Sit down," and he pulled forward a gigantic leather armchair suitable for a hippopotamus. "When I saw your engagement in the paper, I was as pleased as Punch. I didn't ever meet Lady Emily Leslie that you used to live with but the once, and a very great lady she was, and when I saw your engagement I said to myself, 'If there's one thing would please Lady Emily, it would be this.' Well, there's no knowing and I daresay she *is* pleased."

"I hope so," said Miss Merriman, feeling almost a pricking of tears behind her eyes. "Only I think she must be a little disappointed that she can't arrange the wedding. She did love to arrange things. And how is Lucy? You must forgive me, but I can't think of her as Mrs. Adams after knowing her so long as Lucy Marling."

"Well, nor can I," said Mr. Adams. "Sometimes I say to myself, 'It's all too good to be true, Sam Adams,' and then I say 'But it's all true and it's good too.' I do sincerely hope, Miss Merriman, that you and Mr. Choyce will be as happy as Lucy and I are, and more I can't say. And Lucy said we must give you something for the vicarage, and we thought perhaps a carpet might fill the bill. A real Oriental one."

Miss Merriman, though secretly rather taken aback, was not the woman to flinch.

"I can't think of anything we would like more," she said. "The carpet in Herbert's study is a disgrace—and we shall mostly be sitting there. About twelve by eight the old one is. And it doesn't really matter what colours. All the good Oriental ones are pleasant. It is *most* kind of you."

"Very kind of you to accept it," said Mr. Adams, evidently with genuine feeling. "I said to my Heth—my girl, Mrs. Pilward Junior that is, though I don't think she'll be Junior long, her father-in-law's in a poor way—well, as I was saying, I said to my Heth, 'Miss Merriman is one of the best and she deserves the best that Mr. and Mrs. Sam Adams can give her.'"

Slightly exhausted by this speech which had the effect—as some of Mr. Adams's remarks not uncommonly did—of making his hearers feel as if they were in a telephone box and couldn't get out, Miss Merriman thanked him again. Mr. Adams asked if she would like to go up to the first floor and see the new offices there and the big restaurant and kitchens on the floor above, so that the smell of cooking never came into the rest of the house, but by this time she was rather tired and said she must get back to Lady Pomfret.

"I'll let you out the garden way then," said Mr. Adams, and he took her into the next room, which had a French window opening onto the terrace.

"Let me know when it will suit you to have the carpet, Miss Merriman," said Mr. Adams, "and I'll get them to send a man along to lay it all proper and a good piece of felt to go underneath it. Those Oriental carpets, they're used to being treated well," he went on meditatively, "and they don't want to be trodden to death. And by the way, Miss Merriman, if your room gets the afternoon sun, don't let it shine on the carpet too much."

"Well, that room does get rather a lot of sun," said Miss Merriman, "ever since Herbert got some men with a tractor who were mending the road to put a chain round the dreadful monkey-puzzle tree and pull it down," at which Mr. Adams laughed loudly and said Mr. Choyce ought to stand for the County Council and keep things going.

"And one thing more, Miss Merriman," said Mr. Adams. "I've only met Mr. Choyce once or twice, but I took a liking to him and I'd like to give him something for his church. It wouldn't seem so personal, that way. Would he feel offended if I asked him to accept a cheque for the church as a wedding present?"

Miss Merriman, in all her life of thinking of others, had never had this particular problem of the rich benefactor to face, but her intelligence made her realize that Mr. Adams's time—of which he had been generous—was also money and that the truest economy lay in accepting at once, without question, what was offered.

"We have a fund for preparing and improving the church," she said. "Things like a better heating system and some improvements in the vestry. I know Herbert will be most grateful—for the church and his parishioners and himself. Thank you very much."

"Then if you will give it to him yourself that will make it all nice and comfortable," said Mr. Adams and he went back to his desk, wrote a cheque, put it into an envelope, and handed it to Miss Merriman.

"Hadn't you better lick it up, Mr. Adams?" she said.

"You'd be bound to want to open it if I did," said Mr. Adams, though not ungallantly. "It's for you both," and he held the door open for her to go out onto the terrace.

"Oh, one thing, Mr. Adams," said Miss Merriman. "What has happened to the jet of water on the top of the fountain in the drive? It always used to work all right."

"That's just what we've all been asking," said Mr. Adams. "My engineers have had a go at it and I've had a go myself and it's got us completely beat. No one knows where that water comes from and we can't trace it. It's a different supply from the pond."

"Oh, but that comes from the Grotto, Mr. Adams," said Miss Merriman. "You know, that little stream at the far end of the garden where the water comes bubbling up through the sand under a kind of arch. I remember old Lord Pomfret talking about it."

"Well, we live and learn," said Mr. Adams. "I'll get a man onto that next week. Thank you, Miss Merriman."

When Miss Merriman reached the far end of the terrace, she found Lady Pomfret on her knees weeding.

"Well, did you enjoy yourself, Merry? I got my business over sooner than I expected so I came back early," said Lady Pomfret.

"Very much," said Miss Merriman. "Miss Cowshay showed me all the office rooms and the chapel. Then I was summoned to see Mr. Adams. He is giving us an Oriental carpet for the study."

"Well done, Mr. Adams," said Lady Pomfret. "The more I see of that man the more I like him. And his wife too, even if she is a bit hearty at times. But her people are good Barsetshire—much older than we are probably."

"Yes—her mother is connected with the Thornes, a very old Barsetshire family. My Lady Pomfret was a Thorne," said Miss Merriman, who though an outsider had come to know her Barsetshire families pretty thoroughly. "Blood does tell." A very true remark, for blood remains responsible for much good and much evil in families, and as for its permutations and combinations of virtues and vices, or good looks and ugliness (in which case the ugly ones are far more conceited than the good-looking ones, boasting loudly of being just like Great-Uncle-Algy whose ears stuck out more than any other ears in the county, or the spitting image of Old Cousin Marcia who had the largest lump—only just short of a wen—on her face with three large black hairs growing on it in East Barsetshire) they almost need a book to themselves.

"And he gave me a cheque for the church, but he didn't lick up the envelope," said Miss Merriman, looking at it.

"Then it won't matter if you look at it now," said Lady Pomfret, consumed with a vulgar and natural longing to know what he had sprung.

"Well—as he didn't lick it up—" said Miss Merriman. She firmly took the cheque from its envelope and looked at it.

"Anything wrong, Merry?" said Lady Pomfret, for expressions were changing in Miss Merriman's face as swiftly as cloud shadows over a meadow.

"It's a hundred pounds!" said Miss Merriman. "Do you think he meant it, Lady Pomfret?"

"Of course he did," said Lady Pomfret, who felt that Miss Merriman might try to return it, thinking that he had made a mistake. "He wanted to help Mr. Choyce and this is a charming way of doing it. How pleased Mr. Choyce will be," she added, which judicious words at once—as she had rather hoped— restored Miss Merriman to her wonted calm.

"I have suddenly remembered something," she said.

Lady Pomfret begged for further information.

"It's only when I first met Miss Cowshay. It was when I was with Lady Emily at Holdings in the war—before Mr. Leslie died—and Miss Cowshay was in the cashier's desk at Pilchard's Stores. I often used to shop there or cash small cheques for Lady Emily. Of course she wasn't so blonde then. And then she was in the Regional Commissioner's Office. Mr. John Leslie took a party of us there. It all feels extraordinarily far away."

"It's more than ten years since the end of the war," said Lady Pomfret, and both were silent, thinking of the passage of Time and the passionless sweep of his scythe.

Lady Pomfret got up, shook her apron, put her gardening gloves and tools into their basket and they went indoors to lunch. Lord Pomfret was in the sitting-room, reading letters.

"Good-morning, Merry," he said. "I've some news for you."

As—apart from the sudden death of Mr. Choyce—there was no one whose fate could particularly affect Miss Merriman, she said with her usual calm that she would like to help if she could.

"It's from Edith," said Lord Pomfret. "She has been having a wonderful time in America with David and Rose—lucky girl and I wish I could too. They want her to stay on a bit and then they will all fly over for your wedding. I expect Lady Graham will be hearing from her about it."

Miss Merriman expressed pleasure.

"Come now, Merry, what are you thinking about?" said Lord Pomfret. "You are the wisest of us all."

"I do often wonder," said Miss Merriman, "what Edith will do. She has never settled to anything since she was born. Lady

Graham did think that her plan of learning estate management at that place in Barchester and being with you might steady her. I wasn't very sure. Then she gave it up and went to America. I rather give it all up myself."

"What that girl needs," said Lord Pomfret, without animus, "is a husband who will beat her. Well, there it is, and I'm glad they are all coming over. Come in to lunch."

But the talk about Edith went on, almost uninterruptedly, all through lunch though coming to no kind of conclusion.

Then Lady Pomfret drove Miss Merriman with her fresh harvest of wedding presents back to Holdings. As Lady Graham would doubtless want to talk with Lady Pomfret about family matters, Miss Merriman decided to go down to the village and see how everything was getting on. For life in a village is far more interesting than life in a large town in that everything is happening under one's nose and is freely if ignorantly discussed by everyone, whereas in London you may live in the same house for years and know practically nothing about your next door neighbours, or even the house opposite.

Ever since her engagement Miss Merriman's walks down to the village had been not unlike John Baptist-Cavalletto's progress through Bleeding Heart Yard. Not that the housewives rushed out at her with domestic implements, saying "Flour dredger, Miss Merriman," but they were too apt to stop her and ask after one or another of the family, notably in the case of Mrs. Panter at 6, Clarence Cottages, wife of George Halliday's carter and mother of Lady Graham's kitchen maid Odeena, so called as a tribute to the Barchester Odeon where Mrs. Panter had sat every Saturday during a long courtship, holding Mr. Panter's hand. And sure enough Mrs. Panter was plucking a fowl at her front door, so Miss Merriman stopped to talk with her.

"Well, miss, they do say wonders will never cease," said Mrs. Panter. "I'm sure I'm ever so glad you and Mr. Choyce are getting married. It's much the best way," which made Miss

Merriman wonder whether Mrs. Panter was trying to warn her against living in sin. "Panter's as pleased as anything. He says if you want your boxes and things moving to the vicarage he'll be pleased to take them for you in one of Mr. George's carts."

This generous invitation at George Halliday's expense nearly made Miss Merriman laugh and she felt, as she had often felt before, how powerful the village was under its calm easy-going appearance. There would never, one hoped, be a Jacquerie in England, but the tyranny of the people, though kindly exercised, could be very great. So she thanked Mrs. Panter, asked after the rest of her family, and continued her progress to The Shop, kept by Mrs. Hubback, mother of the Halliday's elderly maid at Hatch House and reputed to be ninety-one. Here one could buy pretty well anything except the one thing one wanted at the moment and here Vidler's fish cart left its parcels of fish for regular customers.

"I've been waiting for you, Miss Merriman," said Mrs. Hubback. "I saw the piece about your engagement. I was wrapping some fish because Vidler he's a stingy old man and won't put enough paper round his parcels and there was your name and Mr. Choyce's staring at me as bold as brass. I said to Vidler, 'Look here, Vidler,' I said, 'Miss Merriman's going to be married to the Vicar.'"

"I hope he was pleased," said Miss Merriman, finding nothing else to say.

"Pleased is as pleased does," said Mrs. Hubback oracularly, "but when he said 'One marriage always brings on another, Mrs. Hubback,' I slapped his face with a nice bit of cod's tail. At my age too!"

"I'm sure he deserved it," said Miss Merriman and walked on towards the Mellings Arms where Mr. Geo. Panter, licensed to sell beer and spirits to be consumed on or off the premises, was sitting on the bench before his inn, doing his pools.

"Well, miss," said Mr. Panter, getting up and holding out his hand. "All the best to you and the Reverend and if ever you want some beer out of hours, let me know."

Miss Merriman, feeling that she was conniving at something unlawful, thanked him very much.

"And if you want a nice rabbit, or a hare, miss, you just let me know," said Mr. Panter. "In season or out of season as the saying is. Trade isn't what it was. Too much land under corn now. There's Squire gone and ploughed up that field on the hill where a man could knock them over like ninepins if he knew the way to do it, or pick them up with a nice little snare. But I wish you all the best, miss. I'm coming to the wedding. When's it to be?"

Miss Merriman said about Easter time, as Mr. Choyce had to be away a good deal this winter and a friend of his would be taking the services.

"That's all right, miss," said Mr. Panter. "I don't never go to church anyway. A man as works as hard as me needs his Sunday morning in bed. But I'll come to the wedding, Sunday or no Sunday, and you can tell the Reverend so."

This appeared to be a kind of polite dismissal, so Miss Merriman turned her steps homeward again. As she had to pass the church she thought she would go in for a moment. She had gone through the lych gate and was near the porch when to her horror she saw, sitting on a camp stool among the green hillocks that marked the older and humbler graves, the far too well-known form of Mr. Scatcherd, the self-appointed village artist, his sketch book on his knees, dressed as usual in a kind of sporting outfit of belted Norfolk jacket, knickerbockers that buttoned below the knee, and a deer-stalker hat. Luckily his back was turned towards her. She felt that at the moment one more congratulation, especially from Mr. Scatcherd, who could have rivalled Prince Giglio in the length of his exordiums, would make her either scream or have the giggles, neither of which would be seemly in a churchyard not suitable to her position. So she walked quietly away, deliberately closing her ears and eyes to

Mr. Scatcherd's lordly wave of the hand inviting her to come closer, and went back to Holdings.

There would be a good deal more of this to come, she feared, but all should be borne for Herbert's sake, and the foolish middle-aged Miss Merriman found herself saying her betrothed's name aloud and had to laugh at herself for her own happy folly.

CHAPTER 2

The year waned and died amid the over-excitement of Christmas. To everyone's joy the stopgap or locum went back to his own parish for a week and Mr. Choyce returned to his flock. During this time he was able to get estimates for the necessary repairs and painting and distempering for the vicarage and leave the rest in his affianced's very capable hands. He also looked up a great many friends and acknowledged the many presents that had come to the vicarage in his absence. So full indeed were his days that he did not see as much of Miss Merriman as he would have wished, and had it not been for the thoughtfulness of Lady Graham in asking him to lunch or dinner when she and Sir Robert were out, they would never have had time to say all they had to say. Not quite all though and Miss Merriman looked forward with quiet happiness to their life in the vicarage when they would always be able to tell each other everything every day and never be tired of doing so.

But tempus, as a comedian now only remembered by the older among us said in a pantomime, does fuge. He lets the sands sift through his hour-glass with unfaltering hand and if the hours that have passed seem short or long to us, they are really all the same length. Though REALLY as Mrs. Morland said, emphasizing as usual the idea foremost in her fertile mind, they aren't. She then tried to explain what she meant, but having rashly dragged in the word relativity was quite unable to do so.

The Thursday after Easter was chosen for the wedding, as both the consenting parties felt that Holy Week and Easter Day would be no bad preparation for the vows they were going to make. Also because it suited the Dean who was going to conduct the ceremony. As for Canon Bostock, who was to assist the Dean, he would willingly have given up any previous engagement for the pleasure of forwarding Lady Graham's plans, having a great affection and admiration for her in an honourable way.

By the greatest good luck the stopgap vicar had liked nothing better than a bit of amateur painting and plastering and accepted with enthusiasm Miss Merriman's tentative suggestion that he should keep an eye on the work done in the rooms which he was not using until such time as Mr. Choyce came back for good. Lady Graham wondered if this was wise and asked the builder's foreman, rather privately, whether it upset his men or the work to have the Vicar always there.

"Bless you, my lady, not he," said the foreman. "He likes it and we let him. The men like it too. The day he came down the ladder and put one leg into a pail of cream distemper, I'll never forget it, my lady. The men they couldn't keep from laughing, but the Reverend he just laughed too and he stood them beer all round when they'd cleared up the mess. The carpenter he took the trousers straight into Barchester on his bike and they came up lovely at the cleaners. Lucky it was his old grey trousers and not his Sunday ones. So then he stood us beer all round again and we had a bit of a sing-song," which reporting of life at the vicarage was very well received in the village and raised its opinion of the stopgap.

Then, on Mr. Adams's instructions, did men come and lay down a piece of felt on the study floor and on it put the very handsome carpet with contraptions fastened under its four corners which would keep them from rolling up as corners are too apt to do. Then was the furniture polished within an inch of its life, the curtains which had been cleaned put up again, the

Arundel prints re-hung. And, most important of all, Mr. Choyce's books, which Miss Merriman had caused to be removed to another room during the repainting, were one by one cleaned from the accumulated dust of a bachelor's house. With the help of Mrs. Carter from the Old Manor House and one or two other friends each book was opened, slapped together again to drive out the dust, well dusted along its top and replaced on its shelf, which had also been well dusted. As Miss Merriman had piled them neatly in heaps, a shelf at a time, there was no difficulty in putting them back in their proper places. There was one moment of alarm when a volume of Gibbon was missing, but it turned up a few days later among the volumes of Gregorovius' *Rome in the Middle Ages*. And as these had not yet been dusted, we can only suppose that Mr. Choyce had absent-mindedly put it there himself.

So when Mr. Choyce came home everything would be shiningly clean and tidy for him and nothing out of its place. His cat, who had kept aloof from the workmen, taking umbrage at finding the lower orders in Its house, came back like the Prodigal son, except that It had obviously fed very well while away; but whether in someone's cottage, or several people's cottages, or simply by poaching, was never discovered. Mr. Choyce's one anxiety had been that his cat might not take easily to a mistress, having been so long accustomed to a bachelor life. But he had underestimated his cat's fine selfishness. A cat likes to sit on people's laps, particularly of course on women's because of their skirts. Its one complaint, as its friends at the Tiles Club knew only too well, was that Mr. Choyce hadn't a proper lap to sit on. Even if he had his cassock on there was apt to be a buckle, a thing no self-respecting cat could be expected to tolerate. But Miss Merriman had a nice comfortable lap and no objections to his occupying it, so he transferred his venal affections to her for good and boasted about it a good deal at his various night clubs, saying loudly that of course a woman's name was sacred but he knew one woman who understood him and appreciated his finer nature and never troubled to sit up for him. For nothing, he said, was more annoying for a Tom than to come home tired in the early hours and find people bothering about him. Not that he was ever troubled in this way, for Mr. Choyce had constructed for him, down in the skirting board of the study, a Cat-Flap which he could push open from the outside and so enter the house without disturbing any one. But this he did not tell his friends, for to have a low fellow one had only met by chance at the club coming unasked into His house would be unbearable.

Miss Merriman's last two or three weeks at Holdings might have become rather wearing, now that everything was prepared and her occupation gone. But the wedding presents were still coming in and the arrears of thank-you letters growing, so she set herself to answering them all as well as helping Lady Graham with her considerable correspondence, which at the moment still consisted largely of acceptances for the wedding. These had to be carefully gone through because it was doubtful whether the church would hold everyone. There was even a moment when Lady Graham, with a weakness quite unlike her, began to consider the cathedral, but the blood was strong, the heart was Leslie and Pomfret, so Hatch End it was. To her own quiet amusement Miss Merriman found that she was gradually arranging the whole of her wedding, just as she would have quietly arranged any other party that Lady Graham thought of giving. Whether Lady Graham noticed this, we cannot say.

The next stirring event was the final return of Mr. Choyce to his renovated vicarage a few days before the ceremony. Hardly had he unpacked his suitcase and begun to look at the improvements when a deputation from the village headed by Mr. Geo. Panter of the Mellings Arms appeared in front of the house, so he went to the front door and asked them to come in. This invitation caused those behind to cry Forward and those in front to cry Back, just as Lord Macaulay so well describes the Roman crowd doing in Horatius.

"If it's all the same to you, sir," said Mr. Panter, "we'll come in the back way. The foreman he was having a glass with us at the Arms last night and he said see the Vicar we must, but not to go in by the front door because the hall floor was still a bit tacky like."

Realizing that he was a mere puppet for the present, Mr. Choyce obligingly went round to the back door, where such a rubbing of boots on the door mat took place as considerably delayed the entrance of the party.

"The first thing," said Mr. Choyce, when he had got them all into the kitchen passage, "is some beer. If you will wait in the kitchen I'll get some. Come in and sit down."

The deputation, looking extremely sheepish, filed into the kitchen where Geo. Panter, Vidler the Fish, and Caxton, the Hallidays' estate carpenter, hitched their trousers at the knee and sat stiffly down on the three kitchen chairs, while the rest of the party leaned against the dresser and the chimney piece, for the kitchen fire had not yet been lighted. Mr. Choyce went to the little scullery and brought out six bottles of beer.

"It's all I've got in the house today," he said, "so let's drink it."

His guests all looked at one another.

"Well, sir, it's this way," said Geo. Panter with a kind of quiet desperation. "We've brought a present for you. What about bringing it in?" he added, addressing his followers.

Two men, recognized by the Vicar as the local poachers, slouched out of the room and came back with a fair-sized barrel. A third man followed them with what we can only describe as a barrel-stand, not knowing its technical name, on which they put the barrel. There was then an embarrassed silence which Mr. Choyce broke by saying what a nice solid barrel-stand that was and he wished he had one like it.

"Well, in a manner of speaking, sir, you have," said Geo.

Panter. "What I say is, what's the good of a barrel without you've something to put it on. That's right, boys, isn't it?"

Murmurs from his friends, who had obviously been coached in their parts, arose, such as "That's right," and "Without you've got a barrel-stand where do you put the barrel?" and "If a man's got a barrel it stands to reason he'll need a barrel-stand," with several other variants on the same theme.

"So Caxton here, he had a nice bit of wood in his shop and he made it," said Geo. Panter, unable to contain himself and suddenly giving everything away.

"And nice bit of wood it *is*," said Caxton, surveying it with something of the pleasant melancholy a father may have when giving his favourite daughter away. "A pleasure to work with, that wood was. You treat her well, sir, and she'll see you into your grave and all your children too."

"But I haven't got any," said Mr. Choyce.

"Lord bless you, sir, not yet of course," said Vidler the Fish. "Another nine months, sir, and we'll see," which remark was followed by a kind of Noises Off while each visitor told the man next to him that he'd been a six months child himself and the doctor said his parents would never rear him but look at him now, or the doctor had said he'd never live weighing only three pounds the way he did and look at him now, and from Vidler the Fish that his father and mother had been married eighteen years and never a child till the old woman over Starveacres way sold them a charm for a bottle of gin and look at him now.

"Ar, but your father and mother are dead now," said Geo. Panter. "My old mother's alive and a gormed old nuisance she is."

Much as Mr. Choyce would have liked to hear more of these simple village chronicles, he had work to do. His own small stock of beer was finished, so he dismissed his kind friends and went on with his unpacking. We need hardly say that before long Miss Merriman joined him, saying that she had driven over with Lady Graham who wanted to see Mrs. Carter at the Old

Manor House, so she had come on to the vicarage and Lady Graham would pick her up. They had a delightful talk— perhaps a little dull to us—about further improvements to the kitchen and whether it would be worth while having a fridge— for as that horrible word has come to stay one might as well use it. Mr. Choyce boasted about the barrel of beer on its stand, rather proudly, though not because it was a fine upstanding affair so much as in affectionate gratitude to the friends who had subscribed for it and made the stand and filled the cask with beer.

"And I have something for you, Herbert—"

"I do like to hear you say Herbert," said her betrothed.

"And I love saying it," said Miss Merriman, "but what I wanted to tell you is that Mr. Adams, whom I saw at the Towers, asked me to give you this," and she handed him an envelope carefully licked up by her.

"Shall I open it?" said Mr. Choyce.

"Oh, *do*. I am longing to know what it is," said Miss Merriman, which was not exactly telling a lie, because even if she had already seen Mr. Adams's munificent cheque it had been rather in the nature of eavesdropping and she wanted Mr. Choyce to be able to surprise her—or to think that he did.

"A cheque!" said Mr. Choyce. "How kind. How *very* kind. But I can hardly take it."

Miss Merriman, who had rather expected some trouble of a Quixotic nature, asked why.

"I don't really deserve it," he said. "Mr. Adams hardly knows me. I do not see how I can accept it."

"I don't know what it is," said Miss Merriman, telling a whopping lie, "but Mr. Adams said it was in trust for you to use for the church. Nothing personal, Herbert."

"I *do* like it when you say Herbert," said Mr. Choyce. "Of course if it is for the church I accept it gladly. How stupid I am. Of course Adams would not give money to *me*."

Miss Merriman said she supposed that would be simony,

which ignorance her betrothed thought the most charming remark he had ever heard. Then she asked how much it was and put on an excellent presentation of someone being extremely surprised, which entirely deceived Mr. Choyce. And we think she was right.

Then they went to the study where Mr. Choyce was quite overcome by the richness of the new carpet which Miss Merriman described, quite correctly, as a present to herself from Mr. Adams. The cat, who was dozing on the sunlight by the window, got up, stretched, and began to sharpen its claws on a chair leg. Mr. Choyce picked it up by the scruff of its neck and put it out of the room.

"I can't have the furniture spoilt, even by Puss," he said, and Miss Merriman, though she liked the cat, was glad to find that Mr. Choyce was not going to stand any nonsense from it in his renovated vicarage.

Then they walked across the garden, through the little gate into the churchyard, where Mr. Choyce stopped, looking upwards at the tower.

"You know, Dorothea," he said, "this gift, this most kind gift of Mr. Adams's, is a trust for me to use for the church. There are so many things I want. A new altar frontal, perhaps. The choir could do with new surplices—they are so darned and yellow. The stonework in the chancel does need cleaning badly and the stove is almost worn out. It is all most difficult. I almost wish that Mr. Adams in his kindness had specified his wishes as to its use—or even made it smaller. What do you think, my dear?"

Miss Merriman, who had really given considerable thought to this, said she had had one or two ideas if he would like to hear them. Luckily, she said, the altar did not need anything at present. The embroidered hangings were in good condition and the altar plate of good quality and quite enough for their wants. The vestry could certainly do with a good turn-out and repainting and the great iron stove that heated the church in winter had some ominous cracks in it. Of course a hundred pounds wouldn't do everything, she said, which last piece of common sense impressed Mr. Choyce immensely.

"There is one thing, Herbert," she went on, "but perhaps one oughtn't to think about it."

Mr. Choyce said that anything she thought must be right.

"Well, it's the cushions or squabs or whatever you like to call them, in the pews," said Miss Merriman. "You couldn't know about them, Herbert, because you never sit in a pew. I can assure you that any stuffing there ever was has turned into lumps and knobs and places where there isn't any stuffing at all. Lots of people bring a cushion, or even better an air-cushion, only then you have to blow it up outside the church, otherwise it would make the children laugh."

She then looked at Mr. Choyce and was much distressed to see anguish written on his face.

"What is it, Herbert?" she said, wondering if her strictures on the cushions had somehow touched him on the raw—though this seemed unreasonable.

"I cannot bear it," said Mr. Choyce vehemently. "To think that you—that *you* of all people—should have had to suffer discomfort in the church where I minister. I have failed in my duties," and so distraught did he appear that Miss Merriman, with hazy recollections of historic novels, half expected him to beat his breast and say Mea maxima culpa.

"If Lady Graham can stand it, I can," said Miss Merriman stoutly. "She did once say something about having the cushions picked over, but nothing came of it."

"Most certainly the remaking of the cushions shall be a first charge upon Mr. Adams's gift," said Mr. Choyce. "For you, dearest."

"Then," said Miss Merriman, rather cleverly we think, though not illogically, "you must have six new surplices to do justice to the new cushions."

Mr. Choyce said surely two would be enough, but his be-trothed was adamant, pointing out that if three were at the wash and one had a little tear in it, he would only have two left. And if there were only two, something was *bound* to happen to one of them, like the time when the laundry had starched them almost as stiff as a board and they had to be unwashed by Mrs. Panter and re-ironed.

"You think of everything, dearest," said Mr. Choyce.

Miss Merriman said Why not ask Sir Robert Graham, as he was a churchwarden, and luckily Lady Graham drove up at that moment and finding Mr. Choyce there asked him to come back to Holdings and stay to lunch, an invitation which he accepted with pleasure, for he had always admired Lady Graham and though Miss Merriman must now take first place in his allegiance, Lady Graham would still have a throne of her own.

"Only just ourselves," said Lady Graham. "Robert said he would be back to lunch and he does so want to see you. I do not quite know why, but it will be very nice," which foolish words seemed to Mr. Choyce the very essence of kindness, as indeed they were intended to be. Then they were at Holdings and went indoors. Lady Graham said they would have some sherry and rang the bell; an act of glad confident courage which deeply impressed her guest. Odeena appeared.

"Sherry in the drawing-room, Odeena," said Lady Graham, "and tell Cook we shan't be ready for lunch for a quarter of an hour. Is Sir Robert in?"

"I'm sure *I* couldn't say, my lady," said Odeena, apparently imagining that Lady Graham suspected her of having secreted him in a cupboard. "Shall I ask Cook?"

"No," said Lady Graham, quite kindly. "Go and look in Sir Robert's study and if he isn't there, ring the outside bell." For an old bell with a long wrought-iron handle was fixed to an outer wall, with a little wooden penthouse over it, and was used to warn the family of meals when they were in the garden or the stables or the piggery or even—if the wind were in the right direction—on the river.

"Yes, my lady," said Odeena and went away.

"I have never heard her say My Lady before," said Mr. Choyce, considerably impressed.

"I don't think anyone had," said Lady Graham. "It was Mrs. Carter who thought of it. You know, that nice Mrs. Carter at the Old Manor House. She has had the same trouble with her foreign servants about speaking properly to people. So she very kindly took Odeena to the Barchester Odeon to a film about a sort of Scarlet Pimpernel hero where everyone said Sir or Madam and danced minuets on the slightest provocation. Of course Odeena came back perfectly enraptured and we have had nothing but Sirs and Madams ever since."

Miss Merriman, nearly always practical, asked if Lady Graham thought it would last.

"Now that it has begun, it is *going* to last," said Lady Graham firmly.

Then Sir Robert, summoned by the bell, came in and shook hands warmly with his vicar, saying how glad they all were to see him back, and they went in to lunch.

It was a very comfortable party of four who temporarily had a strong common interest, namely the approaching marriage and how nice it was of the Dean to marry them and how nice it was that Mr. Gresham would be best man, and the wedding was discussed all through lunch in an impartial way, each speaker trying to see it from someone else's point of view. Miss Merriman waited to get round to the question of how best to spend Mr. Adams's gift, but every time a change or a gap in the conversation seemed to make this possible someone was sure to sidetrack it. But while Odeena was out of the room fetching the pudding, Mr. Choyce, summoning up his courage and remembering that though he was not the Vicar of God on earth he was Vicar of Hatch End (which seemed to him the higher point of honour), told Sir Robert about Mr. Adams's cheque.

"Adams, eh?" said Sir Robert. "Never could abide the man, but he's a very good citizen and a remarkable character. Self-

made of course and it does him credit. Glad one of *my* daughters
didn't marry him, all the same."

"But Robert, they *couldn't*," said Lady Graham.

"Of course they couldn't," said Robert. "No one asked them
to, my dear. Well, Vicar, what are your ideas?"

"Dorothea—I mean Miss Merriman—" said Mr. Choyce—

"Never knew your Christian name, Merry," said Sir Robert.
"Never thought about it. A charming name. Much better than
Dodo."

This introduction of an unknown quantity struck the party
almost dumb.

"Do you mean Rose's mother?" said Lady Graham. "She is
dead, you know."

"Of course she's dead," said Sir Robert. "Didn't I go to her
funeral and have to stand half an hour in the rain with my hat
off. Can't think what made me think of her. She was Dorothy,"
he added, turning courteously to Miss Merriman, "and you, I
learn, are Dorothea."

Miss Merriman admitted it, with a smile to her betrothed,
who said, rather nervously, that the heroine of George Eliot's
Middlemarch was Dorothea and called Dodo.

"Eliot? I thought he wrote about religious things," said Sir
Robert. "Murder of Becket and all that. More in your line,
Choyce, eh?"

Mr. Choyce, flattered by being drawn into this discussion,
and how surprised he was in reading a recent life of Becket to
find that he was nearly seven feet high, which, he said, seemed
to him impossible.

"Ah well, Choyce, you know we are told that to God all things
are possible," said Sir Robert. "What the dickens were we
talking about, my dear?" he added, turning to his wife.

"How best to spend Mr. Adams's generous gift to the
church," said Lady Graham. "The money he gave to Mr. Choyce
for it."

"Then," said Sir Robert, looking accusingly at the company,

"we'd better discuss it. Miss Merriman, will you tell us what your feelings are," he added, very courteously.

Miss Merriman, always mistress of herself, said quietly that she had suggested some new cushions for the pews, or at any rate that they should be renovated, as they were so very lumpy.

"Excellent idea," said Sir Robert. "Only one thing against it. We had that bed on the top floor made over—the one your mother's maid Conque had—" he added, turning to his wife, "and in a year or so it was just as bad."

"If I might make a suggestion," said Mr. Choyce, "would it not perhaps be better to have new cushions made of that stuff like rubber sponges? They had some in the church where I was taking my friend's duties for a time lately and I thought them excellent. Very comfortable and do not collect fluff and dust as ours do. They have covers of some kind of plastic or rubber that only need to be sponged, or even wiped with a damp cloth, so there is never any dust or fluff flying about. When the League of Church Helpers beat our cushions once a year they have to tie handkerchiefs over their mouths and noses. I believe the rubber ones are expensive but they will last more or less for ever. Latex? I believe that is the name. Or if not, it is something like it," he added cautiously.

"Now who was it who used to say he always liked to hear persons talk because you were bound to get a surprise some-where?" said Sir Robert. "Extraordinary how one forgets things. I believe it was Adams. That man crops up wherever you go. Well, it's your cheque, Vicar, and what you say goes. Does everyone agree on this?" and he looked round the table, as he had looked round so many tables at so many meetings.

"Then the Ayes have it," said Sir Robert, who was celebrated for managing to ignore the No faction on any measure which had his approval, yet somehow without giving offence. "There's a man on one of my boards who has a large interest in whatever that stuff is. I'll get him to send a man and give us an estimate, Vicar. Trade price, of course."

"If," said Mr. Choyce, with unusual diffidence, "there were some money left over, would it perhaps be possible to put a small stone, or a brass plate, above the Holdings pew, to mark where Lady Emily Leslie used to sit while she was living here? I think the village would like it. I would."

"Oh, Mr. Choyce, how very kind of you," said Lady Graham, gently dabbing her eyes. "Darling Mamma. She did so love your services."

"And I loved and honoured her presence at them," said Mr. Choyce. "But one *never* knew what she would do next," which words broke the slight sentiment and everyone laughed— though most lovingly—remembering Lady Emily's various intromissions and her habit of winding herself in scarves only to unwind herself again and her sometimes too audible comments on the service; though only upon the words that were being read or sung, never upon the officiant.

So it was decided that Mr. Adams's gift should be put to these two uses and the money left over—if there were any—to be used for the general upkeep of graves, which all led to a very interesting conversation about cemeteries and their charm, Miss Merriman being adjudged the winner by her description of Brompton Cemetery when as a little girl she was staying with cousins near by, and on the west side you could walk on a long terrace overlooking a deep railway cutting, or run along the great curved corridors of the central building, and there was a tomb somewhere with the terrifying inscription "I am hiding in thee" so that the little girl Miss Merriman had been had nightmares about it.

It was a warm day for so early in April and Lady Graham said they might go and sit in the parlour, which faced the afternoon sun. So they went there and it was quite pleasant, even with one of the glass doors onto the terrace open. A noise, beginning far away, began to increase and become almost alarming.

"If it's one of Pilward's big lorries I'll speak to him about it," said Sir Robert. "I often see him at the Club," for by now the

County Club, a very old and once select Barchester institution with a handsome early nineteenth-century house in the middle of the city, had been forced to open its doors to many members who would never have been considered, nor indeed considered themselves, as eligible for election.

"It's not a lorry," said Mr. Choyce, who knew a good deal about motors though he could only afford a modest car. "It sounds to me more like a Hobgoblin. The new model. They've got the finest engines going and their body-work is first rate. It's coming up the drive, I think," and indeed the loud purring noise had increased and then died down with a comfortable hum to silence. Voices were heard and round the corner of the house Edith Graham came, almost running in her excitement, and hurled herself on her father and mother.

"Oh, mother, it's marvellous," she said. "Uncle David and Aunt Rose said we must come over to Merry's wedding, so we flew over and Uncle David had ordered a new car in England so he cabled that he'd take delivery at the airport, so we came straight to you. Here they are."

And there were Mr. and Mrs. David Leslie, much as we remember then when we last met, except that David was a little balder and perhaps a little stouter. His wife appeared to have come straight out of a beauty-parlour-cum-hairdresser-cum-dressmaker-cum-modiste and her silken legs were as unexceptionable as ever. There was a tremendous kissing and hugging and handshaking among the family and Miss Merriman wondered if she had better remove herself and her affianced till things were quieter, but the affectionate greetings of the newcomers put her mind quite at rest.

"Merry, my adored one, you look years, years younger," said David.

Miss Merriman said, very quietly, that it was happiness.

"When you say that, my precious Merry, I am dancing with tears in my eyes," said David, quoting a rather out-of-date song of nostalgic attractiveness.

"There is no need to," said Miss Merriman.

"Bless your heart, Merry, it is like old times to be snubbed by you," said David cheerfully. "Now tell me all."

"You know quite well that you don't want to hear," said Miss Merriman quietly. "Mr. Choyce and I have known one another for a long time and are both very happy. And I am so glad you and your wife and Edith have come. I know Lady Emily would have liked it."

David was silent for a moment, looking away towards the river.

"You know, Merry," he said, "when we were coming up the drive I somehow wondered if I could see darling Mamma. I didn't know I would go on missing her like this."

"One does," said Miss Merriman. "Even I do."

"Don't say 'even' like that," said David indignantly. "You were nearer to her than anyone. Oh, she loved us more of course, because we were her children. But you were the rock among us all. Choyce, you are a lucky man," to which Mr. Choyce, though much affected by David's words, answered quietly that his luck and his happiness were more than he had ever imagined. Then he was drawn into the general conversation and there was a great noise of everyone speaking at once. Lady Graham wanted news of Rose Leslie's children: Dorothy (after Rose's redoubtable mother, Lady Dorothy Bingham, now no more), known in the family as Dodo, and Henry (after David's father). Both were very well, said David, but it didn't seem worth bringing them for so short a visit, especially as they both went to a day school now and would be having a wonderful holiday in a Children's Camp, near a river. Lady Graham said wouldn't they be homesick, or get drowned.

"Bless your soft heart, Agnes," said David. "After all, they are ten years old or as near as makes no odds and citizens of the New World. Not the Brave New World which I cannot abide and long for four-wheelers and fogs and *really* poor people in rags and gin at twopence a go, but the New World, U.S.A. I must say that the joy of getting one's darling children into holiday camps almost makes up for everything. And don't say 'Wicked One' to me, Agnes, for I couldn't bear it. It would remind me of Rushwater and Mamma" he added, looking away.

"Darling Mamma," said Agnes. "One still misses her. David, tell me about Edith. We have missed her."

"We shall miss her, too, when we go back," said David. "Unless you want her to go back with us. We love having her," but his sister said very firmly that Edith really must settle down at home now and find something to do.

"I expect you are right," said David. "But you won't find it easy to make her stick to anything. All our friends adored her and she had beaux—such a delicious expression—by the dozen. But she is unsatisfied. I don't mean dissatisfied, I mean un. What the dickens the girl really wants, I don't know. Rose thinks she ought to be married."

"Rose has a very good head," said Lady Graham. "So has Hermione. You remember her sister Hermione, David, when we had Martin's seventeenth birthday dance at Rushwater. She married Lord Tadpole and lives almost entirely at their place near Tadcaster."

"I am enchanted to hear it again," said David. "But that isn't exactly what I'm talking about. Aren't there any beaux for Edith here?"

"Several," said Lady Graham. "And likely to be more. Really a daughter can be very trying. Emmy and Clarissa married so sensibly when they were about her age, or perhaps a little older, and they are so happy. Edith is an anxiety to me. There are at least three young men who are fond of her—though how deep it goes I couldn't say."

David enquired with real interest, who they were.

"Well, that nice George Halliday for one," said Lady Graham. "His father died, you know, and he is running the farm and being a good landlord. It's a lonely life for him. His mother goes away a good deal to relations, but I think he feels less lonely when he is alone."

"Therefore post hoc and ergo propter hoc," said David, "he ought to marry Edith."

"And if you really want to hear about the others," said Lady Graham, ignoring his last words, "there is that nice young Crosse, Lord Crosse's son over at Crosse Hall. He is in a bank and has prospects. I like him."

"That is rather a help," said David.

"Oh, but I like poor George Halliday too. Very much," said Lady Graham with decision.

"Well, we'll leave it at that," said David, who was beginning to feel a little bored already, as indeed he had always been too quickly and easily bored if decisions had to be made; but never by his Rose. "And who is the tertium quid?"

"But can't you *see*?" said Lady Graham. "And they are quite *distant* cousins."

"Not that boy of the Duke of Towers?" said David, "though when I say boy he isn't all that young. I hated him at dancing class when we were small. Thank God we didn't go to the same public school."

"Of *course* not," said Agnes with some dignity. She looked round, and seeing that the rest of the party were busily talking, she said, "Ludo, of course."

"If there were a garden path here, I would sit down on it," said David. "Agnes, you don't really mean it?"

"I shouldn't have said it if I didn't," said Agnes, without rancour, merely as one stating an ineluctable fact. "I don't think either of them know it. I can't tell you what Sandhurst has done for Ludo and he will be passing into the Brigade soon."

"And very nice too, darling," said David. "There is still a faint aroma of Ouida about the Brigade."

"Robert says—" Agnes began.

"Bless your heart, I was wondering how soon you would say

that," said David. "Rose never says David says to any one. She says I told David—"

"Which I am sure is very good for you," said his sister.

"Leaving that aside for the moment," said David, "what does Merry think?"

"Now, I will *not* have Merry bothered," said Lady Graham. "She is just going to be married and has quite enough to think of without our private worries. Ludo is a darling and he will, we hope, be in the Foot Guards. But Robert will arrange all that. And they are both very young. Edith is nearly nineteen. Mellings a little older," and she looked away into some far distance.

"Well, if it prove a girl, the boy Will have plenty; so let it be," said David. "And that, darling Agnes, is Lord Tennyson. Don't meddle too much."

"I *never* meddle," said Lady Graham with great dignity. "And as for money, if that is what you mean, I should think Ludo will have to work pretty hard. Death duties are killing England. Of course Robert has been insuring against them and doing everything legal he can to make it easier. I daresay Gillie has too, but if you make all the best arrangements about your property and make it over to your heir, then he dies first—or is killed in the next war in Ludo's case—and there you are without a son and all the death duties to pay."

To this David could not at once make any answer. Never before had he seen his beloved elder sister so moved, and to be moved was not part of his scheme for himself.

"And now we must talk about Merry's wedding," said Lady Graham, getting up and joining the rest of the party. "How are the arrangements going, Mr. Choyce?"

"Excellently as far as I know," said the vicar. "I can't tell you, Lady Graham, how kind people have been. You and the Pomfrets and Mr. Adams whom I hardly know, and so many other friends. And Panter at the Mellings Arms has given me a delightful present. A fur foot-muff for the winter, when I am trying to compose my sermon—for I made it a rule quite soon after taking Holy Orders to prepare my sermon on paper but to speak it extempore. It is made of quite beautiful skins. I cannot tell you how touched I was. I fear it may have cost a good deal."

"Good old Panter," said David aside to Sir Robert. "I don't know a man in West Barsetshire that can trap rabbits—and hares—as he does—and cure them too," to which Sir Robert only answered by a smile; but to anyone who knew him that smile would have meant as much as Lord Burleigh's nod.

At this moment Odeena appeared with a parcel.

"Please, my lady," she said, "the post's just come and there's a parcel for Miss Merriman so I thought I'd better bring it at once."

"Tell Cook," said Lady Graham, "that we are three more for tea. Here is your parcel, Merry."

"I don't know the writing," said Miss Merriman, trying as one so often does to guess who one's correspondent is with absolutely nothing to go upon.

Sir Robert very sensibly suggested that if she opened it she would probably find the sender's name inside.

"Besides, we are all panting to know who has given you what, Merry," said David.

Encouraged by these remarks Miss Merriman undid the parcel and took out a book rather badly wrapped in a piece of tissue paper which had obviously seen use before.

"To use a very démodé phrase, I can't wait to see what it is," said David, to which his niece Edith replied that she wished Merry wouldn't open it so that she could see what would happen to David. Probably there would have been a sparring match between David and his impertinent young niece, but all was forgotten when Miss Merriman uttered the words, "The Palace."

"What *do* you mean, Miss Merriman?" said Rose. "Has the Queen sent you a present?"

"Oh, I don't mean a *real* palace," said Miss Merriman, "I mean the Close."

There was a brief and pregnant silence.

"Do you mean the *Bishop*?" said Mr. Choyce.

"Well, it says on a card from them both, but I expect his secretary did it up," said Edith, who had been looking at it over Miss Merriman's shoulder. "It's that book he wrote about their cruise to Madeira."

There was complete silent for a moment.

"Let me see it for a moment, Edith," said David. "I must say the Palace has surpassed itself. Second-hand copy. I can distinctly see the words two and sixpence which have been written in pencil on the back page and rubbed out rather carelessly by some one," and he handed it back to her.

"Canon Joram's butler Simnet always speaks of the bishop's wife as the old cat," said Lady Graham, addressing apparently the circumambient air, but looking gratified when people began to laugh.

"Even a cat wouldn't do that," said David indignantly. "I mean if it *could* it wouldn't."

A fascinating discussion then took place as to how such a present should be acknowledged and several suggestions were made.

"I shall write to the Bishopess and thank her so much for the kind thought," said Miss Merriman firmly. "But I shall tell *everyone*, of course," which statement was loudly applauded.

"And then," she continued, "I shall give it to the next sale in aid of something. As she hasn't written my name in it, I think I shall be justified."

Her hearers agreed that this would be a good course to pursue and though they were sorry that Miss Merriman was going to be polite, they felt she was living up to her own standards and respected her. Then they all went in to tea and Miss Merriman, smiling at Mr. Choyce across the table, thought how delightful it would be when they were alone together at their meals in their own house.

After tea Rose and David Leslie bade an affectionate farewell to everyone and said Edith must come to America again soon, which she promised to do. They then drove off to The Towers and apparently thence to the whole of West Barsetshire, before going back to London for a play and supper at the newest night club. Lady Graham was sorry they had to go, but they promised to come for Miss Merriman's wedding, and so drove away.

After the excitement of Edith's homecoming and the lunch party, Lady Graham, having sent Miss Merriman upstairs to rest, felt that a short rest for herself would not be disagreeable, but first asked Edith what she would like to do.

"I know *exactly* what," said Edith. "I'll just hang up my new dresses that Rose gave me and then I'd *frightfully* like to go round the farm. Could we, father?"

Nothing could have been more pleasant, more flattering to Sir Robert. He also gave his daughter a good mark for hanging up her dresses instead of letting them lie about. Sir Robert had never, as we know through our long acquaintance with him, been a father who showed great outward affection for his children, but he thought much about them, none the less. That his boys were following or preparing to follow his own profession gave him much quiet satisfaction. Of his daughters the eldest, Emmy, had married Tom Grantly, son of the Rector of Edgewood, and they farmed at Rushwater with Martin Leslie, Agnes's nephew. His second daughter, brilliant, charming, unsure of herself, had been won and tamed by Charles Belton of a family as good as any in Barsetshire, now a master at Harefield School. Now there was this youngest, naturally the spoilt one of the family, who had so far never stuck to anything. She was very young and her parents thought a visit to her Leslie cousins in America would help to civilize her. Well, in a way it had. She seemed to be her old affectionate self, with some experience and poise added, which was so far all to the good, and for these last Lady Graham felt the Pomfrets were largely responsible.

"But what are we going to do with Edith now, Robert?" said Lady Graham, when Edith had gone upstairs to unpack. "She went to stay at the Towers so that she could go into Barchester every day to learn estate management and just as we thought she was settling down to it, David and Rose asked her to go to America. And what she wants to do now I cannot imagine."

"We shall just have to wait," said Sir Robert. "I shan't mind having a daughter at home for a bit. The last we've got, you know," to which his wife replied that she wouldn't mind having a daughter at home either, but Edith would have to do *something*, or she would never see any young people of her own age. Which seems now to be sadly true. "Are you ready, Edith?" he called up the stairs and in a moment down came Edith in her comfortable shabby English coat and skirt and her sensible brown shoes.

"You look very nice," said her father approvingly. "Come on," and off they went towards the farm where Sir Robert's bailiff, Goble, was delighted to see Miss Edith safely back and to show her the latest additions to the pig-world, who were sixteen in number and all trying to have their tea at once while the beneficent donor of the tea lay flatly upon her huge side and looked malevolently at her owner and her daughter through her small eyes.

"I say, Goble, it's lovely to smell pig again," said Edith. "Rose and David have lots of friends in America with gardens but none of them had pigs like ours. How is Holdings Goliath?" to which Goble replied that handsome was as handsome did and if Miss Edith would come along she would see something. Accordingly they went to the far end of the pig-sties and there was the great boar, Holdings Goliath, lying on his side waiting to be scratched.

"Can I have your stick, father?" said Edith.

"You take mine, miss," said Goble. "Sir Robert, he'll be wanting to scratch old Goliath himself," so father and daughter poked and scratched and tickled the great monster, who grunted his pleasure and from time to time turned his great bulk to indicate a fresh spot that required treatment.

Edith asked if Goble was entering any of the pigs for the Barsetshire Agricultural Show in the summer.

"Old Goliath he's going up again," said Goble, "and I've got a nice young boar I might send and I'm hoping for a nice lot of piglings. Her ladyship here," he went on, pausing before a sty a little further along, "has done us proud" and he stood aside to let Edith see an immense matron, reposing on her side, surrounded and overrun by piglings. On seeing Goble all the piglings began to shriek for help, saying that they had had nothing to eat or drink since last Tuesday, which very untrue statement left Goble unmoved. Their mother, probably annoyed at being disturbed in her afternoon nap, ponderously rolled herself over and engulfed her brood, who however almost immediately reappeared on the far side of her bulk and re-arranged themselves for another meal.

"They are *lovely*, Goble," said Edith, "I didn't see anything in the least like them in America," which in its literal sense was perfectly true, for if any of David's friends had pigs, she had not seen them.

"No, nor you won't, miss," said Goble, "unless it was some of young Mr. Halliday's pigs over at Hatch House. He's got a tidy lot of little 'uns."

"Thank you, Goble," said a voice, and there was George Halliday. "Welcome home, Edith. I met Choyce in the village and he told me you were back. You are looking very nice. I thought you might come back looking like the American *Vogue*."

Edith, who privately thought she did, was almost annoyed, but her real pleasure at seeing George got the upper hand and she welcomed him warmly.

"You're the first friend I've met," she said. "I only got back after lunch. Of course I don't count Miss Merriman and Mr. Choyce."

"I do," said George stoutly. "But I'm very glad to see you. My mother always asks after you. She is still at Rushwater with Sylvia."

Edith said she hoped she would go to Rushwater soon and see Mrs. Halliday. There was a pause. George Halliday had not expected to see Edith (as why should he when she had so lately arrived) and was trying to find his bearings. The pretty, pert, rather spoilt Edith had been replaced somehow by a better groomed and dressed Edith; one with poise (if one must use that word) rather than a slight cockiness. But where he stood he did not quite know.

"Was it fun in America?" said George.

"It was *lovely*," said Edith. "Rose and David were angels to me."

"And did you have heaps of beaux?" said George, having gathered from American literature that it was the right equivalent of admirers, or prétendants.

"Of course," said Edith. "Rose wouldn't have allowed me not to. I liked them all awfully, but I found them a bit young."

"Young yourself," said George cheerfully. "Wait a minute. I want to ask Goble about a tractor," and at once he was deep in technical talk with the bailiff, Sir Robert standing by to see fair play.

To Edith, accustomed lately to homage, to gifts of flowers and what she still thought of as candies (soon to turn into sweets now that she was home again), this was almost the equivalent of a snub. The three men were having a pig-talk and no one was paying any attention to *her*. She turned away rather pettishly, didn't look where she was going, and almost ran into a tall young man with a pleasing though rather melancholy face.

"Hi! hold up!" said her cousin Ludovic, otherwise Viscount Mellings.

"Ludo!" Edith shrieked, standing on tip-toe to kiss her tall cousin. "You've been growing again while I was away."

"Wrong again," said Lord Mellings. "It's only because I stand up straight. You can't slouch at the Shop. I'm only six foot two really, but there's a fellow who's six feet four and a half and he thinks he's still growing."

"Do you *have* to be tall in the Brigade?" said Edith. "When I see them marching it's always the privates who are so tall and the officers are often quite un-tall," over which last word she had hesitated, thinking "small" to be perhaps rather tactless.

"Oh, they take us as we come," said Lord Mellings loftily. "Mother sent her love to everyone. I'm really here on business, a kind of ambassador. Uncle Roddy wants to know if Holdings Goliath will oblige, but he won't hear of it unless your father will take a proper stud fee. It's always better to do things on a business basis."

At these very sensible and practical words, Edith almost burst. Here was she, just back from America and beaux and bouquets and in general a high old time, but when her cousin Ludo met her, fresh from her triumphs, all he wanted to talk about was a stud boar.

"Well, he's over by Goliath's sty, talking to George Halliday and Goble," said Edith, rather sulkily.

"Good. I'll go along and see what I can do," said Lord Mellings and went off to the sty.

If Edith had been an amateur of melodrama, she might have said "Foiled Again." But being a nice, rather spoilt young woman, she only kicked a stone into the side of the lane. This did her good, so she kicked it again.

"Hi, Edith! Look where you're kicking," said a cheerful voice, and there was Mr. Crosse, a pleasant friend to the Grahams for some years now and son of the widower Lord Crosse over at Crosse Hall.

"Oh, sorry. I didn't mean to kick *you*, John-Arthur," said Edith, for somehow by this hyphened name young Mr. Crosse was known to most of his friends.

"Whom *did* you mean to kick, then?" said Mr. Crosse, not unreasonably.

"Oh, I don't know—anybody," said Edith, and suddenly she saw how silly it all was and began to laugh.

"That's better," said Mr. Crosse. "Come to the sties with me. Father wants me to ask Goble about some young pigs."

So back to the sties they went, where George Halliday was talking to Goble about the tractor, while Lord Mellings waited his turn to enquire about getting Holdings Goliath in his capacity as future father to a large progeny whom he would probably never see and certainly would not recognize if he did. Mr. Crosse took his place in the queue to ask Goble about some young pigs. Sir Robert, intelligently interested in all these subjects, stood by as a kind of arbiter in case of need.

It was all too much. Edith would have liked to drown or stab herself on the spot just to show them what she thought of their behaviour and was only deterred by being at some distance from the river and not having a sword or knife. So she went away rather loftily, looking round from time to time to see if anyone had missed her. Busy talk with laughter from time to time reached her ears. A horrid prickling behind her eyes meant that she was going to cry, so she hurried back to the house, rushed upstairs to her bedroom, shut her door (though, we are glad to say on her behalf, *not* with a bang) and delivered herself to Misery. This was her welcome home! If people liked to talk about pigs, let them! If tractors were more important than politeness, that was that. If Holdings Goliath wanted to be the father of lots of piglets, well let him. She hated piglets and she hated Goliath and John-Arthur and Ludo and George Halliday. It then occurred to her that she also hated herself for being so silly, which made her laugh. It was rather a poor kind of laugh, but it helped, so she unpacked the rest of her luggage, laid or hung everything in its right place with her usual precise neatness, collected the presents she had brought from America for her family and the villagers, and then looked at her face in the glass.

"Idiot!" she said to it, and it looked as if it were saying Idiot back to her and they both laughed.

"Well, I'm sorry," said Edith to her reflection, "but John-

Arthur and Ludo and George were rather trying. Sherman
Concord and Lee Sumpter wouldn't have been so rude. I wish I
was back in America," she added defiantly. But somehow these
words, instead of lashing her to further fury as she had meant
them to do, made her laugh even more. And when she had
laughed enough she went downstairs again, at peace with the
world. It was nearly teatime now. She found her mother with
Miss Merriman. Her own troubles and the slights put upon her
were all forgotten in a moment and she asked how soon she
could see the vicarage.

"At any time you like," said Miss Merriman.

"Could we go after tea then?" said Edith. "Oh, and mother
this is for you," and she gave her mother a parcel wrapped and
tied with a skilful prettiness that we have almost forgotten. In it
was a soft silky scarf, warm, yet delicate enough to draw through
a wedding ring. Lady Graham was delighted with the present
and kissed the giver.

"Oh, and I've brought you a wedding present, Merry," she
said. "I *do* hope you will like it," and she offered her a package
wrapped in enchanting flowered paper and tied with the gayest
of tinsel ribbons.

Miss Merriman undid the ribbon, smoothed it, rolled it
neatly and put it aside. Then she unwrapped the parcel,
smoothed and folded the pretty paper, undid the inner wrapping
of tissue paper, and took out a grey silk bag, piped with silver,
with three different silvery zip fasteners for three pockets containing a little of everything that a bride could want in the way of
discreet made-up, powder, lotions, tissues and in fact all the
things we want and never seem to have when we need them,
including a special damp-proof compartment for the soft
sponge and pretty face-cloths that were nestling there.

We regret to have to write it again, but facts are facts, and
Miss Merriman did begin to cry. But she stopped almost at once
and thanked Edith with a warmth that was perfectly truthful.

"I remember when I was engaged," said Lady Graham, "someone sent me a lovely little crystal heart on a chain."

"Who was it?" said Edith.

"I never really knew," said Lady Graham. "There was no name in it, only a poem."

Edith and Miss Merriman begged for the poem.

"It was quite silly," said Lady Graham. "It said:

> "'Two little feet, unconscious they,
> Trod on the heart of a man one day,
> Two little feet ran gaily on,
> But the heart of the man was for ever gone.'"

"Oh, mother!" said Edith, deeply surprised that anyone as old as her mother should have had so romantic an experience—for there is something about our beloved parents that sets them to us, quite apart from romance; just as we appear now to our children and so it will always go on. "*Who* was it?" but Lady Graham laughed and said it was all very old history now and might have been any one of several men with whom she had danced and who had come to her mother's parties. Edith teased her mother for a little, but Lady Graham, though not resenting the teasing, would not tell. And if our reader thinks we are being unfair, we can only say that we have not had time to invent this prétendant to the lovely Agnes Leslie's hand. If he existed we fear he must have been a Detrimental—delightful expression now no longer in use.

Miss Merriman then said that she must go to the vicarage and Edith asked if she might come too and see the improvements, which pleased Miss Merriman very much. So they walked down to the village, making a kind of royal progress as one old friend after another stopped Edith to ask if she had had a nice time, and whether she had seen their Jack who was in a lumber camp in Oregon, or their Doris whose husband was a builder in Houston, splendidly ignoring the improbability of Edith, whose

visit had been limited to New York City and the surrounding
country (a fairly large radius, given good roads and mammoth
cars and two hundred miles as a pleasant afternoon's run),
having ever visited any of these places. But as none of her
questioners had the faintest idea where in the United States
these places were, no bones were broken.

Mrs. Panter at 6, Clarence Cottages, wife of George Halliday's carter, who as usual was doing her ironing at the front door,
partly because the light was better, partly to talk with any passing
friends, was the next to see Edith, so she put her iron back on the
stove and came out to shake hands.

"So you're back, Miss Edith," she said. "Nice to see you
again."

"It's nice to see you too, Mrs. Panter," said Edith and asked
after the children.

"Still at school," said Mrs. Panter, "and high time they wasn't.
If *I'd* been at school till I was their age, mother she'd have told
the teacher what she thought of her. Trouble is they keep them
at school too long, learning them things they don't want to
know," with much of which Miss Merriman privately agreed,
but felt it better not to say so.

"I brought some presents for you and the children, Mrs.
Panter," said Edith, offering her a parcel.

"Well, Miss Edith, that *is* a treat," said Mrs. Panter. "It isn't
often I get presents. Can I open it?"

Without waiting for permission she carefully untied it, rolled
up the pretty tinsel ribbon, and folded the pretty flowered
wrapping paper. Not till this was done did she look at the
contents.

"Oh, miss, they *are* lovely," she said. And indeed very pretty
they were. Printed scarves of gay colours for the girls, trappers'
caps made of sham fur for the boys, and for Mrs. Panter a long
plastic clothes-line with plastic attachments for hanging the
washing on.

"Oh, it's *lovely*, miss," said Mrs. Panter, deeply moved. "I'll keep it wrapped up careful and only use it for the best wash. You know I do some of Mrs. Carter's things at the Old Manor House. Her smalls are beautiful and real handsewn," and then she picked up her iron and her visitors went on their way.

As they had to pass the church, Edith said she would like to go in and there was Mr. Choyce talking with the verger and delighted to see them.

"We were discussing flowers for the wedding," he said. "I am not any good at that kind of thing."

"Nor am I," said Miss Merriman, "and I would rather marry you without flowers than have flowers and not marry you."

"Lovely flowers there were when Miss Clarissa used to do them," said the verger. "Lady Emily Leslie too, she always mentioned the flowers. And a rare time we had sometimes when her ladyship wanted to do the flowers a bit different. It was a happy time, miss, when her ladyship was living at Holdings."

"It was," said Miss Merriman. There was a silence, broken by Miss Merriman who said, "Herbert!"

"What, my dear?" said Mr. Choyce.

"What have we been thinking about?" said Miss Merriman. "Of course Mrs. Charles Belton—Clarissa that is—is coming to our wedding. Why shouldn't we ask Lady Graham if Clarissa could come to Holdings for the night before the wedding and do the flowers for the church? There is nothing that she can't turn to favour and to prettiness."

"My dear, you are always right," said Mr. Choyce, which words came so often from his mouth that his less reverent young friends made rather a joke of it, comparing his attitude to Miss Merriman (though in the most loving way) to Miss Betsy Trotwood's attitude to Mr. Dick.

"Then I will ring her up from Holdings if Lady Graham agrees," said Miss Merriman, though she had very little doubt of Lady Graham's acquiescence in anything that could help to make the wedding glorious without and within.

Edith, who had been wandering about the church, came back

to them and said she had been sitting in some of the pews and the cushions were far, far worse even than the cushions in the Holdings pew. This appeared to depress Mr. Choyce, who said he had been a careless shepherd in that he had allowed his flock to be in conditions of discomfort.

"Lord bless you, sir," said the verger, "that's nothing. Gives them something to think about. Makes them too comfortable and they'll go to sleep."

Miss Merriman said she believed people often did go to sleep in those old square pews, some of which had a fireplace in them, but it must have been very pleasant in winter. Then they told the verger about Mr. Adams's generosity which was going to enable them to get new hygienic cushions for the pews. It was but natural that the verger should at once disapprove of so drastic a change, but when he saw how pleased Mr. Choyce and Miss Merriman were, he allowed his better self to get the upper hand and said anyway it would mean less dust as what with them cushions and the coal dust from the stove in winter a man was fair choked.

"Do you think, Herbert," said Miss Merriman, "that Mr. Adams's kind gift might run to a new stove as well?" Mr. Choyce was doubtful, but Miss Merriman determined to find out what could be done. Not at once of course, but quietly, as time went on.

Then Mr. Choyce went into the vicarage and Miss Merriman with Edith walked back to Holdings, sometimes talking comfortably, sometimes in a comfortable silence. The evening passed quietly. When they were going to bed Lady Graham came up to see if all was comfortable in Edith's room and admired the lovely heavy jersey-nylon nightgowns that Rose and David had given her.

"Good-night, darling," she said. "It is lovely to have you back."

"For me too," said Edith. "I adored America and all Uncle David's and Aunt Rose's friends, but Holdings is best, and however often I go to America it will be lovely to have Holdings to come back to."

Lady Graham felt that life was not so permanent as that. Holdings must some day change. Edith's life would very probably some day change. But no need to think of these things yet, so she kissed her daughter and went away, glad at heart that Edith loved her home.

CHAPTER 3

The nuptial hour, as Mr. Choyce rather dashingly said, and then wondered if the words were in keeping with his cloth, was drawing on apace. Everyone had accepted and it was very probable that everyone would come. The mistress of the Infant School, who was very littery, at least that was how she described herself, said that Journeys Ended in Lovers' Meeting but this time the meeting was at Hatch End, at which moment she began to realize the possible implication of what she was saying and lost consciousness, while one of her colleagues giggled and the other said, What was she giggling about.

Easter obliged—in West Barsetshire at any rate—with three days of torrential rain, so that Lady Graham was quite seriously contemplating a reception indoors instead of the marquee that she was having in the garden. But on Tuesday evening the sky began to clear, and by Wednesday there was sun and a good drying wind. On Wednesday afternoon Messrs. Scatcherd and Tozer, the well-known Barsetshire caterers, came with vans and skilled workmen and put up on the lawn beside the river the largest and most beautiful marquee that had yet been seen. Its roof was made of hundreds of very long, thin triangles of white and of green sewn together, and when erected, with a kind of brass ridge along the top of it shining in the sun, everyone said "Oh," which, as our educated reader will remember, was what Man Friday said to his Unknown God. The rest of it was plain white canvas and along one side an awning propped on stout green poles gave extra room and shelter. Stacks of long trestle tables were brought in, unfolded and erected. Hampers of white tablecloths, great cases of glass and china and cutlery were unpacked, and a huge and horribly named fridge was planted in a corner. Electricians rushed about looking for the mains and tripping over each other's wires, and all was bliss.

Lady Graham's daughter Clarissa Belton came over from Harefield the day before the wedding, bringing branches of young foliage and spring blossom to which she added everything she could find in the Holdings garden and spent the afternoon decorating the church. Lady Graham's storeroom provided a number of large glass jars which Clarissa filled with flowers and greenery to stand on window sills and on the chancel steps. White lilac and fresh young beech leaves embowered the altar and for the tablet which marked the pew where Lady Emily Leslie used to sit Clarissa had drooping sprays of young willow.

The night was calm and the wedding day dawned with just enough morning mist to make a warm if not a hot day almost a certainty. More vans arrived, disgorging waiters. Mr. Tozer himself—for Mr. Scatcherd, who was still the ruling brain, had been bedridden for the last seven years at least and enjoyed bullying his staff from a place of safety—had come over In Person to honour the feast, which was now being carried out of the vans into the tent.

It is not for our pen to describe the descent of the Dean of Barchester, the Very Reverend Josiah Crawley, upon the vicarage accompanied by a verger with what George Halliday, who saw them go by, described as the Doings, and shortly followed by Canon Bostock. Rather let us tell how Mr. Gresham from East Barsetshire joined them, magnificent in his deliberately old-fashioned morning jacket, shepherd's plaid black and white trousers and a black-and-white check cravat (for no other word would do justice to his neckwear), the whole crowned with a grey top-hat. There were those who said that he was sporting a fob, but these were—in the fine words of Milton—blind mouths, for it was only two family seals set in heavy wrought gold, a watch key with a chased gold handle and an old family agate ring which had belonged to no one knew whom and had an unidentified crest on it.

The Dean, who had personally superintended every marriage of his large family and was in hopes of doing the same by his many grandchildren, was delighted to see the new decorations at the vicarage, and such was the interest felt by all the party in Mr. Adams's carpet that Mr. Choyce had to tear his guests away and lead them into the church, there to await the bride in the front right-hand pew, at which point Mr. Gresham took command. The Dean with Canon Bostock disappeared into the vestry. Lady Graham's guests gradually filled the other side of the aisle and luckily there were so many of them that they overflowed into the bridegroom's side till the church was quite full. And we may say that this is no uncommon event at weddings. Why the bridegroom's friends should so often be in a large minority (which sounds like a contradiction in terms) we do not know. Mrs. Morland, who was fairly near the front of the church, said to Lord Crosse, who was sitting by her, that when she went to weddings she nearly always sat on the bridegroom's side, just to help.

Lady Graham with her family, followed by the Leslies, filled the Holdings pew and overflowed into the pew behind by kind permission of Mrs. Carter from the Old Manor House. The young man from the *Barchester Chronicle* who was collecting names at the door dropped his pen in his excitement, trod on it by mistake and had to borrow a purple indelible pencil from Vidler the Fish, who was among the lookers on. And so the County gently took possession of the church and talked in reverent whispers to such an extent that Caxton, in his official capacity as sexton, took it out on the village boys at the back of the church, threatening them with excommunication in all its forms if they didn't shut up and behave theirselves.

Mr. Choyce, standing with Mr. Gresham in splendid isola-
tion, looked round his church in great thankfulness to all the
friends who were there, yet at the same time with a little sadness
that the church, so crowded now, should be so poorly attended
at other times, but reflecting that it would be unreasonable to
expect the present congregation—many of whom lived at some
considerable distance and went to their own churches—to turn
up at Hatch End, he contented himself with a prayer of gratitude for all the blessings so far vouchsafed to him. When we say
so far, it is because Mr. Choyce had made a mental reservation in
his trust and gratitude, namely that although so far everything
had gone well, there might be some shattering blow in store
against which it would be well to be forearmed. In more than
one novel (and Mr. Choyce was an omnivorous reader) a bride
had been found dead on her bridal morn or—though this was
less common—had swooned at the very altar steps. There was
also the unfortunate case of Lucy Ashton, brought trembling,
chill, distracted to her wedding and found on her wedding
night, a blood-spattered, mowing and mopping idiot, in the
fireplace. But his excellent common sense, fortified by a short
silent prayer, came to his aid, the more so as already there was a
stir at the church door and Sir Robert Graham entered the
church with the bride on his arm.

As they came slowly up the aisle Mr. Choyce, though realizing what was happening, lost consciousness. Mr. Gresham, who
had been best man more often than anyone in the county,
propelled his charge into the right position, reminded him in an
aside that would have done credit to Irving that he had the
wedding ring in his waistcoat pocket and that Mr. Choyce need
not feel nervous. Mr. Choyce saw land ahead and tried to
concentrate his mind without any visible sign of success, but as
no one ever looks at the bridegroom, who is but an extra in a
superb production, he was perfectly safe. All eyes were riveted
on Miss Merriman, calm as ever, coming up the aisle with Sir
Robert, looking neither to the right nor the left, nor even

towards her betrothed, but towards the altar in the dim East End. The seconds withdrew and the plighted couple were alone, the Dean and Canon Bostock barring, as it were, the way to the altar.

It was universally admitted, except by the Palace who were not represented and therefore do not count, that never had the Dean spoken so well, never had a bride been more beautifully composed in her bearing, clear in her responses, and uplifted with quiet happiness. The Dean, with the wholehearted approval of Mr. Choyce, then read the noble marriage service as it used to stand before THEY began their intromissions; a form of prayer which states clearly and forcibly the reasons for the state of matrimony and its beauty as a sacrament. The ring slipped easily onto the bride's finger. The couple followed the Dean to the altar and there was silence, broken only by a foolish young bird who had forgotten how it got in and paid no attention to its mother who was shrieking to it from a window while it fluttered madly about.

Then they came down from the chancel, looking, as Mrs. Panter said, quite a picture, and so into the vestry, followed by a great crowd of Grahams and Leslies and their kin. Here the register was signed and everyone admired the firmness of Mrs. Choyce's writing. Lady Graham, as acting nearest of kin, kissed the bride—a thing that in their long relationship had never before occurred and probably would never occur again. The bride's hand was taken by so many friends that she was almost bewildered. And meanwhile there was so much conversation in the church—though with a respectful lowering of the voice— that but for Caxton who walked down the aisle announcing in a stage aside the imminent arrival of the bride and bridegroom, they might be talking yet. Now was every eye on the entrance to the vestry and out came the married couple. Mrs. Choyce—late Miss Merriman—with her veil thrown back from her quiet radiant face; Mr. Choyce—for the man rarely comes out so well on this occasion—with an expression of what we can only call sheepish bliss. At the top of the aisle Mrs. Choyce paused, to smile at her friends in the Holdings pews and to give a loving glance at the tablet in memory of her dearly loved Lady Emily Leslie, and then they went down the aisle and out of the church into the porch, where they were at once surrounded by the friends who poured out behind them, and held a kind of court.

"Excuse me, Mr. Choyce," said a young man, unknown to anyone present, wearing a rather dirty khaki mackintosh, "I'm the *Barchester Chronicle*. Would you like to say a few words?" and he produced a dirty notebook and a purple pencil.

Mr. Choyce hesitated. Luckily he had a supporter who knew exactly what to do and how to do it.

"Not here, young fellow," said Sir Robert in the voice that, when he used it, had quelled not only his soldiers but everyone with whom he had come in contact during his distinguished career. "Come down to the reception and I'll see that you are looked after."

"Oh, well," said the young man, at once taking a journalist's interest in something new, "I don't mind if I do. What is the name?" and he opened his pad.

"Caxton!" said Sir Robert. The sexton sprang to attention. "See that this young man gets down to Holdings and has some lunch. I'll look after him there" and he continued his progress.

The newly married couple were then wafted into the Holdings car and driven away. Gradually the other guests followed, by car, or on foot. The weather had settled to one of those spring days when we think that summer has begun—and if it lasts until the evening we are grateful for these small mercies. Holdings was looking its best with the young green of the lawns and trees, many of which were blossoming in pink and white in spite of the inclemency of the last weeks. The company spread out on the lawn, expressing loudly its admiration of the marquee and rather greedily looking to see if there was champagne. Mr. and Mrs. Choyce were planted by Lady Graham under a flowering white double-cherry and as the guests walked past them with handclasps and kindly words of greeting they were delighted to see many old friends, not to speak of friends of Lady Graham, people who had known and respected and liked Miss Merriman.

Among the first to greet the newly made Mrs. Choyce were Lord and Lady Pomfret, who had not been able to get away from their duties in time to go to the church and now only had time to put in an appearance for the pleasure of congratulating their faithful friend and helper. Both of them kissed the bride, shook hands warmly with Mr. Choyce and passed on. Mrs. Choyce laughed very gently.

"What is it, my dear?" said Mr. Choyce. "I do like your laugh."

"Oh, just something I thought of, Herbert," said his bride. "I'll tell you some day," and then they had to greet the other guests who passed them in what seemed an endless line, all bringing most genuine regard or affection. With her usual methodical approach to anything she undertook Mrs. Choyce managed to say to almost every guest a special word of remembrance, or gratitude, or an experience shared in old days, and the procession went on and on.

Among the guests were of course Lady Graham's brother John Leslie and his nice wife from Greshamsbury with their three sons, all old Southbridgians, whom we met at the school a year or so ago. They were and always had been known to their friends as Major, Minor, and Minimus, and the names seemed likely to stick. We need hardly say that the three Leslies and their rather older Graham cousins at once coalesced, reminding Mrs. Crofts, the wife of Colonel the Reverend Edward Crofts, Vicar of Southbridge, and a bitter philavian (if that expresses correctly some people's devotion to birds) of the swallows who were popularly supposed to fly round and round as the cold weather approached till, tightly packed into a ball, they dropped into the nearest pond and there hibernated peacefully. The three Graham boys had slightly the advantage in age and the moral superiority which being in the Brigade of Guards can give, but their Leslie cousins were perhaps stronger in these eccentricities which are still, we are glad to say, practised at the two Universities. Major, so does time pass, was doing well at Oxford and considered a certainty for a good degree, and what is more had made at Southbridge School in the previous summer, during the Old Boys v. The Rest, the spectacular catch off Mr. Feeder's bat that had finished the innings. His brother Minor was due to go up in the autumn with a scholarship for which he had swotted with an energy never before given to his work, his aim therein being to beat the Oxford Alpine Club's record by walking round the quad of St. Jude's along the face of the building on the second floor, thus also doing better than George Halliday, who had only done it on the first floor. Minimus was on the whole a dark horse, as the youngest often is, but he had a way with animals and his father thought he might later be an addition to the farm their Cousin Martin Leslie owned at Rushwater.

The six cousins then constituted themselves a kind of internal police, handling refreshments and being—in Kitchener's words to the First Expeditionary Force—courteous to women but no more. For though they all had excellent manners when they wished and could make themselves popular wherever they were, Cupid's darts had not yet touched their hearts. We do not of course exclude Captain James Graham's passion for the enchanting actress Jessica Dean (a passion shared by all theatregoers), Lieutenant John Graham's devotion to the still lovely Rose Fairweather, who was almost old enough to be his mother, or second Lieutenant Robert Graham's romantic sentiments towards Glamora Tudor, at present starring in her latest film *Pearl of Paris* as Cora Pearl, supported by her latest co-star, Buck Pickaback, scion of a very old Pennsylvania-Dutch family.

Edith Graham, who had up till now been much interested in the wedding and the marquee and the excitement, was not in a good mood. Everyone was talking to someone and no one was talking to her and she jolly well wished she were somewhere where people were POLITE. She might be the youngest of the family, but she was now the only unmarried daughter and as such, in a CIVILIZED country, she said bitterly to herself, people ought to pay attention to her. One didn't expect one's brothers to bother, but her cousins Major and Minor ought to have better manners and Minimus was just a stupid boy who didn't know better and she hated them all. Even George Halliday or John-Arthur Crosse would be better than nothing—or even Ludo. But Lord Mellings had not been with his parents so she supposed he wasn't coming and hated him with black hatred. So black was it that she could not see where she was going and almost banged into her uncle David with her aunt Rose.

"Hold up, Edith," said David. "What on earth's the matter? Here am I and Rose, our journey home postponed, our starving children at home in their empty bassinets. Is this all you can do for us? What's up, my girl?"

Edith said everyone was awful.

"Very well, they are awful," said Rose. "Now tell us the rest."

By this time Edith was rather ashamed of herself and didn't know what to say, so she spoke the truth.

"I thought it was going to be fun," she said. "But the boys only want to talk to the other boys and I'm out of it. And George Halliday isn't here, at least I can't see him, and John-Arthur isn't either. I wish I could go back with you to New York."

"Well, we don't," said Rose, not unkindly. "Not till you can behave like an English lady and not have the tantrums."

There was a silence. David and Rose looked at each other and Rose shrugged her elegant shoulders.

"I'm sorry," said Edith. "I expect they are talking to Merry," to which she added generously, "After all it's *her* wedding day. Let's go back."

So they all walked back towards the party. Rose and David looked at each other over Edith's head with a kind of amused resignation. And as if she had felt their look she was rather silent.

"Sorry, Rose. Sorry, Uncle David," she said presently.

"It hurt you a great deal more than it did us" said David.

"Would you like to come back with us? We are flying next week."

"Oh, Uncle David, I'd—" and then she stopped.

"Well?" said David.

"I thought I ought to stay here and make up for being so rude," she said. "Besides, Gobel may be showing some pigs at the Barsetshire Agricultural. But thank you, *awfully*, both of you."

Rose said nothing, but in a friendly way. David clapped his niece on the shoulder in approval and they walked back to the lawn. Here, with brilliant sunshine, they were just in time to see the arrival of Captain and Mrs. Fairweather from Greshamsbury.

We need hardly say that as Rose Fairweather and her husband walked across the lawn to join the queue and greet the newly wed couple, everyone turned to look at them. And when we say Them, we are told that husband and wife are one flesh, but luckily they still manage to put up a good show of being two people.

In the words of their old nurse, none of the Leslie boys were backward in coming forward and Rose Fairweather was at once surrounded, not only by them but by some dozen friends and admirers. Nor, we are glad to say, was her husband neglected. The blue eyes with wrinkles round them from so much gazing at the heavens and the waters, the well-shaven face and seaman's bearing, not to speak of the responsible look of one used to being in charge of a ship and her complement of men, made several young female hearts quicken, nor did he check their artless admiration. Not that his wife would have minded in the least, for if she had he would have sent them all packing. But just as it amused him to watch his Rose surrounded by her adorers wherever she went, so did she regard with mild benevolence his efforts to conceal how bored he was by his female fans.

The line of guests was now almost at an end, when Mrs. Morland appeared, bringing with her, as she often did, her old friend Lord Stoke, an arrangement by which both benefited as Mrs. Morland much enjoyed driving with Lord Stoke in his dogcart or his brougham, according to the weather, while Lord Stoke, who had no nerves at all, found being driven in her car by Mrs. Morland an interesting experience. Not that the gifted authoress was a bad driver, but such incidents as two large tortoise-shell hairpins falling out and getting mixed up in the gears, or her bag falling off the seat, bursting open and disgorging its contents over the floor, were not uncommon.

"A *lovely* wedding," said Mrs. Morland enthusiastically. "I don't know *when* I have cried so much. It couldn't have been better."

Mr. Choyce expressed the hope that it was not anything in the service that made her cry.

"Oh, not a bit!" said Mrs. Morland. "It was a most uplifting kind of service, and so lovely to hear all the proper words. Not that it matters if you are being married yourself because words simply go over your head like water off a duck's back. After all there is nothing in a *word* to annoy anyone, and anyway when you are being married you really wouldn't notice if they were reading the Commination Service, except that of course it would sound a little peculiar because one isn't used to it. I mean it seems to have got neglected somehow, probably because of being out of date. I mean a lot of the things we would be cursed for doing we certainly wouldn't do and really what some of them are one never exactly knows. Especially all the people one has to curse, though I don't really *know* anyone who does all those things any more than I know the exact difference between fornicators and—" but at this point her old friend Lord Stoke, who, though he could not hear very well, thought that Mrs. Morland had been talking long enough, interrupted to say in the voice of the increasingly and also deliberately deaf:

"Congratulations, Choyce. Glad you didn't have any of these new-fangled improvements. 'Remedy for sin,' eh. That's good enough for most of us. Never got married myself, I don't know why. But if I had, I'd have liked a wedding like yours, just in the village church and only old friends, eh? And then just jog off home quietly."

Mr. Choyce said that Mrs. Morland was very kindly lending his wife—at which word, said for the first time in public, he looked at her most affectionately—and himself her house at High Rising for the weekend after which they would be settling into the vicarage.

"And so to bed, eh?" said Lord Stoke, at which point the bystanders felt they would have the giggles if they weren't careful. "Well, well, it will all be the same in a hundred years. Oh, by the way," said Lord Stoke. "I never sent you a wedding present, Vicar. I remembered that just as the dogcart came round. I did think of the brougham as there were a few drops of rain over my way, but I said to myself 'No, damme' I said— sorry, Mrs. Choyce, you must forgive an old dog who can't learn new tricks—'if it rains it rains.' Now what the deuce was I saying—oh, yes, about a wedding present. I found something in the safe that you and your good lady may like to have—don't often see things like that now," and from one of his many pockets he lugged a wash-leather bag which gave a chinking sound in his hand. "Worth between thirty and forty shillings or more now, I think," he went on. "Well, God bless you. Not my place to say that, padre, but you know what I mean," and having shaken them both warmly by the hand he put on his low grey rather flat-topped bowler and went away. Both Mr. and Mrs. Choyce would gladly have looked inside the bag, but there was by now still a considerable queue to follow. Mr. Choyce tried distractedly to put the bag into a waistcoat pocket, but his wife quietly took it from him and put it in her silver bag.

"You always come to my help, my dear," said the Vicar, and then the remaining guests, rather impatient by now, surged onwards.

Mr. Tozer then approached Lady Graham.

"I think, my lady," he said, in much the same clear yet reverent voice that the undertaker used in *Huckleberry Finn* to explain to the funeral guests that the unexplained noise was a dog after rats in the cellar, "it is about time for the healths to be drunk. I Myself am superintending the champagne. The pop which the cork makes when being drawn is quite unnecessary if properly handled, so your ladyship need have no apprehension."

"Thank you, Mr. Tozer," said Lady Graham. "That will be very nice."

"Then if your ladyship would have the bride and bridegroom well placed before the tent, your ladyship, we can proceed" said Mr. Tozer and went off to the marquee.

By this time all the young cousins were congregating near the marquee in joyful and confident hope of drink, and under Lady Graham's instructions they gathered in the guests. The bride and bridegroom were delivered to Sir Robert, who stood in soldierly exactness between them, and addressing the guests said in his parade voice, warranted to be heard at any distance, that he was glad to have two such old friends married from his house, paid a short and sincere tribute to Mr. Choyce's work in church and village and Miss Merriman's invaluable services to so many of his wife's family, wished them health and happiness and raised his glass. Everyone followed his example and the younger members of the party at once had theirs filled again in confident hope of another toast. Nor were they disappointed, for Mr. Choyce, in as few words as possible, thanked everyone, expressed his and his wife's gratitude to the host and hostess, and asked the company to drink to their health and to the memory of a beloved friend now no more among them, Lady Emily Leslie.

Almost (as in Horatius the story was told) with weeping and with laughter did everyone drink the toast. Those who did not really like champagne, or found it did not improve the rheumatics, drinking a token sip, the younger members tossing off their bumpers like good 'uns, though not without one or two explosions, notably from Leslie Minimus who spluttered and choked and was led off whooping by one of his Graham cousins, who kindly hit him on the back and told him not to be a guzzling little fool.

Then did Mrs. Choyce, ably assisted by Mr. Choyce, pretend to cut the wedding cake which had really been pre-sliced. Then did Mr. Tozer and his head myrmidons cut up the slices and hand them to the guests. It is always difficult to manage the slice or finger of cake which by this time is rapidly breaking into its component parts of rather hard sugar, extremely glutinous almond paste, and some cake disintegrating into crumbs, and in a drawing-room can become a messy affair; but in the garden that did not matter.

Sir Robert, who as far as we know had never in his life broken his word, had not forgotten the young man from the *Barchester Chronicle*, whom he found in the tent, a half-empty glass of champagne in his hand and two or three more on the table near him.

"Now, young fellow," said Sir Robert, "let's see what you've been scribbling. Must get everything correct. If you don't you'll offend people and they'll complain. And if you want champagne there's plenty."

"I'm really very sorry, Sir Robert," said the young man, his teeth almost chattering with nervousness. "I don't often see champagne."

"Daresay you don't," said Sir Robert. "Now, let's see what you've been scribbling."

"It's all in my head, Sir Robert," said the young man.

"H'm," said Sir Robert, which monosyllable terrified the young man more than ever. "Here's a typed list of guests. You needn't put 'em all in, but at least they'll be correct. And here, take this, and don't go about drinking heel taps again. It lets the *Chronicle* down." With which words he pointed to an unopened bottle of champagne and went away.

Lady Graham, with one or two select friends, had now withdrawn Miss Merriman from the feast and accompanied her to the house where her suitcase was already packed and her ordinary clothes waiting, for she had decided, sensibly we think, to go on wearing the clothes she had and liked, and only gradually to buy new things as she found she needed them. Only on one point was Lady Graham adamant. One good three-quarter length evening dress, she had said, Miss Merriman must have, as they were sure to be asked to dine by the neighbours. Miss Merriman had meekly submitted, and no one knew with what excitement and joy she bought the discreet black frock of stiff moiré silk with three-quarter sleeves and a little jacket that went with it and then, greatly daring, had spent part of the cheque that the John Leslies had given her on an equally discreet fur capelet or tippet.

Her preparations did not take long. With a great deal of cheering from the younger members, Mr. and Mrs. Choyce got into his little car and drove away to High Rising where Mrs. Morland's faithful if bullying maid Stoker was awaiting them. She gave them an excellent dinner and having seen them comfortably settled in the drawing-room, went back to the kitchen where she hospitably entertained her various helpers from the village and they drank a whole bottle of not very good champagne from the grocer.

The married couple spent a pleasant hour or so, talking like old married people about their wedding and the party and how kind everyone was.

"You did promise, my dear," said Mr. Choyce, "to tell me why you laughed when Lord and Lady Pomfret congratulated you."

"So I did," said his wife. "But perhaps I'd better not."

This was of course exactly the way to whet Mr. Choyce's curiosity.

"I don't want to intrude, dearest," he said—

"You called me dearest," said Mrs. Choyce.

"Well, so you are," said her husband. "As I was saying, I do not in the least wish to intrude, but your laugh is so charming and I just happened to wonder what made you laugh so sweetly."

"I suppose I oughtn't to tell you—" said Mrs. Choyce doubtfully.

"There will never be an Ought between us," said Mr. Choyce. "But just as you wish, dearest."

"I do love it when you say dearest," said his wife. "It was only that years ago, when I was secretary to old Lady Pomfret—*my* Lady Pomfret, though I admire and love this one—when Lord Pomfret was only Mr. Foster and staying at the Towers—"

"Yes, dearest?" said Mr. Choyce.

"—and I felt very sorry for him," Mrs. Choyce went on. "He was a cousin—you know the Pomfrets' only son was killed in India years before I went to the Towers—and then suddenly his dreadful old father died and he became the heir. He didn't want it, but there it was. I was able to help him a bit—about the estate and things. I know I was a good deal older than he was, but—oh, it all sounds silly."

"Nothing you have ever done in your life could be silly, my dear," said Mr. Choyce. "I expect you cared for him a little and I don't wonder. There isn't a better, more hard-working, honest, sincere, selfless man in West Barsetshire."

"Oh, *thank* you, Herbert," said his wife. "How *did* you guess. Yes, I did care a little. But of course when he got engaged to Miss Wicklow—Lady Pomfret now—I was delighted because it was right for him and right for the Towers and the county. He told me himself, which was very nice of him. But I didn't sleep that night. And that was all. And then this afternoon, when he very nicely kissed me, I couldn't help thinking of the silly secretary who cried all night because a young man half her age was going to marry the right girl. Then I thought how lucky she was to be marrying you and I couldn't help laughing."

"Thank you very much, dearest," said Mr. Choyce. "I am sure he deserved your affection and I wish you hadn't been unhappy. And I shall do my best to make you happy and keep you happy as long as we live. Where *did* I put my pipe—you don't mind a pipe, do you?"

Mrs. Choyce said she liked pipes but couldn't bear cigars because you couldn't get the smell out of the room and Mr. Choyce said he had smoked a cigar when he was at school and that was enough to last him till the end of his life.

"Where the *dickens* did I put my pipe?" he said, rummaging in all his pockets. "Oh, I've got it. And where is the present Lord Stoke gave us?" His wife took from her bag the wash-leather bundle and gave it to her husband, who untied the tape that fastened it. "Oh! look!" he said as he poured onto the table beside him a pile of glittering gold. "Sovereigns—and half-sovereigns," he said, awestruck. "I'd forgotten how lovely gold is."

His wife very sensibly asked what a sovereign was worth now. She had, she said, illegally kept a half sovereign for a long time and then sold it to a pawnbroker in Barchester for fourteen shillings to which her husband replied that it served her right for not taking it to a bank where she would have got more. And both being rather tired they soon went to bed.

Mrs. Choyce's last remark before going to sleep may be recorded.

"Herbert," she said, "I do wish my sister could see how happy I am," and we think this is the only occasion on which she had ever shown any exultation over those who had not been particularly kind to her.

At a London wedding things are usually flat when the bride and bridegroom have driven away in the bridegroom's rather shabby two-seater with a couple of suitcases. The bride's mother, exhausted by standing and being agreeable to all her daughter's new in-laws and all the in-laws' friends whom she is certain she will not know if she meets them again, only wants to go home, take off her finery, put her feet up and perhaps later go out with her husband and dine at that nice little restaurant we have just found so we are going there quite a lot as it is sure to be spoilt as soon as it gets really popular. But in the country, even in

early April when the day may be warm but the evening is pretty
well bound to be cold, life seems to go on much as before.

Messrs. Scatcherd and Tozer's men had with incredible
swiftness dismantled the tent, packed up all their impedimenta,
and were ready to go, only waiting for Mr. Tozer, who after a few
amorous passages with Cook of the "I'd like to see you do it
then" with the riposte "Well, if you don't take care, you will"
type, had left an unopened bottle of champagne in the kitchen as
a token of esteem.

"O.K., now, boys," said Mr. Tozer, getting onto the front seat
of the van. "His Nibs has done us nicely. A pound each for each
of you lads. Here you are."

"What did he give *you*, Mr. Tozer?" said the youngest of the
men, who was at least forty, to which Mr. Tozer replied that
findings were keepings, but Cook had given him half a dozen of
beer and if Eddy could lay his hand on the glasses they might
make the beer look small. Which they accordingly did.

It was not for nothing that Scatcherd and Tozer were ac-
counted the best caterers in West Barsetshire. Not a crumb was
left on the lawn at Holdings. The places where the tent poles
had been and where the ropes that tethered the tent were
picketed had been filled up and the grass well trodden into the
hole. In a few days all would be exactly as it was. A large
contingent of sparrows were dealing with bits of cake and bread
and any other odds and ends that had escaped Mr. Tozer's men,
and to the sparrows were added some pigeons who had heard
about the wedding in Barchester and had rushed over to gobble
what they could, even if it meant missing evensong. Peace lay
upon the garden and the water-meadows and the river, but only
until the younger members of the party, reinforced by George
Halliday and young Mr. Crosse, who had gone up the river in
the punt and the rowing boat, should come back, which they
were bound to do soon.

Lady Graham with her brother John Leslie and his nice wife
had gone indoors, taking with them the guests from Greshams-

bury, Captain Fairweather, R.N., and his wife Rose, to whom were added Captain Francis Gresham, R.N., and his wife, whose people were also navy. These Lady Graham pressed to stay for supper, on the grounds that the caterers had left a lot of food behind and it seemed a pity not to eat it, but they had to decline regretfully, as they were all dining with the Rector.

"Oh, that delightful Canon Fewling," said Lady Graham. "He is nearly as nice as Mr. Choyce only he isn't married. I wonder why," and so had many other people, but Canon Fewling's heart had its own reasons.

There was a sort of bang on the door.

"I do wish Odeena could remember not to knock," said Lady Graham.

The knock was repeated. Lady Graham said resignedly: "Come in."

Odeena appeared on the threshold and stopped, apparently struck motionless and dumb by the sight of company.

"What is it, Odeena?" said Lady Graham, who had found that her henchmaid was incapable of speech unless prompted.

"Please, my lady, it's Cook," said Odeena. These words of fear, unpleasing to a housewife's ear, fell heavily on the guests, except for Rose Fairweather who was invulnerable to all domestic shocks.

"What does she want?" said Lady Graham calmly.

"Please, my lady, she says she's getting you a lovely buffer supper and when will the young ladies and gentlemen be back," said Odeena.

Rightly interpreting the buffer supper as a buffet, or in other words everything that was left over from the wedding, Lady Graham said that would be very nice and would Odeena ring the outside bell to warn the guests who were on the river, which she did with heart and soul.

"And now, Mrs. Gresham, do tell me about your children," said Lady Graham, who really meant what she said, having so many herself.

"Rather an odd lot," said Mrs. Gresham. "We had one boy, Frank, and then Francis was a prisoner of war in the Far East," and her eyes darkened at the remembrance of those dark years. "And then we had two girls, so of course they are a good deal younger—almost like a second family. Frank doesn't think much of them at present, but they are really very nice. They are called Jane after me and Mary for no reason at all except that there was a sort of ancestress called Mary Thorne who brought some money into the Gresham family, though where it is now I do not know," which explanation drove several of the company into trying to explain to each other who was who, and when.

"I know," said Rose Fairweather suddenly. "The money belonged to somebody called Scatcherd who was frightfully rich and left all his money to someone who no one quite knew who she was, but she turned out to be someone called Mary Thorne only that wasn't really her name because she was illegitimate only a Dr. Thorne adopted her. Scatcherd's Stores at Northbridge are the same family, of course very distant now and anyway she married somebody Gresham," after which almost correct if confusing elucidation she opened her bag and took out a powder compact. Her husband reached out a large powerful hand, took the compact, and put it in his pocket, saying "Not in the drawing-room, my girl."

"And we are Greshams and live in a bit of the big house," said Captain Gresham. "It's fascinating how these county connections go on going on. Some old cousins of mine still own it but they can't afford to live in it all. I hope you will come and see it, Lady Graham," which Lady Graham, who inherited her mother Lady Emily Leslie's passion for poking about in other people's houses, said she would be delighted to do.

"It is so curious," said her ladyship, "how you know some people and don't know other people," a truth which was incontrovertible. "I mean," she went on, "there are people like Victoria Lady Norton, who have lived in West Barsetshire for quite some time, but somehow we have never got to know each other.

Really, one hardly *can* know people when they are so dull that they make you squint," which comparison made the party laugh and there was a delightful conversation about West Barsetshire Bores during which Miss Frances Harvey at the Ministry of General Interference, still housed at Gatherum Castle, was given brevet rank as a Barsetshire woman so that she might be included.

"Of course, there *is* Mrs. Tebben," said John Leslie, "over at Worsted, who will wear homespun and has never got over taking a degree at Oxford."

"But she is kind, John," said his wife. "You remember she asked us to supper after the Worsted Flower Show."

"If you call that kindness," said John Leslie. "Cold pressed beef only it was rather warm and damp, and a salad which I can only describe as tired—"

"But that's *French*," said Rose Fairweather. "You remember, John darling, that nice French naval man we met at one of those conferences and he asked us to dinner and made the salad dressing himself and when he was mixing it he called it fatiguering the salad."

"I do, my girl," said Captain Fairweather, "and what's more I won about ten thousand francs off him at the Casino—I think it was about a million francs to the pound then," he added cheerfully and with what looked suspiciously like a wink. "And now we must really go. Come along, my girl."

So they and the Greshams went away.

"It is extraordinary," said Lady Graham to her husband, "how when one changes the conversation one can never remember what one was talking about. I think I hear the children," whose homecoming had indeed been very audible for several minutes, and then the river party came tumbling in like the Cat and her Kittens when Miss Mouse was entertaining Mr. Rat and Mr. Frog, and all was confusion and talking at once till Lady Graham uttered the words Supper and Saloon.

The younger members of the party behaved very well, waiting

for their elders to go first, and if the Leslie boys did dance a kind of fandango, linking hands as they went, they did it high and disposedly, without any noise.

"Please, my lady," said Odeena, who was waiting in the Saloon, "Cook said to say the soup's nice and hot so please to eat it—leastways I mean drink it—carefully. Cook's auntie drank some soup too hot, my lady, and had to go to hospital. Dreadful it was, Cook said, all—"

"That will do nicely, Odeena," said Lady Graham.

Everyone was now seated and for a short time there was peace. Lady Graham, looking round the table with an indulgent but motherly eye, saw that Mr. Crosse was on one side of Edith and George Halliday on the other. Having had many admirers in her own youth, she was not surprised that her daughter should attract the gentlemen and very sensibly felt that the more the merrier.

"Oh, I say, I'm sorry I'm late, Cousin Agnes," said Lord Mellings, who had only just come in. "I thought I'd better put the oars on the racks. Can I squeeze in by you?" which he did.

"Ludo!" said Sir Robert, in such a parade voice that Lord Mellings almost sprang to attention. "Why were the oars *not* on the racks?"

"Oh, Sir Robert," said George Halliday, "I'm awfully sorry. I did ship them and then—"

"You forgot, of course," said Sir Robert, not unkindly, but as one expounding an ineluctable law of nature.

"I'm awfully sorry, sir," said young Mr. Crosse. "I did put the cushions out of our boat on the racks but I forgot the oars."

"If Wellington had forgotten to form his men in the square at Waterloo we should have been in a pretty kettle of fish," said Sir Robert, at which both men went bright red in the face. As for Lord Mellings, he went even redder, feeling that he was now marked down as the Virtuous Prig. We doubt whether the rest of the table noticed particularly, except Edith, who said, quite audibly, that people who went in boats ought to be more educated, and was brought to heel by one motherly look from Lady Graham, who had no use for Apples of Discord in her house.

"And what about you three?" said Sir Robert, still in the judge's chair, addressing the Leslie boys.

"I'm awfully sorry, Uncle Robert," said Leslie Minor, who always got in ahead of his brothers, "but Major and Minimus and I wanted to see if we could walk across the weir as the water's a bit low, so we took our shoes and socks off and turned our trousers up."

"And did you get across?" said Sir Robert, his judicial ardour now tempered by a sportsman's feeling.

"*Rather*," said Leslie Major. "It was ripping, Uncle Robert, with all that slippery green weed and the minnows squelching about under one's feet. I nearly fell in but I got hold of a branch of that hazel that sticks out on the home side. My two silly young brothers got a bit wet, but they'd turned their trousers right up, so it didn't really matter."

"Well, next time you want to do something silly, don't do it in your best trousers," said their father, who was not displeased to see his effervescent sons slightly squashed. "You'll all have to pay for having them cleaned and pressed yourselves. And now be quiet."

"I told the boys they were being silly," said Edith virtuously, and was rewarded by a motherly look from Lady Graham.

But these were mere daily nothings in the life of a family as united as were the Grahams and Leslies.

"I say, Uncle Robert," said Leslie minor. "What's happened to the Three Musketeers?" for so the Leslie boys wittily called their Graham cousins.

"They have gone back to their duties," said Sir Robert, rather grimly.

"So would we, Sir Robert, if we had any," said George Halliday, speaking for himself and young Mr. Crosse. "But it's much nicer to be here. Oh, and Sir Robert, do you think I could have a word with Goble afterwards? It's about my boar. I want to show him at the Barsetshire Agricultural, but I've had a very good offer for him from Mr. Gresham."

Sir Robert said that Goble was probably at the Mellings Arms and if George went in there just before closing time, he would either meet him on the road or find him there.

"Gresham is perfectly straight," he added. "If he offers you a price you needn't try to haggle. He'd beat you at that in any case. Even Lord Stoke can't get the better of him. If it comes to that, nor can I," and he gave himself another well-deserved glass of port. It had been a long day and some of it rather boring, but worth it. Miss Merriman was safely married, thank goodness, to Choyce, who was a very good sort of fellow and now perhaps he would have his house to himself. And if this sounds selfish, we must remember that he had sheltered his wife's parents all through the war, during which old Mr. Leslie had died; that Lady Emily had stayed on as his guest, in increasing need of help till she too died; which had meant that Miss Merriman was always there too. On the whole he had always liked Miss Merriman, for whom he had indeed a certain admiration, as for a woman—in the great words of Mr. Sparkler—with no bigod nonsense about her, but the dependent who is also a friend, and what is more, a lady, can become a bore. Not that she need bore one personally but the mere fact of her existence means a little extra planning all the time. Whether Sir Robert ever reflected that his wife had had to bear this through and after the war while he was as often as not in London, or abroad on a mission, we do not know; but as he was essentially a just man, we think he did.

As it was now almost dark, Edith suggested going out in someone's car, but met with no enthusiasm. Lord Mellings had promised his father to come back early. The Leslies, with many thanks for a delightful treat, had taken their leave. George Halliday had gone off again Goble-hunting. There only remained young Mr. Crosse and he was talking to Sir Robert about the Barsetshire Agricultural. Edith hung about in the room for a time, was told by her father either to come in or go out, and sulkily went away into the dark garden. Life was dreadful. Why hadn't she gone back to America with David and Rose? In fact why was she alive at all and what was the use of anything? One might as well be dead, only then perhaps one would miss something, so *everything* was horrible. These last helpful words she said aloud, with great vehemence, several times, not looking where she was going, and banged into George Halliday in the growing dusk.

"Look out, Edith," said George, not unkindly. "What's up?"

Edith said, Just horribleness.

"If that's all," said George, "you'd better think of something else. You are behaving badly, my girl."

Edith said she hadn't said anything.

"But you've been *behaving* abominably," said George Halliday. "Dumb insolence we called it in the Army and you had to snap out of it or you were for it. What you need is to stop thinking about yourself."

"But how *can* I?" said Edith, so piteously that George had to laugh.

"You could teach the orphan boy to read and teach the orphan girl to sew," he said, to which Edith's answer was:

"Oh, don't be silly."

"I didn't say that," said George. "It was a poet called Tennyson. A jolly good poet. Why the hell didn't you go on with your estate management course or whatever it was?"

Edith said David and Rose had invited her to America.

"Oh, Lord! does one have to talk to you in words of one syllable?" said George. "I like you, my girl, but I shan't like you much longer if you go on like this. Now listen. You know my sister Sylvia that married your cousin Martin Leslie and helps him to run the farm at Rushwater."

Edith said yes.

"She is having another baby, bless her," said George, "and it hampers her a bit. She and Martin do wonders and Emmy

Grantly and her husband do wonders. But they could do with an extra hand. What about it?"

"But what would father and mother say?" said Edith.

"Now *do* listen, my girl, and be your age," said George. "Your father and mother are busy people. All their children are working at something if it's only looking after a husband and babies—and one might do much worse," he added meditatively. "All except you. You've had your chance of a good estate-work training, though mind you there's a lot to be said for learning it on the premises. You tell your respected parents that you want to go to Rushwater for a bit and they'll jump with joy. Think about it. Now I must find Goble. I've been down to the Mellings Arms and he wasn't there. I expect he's in his cottage," and without as much as good night he went off into the gathering darkness.

By now it was chill, as it so often is near a river. Edith went back to the house and up to her bedroom, where she made a hideous face at herself in the glass.

"You are horrible," she said aloud to it, "and I'm horribler and George is a Beast and I'll jolly well go to Rushwater, just to *show* everyone!" after which she undressed crossly, had an angry bath, and got into bed in a temper and was fast asleep in five minutes. What would one not give to be young—perhaps to have troubles that seem like black eternal misery, but to be able to sleep them off.

CHAPTER 4

The Amazing Marriage, as George Knox the well-known writer of historical biographies had called it (though most of his hearers being illiterate did not take the allusion), was soon forgotten. We are as certain as one can be of anything in this Pilgian's Porjiss of a mortal wale—to use Mrs. Gamp's immortal words—that Mr. and Mrs. Choyce will be as happy as two good, kind people ought to be and will go on feeling more and more love and respect for one another. Now the wedded pair were back and moving round in their diurnal course—but not in the least like rocks and stones and trees; rather, like two people whose happiness is in one another and in sharing that happiness with as many people as possible.

The only contretemps we have to chronicle was the young man from the *Barchester Chronicle*, who through sheer lack of intelligence had put down Sir Robert Graham's name as Mr. Caxton. And if our reader will turn back a few pages, she will see exactly how this happened. Several people wrote letters to the *Chronicle* to point out the error, but as the sub-editor, not seeing any news value in them, put them all into the waste-paper basket, the affair died a natural death. The young man went, like Fair Leslie, to spread his conquests further, quite surpassing himself a few days later by his description of Councillor Budge of the Gas Works as the Wicked Uncle of Mr. Therm. But alas! Mr. Therm, that engaging invention of Gas Advertising, was by now almost entirely forgotten. The allusion fell quite flat and the sub-editor said if the young man couldn't do better than that he had better take his valuable talents elsewhere; after which they each stood the other a beer and there was no ill-feeling.

Shortly after the wedding Edith Graham, a little chastened by the very plain words that George Halliday had spoken to her, was rung up by George's sister, Sylvia Leslie, who said it was much too long since she and her husband had seen Edith and what about her coming to stay with them for a fortnight, or longer if she liked, and see estate management at close quarters. Edith said she would love it and would ask her mother.

"Quite right," said Sylvia. "Mother knows best. I've got to come over with the station waggon to collect a pig from Goble next week, so you can come back with me. Have you any breeches? If not, Emmy will lend you a pair. She's just burst out of her second best ones and I'm having them mended. They'll be about right for you. You'll need them."

Now was it that Edith, who had no great aptitude as a rider and always secretly wished that she could have a horse with a pole sticking out of its neck like horses on a round-about, suddenly felt small and wished she had taken advantage of her cousin Rose Leslie's offer to give her a cast-off pair of her own very well-cut breeches. It was, she admitted to herself, entirely her own silly fault. She had refused the breeches because she was secretly afraid to ride. But perhaps at Rushwater, with her cousin Martin, who was kind and patient, it wouldn't be quite so awful to ride. On the other hand, to ride in Emmy's cast-off breeches would be a mortification, especially as they were bound to be too large for her. Anyway, if she went to Rushwater it would serve George Halliday right, so she would jolly well go and that was that.

A few days later Sylvia Leslie drove over from Rushwater in the station wagon. Ten years of married life and several children had made very little mark upon her golden beauty. That she would in time be Juno was obvious, but for the present she was still in looks and carriage a young goddess, even in breeches and a turtle-neck jersey.

To Lady Graham, who had a deep love for Rushwater, her girlhood home, anyone who lived there was welcome and Sylvia was very welcome, not only as the capable, affectionate wife of Lady Graham's nephew Martin Leslie, but also as a good purveyor of babies. The eldest, Miss Eleanor Leslie, we know fairly well, now about seven years old with two choice successors, but though we have given them a local habitation we are not sure of their names.

Of course the whole question of names is a difficult one. Christian names are extremely limited compared with surnames, as can easily be seen by looking at the London Telephone Directory, now in four fat volumes, which are brought up to date at varying intervals. And we may here add that the renewal of these volumes roused very strong feelings among Barsetshire housewives, because the Postmaster-General had decreed that all the old books must be collected by the unfortunate deliverer of the new ones. As every housewife knows, an out of date directory is essential in the kitchen. On it you can put the saucepan that has just horribly boiled over, or the plates hot from the oven. Then you tear off the scorched or dirtied page and so on till the book is finished.

Heartily did the postmen curse their headmaster for this piece of cheese-paring which added considerably to their normal duties, and even more heartily did the housewives curse him for a gesture which impressed nobody and annoyed everybody. Old Mrs. Hubback at The Shop, popularly reported to be ninety-one and a witch (of the beneficent, wart-curing species), was known to have at least six back numbers under her mattress, so it wouldn't sag in the middle the way it did, and had personally invited the local postman who was also her grandson-in-law to fetch them if he liked and see what would happen.

A number of voluntary observers reported that they had seen

with their own eyes, or been told by someone who had seen it with her own eyes, or heard from an informant unspecified, that those telephone books they was being taken away in a van all locked up tight and no windows so you couldn't say what was in it though it was plain enough what it was; and that all the old telephone books were (a) burnt, (b) thrown into the river and (c) sent to the factory to make new paper. All of which, being faithfully passed on by word of mouth, with such errors and accretions as suggested themselves to the speakers, had become Gospel Truth.

When old Mr. Halliday died in the previous year, Sylvia had taken her widowed mother to Rushwater for a long visit, while her brother George wrestled with the endless death-duty formalities. The estate was a full-time job in itself. Two of the old farm hands had died during the winter and though George was in a way relieved not to be paying weekly the statutory wages plus a good deal in kind for very little work, he had to work himself far harder than any of his men, who went home when their stint was done. With his mother away it was not unpleasant to come home to the good meal that the old cook Mrs. Fothergill never failed to give him, to smoke and laze for a little before setting himself to the necessary office work, or in summer in saddle the younger of the farm horses—for two were still kept, as well as the tractor—and go up onto the downs, there to breathe the clear air, to watch the clouds above the coloured landscape, to hear if the wind were in the right quarter from the distant cathedral bells, and to allow himself to dream a little of an improbable happy future.

When his mother, not unnaturally, began to think of coming home again from Rushwater, Hatch End said, according to the speaker, that it would be nice for George, or Mr. George, or the young Squire, and gradually just the Squire, to have his mother back. And so of course it should be, for he loved her and felt sorry for her; but he would himself far rather have been lonely in his own way; not to have to make talk at meals, not to be questioned about his comings and goings, not to wonder if he could ever manage to take a real holiday.

But he was a good son and did his best. Rarely did he talk about himself, save once or twice to his sister Sylvia who, much as she too loved her mother, was finding her continued presence at Rushwater almost as wearing as the drop of water on stone. Nothing one could honestly complain of, nothing to put one's finger on; but it remains true that comparative age (though not necessarily in the least crabbed) and youth (even if the young are in their thirties now) do better on the whole if they are not living together in the same house. And the more so if the parent who used to be head of the house cannot, except in rare cases, bring himself or herself to realize that the sceptre and the responsibility are in other hands.

If George had been less dutiful—a dull word, but it has its meaning—he could certainly have gone out three or four times in the week to various houses in the neighbourhood, but he knew that his mother, with the best intentions in the world, would take so much trouble to explain to him how quite happy she was to be alone, and there was the wireless and she would get on with her gardening, or get on with her exquisite darning and patching of the house linen, or get on with something else, that it was bound to end in his staying at home.

It was all a pity, for the mother-plus-son relationship can be extremely pleasant and a real comradeship as well, but this demands a mother who shows by visits to friends or excursions abroad, taken on her own initiative, that she is by no means tied to her old home; or a son who can announce at breakfast that as soon as the wheat, or the cows, or the turnips are doing whatever they ought to be doing, he means to take the small car and run over to Spain with a couple of men, or share a large car with those nice Carters and Young Crosse and tour Italy for two or three weeks. But nothing was going on quite as it should. George's old army friends were mostly knee-deep in families or business now. John-Arthur Crosse, brother-in-arms at Vache-en-Écurie and Vache-en-Foin, was working all through the holiday period that he might take a longer leave at Christmas and go to the Swiss or Austrian Alps. The Graham boys, though very fond of George and admiring him as a hero of a real war, such as they, professional soldiers, might never see, were already heavily booked ahead by their many relations and friends. The thought of the long days of summer, when all his friends were abroad, was lying heavy on George, though he tried to pretend to himself that it wasn't. And he steadfastly refused to let himself think about Christmas.

Upon these true, depressing, and unprofitable musings, there broke in his sister Sylvia.

"Hullo, Sylvia," said George. "Bless your heart, you look nicer every time I see you. Rum shape, but it suits you."

"Well, why not?" said Sylvia, with what we can only describe as a pleased if slightly shame-faced simper. "Three isn't a family, you know."

"Serve you right if it's triplets," said her brother cheerfully. "Good old girl!" and he put a fraternal arm round her with a hug. "How has mother taken it?"

"Oh, she's frightfully pleased," said Sylvia. "Look here, George. About mother. I mean—" and she stopped, looking uncomfortable.

"So do I," said George. "Let's face facts, old girl. We're both very fond of mother and we'd both awfully like not to live with her—or be lived with by her."

Sylvia said that was exactly what her husband Martin said.

"Good old Martin," said George with sad want of filial feeling. "But look here, old girl, what can one do?"

"Martin and I have been thinking about it till we're black in the face and we don't know," said Sylvia. "Martin has been an angel about it. But honestly, George, it does make things a bit difficult. I mean when we've finished work he and I usually just sit and do nothing for a bit. Often we don't even talk, unless it's about the children—they all sent Uncle George their love. But mother thinks one ought to talk."

"And you," said George, "are telling *me*. I say, I do sound a beast. But it's tough luck for you and Martin."

"It would be worse for you if she came back here," said Sylvia stoutly, "because you're alone. I mean you haven't anyone else to talk to and I have. You can't escape. I say, does mother mind if you go out much in the evening?"

"She always *says* she doesn't," said George, not looking at his sister. "But she really does. I don't mean complaining or anything—"

"Oh, Lord! you needn't tell *me*," said Sylvia. "What Emmy calls an Atmosphere. George, shall *we* get like that?"

"You won't," said George, "because you've got Martin," to which his sister replied with great vehemence that he made her feel mean and surely there must be someone he would like to marry.

"In the abstract, yes," said George. "I'm all for marriage. But there would be mother again and I don't quite see a wife taking it on and I don't see how we could divide this house. I've often thought about it and I always feel a beast if I do."

"I don't see any sense in a house that hasn't a Dower House," said Sylvia. "Of course there is the Old Manor House, but as it's let so well to those nice Carters you can't very well turn them out. And anyway mother couldn't live there alone. It would be too expensive."

"I do sometimes wonder where she would like to live," said George. "She wasn't very happy here. I simply can't be with her much, Sylvia. I don't mean I don't want to—no, that's a lie—I do *want* to want to, but I can't," which explanation made his sister inclined to laugh and cry in one breath. "Those blasted forms and accounts take up half my spare time. And she hasn't many old friends here."

"I know what you mean. Not the friends of when she was young, only the ones of after she married father," said Sylvia thoughtfully. "Her old friends are Northbridge, of course. Granny was Northbridge, but I don't remember her."

"I just do," said George. "I remember her giving me one of those things you put two photographs of the same place in and it all looks solid," which description his sister accurately diagnosed to mean a stereoscope. "She lived at Hovis House in Northbridge High Street. It must have been rather a nice bit of eighteenth century, but the front got decayed and had to be refaced. Some kind of relation of Granny's, Mrs. Dunsford, lives there now, but I hardly know her. Mother always goes to see her when she goes to Northbridge and she comes here sometimes with her daughter—a nice dull old maid."

Sylvia said what a funny name Hovis was for a house.

According to Granny, George said, the land originally belonged to a Danish settler called Offa and Hovis was a kind of corruption of Offa's; or else the original owner was a wool-stapler called Hover and it gradually became Hover's and then Hovis.

"They've got a portrait of Granny's mother there," said George. "She must have been a good-looking woman when she was young. Of course when you are small you don't think about people's looks much, except if they're nice or nasty. I always thought Granny was about a hundred, so her mother must have been about a hundred and fifty."

Sylvia laughed and said she must ask Mrs. Villars, the rector's wife at Northbridge, about it when she next went over.

"And of course those nice nurses who came when father died," she said, "live there too in a quiet awful old house, all ingle-nooks and banging one's head on the ceiling," which made George laugh.

"Now, look here, I must be going," said Sylvia, "or I shan't catch Goble before his dinner. I'm collecting Edith and taking her to Rushwater for a bit. I'll have to go to Northbridge soon to see the rector's wife about a possible cook and I'll get the low-down on Mrs. Dunsford from her. Or, I know, I'll take mother too and we'll go and call on Mrs. Dunsford. Of course the great thing is to get mother comfortably settled so that you can get married."

It was as well that George's back was to the light.

"Oh, I'm too busy to get married," he said. "And anyway who would want to live here?" to which his sister very lovingly replied, Would he rather be a bigger fool than he looked, Or look a bigger fool than he was, which well-worn nursery joke made them both laugh. His sister enquired after the Grahams.

"Lady Graham is as enchanting as ever," said George. "She ran the whole of the Choyce-Merriman wedding and we all had dinner at Holdings afterwards. I met those Greshams at the wedding and some nice people called Fairweather."

"Oh, good!" said Sylvia. "I adore Rose Fairweather. I never knew anyone who looked so lovely and talked so sillily and yet was so awfully good at housekeeping and children and all that sort of thing. And she is so in love with her nice husband whom I adore. I adore Martin too—and you, you old idiot," she added, with a very affectionate hug. "I wish I could have been at the wedding, but there was trouble with a heifer and we had to wait for the vet. I telephoned to Agnes and she was *most* understanding. Good-bye, old thing," and away she went.

Sylvia drove down to Holdings, parked the station wagon in the farm lane, and went in search of the bailiff. A large corduroy back bent over the wall of a pig sty straightened itself at the sound of her steps and turned round as Goble.

"Hullo, Goble, what's the price of pork today?" said Sylvia. "I hear you're sending Holdings Goliath up again."

"That's right, Miss Sylvia," said Goble. "It's his last try, poor old fellow. He did feel it the time the Agricultural was at Lord Bond's place and he only got a second. Mind you, I don't say there was any prejudice, not so as you'd notice, but Mr. Marling's Marling Magnum he's not the boar old Goliath is. Come now, is he, old fellow?" and leaning over the sty wall he poked at Goliath with his stick. The great monster opened one very small malevolent eye, gave a look of resentful disgust at Goble, and went to sleep again.

"Ar," said Goble. "*He* knows. All well over at Rushwater, Miss Sylvia?"

Sylvia, who was accustomed to Goble being about ten years behindhand in his mode of addressing her, said everyone was very well and her husband sent his best wishes and had a nice little lot of piglings if Goble would care to come over. Not champions, of course, but a good lot.

"Ar, champions are all very well," said Goble, "for the shows, but it's baconers we've got to breed now. Just look here, miss," and he conducted her to a sty where seven or eight teen-age pigs (for we do not know the right word for that class) were having great difficulty in getting their dinners. Not that the trough was too short, nor too small, nor the supply of food inadequate, but each pig was convinced that the food among which he was rootling was not so good as the food to the right or the left; all of which led to such shrieks and grunts of greed as sounded like the whole of market-day in Barchester.

"Prime, they are," said Goble, benevolently scratching the largest pig's back with his stick. "Prime porkers. Lord! when I think of the eating on a pig, I bless the Lord. Male and female he created them—and the little 'uns."

"And one that you've left out, Goble," said Sylvia.

The bailiff stared at her and then burst into what we can only call a guffaw.

"You *are* a one, miss," he said, wiping his eyes. "That's as good a one as ever I heard. Left-one-out! I'll give them a good laugh with that at the Mellings Arms. Left-one-out, eh? That's as neat a thing as you'd find anywheres" and in his ecstasy he slapped his corduroys with a resounding slap, at which each of the young pigs suspected that the pig on one or the other side of him had made that noise to frighten him and thereby guzzle his food, and another great squealing arose, including a kind of squeal-grunt from the older piglets, whose voices were beginning to break and who thought they ought to be allowed to shave, even if it was only once a week.

Sylvia took Goble's tribute calmly. Then, having observed the proper preliminaries, she entered upon her main theme, which was What about a nice couple of young pigs for fattening. This transaction moved with proper slow solemnity, during which the church clock sounded its bell once.

"What's that?" said Sylvia. "You never know if it's half-past twelve, or one, or half-past one with that clock. It ought to have chimes as well."

Goble said he didn't hold with chimes, but gave no reasons. Then pulling his watch out of his waistcoat pocket, he said it was one o'clock.

"That Odeena, she's late with the dinner bell again," he said. "Now my mother, if I was late, she'd lay into me with the rolling-pin, or anything else handy. If I was Cook I'd give that Odeena one with the rolling-pin."

Sylvia, said, Or the nutmeg grater and would Goble put the piglings in her van, and so left Goble still shaking with laughter at her wit and went round to the kitchen door.

"Hullo, Cook," she said. "Is there some lunch?"

"Well, Mrs. Martin, I'm sure!" said Cook. "A nice surprise this is. Lunch is just going in. Some lovely sausages I made last time Goble killed and they've been in the deep freeze. Go in, miss."

So Sylvia went through into the house and found her Aunt Agnes in the dining-room, delighted to see Martin's wife and have her to lunch. Edith, she said, was looking forward immensely to her visit to Rushwater and was going to bring some of the pretty American frocks that Rose Leslie had given her.

"I must say I'd love to see them," said Sylvia. "Martin and I rather forget about clothes sometimes. I say, Aunt Agnes, what *is* Edith doing? I get a bit mixed with all her plans."

"So do I," said Lady Graham. "Of course Emmy knew exactly what she wanted to do and did it."

"And what we would do without her and Tom, I don't know," said Sylvia. "Martin is going to take Tom in as a full partner. It seems funny to turn one's home into a business, but it's the only way now."

"Clarissa was *very* difficult," said Lady Graham who, following her own train of thought, had not paid much attention to what Sylvia was saying, "and now she is so settled and happy being a schoolmaster's wife and we do love Charles Belton. But Edith—" and she paused.

"There's nothing wrong, is there, Aunt Agnes?" said Sylvia, her mind at once—as our silly minds do—flying to the worst possibilities. "I mean like being in love with a Russian or something?"

"Oh, dear me, no," said Lady Graham. "She is as good as gold if that's what you were thinking of. I really wish she *were* in love with someone. I do miss Merry. She could always control Edith. *I* don't know what Edith wants—and she doesn't know either—and it annoys Robert, of course. All these young men. It is most difficult and I sometimes think I'll take her abroad for a bit. Sally would always lend me the villa at Cap Ferrat. But I do so dislike going abroad now, with all the fuss. Robert says if one goes by the night ferry you don't notice it at all, but I am *certain* that if there is really a storm they couldn't control the train and everything would break loose and rush about the deck like that *very* stupid book of Victor Hugo's that we had to read in the schoolroom—Vingt-et-un or something of the sort."

"Oh, I don't think it would really be as bad as that, Aunt Agnes," said Sylvia. "I expect Edith needs someone who can bully her."

"I often feel like the mother in that poem of George Meredith's," said Agnes, "who looks at her pretty daughter and thinks how *heavenly* it would be if she were married and off her hands."

Sylvia, not much of a reader and unacquainted with *Love in the Valley*, said it seemed a funny thing to write about, but she quite agreed with the mother and she would certainly marry her daughters off as soon as possible and then their husbands could work on the farm—a point of view which Mr. Meredith had overlooked.

"You know, darling Sylvia, I always feel you are just as much one of the family as Martin," said Lady Graham. "I mean you get more and more Rushwater every year. How darling Mamma would have loved you. That's why I want to talk to you about Edith. Robert says it is my business to look after the girls and I daresay he is right, as he has looked after the boys. Edith is rather young and very silly," said her ladyship, with a fine gesture of impartiality towards her trying daughter. "Of course I hope she will get married too, but she can't just sit waiting for someone to marry her, so she might as well get married soon. I did have a kind of idea that young Mr. Crosse—the children all call him John-Arthur—was épris of her, but she certainly isn't éprise of him or anyone else. If only she would find the right man I am sure she would settle down. Someone like George, only of course he is far too busy to think of such things besides being nearly twice her age."

How much easier—or at any rate less trying—the world would be if people did not suddenly put into words something that has been simmering in one's mind for a long time. During the last years Sylvia Leslie had not been too busy to cast an eye over her dear brother George's affairs from time to time, especially when their father died. After his death she had taken her mother to Rushwater for a long visit and if she was to be truthful, which she usually was, she must say that though she was not altogether enjoying the visit, it might have been much worse. What Mrs. Halliday thought, no one, as far as we know, had enquired, nor was she the woman to criticize aloud the house that sheltered her. But the position of queen-mother is not easy. If she came back to Hatch House no one could say how things would go. If George were married it would simplify things. The Dowager would naturally yield her place—and with dignity and good will—to the new mistress. But George remaining unmarried with a house too large for him and a mother in exile would not be well looked on. If only it were London, Sylvia and Martin had said more than once to one another, where you can do what you please, as you please, when you please, and no one—unless invited—will approve or blame. But it was West Barsetshire, and if the widow left her unmarried son's house to live elsewhere, there would be talk. People might even say that George Halliday had turned his own mother out of her house.

And now Lady Graham had implied that what Edith needed was someone like George, and Sylvia found it difficult to concentrate further upon what her ladyship was saying. She had never much troubled to consider George's affairs of the heart, if any, being very busy with domestic affairs of her own. But if George needed help, help he must have.

"There are very few families that can live together in England," said Lady Graham. "Foreigners do, though I really do not know why. Our Italian cousins, the Strelsas, live together like anything in a large palace with no central heating. Old Lord Pomfret used to say that Guido Strelsa had been turned out of every gambling hell in Europe," which statement, though full of interest, did not help matters much.

"Well, anyway, there's nothing we can do," said Sylvia. "When the Barsetshire Agricultural is over perhaps we can settle something. Things do turn up and poor old George needs a bit of good luck. Where's Edith?"

Her mother said she had been to see Mr. and Mrs. Choyce at the vicarage and would be back at any moment and hardly had she spoken when Edith came in and hugged her cousin Sylvia violently.

"Sorry I'm late for lunch, mother," she said. "All my luggage is ready. Oh, and mother, I went to say good-bye to Mrs. Carter at the Old Manor House and John-Arthur was there and he said he would love to see Rushwater because you used to live there, so of course I said Sylvia would love him to come," at which unexpected praise from young Mr. Crosse Lady Graham felt quite set up for the moment, though later she reflected that if a young man wished to see a young woman, any excuse would do.

So Sylvia and Edith got into the station wagon and drove away to Rushwater.

As we know, Rushwater, now the property of Martin Leslie, was very much a family affair. Always hampered by a leg badly wounded on the beachhead at Anzio, Martin had run the estate for more than ten years now, helped by his wife, who had been Sylvia Halliday and his young cousin Emmy, Edith's elder sister, happily married for some years now to Tom Grantly, of a very good clerical family. By the greatest good luck, not unaided by general willingness to fit in anywhere and anyhow and give a hand, the Rushwater Estate was doing very well. Still were their best stud bulls sold to the Argentine for what sounded in the currency of that country like millions; their pigs though only a side line were flourishing. From the large walled kitchen garden they sold fruit and vegetables locally at very good prices all the year round while the home farm produced a very reasonable amount of food and bedding for the animals. And, though this had been a heavy charge on the estate, nearly all their working people were now well housed and Tom Grantly saw to it that they did their proper share towards keeping their houses in good condition.

Owing to the way generations will overlap one another, the relationships of Leslies, Grahams, and Pomfrets were like a kaleidoscope to outsiders and even old Lord Stoke, a stickler for pedigrees, had once or twice failed to determine the exact degree of kinship between—say—the late Lady Dorothy Bingham, who was David Leslie's second cousin once removed as well as his mother-in-law, and the well-known novelist Mrs. Rivers, whose husband the Honourable George Rivers was a distant cousin of the Pomfrets with a place in Herefordshire and never left the county. As his wife was always (unless cadging a visit to some of her husband's relations) in London, this suited both parties very well, only marred by the time when George Rivers had changed his bedroom and his wife, arriving unexpectedly and very late with the servants gone to bed and George Rivers fast asleep, could not find her bedroom or his and nearly fell downstairs in the dark. How this story got round we do not know, for George Rivers was a gentleman, but get about it did, to the great joy of Mrs. River's friends.

"It makes all the difference to have this car instead of the old Ford van," said Sylvia. "There's more room in front and if we don't have pigs or anything at the back we can put in two seats and take all the children, and then if we want to go further they can sleep in the back quite comfortably. Martin says he's working out a way for us all to sleep in it and then we can go all over Europe, only I'd rather stay at home."

Edith, looking at the back of the car, which contained a useful mixture of potatoes, an oil drum, spare parts, mangolds, a large sack of Holman's Vita-Sang Manure, a ladder, three angry geese in a barred crate, the piglings, and a huge roll of chicken wire, wondered where one would sleep under these conditions and gave it up. Leaving the river valley they mounted the downs, drove along the ridge where juniper bushes on the short sweet turf looked like armies of dwarf invaders, down again and so by the little Rushmere Brook, tributary to the Rising, through the village, into the park, where they crossed the brook and drove into the stable yard.

Here in the valley the sun was so warm that the mounting-block on which Edith had perched while the van was being unloaded was almost uncomfortably hot. There was a quiet cooing from the white pigeons on the coach-house roof. The stable cat, lying flat on the warm tiles, looked tolerantly at them, opened its mouth and yawned, gave itself a slight wash and brush up, and yawned itself to sleep again. Then Martin Leslie came out of the estate office on the far side of the yard, as always limping a little, to greet his cousin Edith.

"Is your leg hurting today?" said Edith.

"I really don't know," said Martin. "Why?"

"Because you were limping a bit," said Edith.

"Oh, that's only my leg," said Martin, as if that explained everything.

"Yes, I *know*, but is it hurting?" said Edith.

"Well, now I come to think about it," said Martin, sitting down on a horseblock, "I suppose it is. You know, you get so used to a pain in one special place that you can pretend it isn't there. Quite often it works."

"Good old Martin," said Edith affectionately. "I say, how's Mrs. Halliday?"

Martin said he thought she was very well, but he did not say it with any enthusiasm, nor did he pursue the subject. When the station wagon was unloaded Sylvia joined them and they all went along the stone-floored passage to the other side of the house. A black beetle who had been reading the newspaper in a corner, threw it down, rushed madly away from the invaders, and disappeared down a hole under the skirting board.

"Oh, bother, I'll have to put some more beetle-powder down," said Sylvia.

"Uncle David," said Edith, "said that when he was a boy he and Uncle John used to come down at night when the servants had gone to bed and there were *millions* of beetles and they used to tread on them and squash them and next day they were all swept away."

"Echo du temps passé," said Martin. "I do just remember the uncles doing that when I was a boy. I thought it the most dashing thing then. But you can't stop beetles once they've begun, at least amateurs can't. I have the beetle-killer out from Barchester from time to time and he settles their hash for a bit."

"Is there *really* a beetle-killer, Martin?" said Edith.

"Quite really," said Martin. "He is an honoured employee of

the Barchester City Council but his name isn't beetle-killer now. He is vermin- and rodent-exterminator. Here's Emmy."

And there in the door which led from the old servants' quarters to the house was Mrs. Tom Grantly, otherwise Emmy, in jersey, breeches, and gum boots, who welcomed her sister Edith warmly.

"I say, you've grown since last time," said Emmy. "How is Goble? I want to get him over here to look at the last litter. Sylvia said you'd want some breeches, so I've put my old pair in your room. I can't get into them now, so you'd better keep them. I say, we couldn't get to Merry's wedding because we had a heifer in trouble. Martin wants to hear all about it. Tom's gone to Barchester but he'll be back before supper. You must come and see your nieces and nephews. They think Aunt Edith is so funny because of you being so young. I say, how old are you now? Nineteen?"

Edith said eighteen, but she didn't like eighteen because it was a dull number, which led to an interesting discussion as to which numbers were dull and which interesting. Edith said rather sadly that nineteen and twenty were both dull, but twenty-one would be nice, only it was such a long way off.

Sylvia, who had been delayed in the kitchen quarters, then joined them and they all went into the sitting-room where Mrs. Halliday was darning house-linen, very beautifully.

"I thought I darned pretty well," said Emmy, "but Mrs. Halliday does it much better. I say, Edith, do you remember how well old Conque used to darn, Gran's maid? She could darn like the pattern in table napkins and things, if you see what I mean. I mean the sort of light and shade."

Everyone saw exactly what she meant, but not one of them could give a name to that kind of darning.

"Clarissa can do it," said Edith, remembering her sister's gift for the needle. "Conque taught her. Did you know Conque, Mrs. Halliday, ever?" which was a piece of polite kindness on

Edith's part to bring Mrs. Halliday into the circle of younger people.

Mrs. Halliday said she did remember her very well during the war, when Lady Emily was living at Holdings and Conque was with her, but she had never known that Conque was such a good needlewoman.

"And a needles-and-pins woman when she was cross," said Emmy, who had known Conque better than Edith and acquired from her a fluency in rather unacademical French which she found very useful when in France for dealing with porters, waiters, shopkeepers, and others to whom the public school French of most English travellers was almost unintelligible. "I say, what would you like to do? There's always plenty to do in the kitchen garden, weeding and things. I say, Martin, do you remember when I pulled up half the spring onions because I thought they were weeds?"

Martin said he did.

Then Sylvia said she must fly or she would be late for the Women's Institute meeting where she had promised to go through the accounts. Tom and Emmy also had jobs on hand. Edith was left with Mrs. Halliday, who asked her if she would like to unpack her suitcase now and offered to show her the room she was to have. So they went upstairs and Mrs. Halliday took her to the Tulip Dressing-Room, so called from the wall-paper.

"I am next door in the Tulip Room," said Mrs. Halliday "and the bathroom is opposite. Shall I help you to unpack?"

Edith said politely that she hadn't much to unpack and should she come down to the sitting-room when she had finished, but Mrs. Halliday said she would stay with her. Edith rather wished she wouldn't, for one's clothes, chosen and packed with care, look pretty silly when they are coffined in a suitcase and come out rather creased because one hasn't bothered to put enough tissue paper in. Mrs. Halliday asked about Edith's people and other friends at Hatch End and enjoyed any bits of local gossip and was delighted to hear that the new cushions in the pews were to be made of that stuff like rubber sponges so that they wouldn't be lumpy. Then she enquired after her son George.

"Oh, George is awfully well," said Edith. "And he's awfully busy because of all those forms he has to fill in. I can't think why farmers should be persecuted like that."

Mrs. Halliday said Nor could most people, but once that sort of thing began there was no end to it and it was a pity paper was ever invented, to all of which Edith paid what we can only call Token Attention, being much more interested in what she was going to do at Rushwater.

"How neatly you unpack," said Mrs. Halliday, when Edith had refolded the last piece of tissue paper and put her suitcase in a cupboard. "What would you like to do now? We might sit on the terrace."

What Edith not unnaturally wanted to do was go out and find some of her hosts and hostesses and have a good family gossip, but her kind heart bade her show courtesy to the old (though Mrs. Halliday would hardly have thought of herself in that category), so down they went and sat on the terrace outside the great drawing-room, in the afternoon sun.

"And now," said Mrs. Halliday, "I want to hear all about Hatch End."

There is a chapter in *Little Dorrit* called Taking Advice in which Fanny Dorrit asks advice from her younger sister Amy; her method of enquiry being to talk about herself and what she means to do, with an occasional and rather perfunctory appeal to her sister for support in whatever plan she has in hand and with no intention whatever of listening to what she says.

So did Edith, who would far rather have been outside with one or other of her relations, find herself pinned down as listener to Mrs. Halliday's complaints. Complaints is a hard word and we wish we could think of a better, but almost everything Mrs. Halliday said was tinged with wistful looking back to the past, or slightly disparaging references to the present. So long as Mrs. Halliday was regretting her old life at Hatch House Edith could truly sympathize, but when she began to speak of her own lonely condition at Rushwater Edith felt extremely uncomfortable.

To begin with—and we should all, including the present writer, try to remember it—crabbed middle-age (for we cannot call Mrs. Halliday aged by any means) and youth can less than ever live together. Cushioned and bumper-barred by bigger houses and more servants it was comparatively easy. Granny, or mother-in-law, could have her own bedroom and sitting-room, join the family, or stay in her quarters and there receive her own friends; even sometimes have her own carriage and her own personal maid. Now all had to be communal. In any case there was not much privacy at Rushwater because everyone was working so hard at the same object, the upkeep and improvement of the estate. It was all very well to establish oneself as the widowed mother when black crêpe was anything up to a foot wide, but when one just went on wearing one's old tweeds and one's old gardening clothes, one became part of a very busy working family party. Possibly Sylvia could have been a little more with her mother—but not much. Possibly Mrs. Halliday could have roused herself to go more often to the village, where the mere act of sitting in a rather stuffy cottage and letting the occupant talk to one is a true kindness, for the great point of a charitable visit is to listen. The recipient of your kind impulse does not in the least wish to hear what you have to say, only to talk about him- or more often herself, but we do not think this occurred to Mrs. Halliday.

The case has been summed up by old Mrs. Panter who, when Mrs. Carter at the Old Manor House had rather nervously gone to see her, said afterwards to her friends, "Poor lady, she liked to talk, so I let her." So visiting the cottages was not part of Mrs. Halliday's normal life. Her one and very pleasant outlet for energy had been her garden, at least that part of it near the house, where flower beds still were well stocked and plots of

fragrant herbs surrounded the sun-dial and there was no one else
to weed or hoe. And we may say that her chief regret for not
being at Hatch End was her flower garden, but very sensibly she
tried not to think about it and mostly succeeded.

So Edith did begin to tell Mrs. Halliday about Hatch End,
but before long found herself listening to Mrs. Halliday on
Rushwater. Or perhaps not listening—just having a polite face
of interest and letting her mind stray to other things.

Presently the family drifted in for tea round a large table in
the morning room. Edith was between her sister Emmy Grantly
and her cousin Martin. The talk was almost entirely about the
approaching Barsetshire Agricultural Show and the question of
road transport for livestock. In this Edith readily joined, for
through Goble she had picked up a good deal of information
and could probably have taken the Holdings pigs to the Show
single-handed if necessary. Her cousin Martin was much struck
by her knowledge and asked her if she would like to go to the
Agricultural with him and his hopeful bull and his two Grade A
milch cows (and if this description is not accurate, we cannot
help it. Our only cow acquaintance in Riverside, S.W.3, is a
gilded model of a cow over a local dairy: alias a shop where milk
is retailed in glass bottles). Of course Edith was much elated by
this invitation, the more so that she would also see the Holdings
pigs and the young boar in their glory.

"And then I could go home with Goble," she said.

Martin, amused, asked if she were in a hurry to leave Rushwater.

"Oh, I don't mean that a bit," said Edith. "I was only thinking
it would be an economy," and her sister Emmy who had heard
the talk said "Little prig," but quite kindly and Edith laughed
too.

"Oh, bother," said Sylvia suddenly. "I've got to go over to
Northbridge tomorrow. Anyone want to come?"

Edith said she would love to. Everyone else was busy with
children, or the farm, or the accounts, or seeing the man from

Mr. Adams's works about that spare part for the tractor. So it
was settled that Edith should go with Sylvia.

The rest of the day seemed to last forever (as one's first day in
new surroundings mostly does) and after an exhaustive (and to
her exhausting) visit to the cows with Emmy and an endless
discussion at supper between Martin and Tom Grantly about
the possible importation of some of the Scandinavian prefabri-
cated wooden houses for the growing population of Rushwater,
Edith was already half asleep and very shortly afterwards Sylvia
packed her off to bed where she at once went to sleep and slept
dreamlessly.

When we say we sleep dreamlessly, we probably mean that we
have forgotten already the far lands in which we have spent the
night. Others among us remember them so clearly that they
almost obscure the first moments of our waking. Whatever
psychologists or psycho-analysts or pseudo-anythings may say,
dreams remain dreams, and most of them, as we learnt very
young in church, fly at the opening day: as indeed the wise in
every land and generations have said. But we cannot help
thinking about such shreds of our dreams as survive the opening
day, and wondering how we could be such idiots (or occasionally
so miraculously inspired) as to invent the wonders we have seen
and heard—but curiously enough hardly ever felt physically.
Fire does not burn, nor water quench, nor do we feel heat or
cold. All very unlike real life—if life is real.

CHAPTER 5

Accordingly next day Sylvia Leslie drove with her young cousin-by-marriage over to Northbridge, this time not in the station waggon but in the one rather respectable car which was kept for what newspapers call social functions. The ostensible object of her visit was to ask the rector's wife, Mrs. Villars, about the character of a possible cook, and she also intended to pay a visit to her connection (for the degree of cousinship would have required Scotch blood to explain properly) Mrs. Dunsford at Hovis House.

Of course the Plashington Road end of Northbridge is now council-housed and bedevilled in every way, but the High Street with its lovely curve leading down to the river, here spanned by the graceful Rennie bridge, remains on the whole untouched. Just where the street swings round the curve is the little Town Hall on twelve stone legs with an open market place below it. Then there are some handsome late eighteenth- and early nineteenth-century houses with fine carved porches and great sash windows. Among these not the least handsome is Hovis House, now the property of Mrs. Dunsford, a widow, nearer seventy than sixty, with one unmarried daughter. They were always dressed exactly as a widow and her more than grown-up daughter should be dressed, never looked their best (if they had ever tried to), and were practically indistinguishable from hundreds of quiet, well-bred, useful ladies of the same kind all over England.

Both ladies had been much to the fore in the Coronation Year festivities. In the back drawing-room on the first floor of Hovis House most of the dresses for the Pageant had been made. There had been seen for the first time that high light of theatrical dressmaking, the pale pink cotton cap, closely fitting to the head, with a rim of hair (combings from a friendly red setter) round the edge, manufactured by the curate, Mr. Highmore, for his own appearance as Becket.

"Rushwater is divine and I love it frightfully," said Sylvia as they drove up Northbridge High Street "but it takes some living up to. I should like to retire to a house like Mrs. Dunsford's. One could be a dowager there quite cheaply and there are a lot of nice people."

"But then you wouldn't be at Rushwater?" said Edith. "I mean," she went on, "you and Martin *are* Rushwater."

"I believe we are," said Sylvia, smiling at her young cousin's vehemence, "but if Martin dies before me—not that either of us is thinking of dying, but you never know—I shall be the Dowager and have to move out. Or the Dowager and live there till my son is twenty-one."

Edith said there was heaps of room for a Dowager at Rushwater.

"Oh, yes, there are plenty of *rooms*," said Sylvia, "but I don't think it would work. We'd have to do a sort of General Post. I wouldn't mind living in what used to be the agent's house—old Mr. Macpherson who adored Lady Emily. It was very well done up for Tom Grantly and Emmy and so far they fit in quite nicely, but if they have any more children we shall have to think again. We might put them in one of the new houses Martin is building on the other side of the spinney. Nice big rooms, built-in cupboards, central heating under the house, all mod. cons."

"I say, Sylvia," said Edith. "Do you *mind* about Rushwater?"

Sylvia begged Edith to make her meaning clearer.

"I mean—what you were saying about if Martin died— would you go on being at Rushwater?"

"Quite likely," said Sylvia. "Just as mother goes on living at Hatch End. Though I sometimes wonder—" and she stopped.

Edith said Wonder what? But Sylvia was taking the turn on the narrow road that leads to the Rectory and didn't hear her: or perhaps did not wish to pursue the subject.

It was one of the charming peculiarities of Mrs. Villars, the rector's wife, that she was always at home. Not that she was a recluse, for she went about the village and to Barchester, but seemed somehow to permeate the rectory or the rectory garden. So has time passed since we first visited Northbridge some fifteen years ago that Mrs. Villars was now not only several times a grandmother but also beginning to look it, though in the nicest way possible, as we all hope we may be allowed to do. Of course sons are a bad investment for Grannyhood, for as a rule they marry later than girls and so set one back in the Granny Stakes. But, as Hamlet so truly said, The readiness is all. After that we must take what the gods give us, and Mrs. Villars was always delighted to have her darling grandchildren to stay and almost equally delighted by—or shall we say resigned to—their departure. To her husband and her old friends she of course looked much the same. Rabbi Ben Ezra must have had something of that feeling when he invited all his friends to grow old along with him—for then they would not notice so much each how the other was aging and there would be less unpleasantness.

Mrs. Villars was not only at home but extremely visible, on her knees in her garden, planting something or other. Hearing a car stop she looked up, saw Sylvia, got up and came to the gate.

"Well, Sylvia, this is very nice," said Mrs. Villars. "And this is Edith isn't it?" which it was and Edith said How do you do very prettily. Mrs. Villars took her gardening gloves off, slapped them together, laid them in her trug—which useful garden baskets or carriers were still made locally from what we can only

describe as strong shavings of wood, as any Sussex gardener will
know—put her trowel and fork in it, and prepared to be the
Rector's wife.

Sylvia was carrying a small parcel which she offered to her
hostess.

"I've brought you some of the stuff I told you about that if you
remember to wash your hands *first* and put it on, you can get as
dirty as you like and then all the dirt peels off like an onion skin
when you wash your hands," she said.

Mrs. Villars thanked her, and we feel that credit is due to both
ladies. To Sylvia for having remembered a promise, perhaps
rashly made at a sherry party, and to Mrs. Villars for not having
completely forgotten what it was she wanted, and why, and then
having to have it all explained to her.

"You will stop for tea, won't you?" said Mrs. Villars.

Sylvia, though sorely tempted, said she had to go and see Mrs.
Dunsford; and as she was sure Mrs. Dunsford would offer her
tea and feel hurt if she refused and quite equally sure that Mrs.
Villars would not be hurt if she did refuse, that seemed the best
thing. Which was a bit addling to the intellect, but Mrs. Villars
took it all in good part and said at least they could look at her
garden. It was indeed worth looking at, beautifully kept, sloping
slightly towards the river with an embanking wall of old rose-red
brick. On the opposite side of the river, further up its course,
there were glimpses of Northbridge Manor, the home of Sir
Noel Merton, Q.C., and his wife, once Lydia Keith. From the
middle distance came the sounds of fine Saxon objurgations.

"The Bunces again?" said Sylvia.

Edith asked who the Bunces were.

"Old Bunce was born in the reign of King Alfred or thereabouts," said Mrs. Villars, "and has remained pure Anglo-Saxon
ever since. Both his daughters are delightful women with lots of
delightful intelligent illegitimate children and they all fight
from morning to night and enjoy life immensely, and old Bunce

beats his wife. He daren't beat his daughters now. They'd beat
him."

We fear that Mrs. Villars in giving this brief but very correct
conspectus of the Bunce family's fortunes was rather wondering
how Edith would take it. And we may add that if she had
thought it would shock or distress Edith she certainly would not
have put it in those words.

"Like Ted Poulter and Lily Brown," said Edith. "Emmy was
telling me about them. But they got married, so it's all right."

"Well, Effie Bunce and her sister didn't," said Mrs. Villars
calmly, "but it seems to work out all the same. They are both
splendid workers and get plenty of jobs and the children are very
handsome. One of them has just got a scholarship to a higher
school—I really don't understand the names all these schools
have now."

"Would it be a comprehensive school?" said Edith. "The
newspapers are always talking about them and I don't know
what it means."

"It's just a word," said Mrs. Villars calmly. "What was it you
wanted to ask me, Sylvia? I couldn't quite make out when you
rang up."

Sylvia said it was to ask if Mrs. Villars knew anything about
Doris who used to be with Mrs. Turner before she married Mr.
Downing.

"Doris?" said Mrs. Villars thoughtfully. "Oh, yes. A curious
girl."

Sylvia asked why.

"She was never an unmarried mother," said Mrs. Villars.
"Most of them are. It seems to pay on the whole. But a good
worker and quite honest."

Sylvia said she was sure she would not feel comfortable if she
had children and wasn't married.

"Well, I am going to have six children," said Edith. "I shall
adopt them. Then I needn't get married," which made Mrs.
Villars laugh. Sylvia laughed too, but felt rather uncomfortable.

Edith was at the moment her responsibility and she did not want any showing-off from her young cousin and determined to speak to her for her good later on; though whether it would have any effect she did not know. Then she said good-bye to Mrs. Villars and drove away with Edith to Hovis House.

So long had Mrs. Dunsford and her daughter been at Hovis House that they had, as it were, assumed protective colouring and become part of the town. No one could have taken them for anything but the well-bred English gentlewomen that they were. In China or Peru they would have been the same; in well-cut, well-worn tweeds, each with a necklace of small but real pearls, each well shod with sensible country shoes, and in the evening a black moiré silk (Mrs. Dunsford) and a rather hideous beige silk (Miss Dunsford). They went to church regularly, subscribed to various worthy objects, were always ready to lend their large drawing-room on the first floor for any charitable purpose and were pillars of Northbridge Church, thinking but poorly of St. Sycorax, which had High Church, not to say Romish tendencies.

In pleasant country town fashion the front door of Hovis House was open during the day and friends went straight in and opened the glass door into the hall.

"Anyone at home?" said Sylvia. There was no answer.

"I expect they are in the garden," said Sylvia. She went through the house, followed by Edith, and sure enough there were Mrs. and Miss Dunsford hard at work on a herbaceous border, weeding, removing dead leaves, loosening the earth with small forks and being extremely busy. At the sound of steps on the gravel path Miss Dunsford got up.

"Oh, mother," she said. "It's Sylvia Leslie."

Mrs. Dunsford, who was kneeling on a small waterproof pad, looked up, took off her gardening glove, and extended the hand of friendship to Sylvia, and then to Edith.

"You have come at the right moment," she said. "My new blue poppy is just flowering. I got some seeds from Lady Norton—I mean the Dreadful Dowager, not young Lady Norton—and they have really done very well. Look at them."

And certainly they were very lovely in the sunshine in the long bed under the rose-red brick wall.

"I'll let you have some seeds, Sylvia," she went on. "And I wouldn't say that to everyone."

Sylvia, who was no gardener, though she loved gardens, was trying to express at once her gratitude for the offered gift and her complete unworthiness of it, and finding it difficult to put these conflicting statements into English, when Edith said, "Oh, that's the poppy Mrs. Halliday tried to grow, but she hadn't any luck. I think her garden had the wrong soil."

"Your mother, Sylvia?" said Mrs. Dunsford. "How very interesting. I would like to hear what she did. Did you know that my husband's grandmother and great-grandmother were sisters? I have a lot of old letters that I have always been meaning to go through. Barbara, where did I last put those old letters of Granny's. I *know* I put them somewhere."

Miss Dunsford said in the Sheraton escritoire.

"I must show them to you after tea," said Mrs. Dunsford. "They are in a most beautiful handwriting, almost copper-plate, so clearly written that you could read them just as if they were written yesterday except that they are crossed, which makes it almost impossible. Of course *my* grandmother's letters were crossed and re-crossed, but then she was in India where her husband was stationed at Madrepore. We had an Empire then."

This was so true that there was nothing to say, so no one said it.

"Barbara dear, will you get the tea," said Mrs. Dunsford, adding to her guests, "Come and see the house," and she led the way towards a side door.

Sylvia looked at Edith with an expression of mock despair, a look returned tenfold by Edith who felt that of all the dull afternoons this was perhaps the dullest.

"We keep our old-fashioned ways," said Mrs. Dunsford, with

an air of graciousness which nearly made her guests have the giggles, "and have our drawing-room on the first floor. Come up," and she led Sylvia and Edith upstairs, while Miss Dunsford went to the back regions, obviously to get tea. Not that this was surprising, for during the war very few houses had been able to have a maid and those who had for the first time learned to do without one found life so free and so simple that they went on being maidless. Luckily Northbridge was full of women who wanted a half-day's work, so nearly every gentry house had its morning helper and they managed on the whole pretty well.

The drawing-room was a handsome apartment with a large room overlooking the street and a smaller one overlooking the garden, rather too full of family pictures and family furniture, but a lady's room, well kept and loved.

"It was in this room that we did most of the dressmaking for the Coronation Year Pageant," said Mrs. Dunsford. "We turned out some really good work. Commander Beasley who worked with us could make stencils which we used with great effect for the costumes. And our nice curate, Mr. Highmore, made a wonderful cap for his part. He was Becket and he made a flesh-coloured cap with a fringe of hair from a red setter and looked *exactly* like a monk. He often drops in about teatime. Ah, here is Barbara with our tea."

Miss Dunsford brought in a tray with some pretty old silver on it, opened a folding table, put a fine lace-edged linen cloth on it, and laid the tea.

"The kettle is just on the boil, mother," she said. "I'll bring it up."

Downstairs a bell jangled.

"It's the front door," said Mrs. Dunsford. "Barbara will see to it."

There was the noise of a door being shut and voices in the hall. Then Miss Dunsford came up with the kettle, followed by a pleasant-faced young clergyman.

"This is Mr. Highmore," said Mrs. Dunsford. "Mrs. Martin Leslie from Rushwater and her cousin, Miss Graham."

Mr. Highmore, who was well used to the society of ladies, as indeed most clerics are in a small country town, shook hands warmly and said it was his privilege to have made the acquaintance of Canon Bostock, the incumbent of Rushwater, a splendid fellow in every respect, which at once smoothed the way. He and Sylvia fell into clerical talk very comfortably while Mrs. Dunsford asked Edith what she was doing. Edith said she had been in America with her cousins and had come back and didn't quite know what she wanted to do.

"A real home-lover," said Mrs. Dunsford. "Just like my Barbara. She and I are just like sisters, aren't we, Barbara."

"Oh, yes, mother," said Miss Dunsford. "We do everything together. It's such fun."

The not-so-young daughter living with, and often lived on by, a more powerful mother is perhaps a stock figure and is certainly a real and human one. Northbridge had never troubled itself much about this question, taking things as they came. Mrs. Villars had sometimes wondered; but as Miss Dunsford did not look cowed, not starved, and sometimes went up to London with a day return to attend a performance at the Old Vic with a school friend, she did not give much thought to the matter. There was a small but pleasant society in Northbridge, with many hospitable houses, from the rectory to the Hollies where Mr. Downing, the well-known authority on old Provençal poetry, and his delightful wife lived; or Punshions where those nice retired Nurses, Miss Heath and Miss Chiffinch, lived; or Glycerine Cottage, the abode of Miss Hopgood and Miss Crowder, who had lived on the Riviera, and much admiring the wisteria that flourished there, had planted a Virginia creeper against the porch and done their best to give their house a French name.

"Oh, mother, I have forgotten Mr. Highmore's special cup," said Miss Dunsford. "I'll run down and get it."

Mr. Highmore begged her not to go downstairs on his account, but with a beautiful selflessness she insisted on going. Her mother said Barbara was always so thoughtful for others. Miss Dunsford came back bearing a very large white cup and saucer. On the cup the word Father was emblazoned in Gold with Olde Englishe lettering.

"Here is Your Cup, Mr. Highmore," said Miss Dunsford.

"I say, it's most awfully kind of you," said Mr. Highmore. "I'm afraid you think me a terrible tea-drinker."

Edith privately thought this exchange of remarks very silly. To her cousin Sylvia it sounded more like a mild clerical flirtation. Probably it was both, and no harm in that. Mrs. Dunsford was busy pouring out tea for her party. When everyone was comfortably settled Sylvia enquired after various other old friends at Northbridge. All were well, though of course not so young as they were.

"You have read of Professor Talbot's death in the *Barchester Chronicle*, I suppose?" said Mrs. Dunsford to Sylvia. "It was really a blessing in disguise. Those poor girls were nearly worn out."

"I should have thought he was dead long ago," said Sylvia. "His daughters must be nearly dead with looking after him. They are pretty old, aren't they?"

"Well, Miss Talbot is about my age," said Mrs. Dunsford, "and Miss Dolly Talbot a year or two younger," which at once made Sylvia count mentally on her fingers (a thing anyone will understand); but as she had no clue to Mrs. Dunsford's age beyond the fact that her daughter was obviously no longer young, she did not come to any very definite conclusion. And although she was quite enjoying herself, her habit of thinking about and for other people, learned as chatelaine of Rushwater, made her feel that for Edith it must be rather dull.

Mr. Highmore, who had a very kind heart, had formed the same conclusion, and casting about in his mind for something to say, asked Edith if she had been in the Cathedral last Sunday when the Dean was preaching. Edith said she hadn't. Mr.

Highmore said he had noticed some girls in the deanery pew when he went in to Evensong on the previous Thursday, but did not add that he had found them rather attractive; for this, it seemed to him, would be an unsuitable kind of conversation with Miss Graham.

"Oh, Goody! Goody!" said Edith. "I hope it was Grace and Jane."

Mr. Highmore asked who Grace and Jane were.

"Oh, the Dean's granddaughters, didn't you know?" said Edith. "He has lots of grandchildren because he has so many children. Grace is the eldest one, she's quite old. Grace is all right. Her sister is Jane. When I go home I'll ask Mother if they can come and stay at Holdings. I'd ask you to come to tea with them if you like."

Mr. Highmore, with private reservations as to being asked to tea by so young a person whose parents he did not know, said that would be delightful.

"I shan't forget," said Edith.

Mr. Highmore said he was sure she wouldn't. Nor, he added, would he forget her promise. Had she heard, he added, though rather cautiously, about the dinner party the Palace had given for some Russian trades union delegates who were visiting Barchester, and how the Russians brought their own drink with them because they had been told that the Bishop and Bishopess were stingy, and had not come up to the drawing-room after dinner because they were busy teaching the Bishop how to drink healths in Russian and what the Bishopess had said. All of which Edith, as a loyal supporter of the deanery, heard with joy and said she would ask her mother when she got home to ask Mr. Highmore to dinner because her father would like the story; which in turn gave Mr. Highmore considerable pleasure, part of which was the thought that to see this amusing Miss Graham again would not be disagreeable, and so took his leave.

Presently Sylvia said she must be going, but first would Mrs. Dunsford let them see the portrait of her great-aunt, or was it great-great-aunt, she meant the great-grandmother of herself and her brother George Halliday.

"Dear me, how stupid of me," said Mrs. Dunsford. "It is in the end room," and she took them through the back drawing-room into a small third room with a window overlooking the garden and a writing table against the wall, above which hung a woman's head, delicately yet firmly drawn by a master hand.

"What a charmer she must have been!" said Sylvia.

"Drawn by George Richmond," said Mrs. Dunsford. His style is always recognizable and there is what one might call his signature mark—the highlight on the end of the nose."

"It *is* a lovely thing," said Sylvia, who was not as a rule much interested in pictures.

Miss Dunsford said the good looks were still in the family. As this was almost the only original remark she had contributed to the afternoon's entertainment, Sylvia smiled to her and then, suddenly realizing that the compliment was for herself, blushed furiously.

"George would simply love to see it," she said. "Could he come over one day when he can get away from the farm?"

"We should be delighted," said Mrs. Dunsford. "I may as well tell you now that I have left that drawing to your brother George in my will. It ought to be with the family and Barbara quite agrees with me. I have had it carefully cleaned and re-framed by an expert and I hope it may give pleasure to future generations."

Miss Dunsford said she felt Mother was doing just what the original of the picture would have liked, and Sylvia pressed her hand affectionately, at which Miss Dunsford went red in the face with emotion.

"You are very generous," said Sylvia to her hostess, "and I know George will value it and take great care of it. He has a real family feeling. Mine is mostly Leslie now," she added, more lightly.

"And most suitable," said Mrs. Dunsford approvingly. "He ought to get married though. There are far too many unmarried young men about since the war. In the real war—I mean the 1914 war—everyone got married," she added rather severely, as if it were Sylvia's fault.

"I'm sure George would get married if he wanted to," said Sylvia. "I did talk to him about it once and he said he would simply love to get married, but he had never seen any woman that he could bear the idea of being married to. I mean he *likes* them and has lots of friends—"

"Ah, well," said Mrs. Dunsford. "Time will show. And Barbara and I are very glad that your grandmother—I mean great-aunt or whatever it is—will be in good hands. You must come again soon, and I will show you those old letters I have in the Sheraton escritoire."

Sylvia said that would be very nice.

"Just draw the curtain a little, dear," said Mrs. Dunsford as she left the room, followed by Edith.

Sylvia politely waited while Miss Dunsford drew the curtain to keep the level rays of the sun from the portrait. Then Miss Dunsford waited for Sylvia to go back through the drawing-room.

"I'm awfully glad you're going to have it—at least your brother," she said. "It isn't right here."

"But why?" said Sylvia, surprised and rather alarmed by this sudden manifestation of a personality.

"Because it isn't happy," said Miss Dunsford. "It wants a house that's lived in, and young people. Mother and I are too old."

"But *you* aren't old," said Sylvia, who was interested by this sudden development of a personality in the shadowy Miss Dunsford.

"I'm just about as old as mother," said Miss Dunsford calmly. "That is why we are such good friends," and she went downstairs in front of Sylvia as if to protect her if she fell. Sylvia was disturbed by her words. She could not quite understand them and at the same time felt that perhaps she would rather not understand. When they reached the bottom of the stairs Miss Dunsford was again her normal, pleasant, ordinary, rather drab self; the middle-aged unmarried daughter living quietly with her elderly widowed mother, companions in everything. Good-byes were said and the guests departed.

"Now we will just finish the bit of the border, Barbara," said Mrs. Dunsford, "and then we must get ready for the evening service."

"Yes, mother," said Miss Dunsford.

The drive home was uneventful except for an exciting moment when, just at the bottom of a steepish hill, a car came out of a side road a little too fast. Edith was frightened. Sylvia did a very pretty bit of accelerating and swerving and rushed up the hill. At the top she drew in to the side. The other car drew up level with her.

"I am so *very* sorry, Mrs. Leslie," said an agreeable voice. "I was in error, not you."

"Hullo, Dr. Fewling," said Sylvia. "I thought it must be you. Don't say you've got *another* new car. This is Edith Graham."

Edith politely said How do you do to what was, judging by his collar, a clergyman.

"Well—it is," said Dr. Fewling. "I was just trying her. She has that new fluid supersonic rotary drive," or if these were not his exact words, they were others exactly like them. "Would you care to try it?"

Sylvia said not today as she had to get home, but some other day she would love to.

"Perhaps you and your husband—and Miss Graham," he added with a kind of courteous bow towards Edith, "will come over and dine with me one day? The John Leslies are coming next week and one or two others. I always need an odd lady—or should I say an extra lady—owing to being a bachelor, and this would be a delightful party."

Sylvia thought so too and a date was fixed, subject to the

approval of Dr. Fewling's housekeeper and Sylvia's husband, Dr. Fewling disappeared, going far too fast but, we believe, very safely.

Edith asked about this new friend.

"Oh, he is awfully nice," said Sylvia as she started the car again. "He's celibate or something and gives very good dinners."

Edith asked if he was nicer than Mr. Choyce or, she added in compliment to Rushwater, as nice as Mr. Bostock.

"I really don't know," said Sylvia. "They are all so different. Mr. Choyce is married. Mr. Bostock isn't married but he would quite like to be—he told me so himself. Canon Fewling—"

"I thought you said Doctor," said Edith.

"Oh, we say either," said Sylvia. "He used to be called Father when he was at St. Sycorax at Northbridge and then he came to Greshamsbury and was made a Canon of Barchester, and he is an honorary Doctor of Divinity, so I suppose he's both. Anyway he doesn't like the Bishop, so he's all right."

Edith, properly brought up to renounce the Bishop—and more particularly the Bishopess—in all their works, said he sounded very nice and she would ask her mother if she would ask him to Holdings. By this time they were back at Rushwater. Sylvia left the car in the stable yard and went off on some garden or village job. Everyone was out and the house very still. Edith went onto the terrace where there were chairs and sat looking at the beautiful tulip-tree, one of the finest in England and reported now to be even higher than the tulip-tree at the Great House at Woolbeding. Lovely warmth and stillness. On the hill beyond the garden the Temple, a charming and useless monument erected by Martin's great-great-grandfather, stood golden in the last afternoon light in a clearing among the beeches. All was nostalgic and lovely and Edith thought what fun it would be if a Prince on a white horse came out of the woods. So wrapped was she in her fairy story that she was almost startled when Mrs. Halliday sat down beside her.

"I saw you were alone, so I came out to keep you company," said Mrs. Halliday. "Did you have a nice afternoon?"

Edith, still rather in a dream, rather resentful that her dream was being broken, pulled herself together and said she had had a very nice time at Northbridge, and Mrs. Dunsford had said she did hope Mrs. Halliday would come and see the portrait of their ancestress; using the word ancestress because she could not remember exactly what degree of auntship or cousinship it was.

Mrs. Halliday said she would like very much to go and must ask Sylvia to drive her over one day. Or even better, she would ask George to drive her as he would like to see it so much. She might, she said, get Sylvia to take her over to Hatch End to lunch with George and they could drive straight to Northbridge and then George could bring her back to Rushwater and she was sure Sylvia would ask him to stay to supper.

To all this Edith made polite noises of acquiescence, because she felt sorry for Mrs. Halliday; though her more practical self told her that George was a working farmer, short-handed on the farm, and might not find this plan very easy. But coming to the conclusion that Mrs. Halliday didn't listen much to what other people said, she held her tongue; which perhaps showed that she had in her some of that very valuable quality inherited from her mother—worldly wisdom.

As always at Rushwater, at any rate for visitors, time flowed on peacefully, golden day followed golden day. Edith spent most of her time with her various relations, helping in stables, cowshed, farm or garden according to what was needed and her ability to do it. Nor were the pigs neglected. A sow had farrowed (we believe we are correct in saying this) and to Edith's joy and pride one of the litter was given her name. There was some discussion as to whether a boar could be called Edith, but Martin said that Cecil and Esme were used for both sexes, so why not Edith—and anyway they could call him Eddie. It was finally decided that he should be Edward.

"I'll keep an eye on yours for you," said her sister Emmy Grantly, who had assisted in every sense at the interesting event. "If he looks like a winner we'll keep him. If not we'll kill him for you if you say when and send over the best bits. I like a loin best myself, but you can say what you like."

Edith, rather at a loss, said please would Emmy send whatever she thought would be best for Holdings.

"There's one thing about mother's cook," said Emmy, "she does understand pigs. I say, I'll send you a side, then you can have what you like when you like. I say, it would be funny if Holdings Goliath and our boar tied at the Agricultural. Wouldn't it, old man?" and she picked up a stick and prodded the vast bulk of Rushwater Blunderbore.

To Edith brought up on an estate where family came first and the animals were a pleasant, useful adjunct, it was something of an eye-opener to see Rushwater where farm, garden, stream, meadows, woodland were all part of an ordered economy with the family its servants in a manner of speaking. As a child she had taken it all for granted and now, going about with one or other of her relations, she began to realize what an estate in all its ramifications implied. Eager to learn, she even tried to grasp the estate accounts, and surprised the professional accountant who came to look over the books by her quickness. She found it not unpleasant work and decided to take a course in bookkeeping. This plan she laid before her cousin Martin, who, to her great mortification, burst out laughing.

"Look here, Edith," he said. "You don't begin to know what you're talking about. And another thing. Will you stick to it? There was that plan of learning estate management and then you chucked it all and went off to America. Not your line, my girl. What you should do is to marry some nice fellow in a few years and settle down."

"But Sylvia helps you," said Edith.

"Of course she does, bless her," said Martin. "If it weren't for her I'd have gone mad years ago with this blasted foot of mine. But I run the farm with Tom Grantly and one or two men who know the job under us. Sylvia runs the village. That's different. I daresay you could run a village. But you'd have to learn a lot. Not colleges of anything, but talking to your people and helping them and bullying them and being at their beck and call all the time. It's worth it. Very little to show for it, but you pull your weight. Do you know anything about bookkeeping?"

Edith said nothing, but her face grew redder and hotter with shame and misery. For the first time in her life she saw how unlike she was to all the dreams she had of herself and didn't enjoy it. Martin felt sorry for her, but it was just as well for her to face a few facts. A nice girl, a very pretty girl, an intelligent girl, but not like Sylvia, or Emmy, or like Mrs. Samuel Adams, who knew as much about mixed farming as most people and more than a great many. Edith had too much Pomfret in her, that was her trouble. Taking it for granted that she would do what she wanted. Old Lord Pomfret had carried it off with his personality and his wealth, but that time was gone for ever. Land was a master now, not a possession to be used and exploited.

"I'm sorry, Martin," she said in a very small choked voice.

"So am I," said Martin. "Now cheer up. I'll ask Sylvia to find you some jobs you *can* do. I must get on with my own job. By the way, you might talk to Mrs. Halliday a bit. She is feeling rather widow-ish I think," which made Edith laugh and then she felt much better.

After this very salutary talk from her cousin Martin we cannot say that she was a reformed character, but she did sincerely try to help, or if she could not help, not to be a nuisance.

Only the youngest of a family can know the difficulties of that position. One begins by being rather spoilt, perhaps unconsciously kept young by one's parents who cling to the last baby. One's brothers and sisters go into the world or marry and one becomes the important child in the house. Parents are older and perhaps rather exhausted by bringing up one's elders and let one go too much one's own way. Sir Robert Graham had done well by the three sons. His daughters he had left to their mother's care. Emmy had always been a farmer and took to the life like a duck to water. Clarissa had been difficult, but was now most happily settled with her schoolmaster husband Charles Belton. Edith was the youngest, the most spoilt. She could, if she had known the song, have said "Oh thou hast been the cause of this anguish, my mother"; but this her generous heart would never recognize.

We think that Lady Graham did wish that she had been more strict with her youngest; but how many mothers have in all love and good faith hopelessly spoiled the last of the brood.

The present moment is always the important moment. Edith did try to improve, even going so far as to spend a good deal of time with Mrs. Halliday who was sometimes in a rather Gummidge-ish state of mind, "thinking of the old'un." It was not very amusing to be with someone who was being sorry for herself, but Edith persevered and tried to think how Mrs. Halliday might be amused or interested, going as far as to ask Sylvia if she could take Mrs. Halliday to Northbridge to see the Dunsfords and the family portrait. Sylvia, delighted by Edith's request, got one of the men to drive them over. The visit was an enormous success. Mrs. Halliday and Mrs. Dunsford never stopped talking, while Edith helped Miss Dunsford in the garden.

"You *were* lucky," said Miss Dunsford, "to go to America. Mother doesn't like travelling, so we always stay here. Do you know what I want to do?"

Edith said she didn't.

"I want to Go Abroad," said Miss Dunsford. "I've got enough money to go with, but mother is always sick crossing the Channel and she won't try flying. Miss Hopgood and Miss Crowder used to live on the Riviera at a very nice hotel, the

Pension Ramsden, and go for lovely excursions in motor-buses with an English guide. They would give me an introduction. It would be wonderful."

Edith said why didn't she go then.

"Mother wouldn't like to be here alone," said Miss Dunsford. "Even when I go away for a weekend, only I've given it up now, she is so nervous. Some people don't like being alone of course. I should *love* it."

"But surely some one could come and stay with your mother while you were abroad," said Edith.

"Oh, mother is very particular," said Miss Dunsford. "She did try a companion once, but it didn't work."

"But she could have a friend to stay with her, couldn't she?" said Edith. "Someone like Mrs. Halliday who knows her and they could talk about old times. It would be wonderful. After all, it wouldn't be forever."

Miss Dunsford sat back on her heels and looked at Edith.

"You're a pal," she said. "Put it there," and she extended to Edith the hand of friendship, covered with damp earth. Edith shook it warmly and began to laugh.

"What's the joke?" said Miss Dunsford, "and I'll laugh too."

"Oh, I don't know," said Edith, a little ashamed of herself. "One does laugh sometimes, just about nothing. You know."

Miss Dunsford, though she obviously didn't know, appeared to be contended. Then Edith extracted Mrs. Halliday from her hostess and took her back to Rushwater.

CHAPTER 6

We need hardly say that Edith had brought with her to Rushwater a wardrobe of the enchanting dresses her cousin Rose had given her in America. Neither day nor evening, incredibly smart yet simple, suitable for almost anything from a lunch party to a cocktail party, or even a small dance. But there had been no opportunity at all for wearing them. During the artificial Summer Time, when evenings were long, and right up to the time when the clocks were put back (or was it forward? a question which is asked twice a year and is always perplexing), everyone went on working in field, garden, cowshed or wherever a hand was needed up till the late darkness.

Sylvia had asked to see the dresses, had been enchanted by them and said What a shame Edith couldn't wear them, but what was the use if they were going to clean out the hen run after supper, or help Martin to get all that green muck out of the pond. Very sensibly Edith agreed with her and had got so much into the habit of wearing the same dress from breakfast to bedtime that she felt a little shy about dressing up. But Sylvia, as a good house-mistress, thought of everyone and everything and on the day they were to dine with Canon Fewling she made Edith stop whatever work she was doing after tea, go upstairs, have a bath and put on her best frock. The important question then arose: which was the best. Edith had brought three with her, all with a not too low neck, short sleeves, and an ankle-length skirt with a kind of ballerina swirl over its stiff taffeta underskirt. We need hardly say that Sylvia had—as any woman would—tried them on herself; but she was taller than Edith and of a fuller figure, so she laughed cheerfully at her own appearance and told Edith to wear the one that had the tiny black-and-white check and the shiny black belt and the amusing glass buttons down the front and bring her lovely scarf of black wool interwoven with silver and her black and silver vanity case.

There was rather a run on the two bathrooms, as everyone felt it would be as well to wash off the day's toil, but Edith by arrangement had hers fairly early, so when she was dressed she went downstairs to show her finery to Mrs. Halliday. And it must be said in justice to everyone that not only had Canon Fewling rung up and said he had not realized that Mrs. Halliday was at Rushwater and would she come too, but Mrs. Halliday had said she would rather stay at home if no one minded.

Edith, partly from her own good nature, partly from her mother's example, was usually very kind to her elders, looking upon them we think as a species of rather nice undeveloped idiots whom one might as well humour because it gave them pleasure. And to us who are now the elders, if the young are kind and charming we accept it with real gratitude at its face value and do not enquire whether the kindness is from the heart or the head. Both have their value and what the head has begun the heart will often take to itself.

"Do you like it, Mrs. Halliday?" said Edith, when she had strutted and postured and pirouetted before her.

Mrs. Halliday said, quite truly, that it was the prettiest dress she had seen and Edith looked very nice. Then Sylvia came down, magnificent in red, which is not everyone's colour, and Martin, very distinguished with his dinner jacket and his slight limp, which somehow gives cachet. Emmy and her husband had gone home, but Mrs. Halliday was not to be alone, for Sylvia had suggested that Mrs. Dunsford should come over from Northbridge and spend the evening with her cousin—for

though no one could get the relationship quite straight, the
kinship had become a matter of some importance and interest to
both ladies.

Then Mrs. Dunsford arrived in one of the two Northbridge
taxis, which was to have its supper in the kitchen and take her
home again.

"It *is* nice to see you again," said Mrs. Halliday. "What is
Barbara doing without you?"

Mrs. Dunsford said she had gone to supper with those nice
rather dull ladies at Glycerine Cottage, Miss Hopgood and Miss
Crowder. And as no one really cared where Miss Dunsford was
having supper they talked about other things. Then Martin with
Sylvia and Edith drove away to Greshamsbury.

It was a lovely evening after a fine day. In spite of her
American experiences Edith was not at all blasé about parties
and felt almost excited at the idea of seeing the nice Fairweathers again, for Rose's beauty and Captain Fairweather's nautical
manner and good looks had made a considerable impression on
her. The road to Greshamsbury was not very crowded. They
drove swiftly across the downs, into the river valley, and then up
again over the downs, avoid main roads. The old Greshamsbury,
formerly little more than a High Street leading to the Big
House, was now the core of a fair-sized settlement which might
almost be called a town. Luckily the new building was mostly
out at the other end of the main street, and the Old Town—as
newcomers were beginning to call it—had retained a good deal
of its character. Greshamsbury House itself still stood in what
was left of the park. The John Leslies had some time ago bought
the Old Rectory, a good late Georgian house standing in its own
grounds. Captain Francis Gresham, R.N., lived with his wife
and three children in a wing of Greshamsbury House, now
under the National Trust. Captain Fairweather, R.N., and his
beautiful wife Rose had also settled in the town with their
growing family. Captain Fairweather had to go to London every
week to do no one knew what at the Admiralty, but their

lordships seemed to be generous in the matter of working hours and he was mostly at home for a long weekend. Sometimes he would bring an old naval friend down with him and then Rose would invite the rector, Canon Fewling, who had been a sailor himself in the first war, and the men could talk happily, far into the night, about what the Old Man said to Number One.

Providence who, it seems to us, has always taken a very unfair and unnecessary amount of interest in bachelors, had arranged for Canon Fewling to have an excellent housekeeper, one Mrs. Hicks, a widow in whose house he had lodged when at St. Sycorax in Northbridge. When he was given the living at Greshamsbury she had determinedly followed him and installed herself in the rectory and liked nothing better than to cook and serve dinner for any number up to ten, even if it meant putting the extra leaf into the table. She would—so Mrs. Hicks said— never forget the time when the Bishop came to lunch and the extra leaf came down at one end and all that lovely steak and kidney pudding on the Bishop's lap really quite a shock it gave her, a queer turn, and though she had put his apron as they called it first under the cold tap and then under the hot, the way her mother told her, of course you couldn't get not all the marks out and her friend who obliged at the Palace said there was ever such a dust-up because the apron had to go to the cleaner's and they didn't get it back for three days and the Bishop hadn't got a spare one and the Old Cut was in a fine old wax because the cleaner's charged extra for a quick clean as everyone knew.

The Rushwater party were the first to arrive at the rectory and Canon Fewling was delighted to see them. Not that he would not have been delighted whether they were first or last, but he suffered—as most of us do—from an incurable pessimism about his own plans. How often have we not, on the morning of the small dinner party we are giving, suddenly been smitten by a horrible anxiety that it isn't the right day. It cannot have been yesterday, for then our guests would have arrived unexpectedly at the allotted hour. We feel sure it *is* today, yet if by some awful oversight it was really tomorrow, how could we know the stark truth until we had waited for at least half an hour (to give people time to be late) and still had no guests. Luckily this only happens very rarely, but nearly all givers of parties will sympathize with the feeling. There is of course the other side of the question— the guests who (as in one of John Leech's *Punch* drawings) arrive in period clothes only to be greeted by the words: "Missus's fancy-dress ball was *last* Toosday."

However it is luckily not often that these things really happen and we will say at once that the Leslies with their young cousins were cordially welcomed. Captain and Mrs. Gresham and John Leslie with his wife followed hard upon. Canon Fewling gave them a choice of sherries, which impressed Edith very much.

"I say, Uncle John," she said rather softly, "which do I like, do you think?"

Her Uncle John said that he had seldom heard a simple question more complicatedly put and he thought the dry sherry would be far too dry for her and better take the other one, which she did and liked it.

Mrs. Hicks, whose finer feelings had been slightly outraged by the way the Leslies had come in without knocking or ringing (a quite usual custom among the circle of Canon Fewling's friends), was lying in wait for the Fairweathers. There was a pause before the drawing-room door was opened and Mrs. Hicks announced them properly. She then went back to the kitchen, wrapped (more or less in Horace's beautiful words) in her own virtue. And we do not propose to argue about the English equivalent of virtus, for it would waste time and spoil our point.

All those Friends of Barsetshire who have followed Rose Fairweather's progress from the outrageously spoilt, silly, and lovely girl to the kind, capable, and beautiful wife and mother will be glad to see her again, as we always are. Not that she was perfect, nor, we think, did her devoted husband, who was also a martinet in his home, ever consider her for a moment as such.

But they were an unusually happy and affectionate couple and excellent parents, with several very agreeable children, whom Rose, to the surprise of all her friends and relations, was bringing up extremely well. Nor did she insist, as many mothers do, on relating very pointless stories about their gifts and charm.

As the party, with the exception of the Rushwater contingent, were all Greshamsbury, the sherry talk was naturally rather one-sided, bearing largely upon local politics and the balance of advantage and disadvantage of living, as the Greshams did, on a National Trust estate.

"I rather like it," said Mrs. Gresham. "I show the visitors round sometimes and some of them tip me. I like that too," and she looked defiantly at her husband.

"She made seventeen and sixpence last week," said Captain Gresham, with a kind of shamefaced pride.

"But when father was staying with us he was *much* worse," said his wife. "He collected nearly three pounds. I think he said he was at the Battle of the Nile and as no one knew what it was they all believed him."

Canon Fewling said, for the benefit of the audience, that Mrs. Gresham's father was old Admiral Palliser at Hallbury.

Rose Fairweather said she simply *adored* Admiral Palliser.

"And you know what he called *you*, my girl," said her husband. "Sailor's Luck," but as no one was sure whether this epithet, though doubtless merited, was complimentary or opprobrious, no one liked to comment.

"Because," Rose continued, with an adoring look at her husband, "he is so *exactly* like an Admiral. John isn't. He's like a Captain."

Martin very sensibly said that if one was a captain it would be just as well to be like one, and then wondered if what he said meant anything.

"Then you ought to look like a landed proprietor, Martin," said Edith.

This led to an interesting discussion as to what landed proprietors ought to look like, during which it appeared that pretty well everyone thought of them in terms of Washington Irving's *Bracebridge Hall* with Caldecott's illustrations, except for those who preferred to envisage them as Captain Boldwig who, finding Mr. Pickwick sleeping off the effects of cold punch in a wheelbarrow on his estate, had him trundled off to the village pound.

Mrs. Hicks then announced dinner.

The seating of a party of ten, of whom eight are married couples and five are members of the same family, is enough to drive a mathematician mad. Cannon Fewling had made at least four different maps of the seating, got them all wrong, torn them up, made a fifth which was even worse and was sorely tempted to break at least one of the ten commandments. Finally it was more or less settled. Mrs. John Leslie on one side of the host, Mrs. Martin Leslie on the other, Mrs. Gresham at the far end of the table opposite her host, and the rest of the company distributed so that—as nearly as possible—the would not be next to a near relation. This, considering that there were five Leslies present by birth, marriage, or connection, was not easy, but somehow a round table makes it a little easier, why, we really cannot say.

We should like here to chronicle, to the greater glory of our sex (and by *our* we mean the libery reader who has got this book out because the girl at Gaiter's Library said it was ever so nice and is going to take it back tomorrow because she found after she had got half-way through it that she had read it before), that we do not in the least mind being next to our relations at dinner. With a stranger, however charming, distinguished, urbane he may be, we have to make an effort (English), to explore every avenue (Journalese), to tâter le terrain (as the French have it). With Cousin Henry, or Aunt Sibyl, or even our married daughter's sister-in-law, there is at once some kind of common ground—whether of like or dislike—in the other relations and whether Charles is really going to marry that quite dreadful girl, or how on earth Horace and Lesbia can afford to live as they do. So was it at Canon Fewling's party, where half the party were Leslies by blood or by name, speaking more or less the same language. It is true that the Royal navy was also well represented by two naval captains with their wives, one of a naval family herself, and also by the host who had during the first war risen to the rank of commander before entering into Holy Orders, and sometimes thought nostalgically of the happy days when he had been round the Horn in a sailing ship; probably one of the last to do so.

Mrs. Hicks, an excellent cook, prided herself on the Rector's dinner parties. There were only three courses—apart from the dessert of garden fruit—but they were excellently cooked, hot, and plenty of second helpings for those who wanted them. Encouraged by Martin, who had a labourer's appetite, and Edith who was young enough to be frankly greedy, everybody had a second helping of everything.

"It's all right, sir," said Mrs. Hicks to her employer when Edith had had the remains of the superb omelette surprise.

"I've plenty more in the kitchen. Mrs. Fairweather's girl is giving me a hand and so is that Lily that works at Mrs. Gresham's," which audible aside gently interested the guests and Mrs. Gresham said now she knew why her Lily was getting so fat. It became obvious to John Leslie that both the naval gentlemen were thinking of other reasons for this phenomenon, so he asked Mrs. Gresham how her father, Admiral Palliser, was.

"Oh, very well, thank you," said Mrs. Gresham. "Of course he isn't as young as he was and he misses dear old Dr. Dale," but as none of us are as young as we were, and it was at least ten years since the old Rector died, there did not seem to be much comment to make.

Edith said it would be awful if Mr. Bostock at Rushwater died.

"Some people," said Rose Fairweather, "who are quite old enough to die just don't die, like—"

"That's enough, my girl," said her husband. "Always be polite to anyone in gaiters whether you like them or not," at which there was a kind of hum of approval till Sylvia Leslie said there was the Archdeacon over at Plumstead of course, and everyone agreed that gaiters or no gaiters the Archdeacon was so nice and had such reasonable ideas about game-preserving and the Palace, that even his gaiters had acquired merit.

The grown-ups were now well away upon the ever interesting subject of The Close, and Edith felt rather out of it. To be between two real Royal Navy captains and not be talked to by either of them was mortifying. At Rushwater one could talk across the table, but here all the grown-ups (for Edith had forgotten for the time being that she considered herself grown-up) just talked to one another. But she had been well trained to be polite, so she asked Captain Gresham whether he knew Grace and Jane Crawley, the Dean's granddaughters.

"Not as well as I'd like," said Captain Gresham. "You see I'm in London most of the week and we don't go much to Barchester."

Edith said in Oxfordshire where their father was a Rural Dean. Then conversation languished. Edith, feeling the honour of the House of Graham at stake, tried again and asked Captain Gresham if he had been to America, because she had and it was lovely.

"Not the United States, if that is what you mean by America," said Captain Gresham, "but I was stationed at Las Palombas at the beginning of the war when we sank a few German ships—at least one scuttled herself."

"That seems very unfair," said Edith.

Captain Gresham enquired why.

Edith said one ought to go on fighting. Like Sir Richard Grenville she said, with the "Revenge."

"But he *did* want to scuttle her," said Captain Gresham. "He told the Master Gunner to sink her and split her in twain. Perhaps the German captain did give an order to scuttle his ship and the crew wouldn't so he did."

"Well anyway whatever the German captain did he was *wrong* and whatever Sir Richard Grenville did he was *right*," said Edith.

Captain Gresham thought well of the sentiment, but was finding this pretty child rather a bore and was not sorry when Sylvia appealed to him in some small argument between herself and Canon Fewling. Edith turned to Captain Fairweather on her other side, but he was deep in talk with Mrs. Gresham about the County Council's proposal to make an arterial road within a hundred yards of the cross-roads, which would be bound to make a lot of cars go up the High Street because they wouldn't want to use the arterial road. It would be awful, said Mrs. Gresham, but no worse than having sightseers all over the place at Greshamsbury House and leaving their horrible sandwich papers and orange peel about, because however many waste-paper baskets were put for them, they preferred to put their rubbish in a place where it would show more. And as for staying inside your own house, they pushed their faces up against the windows to see what the inside was like.

Really, Edith thought, it was as bad as Merry's wedding all over again, when no one took notice of her. She began to feel a rebellious pricking behind the eyes, in spite of the excellent dessert which included delicious candied fruit and fresh garden fruit and plenty of peppermint creams.

Rose Fairweather, also temporarily stranded but perfectly at her ease, noticed Edith's forlorn face and felt sorry for her. For it was among the pleasant and unexpected sides of that charming creature that she had an eye swift to see a guest in trouble, a quick sympathy for the neglected, and liked the society of her own sex.

"I say, Edith," she said, addressing that young person across the table. "Where on earth did you get that perfectly divine dress? I'm absolutely *envious* of it. It can't be Barchester."

Edith, suddenly feeling rather shy before this unexpected kindness, said she had brought it back from New York with her.

"Good girl!" said Rose. "When John was at Washington I used to fly to New York and get perfectly marvellous dresses at a too divine shop on something Avenue; not frightfully high-class but the most terribly smart clothes and notions."

Edith said did she mean Puddingdale's on Texington Avenue.

"That's it," said Rose. "I bought six divine dresses off the peg and I spent the whole of the voyage home oversewing the seams. I think they were all machined too quickly and you know when the thread breaks in your machine you have to go back and start again, but these were just machined with great gaps in the machining, if you see what I mean."

Edith, delighted to be noticed by the lovely Rose, said she had come back by air so there wasn't time to do any sewing, but she had oversewn all the seams since she got home.

Rose, to Edith's great surprise, said she didn't like flying, because she thought the aeroplane might fall down and she also travelled by sea if she could, which at once gave Edith a rather holy and protective feeling for the beautiful Mrs. Fairweather.

"Look here," said Rose, "if Tubby gets down to the piano after dinner, let's go over to my house and I'll show you my American dresses," which invitation delighted Edith. Partly because she was not naturally musical and would quite as soon not go to a concert; partly from a sudden and most natural heroine-worship for Rose. At Edith's age, standing with extremely uncertain feet where the brook and river meet, her mind rather jumbled by her various excursions into so many changing scenes, from the College of Estate Management and Pomfret Towers to David and the Rose's curious rather homeless life in America, hardly ever more than a week in any one place if that, then home, then to Rushwater, Rose seemed to her to represent something solid, someone who knew exactly where she was and what she would do. And those who knew Rose best, under her still apparently vague and girlish ways could sense an extremely good world sense and a very kind heart and would entirely have agreed with Edith.

At Greshamsbury dinner parties what John Leslie called the Segregation of the Sexes did not often take place and the parties tended to sit over the table for some time and then all go together to the drawing-room or sitting-room, for that dreadful word lounge was not, we are thankful to say, used by any of the people we know. So on this evening did the ladies—marshalled by Mary Leslie, who at her host's request acted as temporary hostess—go across to Canon Fewling's large drawing-room, and were almost at once followed by the men. Mrs. Hicks brought in more coffee, freshly made; glasses and syphons and several drinks were already on a side table.

Conversation was general. The Greshams had lately dined at the deanery, had much enjoyed the evening and had met two very nice granddaughters of Dr. Crawley's, called Grace and Jane. That pleasant Mr. Needham, the Vicar of Lambton, had also been there with his wife Octavia, daughter of the deanery and Beneficent Autocrat of the parish. It was too bad that Mr. Needham had lost his right arm in Africa, but he did wonders with his left arm and Octavia watched over him so kindly.

"We are a pretty lucky lot," said Captain Fairweather, looking round at his two brother combatants. "Not an arm or a leg lost between us."

Canon Fewling said he had always hoped, during the war, that if he were wounded it would be an eye or an arm so that he could share something with Nelson. Everyone felt patriotic and no one knew what to say.

"Well, here's to more and better legs," said Martin Leslie, raising his modest glass. His wife looked at him with sudden affectionate uneasiness.

"I say, I never meant—"

"My *dear* old Martin—" said Canon Fewling and John Leslie almost simultaneously.

"Oh, that's all right," said Martin, acknowledging the apologies by lifting his glass and drinking to them both. "it's not like Robin Dale who left a whole foot at that foul Anzio. I only got a knock," which was a nice speech, but did not make the other men feel much easier.

"Octavia Needham that's the clergy's wife at Lambton," said Edith, "says Tommy often thinks his arm's there when it isn't. I mean he thinks he's going to touch something or pick it up and then he can't."

Seizing upon this escape from a rather uncomfortable position (though we do not think that Martin would have thought twice about it if left to himself), the gentlemen began to discuss the week's cricket, which in turn meant turning on the wireless, only it wasn't the right time for the sports news and all they got was a talk on Owain Gryffudd the Welsh miner poet—*minah*, of course, not *minah*, said the golden-voiced announcer—which Canon Fewling at once turned off. A discussion then took place as to why announcers had to talk like that. John Leslie said that years ago—the year Mary first came to stay at Rushwater, he added, with an affectionate look at his wife—his brother David had picked up a female B.B.C. who had given him a fair sickener, but luckily she entered into a companionate marriage with a colleague, and David had married Rose Bingham.

Canon Fewling said he often wondered whether the word controversy would gradually become contròversy, as that appeared to be the B.B.C.'s authorised version and whether ackcherly would appear in the next edition of the lamented Mr. Fowler's *Modern English Usage*.

The grown-ups were now all away on a hot scent, instancing various horrible instances such as applickable and the gentlemen who had spoken on Iphigeenia in the Third Programme. The

grown-ups were all enjoying themselves immensely and mispro-
nunciations hurtled through the air.

Rose Fairweather in the kindness of her heart saw Edith
trying not to look bored and again suggested that she should
come over to the house and see her American dresses, an
invitation which Edith gladly accepted. So Rose looked at her
husband with a look as expressive as Lord Burleigh's nod and
slipped quietly out of the room followed by Edith.

The Fairweathers' house was a pleasant mid-Victorian
gentleman's residence with a large garden. Rose Fairweather
made no pretensions to period furnishing or being artistic. The
chairs and sofas were very comfortable, there was no particular
colour-scheme anywhere, the curtains were of harmless flowered material, but it certainly felt like a home. And we may say
that wherever Rose had been during her married life as a sailor's
wife, the flat, or house, or villa in which she and her family
temporarily lived had always been extremely comfortable and
well run. Rose took Edith upstairs to her bedroom and showed
her a wardrobe of perfectly ravishing dresses.

"Would you like to put them on?" she said.

"Oh!" said Edith, all the woman in her rising, "may I *really?*"

Rose said very sensibly that was what she meant and laid out
on her bed five or six dashing confections. At the sight of so
much beauty Edith forgot to be self-conscious, slipped off her
own very pretty dress and peacocked about in one after the other
of Rose's.

"Of course I really need some make-up," said Edith, "but
mother won't let me."

"Quite right," said Rose. "I used to use a lot when I was a girl
and mother didn't like it either, so I practically stopped. Of
course I always put a *bit* of make-up on and a little bit extra for
parties. You don't need to. You can have a little bit of lipstick if
you like, but *not* bright red or that awful purply sort. And if you
like you can trim your eyebrows just a little, but whatever you do

don't trim them too much. It isn't every woman that has a good natural line of eyebrow," by which Edith felt flattered.

As Edith had seen the frocks and had some good advice on make-up there was nothing else to do except look at Rose's children in bed. To us that treat is always enchanting, but we quite see that Edith thought it extremely dull and only her politeness sustained her. Then they went back to the rectory, whence the sound of a piano floated on the warm summer air.

"Oh, *good* old Tubby!" said Rose. "He plays too shatteringly well and I always cry buckets when he really gets going. Come on."

They went in quietly by the open French window through the dining-room and so to the large room, a kind of mixture of drawing-room and study, where the Rector was happily playing to himself while the other men smoked and talked; though their talk was in low voices and interrupted as often as Canon Fewling played himself into some of the music that makes one delightfully nostalgic. Echoes of songs that belonged to a vanished age; some to a nation once first of Europe's children, now broken through its own pride and folly; some to the great music-halls, now almost extinct, or revived with a combination of artiness and commonness; some to the barrel organs that the older among us remember, or to the waltzes of a time between the wars when there was never to be war again.

The elder men would obviously have cried if they had not forgotten how to do it; Sylvia and Mary Leslie and Mrs. Gresham were in a kind of nostalgic dream. Canon Fewling saw Rose and Edith come in and smiled to them to sit down, which they did. He drifted into music of the 1914 war, into songs which broke one's heart then and can break it even more now that we are older and do not forget: "Keep the Home Fires Burning," and "The Long Long Trail." Cheap songs, sentimental songs perhaps, but for the heart. Like Mr. Frank Churchill, Canon Fewling took a second, slightly but correctly, to his own playing. When he stopped playing there was silence.

"I think perhaps something to drink," said Canon Fewling and he went to the table where Mrs. Hicks had put the glasses and bottles. The point of emotion was past and the party began to break up, Sylvia making the first move because she saw that Martin was tired. Edith too had nearly gone to sleep while the grown-ups were drinking their stirrup-cups and almost had to be shaken before she could say good-bye to their host, which she did very prettily, for whatever slight weaknesses Lady Graham may have shown in the bringing-up of her youngest, she had always insisted on good manners. A valuable training.

Then Martin drove his ladies home through the warm late dusk and everyone went straight to bed.

Though no one at the moment suspected it, that day had been the beginning of several events extremely interesting to those concerned if not to Barsetshire generally.

Mrs. Dunsford and Mrs. Halliday had both looked forward to their evening together. Kinship is a rum thing and having very few near relations oneself we have always envied those who have a cousin in every county and connections living in really useful places like the Riviera, or New York, or Madeira. Some of them of course may be invalids and expect one to sit with them all the time; or Uncle Tubby who is really a great-uncle may have lapsed into senility since we were last at St. Sebastian with him and not only be a bore (which he always was) but think we are our Aunt Sophy whom we always cordially disliked. But one must take the rough with the smooth.

Luckily in the case of Mrs. Halliday and Mrs. Dunsford there were no such difficulties. Mrs. Halliday being rather silent by nature while Mrs. Dunsford had a pretty constant flow of talk they got on very well. There was the kinship between them—a thing still respected among the older generation. Mrs. Halliday's mother had often talked of her first cousin Mrs. Dunsford's mother. Miss Dunsford's mother had told Miss Dunsford how she had nearly fallen in love with Mrs. Halliday's father years ago, but didn't like to spoil her cousin's prospect and had been rewarded by marrying Mr. Dunsford within the twelve-month. So there was not only kinship, but a kind of sharing of a past romance.

The ladies had a very good dinner and then sat on the terrace for a time till the midges became too troublesome, talking of life and death and servants and how Mrs. Dunsford liked to have two pillows on her bed because it looked so wretched with only one, but never used the second one because her doctor had said she ought to sleep fairly flat if she wanted to rest properly: and how Mrs. Halliday and her husband used to have a large double bed, but after a good many years had faced the fact that Mrs. Halliday liked to read in bed till the small hours and even if she tied a black scarf round her husband's eyes the light still kept him awake; whereas Mr. Halliday usually woke about half-past six summer and winter and liked to draw the curtains or turn on the electric light, according to the season, and then went to sleep again, while his wife remained awake. After which they had—with mutual affection—slept in separate rooms. The only draw-back to this was that the double bed was not in the least "period," being black japanned with four brass knobs, and no one wanted to buy it or if they did they offered twenty-five shillings, saying it would cost them all of that to take it away. So it was still languishing in one of the attic rooms at Hatch House. At least so Mrs. Halliday thought and so she told her cousin Mrs. Dunsford, not knowing that George had sold it for ten shillings to Mr. Geo. Panter, who said it would do a treat for his old mother if they could get it up the stairs and if they couldn't, well it could go in the old stable.

Driven back to the house by the midges, Mrs. Dunsford said she had told the taxi to come for her at ten o'clock and how sorry she was the evening was over because she had enjoyed it so much.

"So did I," said Mrs. Halliday. "It does one good to talk about the old days when we thought we would live happily ever after. There is no one at Hatch End or here that can remember them."

Mrs. Dunsford said she felt exactly the same about North-bridge. Her generation was coming to an end and dear Barbara and her friends were perhaps a little overpowering.

"I have sometimes felt," she said, "that I shouldn't have kept Barbara with me always, but she is such a home bird. I can't imagine her anywhere but in Hovis House."

"I do so know what you mean," said Mrs. Halliday. "George of course loves every corner of Hatch House and the estate and I feel if I am there I can at least see that he is comfortable. It is lonely for me sometimes—but one must think of one's children. And the bedrooms do need repainting and papering and the floors looking at, but it would mean turning out of my room for at least a fortnight. And I don't like to think of George alone. He is such a good boy—he always was."

Mrs. Dunsford, slightly on her mettle about offspring, said Barbara was a wonderful daughter—almost more like a sister.

"I can't say that George feels like a brother," said Mrs. Halliday, "but of course he isn't so much younger than I am as Barbara is than you," and then felt the idea could have been better expressed, but Mrs. Dunsford appeared to understand.

"I have had a thought," said Mrs. Dunsford. "If you want to have the bedrooms done up, why not come and stay with me—just as long as you like. The big spare bedroom looks onto the garden and I had the mattress made over last winter and it has its own bathroom. I haven't used it since old Aunt Sophy died there and I don't suppose I shall. She used to come to us for Christmas and a fortnight in summer. Barbara and I miss her very much."

"Well, that is most kind of you, dear," said Mrs. Halliday. "I should enjoy a visit to Northbridge. The only difficulty is George. The poor boy will be quite alone."

"Oh, I am sure your nice old housekeeper will look after him," said Mrs. Dunsford, with the easy optimism we have about other people's affairs. "Bachelors are always looked after so well. Though I must say my old daily is excellent. She wants her daughter to come because she is a widow and cooks beautifully, but dear Barbara and I are so used to doing things for ourselves that we can't quite make up our minds to have her, though she is longing to come. I must really be getting back now. Barbara quite misses me if I am out. We always do everything together, you know. Really like sisters. But *sometimes* I feel that it would be a good thing if she were not *quite* so dependent on me. At her age she ought to go away on her own sometimes. But I don't like to press her to. She is so sensitive and it might upset her. Now don't forget to settle a date when you will come to me."

Mrs. Halliday said it was most kind and she would really enjoy getting away from Hatch House for a time so long as poor George would not be too lonely, and then the taxi sent in word that it was there. The ladies said good-bye and Mrs. Dunsford drove away. Mrs. Halliday was rather sleepy so she went to bed and did not hear the family come back. Sylvia, who rather disliked the duty visit that her mother still expected if her daughter had been out late, just as she had when she was at home, come softly upstairs, saw that there was no light in her mother's room, and with great thankfulness in her heart went to her own bedroom.

If Mrs. Dunsford thought her daughter was missing her that evening, she was the more deceived. Edith's suggestion that a friend—someone like Mrs. Halliday—should come for a visit to Hovis House had been like the opening of a cage door to Miss Dunsford. Never before in her quiet, dutiful, and not at all unhappy life had it occurred to her that she need not do everything with her mother. She had looked at the cage door and gone on her usual way. Then Edith had, by a word quite carelessly spoken, put a key in her hands. If only someone would come and stay with mother for a bit, she could go to the Riviera—the Dear Riviera as she called it to herself. She had a small income of her own most of which she had religiously put into the Post Office Savings Bank in case—one day—

Something Wonderful Happened and she could use it. Perhaps, if she was very brave, her dream might come true; she might go along the Corniche road in a motor bus, sit at a table outside a nice café with some of the other people from the Pension Ramsden, and even, if she could get someone nice to go with her, see what it was like inside the Casino and perhaps try just a tiny gamble.

With this in her mind she set out for Glycerine Cottage, where Miss Hopgood and Miss Crowder were entertaining in true French fashion. At least they felt that they were, which is the great thing. Neatly dressed in her grey foulard with the pale blue spots and her grey cloche hat of some kind of shiny straw-ish material, her grey imitation sharkskin bag in her hand, Miss Dunsford walked along the village street, down Cow Street to Cow End, where several retired elderly couples and maiden ladies formed a little colony of cottages, all of striking originality and all exactly alike. Passing Tork Cottage, the meaning of whose name no one had ever dared to ask because the owner, Commander Beasley, was so old and so deaf and so cross; the Evergreens which was chiefly remarkable for not having any; the Rooftrees, which we conclude had one at least, she came to Glycerine Cottage. Through the small, leaded, horse-shoe shaped window that gave onto the porch, she could see Miss Crowder laying the supper table while her friend Miss Hopgood arranged some dahlias in a brass jar covered with repoussé work—which was, broadly speaking, a number of dents punched all over it.

Miss Crowder looked up and saw her guest, so Miss Dunsford rang the bell which had a long handle of twisted metal. The handle came off in Miss Dunsford's hand and Miss Crowder opened the door.

"I *am* sorry about the bell handle," she said, taking it from Miss Dunsford. "It needs something doing to it. I will put it on the cassone just to remind me," and she laid it on a kind of small sideboard of shiny yellow and wood with three green china hearts let into its front. "Come in. Miss Hopgood said to me when we heard the bell, 'It must be Miss Dunsford, or else my aunt.'"

"How nice to see you," said Miss Hopgood. "When La Petite told me you were coming, I said 'How nice.'"

"Now, that is not quite exactly what happened," said Miss Crowder. "It was Chère Amie who told *me* you where coming."

Miss Hopgood looked benignly at Miss Crowder and said nothing really mattered so long as Brother Sun shone.

"And here's auntie," she added as a form passed the horseshoe window, and she opened door to a tall, commanding, elderly woman. "Hullo auntie, come in," said Miss Hopgood. "You know Miss Dunsford from Hovis House."

"Of course I do," said Miss Hopgood's aunt. "I was star-watching with Canon Fewling a few nights ago and we mentioned your name. Why I cannot think, but Canon Fewling said he remembered so well the day when we were all on the church tower and your mulberry velours hat blew off."

"Fancy remembering that!" said Miss Dunsford, going quite red in the face with pleasure. "It was in the war when we all did aeroplane-spotting on the church tower. And then when we came down from the tower I had to put my scarf over my hair because of the church and when we went into the churchyard that nice Mr. Holden who was billeted on Mrs. Villars had found my hat in a yew tree and kindly gave it back to me."

Something on the stove boiled over with a sizzling noise.

"Oh dear, it's Le Potage," said Miss Crowder, moving the saucepan. "Sometimes we call it La Soupe and sometimes Le Potage—that is when it behaves badly like this."

Miss Dunsford said like a husband and wife and then wondered if she knew what she meant. Miss Hopgood said it was wonderful how many things you could say in French and it sounded all right, but if you said them in English it would be—well, *rather*.

"It's just ourselves," she said to Miss Dunsford. "We did think of asking Mr. and Mrs. Villars, but they have one of their sons staying with them, so I asked Mr. and Mrs. Downing." By which news everyone was pleased, for during the war Mrs. Downing (then Mrs. Turner, a widow) had been one of Northbridge's best workers, kept open house for all the billeted officers and with the aid of her nieces dispensed endless hospitality. Later she had married Mr. Downing, the well-known Provençal scholar and though nothing could have seemed more incongruous they were extremely devoted and happy and much liked in Northbridge when they were there; which was not so often now, for Mr. Downing's fame had grown considerably and learned societies all over Europe and America wanted him to come and lecture to them, which he much enjoyed.

Two figures passed the horse-shoe window. Miss Hopgood went to the door and admitted the last guests. Mr. Downing was exactly like what a scholar should be, with a slight stoop and distinguished grey hair, and his wife was as pretty as ever though her hair wreathed itself into silver tendrils now; but this appeared to be an added attraction and all over the scholastic world here, in America, and elsewhere, she had elderly—and honourable—admirers.

The soup began to boil over again but was rescued in the nick of time by Miss Crowder and everyone sat down; just wherever they liked said Miss Hopgood, though it was a little difficult to get where one wanted to be, owing to the table which almost entirely filled the small dining-alcove as we believe these things are called. As the space was limited it did not much matter who sat next to whom but those with long legs suffered most.

The soup, except for being slightly burnt, was excellent but to Miss Dunsford any small mischance was just the French atmosphere.

Miss Hopgood's aunt said she had been told that if soup was slightly burnt, it helped to put a piece of toast into it, but as everyone had either finished their soup or made a show of eating it and tried to cover up what was left with the spoon, the advice was too late. Miss Crowder then took from the oven a large casserole full of Irish stew and set it on the table.

"Just Pottofur," she said. "One of the dear French dishes. We had it three or four times a week at the dear Pension Ramsden, only with just a touch more garlic perhaps."

Mrs. Downing said the worst of garlic was there was never the right amount. On being pressed for an explanation, she said that even half of one of those cloves of the garlic was too much, because it gave some people indigestion, but if you used less to rub the salad bowl you didn't seem to get the taste, which was all you needed.

"I know *exactly* what you mean, Mrs. Downing," said Miss Hopgood. "A kind of repeat you get."

"Ein leiser Wiederhall," said Mr. Downing aloud to himself, but as no one knew the Brahms song he was able to pretend he hadn't said anything.

"And now, Mr. Downing," said Miss Hopgood's aunt, "do tell us about your Dictionary. Have you got to Z yet? You know," she added to Miss Dunsford, "Mr. Downing is writing a dictionary about Provençal poems."

"I'm afraid I don't know any," said Miss Dunsford.

"Nobody does. They can't read them," said Miss Hopgood's aunt.

"Then Mr. Downing's book will make us all want to read them," said Miss Dunsford, who was enjoying the literary and Bohemian atmosphere immensely, though in a humble spirit.

Mr. Downing said his book was, alas, not of translations, but, as it were, a conspectus of the origins, the provenance, of the literature of the land of the Langue d'oc, and then wished he hadn't used so many of's.

Miss Hopgood's aunt, a strong-minded woman, said she had never thought much of the French. A country, she added, that said Oil for Yes in one part and Oc in another was, in her mind, a poor effort.

Miss Hopgood, feeling that her aunt was perhaps presuming

too much on what was, after all, her and La Petite's province, said that everyone said Oui now.

And far too often, said Miss Hopgood's aunt. If the French had said Non in 1914, perhaps we shouldn't have had all this trouble now.

Mrs. Downing said one sometimes wished one was back in 1914 when everything was so easy, and though the remark did not mean anything in particular everyone felt a nostalgia for what now seems to us elders the simplicity of a war which was mostly against one enemy and confined to the unhappy countries over which it ranged. Not, as now, preparing to become what is hideously called Global.

The dish which in Glycerine Cottage was called the Pottofur is known in other circles variously as the main course, Spécialité de la Maison, stew, or the rest of that bit of mutton we had yesterday hotted up. But we must say that the hotting up had been well and savourously done. Everyone ate heartily and even greedily.

"We sometimes call it Pemberton Ragoût," said Miss Crowder to Mr. Downing, with a knowing look which made him feel guilty, for what it was supposed to convey he could not imagine. "Out of that cookery book that Miss Pemberton wrote," after which explanatory words he breathed again.

"It is still selling," said Mr. Downing. "And what touched me very much was that the royalties on it were left to me."

Everyone longed to know what the royalties on a successful cookery book were, but did not like to ask.

"Nearly twelve pounds a year I have had so far," said Mr. Downing. "I did not quite know what to do with it but Poppy helped me," and he looked at his wife with much affection.

"What *did* you do?" said Miss Dunsford, who had been so happy in being at an intellectual party that she had hardly said a word during dinner.

"Of course we have spent it all on the Dictionary," said Mr. Downing. "At least on books that I needed in connection with it. At the American end the Dictionary is being financed by Mr. Walden Concord Porter."

Miss Dunsford asked who he was.

"I have never met him," said Mr. Downing, "but I understand that he employs seven thousand workmen on whatever it is he does. When I and Poppy were last in America," and he looked affectionately at his wife, whose pretty silvery hair seemed to wreathe itself into yet wilder curls under his look, "he was on a trip to somewhere but had left orders that if we came to Portersville we were to use his house and his cars and his secretaries."

"And did you?" said Miss Dunsford, to whom this story was like a New Arabian Night.

"It was *lovely*," said Mrs. Downing. "It was just like the films and when Harold lectured lots of women came every time. And they were so kind to me too," she added. "And the men gave me such lovely flowers."

"I wish I could go to America," said Miss Hopgood. "Don't you?" she added, turning to Miss Dunsford.

By this time, what with the bottle of red wine and the intellectual conversation, Miss Dunsford was feeling extremely brave.

"I don't think I do," she said. "What I would really like to do would be to go to the Riviera. By myself."

So surprised were the company by this outburst from Miss Dunsford, who had always been looked upon as her Mother's Daughter and little else, that no one spoke. But Miss Dunsford was not in a mood to notice this. Her talk with Edith Graham, the excitement of so exotic a dinner-party and a glass of red wine, had for the time freed her from the present and she was wallowing happily in a possible future.

"I've looked it all up," she said, "and when I was in Barchester I went to the Cathedral Travel Agency."

"We always get our tickets there," said Miss Hopgood. "Whether it's a day return to London, or going to our dear

Riviera, or auntie's ticket when she went to Portersville for the opening of the new buildings in the Matthew Porter Observatory in Texas where Uncle used to work, it's just the same. You just tell them what you want and they do the rest. And we can pay by cheque," she added, though why this was considered an inducement we do not know and we think the Travel Agency would have been surprised if their customers had all paid in coin—or paper—of the realm.

"And where will you stay?" said Miss Crowder.

"Well, I thought if you wouldn't mind telling me about the Pension Ramsden," said Miss Dunsford, hardly able to believe in her own courage, "perhaps I could go there. It always sounds so nice when you talk about it."

Nothing could have been more to the taste of the ladies of Glycerine Cottage. The party were now having cheese (rather hard Gruyère, a Camembert on the verge of deliquescence and a bit of plain Cheddar for those who didn't care for French kickshaws), so Miss Crowder said she would hurry and hot up the coffee and then they could have a nice talk about it all. As the coffee had been gently boiling over at intervals on the stove and being withdrawn by one or other of the hostesses, it did not take long to establish everyone with an overbrewed scalding drink. To celebrate the occasion Miss Crowder brought in a half bottle of Cointreau which she had hoarded. As the establishment did not run to liqueur glasses Miss Hopgood produced three custard glasses, a small glass mustard pot and two china egg cups with blue dragons on them, relics of an old breakfast set, and everyone had some.

"Now, do tell us about the Riviera," said Mrs. Downing. "I've never been there."

"Nor have I," said Miss Dunsford. "That's why I want to go. I've got enough money and I want to go abroad and see things. Mother doesn't like Abroad much, so I thought, Well why shouldn't I go by myself. Lots of people do. And if I could go to your Pension, Miss Hopgood, it would be *wonderful*."

Nothing of course is more pleasant than to recommend a place you have liked to other people.

"You tell Miss Dunsford, chère amie," said Miss Crowder. "It was you that found the Pension Ramsden."

Nothing loth, Miss Hopgood told the company of her first visit to the Riviera after the 1914 war with a party from the Barchester Polytechnic. She had, she said, fallen in love with the Riviera and when, a few years later, she had taken Miss Crowder there, La Petite had also fallen in love with it, since when they had been every year except of course during the last war. Luckily, she said, the war had not greatly affected the business, as lots of Germans billeted there, and now it was flourishing again under Madame Ramsden and her daughter Mrs. Petitot, who had married a Frenchman during the German occupation; one of those *typical* French husbands she said, a good deal older than his wife, but quite devoted to her as they had no children and if he did stray sometimes, well, in a Frenchman of course it was quite different and really meant nothing. The beds, she said, were excellent and if one was lucky enough to get one of those two bedrooms up in a kind of little sham tower, one could almost see the sea. But the other bedrooms were very nice too and there was running water in several of them. Of course one didn't really expect bathrooms Abroad, but there was a very nice one and you could get a lovely hot bath by asking for it two or three days ahead and only a slight extra charge, and most of the bedrooms had—and she slightly lowered her voice to protect Mr. Downing—a biddy, so useful, she added, when once you had got used to it. But as he was not listening very attentively no harm was done. Miss Dunsford thought she knew what Miss Hopgood must mean and most dashingly determined to take it in her stride.

"I wonder," she said, "if you could write to Madame Ramsden for me, Miss Hopgood, and ask if she could book me a room. She would pay more attention if it was from you. One with a bidet," she added courageously.

Delighted by the prospect of helping Miss Dunsford, Miss Hopgood said she would write at once and would Miss Dunsford like to take whole pension or demi-pension. It came cheaper, she said, to take demi-pension if you were going to do excursions every day, but if not she would recommend complete pension, as the mid-day meal was the better and larger. On the other hand if you took demi-pension you could always get croissants and coffee or chocolate out, as all the excursions stopped at nice places on every trip and often included the meals in their charges. Miss Dunsford said as it would all be a little strange at first, she thought perhaps full pension for a fortnight or so and then she could see what she felt like, which seemed very sensible.

"Oh," said Miss Dunsford.

Everyone looked in her direction.

"Do I have to have a passport?" she asked. "I thought there was something about not needing them for France now."

Miss Crowder, immensely enjoying her rôle of Guide, said she thought you could go to Boulogne for the day without a passport, or perhaps you couldn't now, but a passport was quite easy to get and the Cathedral Travel Agency would do everything for her. All she would need was two photographs of herself, and Jollyfotoes near the archway into the Close would supply you with the exact size the passport people wanted within a remarkably short time and very reasonably.

And what about clothes, Miss Dunsford asked.

Just the same as at home, said Miss Crowder. Wear one suit and pack another and if possible take an extra skirt as sitting in the motor buses or coaches did make the seat sag so. And a nice light woollen frock and a nice woollen cardigan and perhaps one black afternoon dress that one could wear at the Casino.

"Oh, do you think I could go there?" said Miss Dunsford. "Alone?"

Miss Hopgood said one or two of the visitors at the Pension

Ramsden were always gong and she was sure Miss Dunsford could join them.

"I have thought of something!" said Mrs. Downing. "That nice Mr. Greaves who was billeted on Mrs. Villars and used to come to my house a lot—that was in the war when my nieces were staying with me—has an aunt there, at the Villa Thermogène. I'm sure I could get him to give you an introduction to her. He married one of my nieces. Lady de Courcy, that's his aunt."

For a moment Miss Dunsford, good middle-class, safe in her own position, not wishing to climb or in any way to push herself, felt that an introduction to Lady de Courcy might be even more of an embarrassment than an honour. But it would hardly be polite to return Mrs. Downing's kindness by a rebuff, so she thanked her and said if Mrs. Downing would be so kind as to get her the introduction from her nephew by marriage she would be grateful.

"Oh dear, it's nearly ten," said Miss Dunsford. "I ought to go. Mother likes to find me in, and I shall tell her what a nice evening I have had. But please don't say anything about our talk till you have heard from your friend at the Pension Ramsden. It *has* been a lovely party," but her hostesses pressed her to stay, and with a delicious feeling of playing truant she gave way.

"What a nice woman—one ought to say girl perhaps—Miss Dunsford is," said Mr. Downing to Miss Crowder, while he helped her to carry some of the supper dishes into the little kitchen. "One does get that type in English small town life. Good background, good manners, good clothes."

"We like her and her mother very much," said Miss Crowder. "Mr. Dunsford died a long time ago and Barbara has never married. She and her mother are just like sisters," which is never a really helpful recommendation, for while some sisters share everything and are the greatest friends, even after marrying, others will practically refuse to speak to or meet a sister who would enjoy the relationship, while yet again, some thoroughly enjoy a good old family row or dust-up, whether the other party or parties concerned like it or not.

It was agreed by the hostesses that no one should mention Miss Dunsford's plans and we may say that the pledge was honourably observed by all present.

By this time the two hostesses, appearing and re-appearing rather like the man and woman in the weatherhouse of our nostalgic childhood memories, had cleared away, and pressed everyone to come nearer the fire, which included a great scraping of chairs along the ground.

"We shan't need *all* the chairs, chère amie," said Miss Crowder. "Two can easily sit in Inglenook."

Such guests as knew the cottage at once took their own chairs a little nearer the fire. Miss Dunsford, a newcomer to this delightful circle, did not know whether she ought to help.

"Now you shall be the Guest of Honour, Miss Dunsford, and sit in Inglenook," said Miss Crowder, introducing her guest to a rather narrow brick ledge, part of the Olde Worlde Fireplace, with a plastic-covered flat cushion on it. Miss Dunsford sat down gratefully, though rather wishing that the seat were broader and the cushion less slippery. By bracing herself against the floor with her feet she was just able to stay on the ledge, in spite of its tilting gently forwards, and prepared to go on enjoying herself. And enjoy herself she did, for everyone talked at once, or argued in a friendly way, and when Miss Hopgood or Miss Crowder used a French word (as they frequently did), Miss Dunsford felt she was already in the atmosphere of the Riviera.

A dark shadow passed the horse-shoe window.

"There's Mr. Highmore," said Mrs. Downing, in a pleased voice.

The hostess rose as one woman, but Miss Hopgood got to the door first.

"Oh, I say, how do you do, I didn't know there was a party or I wouldn't have barged in," said Mr. Highmore.

"Only a few friends," said Miss Hopgood. "Come in."

So the curate came in and everyone was pleased to see him, most of all perhaps Mr. Downing who was sometimes a little bored by being the only man at a party, much as he liked the ladies.

"Oh dear, there's only that chair with the leg I mended," said Miss Crowder. "I'll get one out of my bedroom. It will be safer."

"Let me do it," said Mr. Highmore.

"It is so kind of you, but I *couldn't*," said Miss Crowder, ready to die for her maiden fortress.

"I'll take you up and show you the chair," said Miss Hopgood to Mr. Highmore. Miss Crowder said nothing in a very noticeable way.

It is well known that many of the most ferocious and prolonged wars in history have had a religious basis. The whole company waited in uncomfortable though agreeable expectation of a slight row, or scene, while the battle hung suspended.

While this conversation was going on Mr. Downing, who was through long practice resigned to being as a rule the only man at Northbridge parties, had gone up the narrow stair, which had two sharp corners and was kept in a state of high polish. Noises off were heard as of a struggle.

"I am so sorry, Miss Hopgood," said Mr. Downing's gentle voice, "but two of the chair legs got through the banisters and I can't get them out and I can't get past the chair."

Mrs. Downing said proudly that her husband had no house sense at all.

"Hang on a moment, Downing, and I'll give a hand," said Mr. Highmore, which courageous words inflamed all unmarried hearts except Miss Dunsford's, which was set on her Princesse Lointaine—FRANCE.

In a moment Mr. Highmore had disentangled Mr. Downing from the chair and the chair from the banisters and got them both downstairs. Miss Crowder said Should she hot up the rest of the coffee. Mr. Highmore said Thank you but he had had an awfully good meal at the pub, which dashing words further inflamed his hostesses' hearts. But men always prefer to talk with men and we regret to say that Mr. Downing and Mr. Highmore fell, conversationally speaking, into one another's arms and could not be unclasped. The wall-clock, which was a blue-and-white plate with a clock face painted on it, a pendulum, and two chains with sham gilded fir-cones at their ends to wind it up with, struck eleven.

"Oh! I must go at *once*," said Miss Dunsford, feeling like Cinderella.

"It's all right, it's only ten really," said Miss Hopgood. "We always mean to let it run down and then alter the hands, but we always forget. But when Summer Time ends it will be right again. After all, the clock is Keeping God's Time," which remark paralyzed most of her hearers. Mr. Highmore wondered if it were his duty as a servant of the Church to interfere, but came to the conclusion that it wasn't. Partly because he had a sense of humour, partly because he rather wanted to get home and get on with *Blood Down Below!* the new thriller by Lisa Bedale, known by nearly everyone to be an anagram of Isabel Dale, the rich heiress, now Lady Silverbridge, wife of the Duke of Omnium's heir.

But Miss Dunsford was obviously rather anxious, so her hostesses said she must come again another day and bring her mother.

"I've got to go too," said Mr. Highmore. "I promised Mr. Villars that I would go through the proofs of the Parish Magazine this evening. Last month the printer was away and his nephew who works for him is mentally deficient—though curiously enough not where type-setting is concerned—and he printed the Mothers' Union as Onion all the way through. Of course everyone knew what it meant, but we don't want other parishes to be able to look down on us. May I see you as far as Hovis House, Miss Dunsford?"

Miss Dunsford's pleasant face assumed a slightly imbecile mottled look, which was her nearest approach to a blush, as she thanked Mr. Highmore and said that would be very nice if it wasn't really out of his way. So having bidden farewell to Glycerine Cottage they walked back to the High Street which was looking as lovely as possible with the late evening light on its golden-brown stone and reflected from each pane of its handsome windows.

When they got to Hovis House Mr. Highmore prepared to take his leave. Miss Dunsford said would he just stay for a moment so that she could see if Mother was in, as if the house was empty she didn't like to go into it quite alone. So they both went in and Miss Dunsford called her mother, but there was no answer.

"She isn't here, so she can't have come back yet," said Miss Dunsford. "Would you like to see the garden?"

In some cases this might have been a Device to Snare a Man but Mr. Highmore, who was no fool, quite understood that it was politeness to a friend who had escorted one back from a party and they walked down the long border which was looking very lovely, full to the brim with flowers that were not yet over-ripe, every shade and shape of the blue and pink and white. The tall tobacco-plants were spreading their scent on the air and the large-leafed magnolia against the high brick wall was showing its creamy, voluptuous flowers among dark shining leaves. In fact a perfect setting, a perfect evening for Romance, except that there wasn't any. Nor, we think, would Miss Dunsford have liked Romance except in books or the rare plays she had seen.

"Wasn't it a lovely evening," said Miss Dunsford, who knew that one ought to keep the conversation going. "I do so like Glycerine Cottage and the lovely French food."

Mr. Highmore said he did too.

"I enjoyed it more than anything since the Coronation," said Miss Dunsford. "Do you remember the Pageant? Mother and I did so enjoy having all the dresses made at Hovis House. The drawing-room isn't a bit the same without those trestle tables and all the dresses being made and your beautiful sham tonsure,

Mr. Highmore. It was really the highlight of our Coronation celebration. Have you got it still?"

Mr. Highmore said he had lent it to his mother, who was very keen on the Wembley Amateur Dramatic Society, to copy, but she had promised to send it back.

"Oh, Mr. Highmore, there's something I want to ask you," said Miss Dunsford.

Mr. Highmore, hoping to goodness that it wasn't anything to do with the Church, about whose female supporters he had almost Pauline feelings, having had (as he said to Mr. Villars in confidence) a fair sickener of them, said he would be honoured by her confidence and do his best to help her.

"It's The Riviera," said Miss Dunsford. "Do you know it?"

Mr. Highmore said it rather depended. Was it the Italian or the French Riviera. Miss Dunsford said it was Mentone only it was called Menton too, so she didn't know.

"Oh, that's all right," said Mr. Highmore. "A great-uncle of mine lived out there. He was a parson with five daughters and he said it was cheaper than England. I dare say it was then. His daughters all married Italian or French and I've a whole lot of half-caste cousins out there."

"Do you mean—I mean were their parents not properly—I mean—" said Miss Dunsford, excited by so near an approach to Life, but unable as yet to cope with its vocabulary—"weren't the marriages legal?"

"Oh, they were *married* all right," said Mr. Highmore. "My uncle saw to that. He wouldn't let them marry unless the English consul and the C. of E. chaplain did it. But there was some sort of arrangement about the children of course with the R.C. padre. Girls C. of E. and boys R.C., or the other way round. Anyway they're an awfully nice lot and I love going there. It makes me feel a bit sentimental though."

Miss Dunsford asked why.

"Oh well, seeing all my cousins and cousins-in-law with millions of kids," said Mr. Highmore. "I'm an only child. I mean

I was always awfully happy, but it would have been fun to have some brothers and sisters."

"I'm an only child too," said Miss Dunsford. "At least," she added, "I'm not a child. Mother and I are very happy and do everything together. Only I *do* want to see the Riviera. I do hope mother won't mind."

Mr. Highmore felt sorry for Miss Dunsford, but his compassion was mitigated by two reflections: one, that she was obviously going to do what she wanted to do, the second that she must have enough money to do it with or she wouldn't be doing it. So he decided not to feel sorry for her. But this was not to exclude his being pleasantly sympathetic, though in a bracing, brotherly kind of way, and he began the bracing by saying good-night and taking his leave.

He had only been gone for a few minutes when the taxi brought Mrs. Dunsford back from Rushwater. Her daughter came out to meet her and took the flowers and fruit she had brought with her into the house.

"Did you have a nice time, mother?" she said.

Mrs. Dunsford said very nice indeed. She and Mrs. Halliday had had a long talk about old times and made some plans. Miss Dunsford asked what they were, but Mrs. Halliday evaded the question and said would Barbara make a nice cup of Horlicks for her, or she knew she would not sleep. Miss Dunsford also was not at all sleepy, so she made two nice cups of Horlicks and took them up to the drawing-room.

"Thank you, Barbara dear," said Mrs. Dunsford. "It's so nice to be home. I have been longing to have a talk with you about something rather interesting."

Miss Dunsford could have answered that she was in exactly the same position, but she was secretly rather nervous as to how her mother might take it—though determined that even a threat from her mother to commit suicide should not alter her fixed purpose. So she said what was it and she was sure it was something nice.

"Well, I hope you will feel it so, dear," she said. "I had a long chat with Mrs. Halliday and of course we talked about her children and that she is a widow. Of course I am a widow too, but it is all so long ago and you have made up to me so wonderfully, Barbara, for what I have missed."

Miss Dunsford said, with the sheepishness that any emotion between near relations produces, that she was so happy at home with her mother.

"Well, Barbara, you and I have one another, which is wonderful," said Mrs. Dunsford. "Poor Mrs. Halliday is so much alone."

Miss Dunsford said, quite sincerely, that after all Mrs. Halliday was at Rushwater with her daughter Sylvia and all Sylvia's babies and Emmy Grantly and her husband.

"That is just it, Barbara," said Mrs. Dunsford. "It is too much for her. I know myself when your dear father died how I longed to get away and be quiet—just to have you with me and feel peaceful. You were too young to mind much."

"Oh mother, I *did* mind," said Miss Dunsford.

"But you were very young and troubles soon pass," said Mrs. Dunsford, rather unfairly we consider. "I felt poor Mrs. Halliday really needed to get right away from her relations and have a complete change."

"Do you mean go Abroad, mother?" said Miss Dunsford, scenting a fellow-Rivierian.

"Oh dear, no. Not abroad. Just a change of scene and to be with friends who don't remind her of her loss. So I have asked her to come and stay at Hovis House for as long as she likes."

Miss Dunsford had never been so much surprised in her life. Although she and her mother kept a very open house for Northbridge friends and had given up the big drawing-room all through the war for Red Cross Stores and sewing parties and had lent it again in the Coronation year for the committee that with old curtains or scarves and bits of paper and anything handy from a saucepan to a nutmeg-grater had manufactured dresses, including armour, for most of the historical scenes for the Northbridge Pageant in the Town Hall, never had they, since her old aunt Sophy died, had anyone to stay. When Miss Dunsford was a schoolgirl she had been invited to other girls' houses, but never had she been encouraged to ask them to stay at Hovis House. For tea or for tennis they were welcome; as house-guests, no. Hovis House, where Mr. and Mrs. Dunsford and their daughter had lived, where after his death Mrs. and Miss Dunsford had lived, would open its front door, its dining-room door, its drawing-room door and its garden door, but never its bedroom doors.

"I shall put her in the big room at the back that gets all the afternoon sun," said Mrs. Dunsford, "and we will do our best to make her happy."

Miss Dunsford felt as if a kaleidoscope were twirling before her eyes, but she refused to be beaten.

"It sounds lovely, mother," she said.

"There is my own Barbara," said her mother. "I told Mrs. Halliday how pleased you would be."

"I am awfully pleased, mother," said Miss Dunsford. "It all fits in beautifully because now you'll have someone to talk to when I'm away."

"What *do* you mean, Barbara?" said her mother.

"I always wanted to go to the Riviera," said Miss Dunsford, "and Miss Hopgood and Miss Crowder have told me all about the Pension Ramsden at Mentone where they go and they are booking a room for me."

Mrs. Dunsford was momentarily stunned.

"I've got a lot saved up in the Post Office Savings Bank," said Miss Dunsford. "It will be wonderful. I *am* so glad you've got Mrs. Halliday, mother."

There was a short silence. Miss Dunsford had said what she had to say. Mrs. Dunsford, very nicely forcing herself to look at the best side of things and beginning to see some advantages to herself which would on the whole offset the disadvantages, said everything came at once, but of course if Barbara really wanted to go, perhaps it would be the best thing. She had those horrid colds so often and perhaps a visit to the Riviera would clear them up and she must *please* find out if there was a good English chemist at Mentone and an English chaplain.

Having gone so far, Miss Dunsford felt she might as well go further and said Miss Hopgood had told her that the English clergyman was very nice and there was a Cercle Anglais where one could see *The Times* and the *Church Quarterly* and ask one's friends to tea.

"Perhaps," said Miss Dunsford, in an almost Sibyllic frenzy, "you and Mrs. Halliday could come out and visit me."

This invitation, almost a command, made Mrs. Dunsford think, If Barbara was going to be so uppish, perhaps it would be as well for her to go abroad for a bit. Then she and Mrs. Halliday could have nice long talks and their own friends of their own age to tea. And, for she was an affectionate mother who, though rather overbearing, had always done her best for her daughter's welfare, it would be nice for Barbara to get away by herself for a bit and not depend on her mother all the time.

"Well, Barbara dear," she said, "this *has* been a surprise and I am just a little worried about your going so far, but if Miss Hopgood recommends the hotel I am sure it is nice. Now, what about money, dear? I had better see the bank manager about how much you are allowed to take abroad. How long do you want to stay?"

Suppressing from real affection to her mother, a desire to say For Ever, Miss Dunsford said she would rather like to spend one winter abroad and see if it would get rid of that horrid cough she always got in the winter.

"Your great-aunt Alice—your father's aunt, not mine," said Mrs. Dunsford accusingly, "was supposed to be dying of slow consumption when she was a girl and she was sent to the Riviera for six months and came back perfectly well. She died the following year, which was very sad, but it was scarlet fever, not her lungs."

This interesting story would not seem to us to prove anything, but it seemed to cheer Mrs. Dunsford up a good deal and Miss Dunsford felt that if she got to the Riviera she would certainly not come back and have scarlet fever. She would stay there for ever.

Mother and daughter kissed affectionately and went to bed.

CHAPTER 7

We do not like quiet good people to be made unhappy and we are sure our reader does not like it either, so we will say at once that Miss Dunsford's plans met with no contre-temps. By doing things methodically and patiently and paying no attention to the one or two occasions when her mother had been rather ostentatiously self-pitying, nor to the moments when she wondered if she would be homesick, she got her passport, her tickets (first on the boat, second on the train) and a brochure from the Grande Compagnie Internationale des Pensions de Menton containing a photograph of the Pension Ramsden; a fine example of Art triumphing over Nature, with the camera so managed that the Pension looked at least a hundred yards long and two hundred feet high. This she showed to her mentors, Miss Hopgood and Miss Crowder, who said it was exactly like and you could always find the hotel so easily, because it was between Cook's and the Église Protestante.

"There is just one thing," said Miss Dunsford, who was having tea at Glycerine Cottage. "Is there a *really* nice church?"

As Mr. Highmore was also having tea, the ladies of Glycerine Cottage with a beautiful gesture of abnegation said she must ask him, as his uncle who was in Holy Orders used to live there.

"Oh, the English Church is all right," said Mr. Highmore. "A bit dull, but you can't have everything and the parson is a gentleman. They've always had a gentleman there, ever since my great-uncle. Would you care for an introduction to this man's wife? She's awfully nice and they have some quite decent children and he doesn't care two hoots whether you go to him or the Holy Romers so long as you go."

Miss Crowder said she did not go to the English church at Menton. Chère amie, she said, went occasionally, but she herself liked to do as the natives did, though of course she drew the line at going to church without a hat on. Miss Dunsford was properly shocked by such an idea and said she *never* went into a church without a hat or some covering, even when once she had to borrow the plastic cover off the saddle of a friendly motorcyclist because she hadn't even a scarf with her. But in France, she understood—as the Reverend Laurence Sterne had understood nearly two hundred years earlier—they ordered this matter better. Mr. Highmore, feeling that he would soon be demented or have a fit of the giggles, said every country had its own customs and in France he had found that while a bare head was considered quite religious, sleeveless dresses were looked on as going a little too far. Miss Dunsford said she didn't like those sleeveless dresses at all.

Having read so far, our reader may feel quite confident that Miss Dunsford's future will be very happy and full of excitements springing entirely from her own want of worldly knowledge and her desire to acquire it.

Mrs. Halliday felt better after her old friend Mrs. Dunsford's visit, with the refreshment and re-strengthening that we derive, without knowing it, from being among people of our own generation. Not but what we love our young and such few of our elders as remain, but most people's natural air is among their contemporaries. Her daughter Sylvia noticed the difference and thought she must ask Mrs. Dunsford over again before long as a tonic. Mrs. Halliday, all her married life a woman of character, was now rapidly becoming her old self and, as her son-in-law Martin Leslie irreverently said, not always thinking of the old'un. And if—in the words of a bard of lost Ireland—spirits can steal from the regions of air, to revisit past scenes of delight, we think Mr. Halliday's spirit would have been truly pleased to find that his wife had not permanently settled into a Mrs. Gummidge.

With real affection and considerable tact, she told Sylvia and Martin that she knew she must leave them sometime adding—very truly—that their kindness had made all the difference to her and she felt quite equal to re-starting her normal life.

It is no unkindness to Martin and Sylvia to say that they were on the whole relieved, for one or the other had felt a pious obligation to spend parts of the day with Mrs. Halliday; and for a working farmer and for his wife who has to manage a large house and a nursery, besides being of considerable help about the estate and in the county, this was not easy. Whether Mrs. Halliday really wished for company we do not know; if it came she accepted and enjoyed it. If it didn't she had many thoughts and remembrances and had occupied herself—first asking her daughter's permission—in going through the linen-cupboard, putting aside such sheets and pillow slips as had begun to wear thin, darning and patching them exquisitely.

George Halliday—feeling an impostor, a hypocrite, and a liar—of course said he was very glad his mother felt like coming home and he would see that everything was in order for her. Visits had been exchanged between mother and son while Mrs. Halliday was at Rushwater, and George had kept her informed of how old Mrs. Fothergill the cook was and how nicely Hubback their faithful old maid was looking after him and how the carpet in her bedroom had been sent to the cleaners and come back looking quite new—and many other small things which rather smote Mrs. Halliday's heart, for any nice woman will feel a kind of loving yet slightly critical compassion for a man who undertakes her side of housekeeping.

George Halliday, rather to his own inconvenience, had arranged to be at home on the appointed afternoon when he had wished to be at a sale of pigs over Gatherum way. The Rushwater small car brought his mother over and went round to the back yard to seek tea and entertainment in the kitchen. George embraced his mother very heartily and they went into the house.

Mrs. Halliday behaved very well and George felt sincerely grateful to his mother for not Having Emotions, or at any rate for keeping them under control. There were many things to talk about. George wanted to know about his sister Sylvia and the children (of whom his mother gave excellent news) and how Martin's new under-cowman was settling in (which Mrs. Halliday didn't know anything about), and Mrs. Halliday had to ask after various village friends. Then he took her upstairs to see some repainting he had done and a room that had been repapered because a pipe had leaked and other pleasant domestic odds and ends. Mrs. Halliday's bedroom was in apple-pie order with everything just as she had left it only—if possible—cleaner.

"It *does* all look nice," she said, looking out of the window across the river valley.

George, his heart feeling more and more heavy and guilty simultaneously, said he and Hubback had done their best.

"And I had a looking glass put inside your dress-cupboard, mother," he said, opening one of the large doors. "How did you manage without a long glass?"

"I don't know," said Mrs. Halliday. "I always did. After all that large looking glass on the dressing table tips backwards and forwards. And I could see myself full length *very* well in that huge portrait of your grandmother that we had to hang on the stairs because it was too big for the drawing-room. How *dear* of you, George."

"Well, I thought you'd like it," said George, feeling Black Guilt in his heart that he was not more delighted by his mother's return. "Let's go down and have tea."

So down they went and Hubback brought in tea and said Mr. George was eating nicely and she hoped Madam was pleased with his looks; and Madam was, and said she would like to come and talk to Hubback and Mrs. Fothergill later about her plans and then Mrs. Halliday sat in the chair where her husband used to sit and poured out the tea and everything was real and unreal at the same time.

George said he did hope his mother wouldn't be lonely as he mostly had to be out all day on farm and county business and often had to work after dinner till eleven or twelve, coping with the many forms and enquiries by which agriculture is State-encouraged; not to speak of working outdoors till well into the evening during the summer and early autumn months. He had thought about this a good deal and come to the conclusion that the farm was a real and valid excuse, as his mother knew, and that county business—which his mother strongly approved—might by a little management include dining with one of his many friends in Barchester or in the neighbourhood.

Mrs. Halliday said they must have a talk about it. She had of course, she said, loved being with Sylvia.

George waited, thinking not unnaturally that the end of her sentence would be that she was also very glad to be coming back. But it wasn't.

"I am so glad you're back," he said, more or less truthfully. "Hubback keeps everything so tidy and we had everything ready for you at a moment's notice. She has cleaned your room until it is black in the face."

"I have been thinking about plans," said Mrs. Halliday. "It has been so restful to be with darling Sylvia and she didn't want me to hurry."

"Nor did I, mother," said George. "I mean—I don't mean—I don't want you *not* to hurry to come back—but just when it suited you—I mean—"

"I have been thinking about it too," said Mrs. Halliday, "and I have made a sort of plan for the future."

"Good!" said George, doing violence to his worse nature which was rather cross. "Let's hear it."

"Do you remember an old school friend of mine—Mrs. Dunsford at Northbridge?" said Mrs. Halliday.

"Oh, *that* one," said George. "She must have been a prefect when you were in the kindergarten."

Mrs. Halliday, not displeased by this reference to her youthful looks, said that of course she had been in the Upper Fourth when Mrs. Dunsford was in the Lower Fifth, but now she felt that they were exactly the same age. To which George's unchivalrous reply was that her feelings must be barking up the wrong tree and she looked years younger than Mrs. Dunsford, which gave Mrs. Halliday a good deal of pleasure—as indeed George had intended it to do.

"We had some very nice talks about old times and other things," said Mrs. Halliday, "and she suggested that I should visit her."

This George heartily approved, partly because he truly wished his mother to enjoy herself and partly from a strong desire to postpone the date of her permanent homecoming.

"I had a talk with her on the telephone this morning," said Mrs. Halliday. "Her daughter who lives with her—such a nice girl—"

George said nice was just the word, but she wasn't all that much girl.

"We all think of our children as younger than they are," said Mrs. Halliday. "When I think—"

"No, mother," said George, quite kindly but with authority. "We are *not* talking about how sweet I looked in my pram with my lovely curls. What was your talk about?"

"As I was just going to tell you," said Mrs. Halliday with a Voice of Patience which made George waver between laughing and going out of the room and slamming the door, "Barbara is going to spend the autumn on the Riviera and Mrs. Dunsford has asked me to come to her for a long visit. We have a good deal in common and Northbridge is a nice place."

George's feelings were naturally mixed. A part of him saw

freedom ahead; freedom from having to talk when one didn't feel like talking or when one was thinking about the cart-horse that had gone lame; freedom from being expected to give a detailed account of what he had been doing in the day; freedom from feeling that if he asked his own friends to the house it would mean a fuss about meals. Another part of him said that his mother was his mother, which was incontrovertible and—as an afterthought—what would people think. Not that he would care what they thought, but it would annoy his mother if any criticism on his conduct reached her ears.

"Well, I'll miss you, mother," he said, hoping that the Recording Angel had not taken a note of this to be brought up in evidence. "But if it's really going to be a nice change for you, I expect it's all right. You'll see a lot of people in Northbridge and it might be rather fun for a bit," which last words he added more than filial piety than for any conviction. "When are you going?"

Mrs. Halliday said Miss Dunsford was going to the Riviera in ten days and Mrs. Dunsford had suggested that Friday week would be a good time as she could settle in comfortably over the weekend. George said that would be splendid, wondered if he had said the wrong thing, tried to improve his words and failed miserably.

"Dear boy," said his mother kindly, "I'm afraid I've rather upset you. The one reason I wondered about leaving you was the thought that you might be lonely."

"Oh, don't worry about that, mother," said George, apprehensive that she might make a Noble Renunciation for his sake. "I'm working all day long and there are always heaps of papers in the evening and people are awfully nice about asking me out—I mean Lady Graham and the Carters—oh, and loads of people. And it's not forever. How long will you be with Mrs. Dunsford?"

Mrs. Halliday said she did not know. It rather depended, she said, how long Miss Dunsford stayed on the Riviera. Possibly she and Mrs. Dunsford might go out there later and visit her.

We are obliged to state that George's spirits were steadily rising while his mother spoke. He loved her very much and wanted to do all he could for her, but to think of having the house to himself was heaven. And what was so delightful was that the whole plan had come from her.

"People may say, of course," said Mrs. Halliday, "that I shouldn't have left you alone here," to which George replied that they could talk themselves black in the face as far as he was concerned and he was glad his mother was going to have a real holiday and have other people looking after his instead of her looking after other people

Then he had to go off to the farm and Mrs. Halliday unpacked her suitcases and had a nice long gossipy talk with old Mrs. Fothergill the cook and the devoted and hideous maid Hubback. They all had strong sweet tea in Mrs. Fothergill's own room and Mrs. Halliday said she was going on a visit to Northbridge soon. Mrs. Fothergill said you always needed a change after a loss, because a loss turned the blood; a terrifying piece of information. It turned her blood, she said, something dreadful when Fothergill died even if he was a poor piece of work and she had felt ever so queer for ever so long and if Madam was to go over to Northbridge the way she said it would do her a lot more good than doctors' bills. Then Mrs. Halliday went back to her own part of the house.

"What did I tell you?" said Mrs. Fothergill. "Them tea leaves in my cup after breakfast this morning, they said as plain as could be there was a Change of Plans to be expected. Well, I can't stand here all day talking," but as she stood very little owing to Her Feet, this need not be taken literally.

We heard at Greshamsbury about the visit that two of Dr. Crawley's granddaughters were paying at the deanery. We have never been able to keep pace with the Dean's growing grand-family and are not quite sure whose children Grace and Jane Crawley were. But that is of no great matter as all the deanery descendants were very pleasant and well brought up. The only one whose fortunes we have followed was Octavia, youngest daughter of the deanery, who had married the Reverend Thomas Needham, one-time Secretary to the Dean and a valiant army chaplain during the North African campaign, leaving his right arm in pledge in that unfriendly soil. And as they are now in a comfortable living and have several children we will leave them there.

The visiting granddaughters, who had been seen by several people at services in the cathedral, were Grace and Jane Crawley, their Christian names being in memory of the Grace Crawley who had married the wealthy Archdeacon Grantly's son Major Grantly and her younger sister Jane. The first Grace Crawley had been a very lovely girl whose quiet beauty had been happily transmitted to this later Grace and to Jane. Both had a face of that Victorian oval which one now so rarely sees, but otherwise they were quite modern and each had a job. Not that they particularly wanted jobs, for they were very happy at home, but whereas it used to be the girl who worked that had no time to make or to entertain friends, unless in a horrible room, with a chop cooked (and probably burnt) in over-the-gas-ring fashion, now it was almost the other way round and the girl who didn't work was out of it. What their jobs were we neither know nor care, for they were having a very happy holiday with their grandparents; and the Dean's secretary, an impressionable young man in Holy Orders, was mildly in love with them both.

When you are a working farmer and going to drink sherry at the deanery, the chief problem is, how much time do you need to clean yourself properly. If you have been doing office work all day—as happened sometimes—you are fairly clean, but rather tired and cross. If you have been out all day on the place, dealing personally with pigs and cows and tractors or—which was even harder work—seeing that other people dealt properly with these valuable possessions, you are pretty well bound to have a sample of every kind of dirt on your hands and well up your arms, not to speak of the end of your nose peeling slightly after those three hot days, and the fact that even after a hot bath—unless you have really had time to wallow and soak—your hands are still unpresentable and your face of a fine manly red-tan shade and you can only hope that the place where you cut yourself while you were having that quick shave won't start bleeding again, because a touch of styptic looks like dirt and sticking plaster looks as if you had a nasty boil.

George did his best and no man can do more. It was a nice clean smooth shave, his hair had been cut in Barchester the week before, Hubback had brushed and pressed his grey suit and seen that all the buttons on his clean shirt were secure. He had three new handkerchiefs untouched since Christmas and put one in his pocket. He did toy with the idea of wearing his father's old seal ring but as he couldn't at the moment remember where he had put it and hadn't time to search every drawer, he gave it a miss. As he had expected—nay feared—his mother was lying in wait outside her bedroom to say good-bye to him and tell him that supper would be left in the dining-room in case he came back late.

"At least it's not good-bye," she said, "only good-night."

"Good-night then, mother," said George, giving her a kiss. "Go to sleep. Drunk or sober I'll come in like a lamb," and he cleared the bottom flight, which was eight steps, in a bound and hurried out to his car.

Taking the less frequented road he rushed up and down its hilly gradients, passed below the great mound that had been a camp probably before the Romans came to Britain, and so to Barchester. As he usually went there on market days it was a pleasant difference to find the streets not entirely blocked by demented live stock who knew quite well that their owners had taken the wrong turning and were trying to walk over each other's backs to put things right. The street which led to the Cathedral Close was fairly clear. As he passed the White Hart he saw Burden, the old headwaiter, standing on the steps. He was almost a family friend, so George drew up to ask after his feet. The old waiter said they would last out his time, but he did feel them cruel sometimes on market day when the hotel was so full. So George got out of his car and asked old Burden to get him a dry Martini and to give himself something, and by a little pumping got a faithful account of what the Dean's two young ladies were like. Miss Grace she was as pretty as they made them and fair and Miss Jane she was dark and as pretty as they made them and he laughed rather wheezily at his own wit. Then George drove on to the deanery where he was well known by the butler and went upstairs to the drawing-room.

If the noise when the door was opened was like the Roar of London in that super-sonic-speed production of the Wahless called In Town To-Night, it was merely a proof of a good party. George Halliday's spirits suddenly rose with a bound. Here one could forget one's beloved home for a while. Octavia Needham, youngest daughter of the deanery, saw him, took him under her redoubtable wing and forced a way through the guests to her mother.

"I say, mother," she said. "Here's Mr. Halliday."

Mrs. Crawley was pleased to see George, remembered to ask after his mother, enquired after his sister Sylvia, and passed him on to her husband all in one breath.

"Ha, Halliday," said the Dean, which greeting, together with his huge bushy eyebrows, had terrified many of the younger clergy. But George, who had known him all his life, found no terrors in his host and asked where his granddaughters were.

"I have eight. Which do you mean?" said the Dean, showing by a smile that this was not a snub.

"Well, you've got some on show that I haven't met, sir," said George, who found the army Sir useful for almost every occasion. "Grace and Jane, isn't it?"

"Family names," said the Dean. "We have had a Grace and a Jane, or a Grace if there were not other girls, in every generation. Very delightful girls. They both have jobs of course, though I do not precisely remember what they are. You must meet them. Octavia," he called to his youngest daughter who was passing, "take George Halliday to talk to your nieces."

"Come on, George," said Mrs. Needham, who had a very good organizing head and a philanthropic heart, but no manners in particular. "I haven't seen you for ages. You've been losing weight. Good thing too. You were a bit too heavy last time I saw you. Do you want to talk to my nieces? Come on then," and she ploughed a furrow through the party so fiercely that George was almost ashamed to follow in her wake, especially as she altered her course several times to bang past people who hadn't seen her coming. "Here you are," she went on and landed George near one of the long windows, where two young women were talking together, a dark and a fair.

"I say, you mustn't talk to each other," said Mrs. Needham severely. "This is a party."

"It may be a party," said the fair one, "but it's no good trying to talk to people, Aunt Octavia, because you can't hear what each other says, so Jane and I were talking to each other."

"Well, now you can stop talking to each other," said Mrs. Needham. "This is Mr. Halliday. This is Grace fair and Jane dark," and sheering off she cut through the crowd, full speed ahead.

"Well, Aunt Octavia is!" said the fair girl. "As if we hadn't known George off and on since he was in Eton suits. You always came to Granny's parties, George."

"And you girls were in party frocks, one pink and one blue, and cried at the conjurer," said George. "Jane cried most and I gave her the clean handkerchief Nannie had given me for show and Nannie said it wasn't mine to give. I'd just gone into Etons for parties. But now I don't go into society much. These sherry parties frighten me. Can I get you another drink?"

"I don't think so," said Grace. "It's impossible to move, but Jane and I have a secret hoard," and she lifted the top of one of the window seats and from its inside extracted a half-full bottle of sherry and some glasses.

"For family friends only," said Grace and filled the glasses.

"May I drink to my old friends?" said George. "I've been to the deanery on and off ever since I was in petticoats—if I ever did wear them—but I have never been a family friend before."

Octavia Needham, returning from her tour of the rooms, stopped to see how they were getting on and took Grace away to leaven a very sticky corner where two canons and a canon's widow were talking about Mrs. Morland's latest Madame Koska thriller.

"Well, now you'll have to talk to me," said Jane Crawley. "Grace is much better at talking to people and I'm better at listening. What do you do?"

George, rather taken by the self-possessed manner of this good-looking dark girl, said he was a farmer.

"A Gentleman Farmer?" said Jane seriously.

George said he supposed he might call himself that. His people had owned the same land and cultivated it since 1721 if that meant anything.

"Wait a minute," said Jane Crawley. "Eighteen twenty-one, nineteen twenty-one, that's two hundred; nineteen thirty-one, forty-one, fifty-one," she went on, putting up a finger for each number, "that's thirty. And five makes thirty-five. Oh dear, I've forgotten where I'd got to."

"Two hundred and thirty-five I think," said George.

"And you have been in the same place *all* that time," said Jane Crawley. "We can't count back more than about a hundred years and even then we weren't much. Great-grandpapa was a clergyman and frightfully poor and he got into some silly kind of muddle with money and nearly went to prison and his daughter married one of the Grantlys who were pretty rich and one of her sons married someone quite nice with some money, so we came up in the world. It's all rather like a novel."

George felt confused. In his circle, or ambience, or whatever one liked to call it, everyone knew more or less who everyone else was. There were of course some people like Mrs. Joram, formerly Mrs. Brandon, now wife of Canon Joram, who were not anyone in particular, but they had earned their place in the sub-county ranks which were what is roughly called gentry, even if the land that some of them used to hold had long since dwindled to what was practically three acres and a cow. And here were the Dean's granddaughters, apparently rather proud of their descent from a penniless and possibly fraudulent clergyman. He gave it up. Whatever the background, the deanery was good enough for anyone and after all what was he himself? A gentleman farmer—though now the word gentleman had almost lost its value, as indeed had the word lady—hoping to make his land pay and not much hope of doing so.

All these thoughts passed through his mind, of course, far more quickly than our pen (an HB pencil) or even a stenographer could record them. Someone with a tray of sherry glasses oozed into their neighbourhood. George and the Dean's granddaughter each took one.

"And what sort of job do you do?" he asked.

"Well, I've not got a real job," said Jane Crawley. "One needs degrees and things and I'm uneducated."

George asked what she meant.

"My kind parents," said Jane, "sent me to Barchester High School. I didn't really mind it much. And then there was an awful exam coming, something you've got to pass if you want to get any good sort of job and I cried so much that father said I needn't do it. So that was heaven."

George, amused and rather impressed by this individualist point of view, said what was she going to do now.

"Oh, I'm not *going* to do," said Jane. "I *do* do," which made George laugh. "My brother farms over Chaldicotes way and I've been there most of this year. It's mixing farming and I simply adore it. The only thing I really properly learnt was hens."

George asked for further information.

"Oh, you know. A sort of hen-compound with lots of hen-houses all exactly alike and they live there and lay eggs. It's awfully like that new satellite town over Hogglestock way."

George was slightly intimidated by the extreme competence of Miss Jane Crawley, but remembering that he had held a commission in the war, he carried on.

"Hens become slightly boring," said Jane Crawley in an off-hand way. "I'm getting more pig-minded. Do you know pigs? Sir Robert Graham has top-grade pigs but I don't know him. I'd love to see his piggery."

"I quite agree about hens," said George. "I loathe them. We keep a fair number but not prize ones—just the sort that spend the day rootling about in the farmyard and are shut up at night if we can get them all. Some of them prefer to nest in the hedge and we don't worry much. The eggs get collected and we don't notice if whoever collects them keeps a few for himself. I was glad enough to pinch an egg or two in France sometimes."

"Oh! Were you in The War?" said Jane.

"Couldn't help it," said George. "Barsetshire Yeomanry. Sometimes I wish I were back there."

Jane said, rather timidly, "Why? Wasn't it rather awful?"

"It was and it wasn't," said George. "One can't explain. I hated it and I'm glad I had it. I miss it, but I couldn't do it again."

"I'm sure you could," said Jane, looking up at him—which is a pleasant feeling for a young—a not-so-young man, with no particular opinion of himself.

"Do you know Lady Graham?" said Jane. "I think she's near you."

"*Rather,*", said George. "She's one of the nicest people I know. Of course, you know her youngest daughter, Edith. She's the unmarried one and rather a character."

Black dislike against unmarried ones who were characters very naturally surged up in Jane's soul.

"Do you mean *difficult?*" she said.

George said difficult was not the word and—after casting an

eye on Jane Crawley's half-full glass—gave himself some more sherry.

"Mother and father wouldn't let us be difficult," said Jane in a rather snobbish voice. "Especially father. He says one ought never to be rude to *anyone*, unless of course it was the Bishop or the Bishopess."

"Now that," said George, "makes my dream come true. I mean it reminds me of something only I can't think what it is. Oh, I know. Wasn't it your great-grandfather or whichever it was that said 'Peace, woman' to the bishop's wife? I mean the wife of whoever was bishop then."

"Mrs. Proudie it was," said Jane Crawley. "That was ages ago, about a hundred years or something. But if father got the chance he'd say it to this one. Father says the Bishop is an old woman in an apron and his wife is an old devil in petticoats. Father told me not to tell anyone he had said that, but I can't help telling people."

"Good for you," said George cheerfully. "And now I'll tell everyone; but I won't say I got it from you."

"That's a bit mean," said Jane Crawley. "I mean I tell you something and you bag it for your own," and she looked at him reproachfully, which had the peculiar effect upon George of making him feel a cad and unworthy. Though of who or whom he was unworthy he had not time to think.

"I'm sorry," he said and took a step backwards.

"Oh, I didn't mean to be spiky," said Jane. "Really not. *Please.*"

"I never thought you did," said George, taking a step forward to where he was before.

"Then why did you begin to go away?" said Jane.

"I didn't," said George almost violently. "At least I did, but then I didn't, so here I am," at which words Jane's colour flooded her clear skin very prettily and she offered him some more sherry which he took, drank at a gulp and put the glass on a shelf which it at once fell off.

"I *am* sorry," said George, full of annoyance with himself for being so clumsy, but luckily the awful noise of a room of well-bred people conversing had covered the little crash of the glass and no one had noticed.

"It doesn't matter a bit," said Jane. "Granny says nothing matters so long as you didn't mean it and don't make a fuss. She said that when Grace put her umbrella in the umbrella-stand when we had to go to tea at the Palace and she put it right through the Bishopess's without meaning to. So she didn't make a fuss and nobody knew."

George asked how she knew that nobody knew.

"Oh, Granny's second housemaid's cousin is the boot and knife boy at the Palace," said Jane. "He's going to give warning just before Christmas, because last year the Bishopess wouldn't let the servants have a turkey and not even a chicken, so he's coming here, because Granny always gives the staff exactly the same Christmas dinner that we have. I say, you aren't *Palace*, are you?" she added.

"Good God, no!" said George Halliday. "I mean I beg your pardon, Miss Crawley. I shouldn't have used such language here, but my feelings got the better of me."

"Oh, that's all right," said Jane Crawley. "Grandfather says his father told him that old Archdeacon Grantly used to say it quite a lot. And I think your feelings do you credit, however you express them," with which words that young lady gave him what we can only describe as a very provocative look and then looked at the carpet.

"Nymph of the downward look and something eye," said George.

Jane said what was that.

"Well, it ought to be a quotation but I can't get it," said George rather pettishly. "It's something very like that only it's different and I can't think where it comes from."

"Nor can I," said Jane. "I say, Mr. Halliday, do you think you could ask Sir Robert Graham if I could come and see his pigs one day? I don't want to be a pusher, but his bailiff Goble did let

me talk to him at the last Agricultural Show and I'd simply love
to go there if no one would mind."

George said he was sure Sir Robert would be delighted and he
would ask about it. Perhaps Miss Crawley would come to lunch
at his house, meet his mother and see his pigs and he would take
her over to Sir Robert's farm and get Goble to have a talk with
her.

Jane's smooth pale cheeks flushed most becomingly and she
said she would love it at which moment Octavia Needham bore
down on them, hit George on the arm, said he wasn't pulling his
weight and carried her niece away with her to the other end of
the room.

Well, that was that. Jane Crawley—an extraordinarily beautiful name—would like to see Sir Robert's pigs. He, George,
hadn't much time to spare from the farm, but it would be only
civil to arrange a treat for the Dean's granddaughter after the
delightful sherry party at the deanery; and good sherry too, he
added to himself and took another glass of it. Then he pulled
himself together and like a good guest went through the rooms
looking for elderly ladies who were neglected, or young ladies
who had got landed with elderly Canons when what they
wanted—in default of film or tennis stars—was young curates,
and in general made himself useful. All of which was not
unperceived by Mrs. Crawley who presently asked him to get
her a cup of tea—for tea was being served for the weaker
spirits—and sit with her for a few moments and tell her about
his mother. So George got the tea and found a quiet corner near
the head of the stairs where they could sit and talk.

"So your mother is going to winter at Northbridge, is she?"
said Mrs. Crawley. "I expect she will be glad to have a change for
a bit. You mustn't be too lonely though, George. Ring up and
come here for a meal whenever you feel like it. Or no. I will ring
you up, because I know you will think you are being a nuisance
if you ring me up—which you certainly never are. My young
people are always glad to meet my old friends—they seem to

have a kind of age-cult now. When I was a girl we used to think all our mother's friends came out of the Ark. I shan't say lunch because you are always working. What about dinner?"

George, in a kind of humorous despair, said she had offered him so many permutations and combinations that his head was swimming.

"But may I have Mrs. Bun the Baker's Wife and Miss Bun the Baker's daughter?" he said, "and ask you to bring your granddaughters to lunch at Hatch House one day. One of them wants to ask Sir Robert Graham's bailiff about pigs, I don't quite know why? It's the dark one."

"Oh yes, Jane. She is very pig-minded," said Mrs. Crawley. "We'd love to come, and then I could have a talk with your mother while you take Jane to talk pigs at Holdings. Is that what you meant?"

She had only put the slightest touch of good-humoured mockery into her voice, but George went as red as his already sun-tanned face would allow.

"Kamerad!" he said. "Yes. Jane did ask me if she could see Sir Robert's pigs and I said we would arrange it. What nice granddaughters you do keep, Mrs. Crawley."

"Yes, they are very good-looking in their different ways," said Mrs. Crawley, "but your sister Sylvia Leslie beats them all, even if she is a good deal older. Whenever I see her I want to give her sixpence for being so handsome. My Grace is rather her type but she will never be the beauty your sister is," to which George Halliday replied that his sister Sylvia was hors concours but he would like to see all three beauties together.

"And who shall give the Apple?" said Mrs. Crawley, and then they had a nice, silly game of who would be least suitable to take the part of Paris, the prize being awarded, nem. con., to Lord Aberfordbury because he was not only the most annoying but also the plainest man in Barsetshire. And the silliest, said Mrs. Crawley firmly. Then, her little holiday from hostess-ship being up, she went away. So George talked to other friends and had a pleasant flirtation with Mrs. Joram, whose lovely eyes still had a devastating effect on the male sex of almost any age, and then drove homewards. But he went back by the right bank of the river to Hatch End hoping to catch Goble somewhere about the Holdings Home Farm. Nor was he disappointed, for Goble was in the Private Ward of the Pig Sties, exulting over a new litter while the litter's mother kept one vengeful eye on him in case he kidnapped one of the family and turned it into bacon.

After the necessary formalities of an aimless conversation on things agricultural, with special reference to the approaching Show, George said he had been to a party at the deanery.

"Ar," said Goble, who was a slow but powerful thinker, that was where the Dean lived.

"Quite right," said George. "That's why they call it the deanery."

Goble said that was right, but why they called the Bishop's home The Palace he didn't know. Bishops weren't Kings, not so far as he'd heard.

George said that was quite true. They were lords.

Lords, Goble said after a pregnant silence, was lords; not bishops. Look at Lord Pomfret, he said. *He* was a lord.

George thought of adding that he was Lord Lieutenant of the County, but the strain was too great and he knew from long experience that Goble could beat him in divagations any day of the week, so he asked after Holdings Goliath.

Goble led the way to the sty where the great boar lay, like the great San Philip of fifteen hundred tons.

"He'll do it this year," said Goble. "They're laying money on him, big odds too, in the Barsetshire Pig Breeders' Association. Won't you, old fellow?"

The boar only said Humph, but he said it far more loudly and decidedly than the swine who was loved by a lady, turned his great bulk and sank to rest again.

"I've got a message for you, Goble, from a young lady," said George.

Goble, with a deliberate archaism which had no effect whatever on George, said he was too old a fellow for they young
maidens. Young maidens, he said, they fared to look at the
young fellows.

"Well, never mind about that," said George. "One of the
Dean's granddaughters, Miss Jane Crawley, wants to see you.
She said you let her talk to you at the last Agricultural."

"Now, thiccy maiden," said Goble, who was rapidly receding
into the Middle Ages, "seems to me like she was black."

"If you mean dark hair," said George prosaically, "that's the
one. Her sister is fair."

"I seed them both," said Goble. "At the Agricultural it was."

Stifling a desire to gag Goble, George Halliday and Miss
Crawley was coming over to lunch at Hatch House, he hoped,
and she would love to come over and hear what Goble had to say
about pigs and before Goble's rather slow though powerful
mind had formulated a sentence about letting they maidens see
his sties, George had said good-evening and was striding away.

"Hurry, hurry, that don't get no one nowhere," said Goble, as
he looked after George's retreating figure. "*You* don't hurry, old
fellow," and he poked and scratched the great boar's back with
his stick till he heaved with ecstasy.

There is always a horrid moment when, after a delightful
party where one has been—at any rate in one's own
estimation—rather popular and brilliant, one is back in one's
own home with its responsibilities and small cares. George
knew this moment was coming, tried to delude himself that it
wasn't and came in as the clock struck nine. At almost the same
moment he heard the time signal from his mother's wireless,
showing that she was safely in the drawing-room. He went
quietly through the service door, down the kitchen passage, out
into the yard, and across to the farm where he sat on an
upturned bucket, communed with nature in the shape of the
yard dog, and listened to the movements of the cows in their

houses and the distant sleepy grunts and squeals from the pigs. From the henhouse came a hysterical shriek followed by a kind of Combined Fluttering and Scuffling. Silence gradually filled the air again. How lovely was silence compared with people jabbering at cocktail parties, or even sherry parties. It might amuse some people to stand and jabber to other people though no one could hear what anyone else said; how much better to commune with nature like this. Lines from a half-remembered poem of Matthew Arnold came into his mind. Is not on some-things like these, lovely the flush? Ah, so the quiet was, so was the hush. In that hush between the dying gold in the northwest and the growing dusk all round him, with one star shining, he thought of a girl with dark hair and dark eyes who understood what one said. And who liked pigs. Oh love! oh fire!

Most of us have, blessedly, been in love once; many of us have been in love many times. But each time is different and each of our times, of course, entirely different from an infinitely superior to any love ever experienced by anyone. She walks in beauty like the night: who had written that about whom? People who wrote about golden girls didn't know what they were talking about. If it came to that his sister Sylvia was golden and she was a smashing good-looker—but there was something about dusky hair and a pale face—no, that sounded like an invalid, and an alternative white face sounded like a pet sheep. Black but comely—well, that was in the Bible and everyone knew that a lot of things in the Bible hadn't been translated properly in whenever it was (from which opinion we beg to dissent pro-foundly, preferring the Bible as translated under King James the First to any later versions and the Prayer Book as we in our childhood knew it to any Mrs. Grundyish emendations), and one never quite knew in love songs who was which or what. But setting all such questions aside, Jane was the beauty of the world, and that was that. And his spirit soared in a silvery dream till his body, which was getting thoroughly bored, nearly made him fall off the bucket. The dream fled. He said HELL in a loud, cross voice and went indoors, where he deliberately lied and told his mother he had had a very nice time at the deanery and when he got back he had to go and look at the ram which had been pumping rather unevenly, but evidently Caxton had seen to it.

His mother asked what the Dean's granddaughters were like. Very nice, he said. One was called Grace and was fair and the other one, Jane, was dark, which last words he tried to say in a kind of not-caring way to put his mother off the scent. Yes, he had seen Octavia Needham and her husband and quite a lot of people, but he hadn't stayed long because he had to go to Holdings and catch Goble, as there was a good deal to be settled about the Barsetshire Agricultural. His mother said How very nice and now she would go to bed, thus hinting (or so George thought, though we do not quite agree with him) that she felt obliged to stay up like The Drunkard's Wife so that she could see the erring sheep safely into its bed. George, feeling that, in the words of an old village woman, it was better to make one scream serve, added that one of the Dean's granddaughters was rather keen on pigs, so he had asked her to come over one day and he would take her to see Sir Robert Graham's pigs.

Mrs. Halliday, envisaging mentally a second Mrs Samuel Adams, a Mighty Daughter of the Plough (in Lord Tennyson's fine words), saw no harm in this. The Crawleys were a good family and so many girls were taking up farming now—even her own Sylvia over at Rushwater.

"Oh, and Mrs. Crawley sent you her love, mother," George said with more wish to please his mother than a regard for the exact truth, and Mrs. Halliday said that was very nice of her, and so they went to bed.

Life went on. The work on the farm needed daily attention, as did the cruel amount of paper work thrust upon farmers by increasing Bureaucracy. George was not the only ex-combatant who sometimes regretted the care-free days at Vache-en-Foin or Vache-en-Écurie, when one's duties were plainly before one and one could not take much thought for the morrow. But the Circumlocution Office has inexorably pulled everything into a machine which certainly grinds slowly—but not to produce, only to complicate and harass by papers and inspectors and questionnaires (of which last They are probably ashamed and have therefore given them a French name) the men who produce our daily bread and its various accompaniments.

Still, the farm paid its way and there was a small steady profit. The large banking concern in which young Mr. Crosse, son of Lord Crosse, was now a working partner was willing to lend money towards modernization and improvements and George Halliday, who had been during the two years of his father's decay, followed by his death, literally adscriptus glebae if the estate was to survive, began to see light. Not that he was less busy. In fact he worked as hard as any of his men and better than most and was also coming to be known in the County Club and on whatever is the provincial equivalent of On Change, or In the City, as a safe man yet one who was willing to look into modern developments of agriculture and agricultural machinery; and the overdraft which the bank guaranteed when George began to bring the farm equipment up to date was a large one. But all this he kept between himself and his old companion-in-arms, Lord Crosse's son, whose influence in the bank where Lord Crosse was a director was very useful to George.

George rang up the deanery, spoke to Jane Crawley on the telephone, and a day was fixed for her to come and meet Goble on the august subject of pigs. George said he could fetch her, but she said she had a small car of her own and where would he meet her, as she didn't know Lady Graham.

"Well—I say—look here," said George. "I told my mother about meeting you and your sister and she said she would love to meet you."

Jane Crawley said she would like that and should she come to Hatch House or Holdings.

"Well, it's awfully nice of you," said George. "It's not very exciting here, but I think mother would like to see you. Do come to lunch early on Wednesday week if you can and we'll go down to Holdings afterwards. How's your sister?"

Jane said Fine.

"So are you," said George and quickly hung up the receiver, but not so quickly but that he heard an amused laugh.

> "'He either fears his fate too much
>   Or his deserts are small,
>   That puts it not unto the touch,
>   To win or lose it all'"

said George aloud to himself.

"What were you saying, dear?" said his mother coming in.

Cold ordinary life had closed in; the golden moment was over. George said in a rather affairé voice: "Oh, just a bit of poetry, mother. I've got to go up to the top field. Back for tea with luck."

So Mrs. Halliday had to be content. Tea was a vague word. It might be at any time between half-past four and half-past six according to what was doing on the farm or even not at all; but her own tea was always brought to her by the faithful Hubback at half-past four and if George came in late he usually went to old Mrs. Fothergill's room and had a kind of schoolboy tea with cold ham, or sausage rolls (for Mrs. Fothergill still had a fine hand for pastry). Sometimes Mrs. Halliday thought of Hovis House where tea was always at half-past four. Mrs. Dunsford's dull girl would be going to the Riviera next week. Mrs. Dunsford had suggested that Mrs. Halliday should pay her a nice long visit. Perhaps it would be unkind to say that the thought of this visit was the one thing that kept George going. It would certainly be untrue, for his heart was in his farming, and though his feelings about it were often Odi et amo, his heart remained faithful at bottom to the land which was in his blood through many generations.

A few days later his mother came down to breakfast with a rather important face.

"I heard from Mrs. Dunsford this morning," she said, for the post began his round at that end of the village.

George asked what she had to say.

"It is about my visit to Hovis House," said his mother.

"I'll miss you of course, mother," said George, throwing such truth into his voice as terrified him, in case his mother should take him at his word. "But I do think the change will do you good. You've been awfully good to me. I mean being here when I have to be out so much. But there's one thing, I'll be so frightfully busy with the farm and with the Agricultural Show coming on that we'd never meet. You know what it's like. Shall I drive you over to Northbridge?"

This was really nice of George, for his mother had never really learnt to drive and didn't like it. He knew it would interfere with his work and he would probably have to stay for ladylike tea with Mrs. Dunsford, but her mother was his mother. Had he been of an older generation he might have hummed to himself. "But I'll never have another mother, If I live ten thousand years." Those who remember the Follies, in the days when there never had been and never would be any war, will remember that foolish song. But one cannot be reminded of what one has never known.

Mrs. Halliday, genuinely touched by her busy son's offer, made the best possible return by saying that Mrs. Dunsford had to be in Barchester on Wednesday and would call for her on the way back and take her to Northbridge.

Well, of course it was on that Wednesday that Jane Crawley was coming to lunch and he hadn't told his mother. Largely because he had forgotten, but we think the forgetting was also because he wasn't sure how Jane Crawley would strike his mother and had therefore shoved the question into the back of his mind.

"That seems all right," said George, only just stopping himself in time from saying it would be splendid, which would have been true but not very tactful.

"By the way, I'd asked that granddaughter of the Dean's, Jane Crawley, if she could come to lunch that day," he added. "She's farming with her brother over Chaldicotes way and wants to ask Goble about some pigs."

"Well, that would be very nice," said Mrs. Halliday. "Ask her for one o'clock, George."

So George said he would and in an inarticulate way thanked Providence for making things easier than he had expected.

For the next week George was thankful that he had pressing business in Barchester and plenty of work on the farm, for the female part of the house was in a joyful and lachrymose flutter about Mrs. Halliday's departure.

Old Mrs. Fothergill said What had she said about a Change of Plans and she never found the tea leaves wrong. Indian tea, of course, she said. She didn't hold with China tea. It didn't draw nice and black and strong the way she liked it and a nasty sort of smell. Now Indian tea, you could fill the tea pot up again four times if the water was boiling and you'd get the whole strength of it every time: but China tea was water bewitched.

Wednesday dawned fair, in spite of George's certainty that it would never come, or would arrive with umbrella and goloshes. The barometer that hung in the hall said SET FAIR, but George had seen a horrid little gap in the long line of quicksilver and was certain that an air bubble had somehow got in and consequently the weather would be wet. He breathed heavily several times on the bulb at the bottom of the tube, as he and his sister Sylvia had often done in their childhood, hoping to make the thin thread run up and join its upper half, but it stood obdurate. Then he rapped on the barometer rather quickly, which is well known to have an exhilarating effect on the

weather, but again without result. So he said Damn and went off
to the farm.

It was one of those days when everything goes wrong. Not
that there were any major catastrophes. The tractor-engine
didn't seize (if that is how it is spelt), neither of the horses had
cast a shoe and gone lame, no one had put a charm on the cows
to prevent their giving milk, the hay was drying nicely and
would with any luck be ready for cocking or stacking (our
agricultural vocabulary is limited on the whole to poetry, such as
We've ploughed, we've sowed, We've reaped, we've mowed.
We've carried our last load. And we've not been overthrowed),
the hens were laying nicely, the oats were doing well, and
George together with his accountant had put in a successful
claim for a rebate on something. But to make up for this the
morning was consumed with small irritations like an idiot sheep
getting by superhuman or superovine efforts onto its silly back in
a ditch and having to be heaved up by two men; by a hen getting
most unnecessarily entangled in an old bit of wire netting and
there going mad and trying to pack her rescuers to death; by a
large comfortable sow using one of her children as a pillow and
the time taken in heaving the matron aside and telling the piglet
it was all right and not to make all that fuss; by the tap in the
farm yard needing a new washer and someone having to go
down to the village to get one while someone else made a
perfectly good one from a bit of leather in Caxton's workshop.
All trifles, no surprise to anyone, part of daily life but an infernal
nuisance. And just as George was going to knock off and clean
himself who should come into the yard but Sir Edmund
Pridham, doyen to the County and much respected in East and
West Barsetshire.

"Mornin' Halliday," said Sir Edmund, who was looking
extremely fit, in spite of his great age. "Trouble with your tap,
eh?"

George said he was delighted to see Sir Edmund (which,

apart from the inconvenience of his arrival at that moment, was perfectly true) and what could he do for him.

"I'll tell you, my boy," said Sir Edmund. "But Lord bless me! I must get my breath first. That car of mine bucks like a Wild West Show bronco. Good for the liver I daresay, but my liver doesn't need it. I'll tell you what, Halliday. A teaspoonful of salts—good strong ones—in a cup of hot, strong tea first thing will make a new man of you."

George, flattered by being called a boy—even if he was then to turn into a new man—said he would remember about the salts, with no intention at all of doing so.

"Now, what the dickens did I come here for?" said Sir Edmund. "I know when I was coming over the bridge I said to myself—what *did* I say? Something about the Barchester County Club—you're a member aren't you?"

George said his father had got him elected some years ago and he only wished he could go more often.

"That's right," said Sir Edmund. "Show yourself a bit. It's as good a lunch at the price as you'll get anywhere. Some fine port—but you young fellers drink nothing but whisky," said Sir Edmund, rather unfairly.

"As a matter of fact, I don't, Sir Edmund," said George. "I don't like it."

"Quite right," said Sir Edmund. "Brandy if you can afford it. Not gin. Ah, I know what it was what I wanted to say to you. We shall be having the West Barsetshire County Council elections. I was talkin' to some of the fellers," he went on, becoming more pre-1914 at every word, "and we were goin' over some likely names and yours came up. I forget who mentioned it. No I don't, it was Pomfret. Good fellow, Pomfret. He will work too hard like all these young men," he added, having himself worked ceaselessly for the west division of the county for at least sixty years. "He said you would be a good man to put up. So I said, 'You're right, Pomfret. He's a good man and we ought to have him on he Council. His father was all right, but young Halliday will do better than his father,' I said. 'I've had my eye on him.' Well, what about it?"

George, by now bright red in the face, tried to speak and couldn't.

"Take your time, my boy," said Sir Edmund, letting himself down onto a wheelbarrow. "I can't stand about at my time of life. I'm over ninety and a gammy leg—that's why I don't get married," and he laughed what George afterwards described to young Mr. Crosse as a lecherous Regency laugh.

"I've taken my time, Sir Edmund," said George, "I'll stand. Thank you, more than I can say. And please thank the people who are supporting me. May I know who they are?"

"Oh, the usual lot," said Sir Edmund. "Pomfret and the Archdeacon and Grantly. Crosse would have done it but he's East Barsetshire, more's the pity. That boy of his is coming on. He ought to settle in West Barsetshire."

George said how much he liked Mr. Crosse, who had been near him during some of the war years in France.

"Well, that's that," said Sir Edmund. "You'll hear all about it in good time. Formal letter from the West Barsetshire Committee and so on. How's the farm?"

George asked if Sir Edmund would like to have a look round, which he was delighted to do, so they made a short tour in an old car kept for rough work. Sir Edmund praised the state of the land and suggested a few alterations and improvements which George said he would like to consider. As they came back into the yard a small car drew up in the drive.

"Who's that?" said Sir Edmund. "I don't know that gal."

"Oh, that's Miss Crawley, one of the Dean's granddaughters," said George, horribly conscious that he was dirty and sweaty and unfit for female society. "She wants to see Sir Robert's pigs, so I said I'd take her over after lunch. I say, Sir Edmund, I'm awfully dirty. I must go and clean up."

"Faint heart never won fair lady," said Sir Edmund, "but I've never found that good farm muck didn't win them. Introduce me, my boy, and I'll see she doesn't run away."

Half of George said Dreadful meddling lecherous old man; but the other and more reasonable half said it was pure kindness on Sir Edmund's part.

"Oh, thanks awfully, Sir Edmund," he said. "Could you talk to Miss Crawley while I go and get my hands clean?" to which Sir Edmund, with what George considered a lascivious wink, said could a bird fly.

"Hullo, Mr. Halliday," said Jane Crawley, such being the formal address of most of our young.

"Oh, hullo," said George. "I say, it's awfully nice of you to come and I don't know where my mother is but this is Sir Edmund Pridham. Do you mind if I go and clean up a bit? I'll tell mother you're here."

"I know about you, Sir Edmund," said Jane Crawley. "You are a great friend of Mrs. Joram, aren't you? She said you were a sort of guardian of hers."

"Oh, did she?" said Sir Edmund. "Did she tell you I offered to marry her when she was Mrs. Brandon—her husband died a long time ago, a poor stick he was—but she married Joram instead."

"How *fascinating*," said Jane Crawley. "Of course she didn't tell me. I don't wonder you wanted to marry her."

"Want? Never wanted to," said Sir Edmund, "but she seemed a bit lonely and all that and I was her husband's oldest friend. I'd have stuck to my offer of course, but it wouldn't have done. Joram's a good fellow and I'm still a bachelor."

Jane Crawley said, with an attractive upward look under her long black lashes, that she preferred elderly men. Sir Edmund at once rose to her bait and a brief and violent flirtation took place which ended in Jane laughing uncontrollably and Sir Edmund laughing till he coughed so much that Jane became grave. The more so that someone who was obviously George Halliday's mother came out of the house.

"How are you, Sir Edmund?" she said. "and you are Jane Crawley that knows pigs. George is just cleaning up after his morning's work. Will you both come and have some sherry? Do stay to lunch, Sir Edmund."

So Mrs. Halliday took them into the house and was pleased by a quiet, well-bred young woman who was obviously happy to talk with her hostess and in no hurry to see her host. Mrs. Halliday was good at families and Jane was well brought up on county relationships, so they got on nicely, uniting in a common dislike of old Lady Norton, the Dreadful Dowager.

Then George came in, rather red in the face from a ferocious wash and a very rapid change of clothes, and lunch was ready. Mrs. Halliday, who had perceptibly younged—if one may use the word—since her decision to visit Mrs. Dunsford, always got on easily with Sir Edmund, who liked to talk with a pleasant woman who belonged to the county and could talk county families intelligently. The food was good, so was the drink, and Hubback approved of the party.

As they were finishing lunch Hubback came in to announce Mrs. Dunsford's car was there and she had put Mrs. Halliday's suitcases into it and Mrs. Dunsford said Not to hurry. But—just in case she began to feel homesick—Mrs. Halliday said she must not keep her friend waiting, and got up. George took her to the car, hugged her affectionately and told her to ring him up whenever she wanted anything doing at Hatch House. Mrs. Dunsford gave him an invitation to come over whenever he felt like it. George hugged his mother again and the car went away. He stood at the door, watching it go through the gate, turn to the right, then again to the left and across the river and for a moment he felt like the little boy first left alone at his prep. school, defenceless before a new world. But guests must be considered, so he went back into the house where Sir Edmund and Jane Crawley were conducting an outrageous flirtation with much pleasure on both sides. George did not see why a girl like Jane Crawley should pander to a lecherous old man—or if not quite in those words the sentiment was the same—but reflecting that the lechery consisted entirely in light badinage of the "You did," "No, I didn't," type and that Jane was quite equal to looking after herself, he cheered up. Sir Edmund then spoke to him again about the West Barsetshire County Council, and hoisting himself and his game leg into his car went away.

"Now for the pigs," said Jane Crawley. "What a nice old man Sir Edmund is. I'd never met him."

George, heartened by the words "old man," said Sir Edmund was awfully good at County work and his leg had hurt him ever since the Boer War, but he never complained and should they go to Holdings now. Hubback was clearing away lunch and Jane said good-bye to her and shook hands, which George saw with approval. It is nice when one's faithful and tyrannical old servants like one's friends—for that was all Jane was of course.

So he drove his guest down the little hill, across the river, as he had driven or ridden or walked ten thousand times before, except that this drive was slightly different. Probably it was the mild excitement of having a new girl—no, that wasn't the way to put it—a new acquaintance perhaps, for one really couldn't say friend so soon—oh, well then, damn it, such a very nice and good-looking girl beside one. As they passed the Old Manor House young Mr. Crosse came out. Probably he had been lunching with his sister Mrs. Carter, but there was no need for him to look at Jane as long as others might but also a little longer.

"Who was that?" said Jane.

Suppressing a desire to say No-one, George said it was Lord Crosse's son who was in a bank.

"Oh, is that John-Arthur?" said Jane. "Mrs. Morland was talking about him at Granny's party. She said he was awfully nice."

George nearly ran over a hen, swerved almost too far, scraped the car slightly against the flint and mortar wall of an outbuilding, and swore.

"I *know*," said Jane sympathetically. "There ought to be

tunnels for hens to cross the roads by. I hope it didn't scratch your car."

"Oh, she doesn't matter," said George, deeply touched by this sympathy. "She's used to it. I say, *your* car looks a useful little one."

"Not bad," said Jane. "I took her abroad this spring with some friends" (whom George immediately hated) "and she did the Pyrenees like a bird," to which George's mental reply was "Golly!" for Jane looked too elegant, too slight a creature to drive cars over Pyrenees. He would have preferred to drive her himself and so be sure that all was well, which beautiful thoughts so uplifted him from ordinary life that he nearly collided with Pilward and Sons' Entire, which was disgorging casks and bottles at the Mellings Arms.

"I say, you'd better look out," said Jane. "You'd smash to smithereens if you ran into that," and indeed the immense dray could have withstood the shock of almost any car. Its paintwork spotless in red and black, every piece of brass on the dray and on the harness glittering, the coats of the enormous grey cart horses shining with grooming, the draymen in the scarlet linen coats and black leggings (over which the A.U.H.P.B.C., or Amalgamated Union of Horse Propelled Beer Conveyances, had nearly spilt, some saying What about Red Spain, other What about the Blackshirts, both parties agreeing in passing a resolution which called upon the Government to reduce taxation, increase the Air Force, abolish militarism, fight everybody, and establish a thirty-hour week with pensions for everyone at fifty) were one of the most impressive sights in West Barsetshire.

This obstacle successfully by-passed, he turned down the lane that led to the Holdings farm and parked his car by the gate.

"Here we are," he said. "I'll see if Goble's about. He's the bailiff. Will you wait a minute," and he went off towards the barn.

Jane, who hadn't got out of the car, sat in the sun thinking of nothing in particular and enjoying herself. Round the corner

came a young man. No, not so young when you came to look
at his face, but he walked youngly. At the sight of—apparently—a female in distress stranded in a car, he stopped.

"Can I do anything for you?" he said. "My name's Crosse. I
was just looking for Goble, the bailiff."

"Oh, how do you do," said Jane. "George Halliday brought
me here to talk pigs. He's gone to look for the bailiff, too."

"I hope he won't find him just yet," said Mr. Crosse gallantly.
"May I ask who I have the pleasure of speaking to?"

"I really don't quite see how one *could* avoid that preposition
at the end," said Jane.

"I was thinking much the same as the words left my mouth,"
said Mr. Crosse. "May I ask whom I have the pleasure of
addressing?"

"The Dean's granddaughter," said Jane Crawley, trying rather
ineffectively not to laugh. "At least one of them, because grand-
papa has about fifty. I'm Jane Crawley and dark. I've got a sister
called Grace who's fair. It's like Tennyson."

Mr. Crosse leaning, though quite respectfully, upon the side
of the car said he liked Tennyson but couldn't place the allusion.

"Oh, 'We were two daughters of one race. She was the fairest
in the face,'" said Jane, in a deliberately prim, quoting voice.
"She is golden."

"Aurea puella, and very nice too," said Mr. Crosse.

"Golden lads and lasses must, Like chimney-sweepers come
to dust," said Jane. "Sixpence please."

Mr. Crosse took some change from his pocket, found a
six-pence and handed it to her. George came back with Goble
and all four walked to the sties. Goble, who liked intelligent
young women (by which he meant such as would let him do all
the talking), took Jane off on a round of the sties while the two
young men sat on a wall and talked—mostly about county
affairs. George Halliday, who had been longing to let off steam
about Sir Edmund's news, told Mr. Crosse that he was being put
up for the West Barsetshire County Council.

"I couldn't be more pleased," said Mr. Crosse. "So will the governor be. He is always saying West Barsetshire hasn't such a good lot of men as East Barsetshire. Pure local patriotism of course—village Hampden. What a bore Hampden must have been."

George said not half such a bore as Martin Luther, always showing off and nailing things on doors and saying he could no other; which led to an agreeable discussion of the prize bores in history; at which point the reader may make her—or less probably his—choice among that great army of impostors.

"That Miss Crawley is very charming," said Mr. Crosse.

George said nothing, in a rather marked way.

"Look here," said Mr. Crosse. "I am not one to butt in if not wanted. Give me the office and I will shake my bridle rein Upon the further shore, With adieu for evermore I don't even know what your Christian name is, my love, Adieu for evermore."

George said not to be a fool.

"No, I didn't mean that," he said. "I don't mind a bit—I mean I hardly know her—I mean there's absolutely *nothing* in it—I mean—"

"Kamerad!" said Mr. Crosse. "You have conveyed to me *exactly* what you mean. The girl is Sacred to me. Are there any more at home like her?" which echo of an old song made them both laugh.

"Well, there's another sister who is fair," said George.

"Fine," said Mr. Crosse. "If I had known your sister Sylvia before she married Martin Leslie I'd have married her myself. Bring out the blondes, let joy be unrefined. Now, look here: can I do anything to help about the County Council? Not bribery of course, not simony—whatever it is—nor barratry which I have a general impression is something to do with wreckage washed up on the foreshore. But any other blinking thing you like"— only he used a slightly shorter word than blinking.

George said it was awfully decent of him, but he really didn't know what one did and had a strong conviction that if he stood anyone a drink at the Mellings Arms between now and the election he would be sent to the galleys or Botany Bay and branded on the shoulder. Then they talked about what George should do when he was on the West Barsetshire County Council and how he would have toll gates on all the principal roads and a special by-law by which Lord Aberfordbury would have to pay twice as much as anyone else and his dreadful son three times as much.

"If I know Goble he will keep Jane Crawley at least half an hour at Holdings Goliath's sty," said George. "Let's go and rescue her." So they went to where the giant lived and found Jane and Goble arguing with great determination about his chance at the show.

"Still at it?" said George.

"You don't know Barsetshire," said Jane. "We've hardly be-gun."

Before George had decided whether to be amused or indig-nant she had enlisted his help on her side and he found her views of pig very sound till she took the wind out of his sails by saying that she was really only an amateur and Goble a first-class professional.

"Well, Miss Jane," said Goble, and George noted with amusement that he had used her Christian name as he had done with all the Graham children, "what I say is if Holdings Goliath doesn't get the Gold Medal this year I'll eat my hat. There's not a boar like him, no, not in the whole county, no, nor in West Barsetshire neether. As for that East Barsetshire lot, they're too long in the leg. No disrespect to Lord Crosse, Mr. Crosse, but his lordship's pigs they haven't what I'd call—well, I don't know rightly what I'd call it, but if you take my meaning they aren't heavy enough in the undercarriage."

His audience were so thankful that he had got to the end of what he was saying that they would cheerfully have subscribed to any heresy and each said, in slightly different terms, that he or she was sure Goble was right.

"Well, thank you very much for all you've told me, Mr. Goble," said Jane. "I'll be seeing you at the Agricultural, I expect. My father is one of the guarantors, so he always gives me some tickets. Anybody want a couple?"

This was dreadful. All three of her hearers belonged to families that had always gone to the Show since it was founded some two hundred years ago by some of the great landowners and the gentlemen farmers of the county. It had kept its status very well on the whole. There had of course been bad years, notably the cattle murrain in 1789 (attributed locally to the French Revolution) and the year when all the big landowners had abstained to mark their disapproval of the Reform Bill. The Show in 1947 had been particularly remembered by what George Knox, the well-known biographer, had alluded to as The Transit of Winston, when a Great Prime Minister who had been staying a couple of nights at Pomfret Towers drove past the Agricultural Society's grounds, foursquare as a White Porkminster, commanding as a Cropbacked Cruncher, but unlike these intelligent quadrupeds smoking a large cigar. He had lifted his hat and waved the cigar and mothers would tell their uninterested children about it for many years to come.

But it seemed ungracious to refuse. George Halliday saw a yawning chasm of embarrassment before himself and his friends, so emulating that depressing Quintus Curtius (and what good his gesture really did, if any, we do not know) he leapt into the social gulf and said he would be very grateful for a couple. For the Vicar and his wife, he added desperately, as they were very keen on—on everything of that sort, he ended lamely.

Jane said she would post them to him and she ought to be getting back.

Mr. Crosse asked if he could drive her back and when she said Thank you but her own car was up at Hatch House he said then he supposed George Halliday would drive her there and winked at George.

This unnecessary familiarity seared George's soul, but one

cannot throw over a brother-in-arms for any woman—or girl—however superficially attractive, so he pretended he had not seen the wink.

"I'll tell you what, as Mrs. Sam Adams says," Mr. Crosse continued, "why shouldn't we ask Miss Crawley to dinner at the White Hart and perhaps her sister would come too," at which Jane manifested such real pleasure that George felt it was quite unnecessary for her to make such a fuss. If Crosse hadn't suggested it, he was going to have suggested it himself. So he said, gaily, that it was a top-hole plan and Mr. Crosse wondered what had bitten George.

"I'm sure Grace would *adore* it," said Jane Crawley. "We do like doing things together. We're practically twins only Grace is a year older than I am. When will it be?" which almost childish eagerness amused Mr. Crosse, though to George it seemed angelic innocence.

"Come on, John-Arthur," said George. "Mother's gone to stay with an old friend of hers at Northbridge and I'm alone. Get in."

So all three got into George's car and drove towards Hatch House. We say towards, because no journey through a village that has known you since long before you were born can be made swiftly—unless it is known that the doctor is needed for an aging parent or the long-desired baby; or, not infrequently in the Halliday family, because someone had had a nasty fall and you can't be surprised the mare slipped with ice on the hill like that and they did ought to have roughed her shoes.

There were parcels of varying degrees of smell or unwieldiness to be collected; Mr. Scatcherd the local artist to be avoided; nice Mr. Choyce and his wife coming out of the vicarage; old Mrs. Hubback at The Shop with the fish that Vidler had left there for Hatch House, wrapped in a rather dirty newspaper which was rapidly disintegrating; Mrs. Panter, wife of George's carter, who was always ironing in her doorway; Dumka, the Mixo-Lydian maid of Mrs. Carter at the Old Manor House,

having a heavy flirtation with the local poacher outside the
Mellings Arms where she had no business to be; all the life of a
village, so far more real and personal than the life in a town.
Most journeys have an end and George could have wished that
this journey were longer; but it wasn't and there they were at
Hatch House.

Jane thanked him very much for the happy afternoon and said
she would tell her sister Grace about the dinner at the White
Hart and ask Granny if they could go, but she was sure they
could. Then she got into her own car and drove away. Bright-
ness fell from the air. True, there was the dinner to look forward
to, but a table at the White Hart was not like a meal in one's own
house. Perhaps Jane would think a dinner at the White Hart
rather dashing; he hoped she would. And afterwards they might
walk in the Close before delivering the girls at the deanery; he
and Jane in one direction; John-Arthur and what was the other
girl's name, oh, Grace, in another. Or they could go to the
second house at the cinema; but it would be practically impossible not to take—at any rate to touch—the hand of a girl who
was sitting next to one.

He went into the house. The usual post; business letters one
and all. No debts, thank goodness, except the ordinary trades-
men's bills. Some of the endless questionnaires from Jacks-in-
Office who think a small landowner has nothing to do but fill in
forms. Advertisements of farm-implements which he couldn't
afford if he wanted them. A letter from Malta which turned out
to be an advertisement for a lottery. An invitation from Lady
Pomfret to a garden party at the Towers in aid of the Barchester
General Hospital's Two Hundredth Anniversary Fund. A letter
with a London postmark and a tuck-in flap contained an invitation to join a society for the Propagation of Mutual Trust in
our Soviet Friends, which led George to considerations of what
a fool people must think one was if they sent one circulars like
that. He thought of writing a rude and sarcastic answer, thought
better of it, tore it up and went on with the farm letters. He must

ring Jane up about a date for dinner at the White Hart. A nice name, Jane. Mrs. Gresham at Greshamsbury was Jane—but that was somehow a different word—less beautiful, less holy than Jane Crawley. Oh, hell! he must get on with those papers. But as at half-past eleven he had made no particular progress he went to bed and, we are glad to say, was soon asleep.

CHAPTER 8

When young men about town ask young women to dine with them, they quite often come and pick up the young woman in their little sports car, or their battered old jeep that they went to the Tyrol in. Then they drive through the congested traffic to the nice little restaurant everyone says is so nice and either the cavalier leaves his lady in the restaurant while he drives about half a mile to find somewhere to park, or they drive together half a mile and she has to walk back to the restaurant in her nice silver shoes. How much simpler is life in Barchester. Grace and Jane Crawley were staying at the deanery and even if it had been raining they could have run with an umbrella through the Close and been at the White Hart in a jiffy. But very kindly it was not raining, so they went out of the deanery door without umbrellas and were at the White Hart within a very few minutes. Burden, the old headwaiter, who looked upon all children and grandchildren of the Close as an old Nanny may look on her ex-charges, was in the hall when they came into the hotel.

"Hello, Burden," said Grace and Jane.

"The gentlemen are here, miss," said Burden. "In the bar. They said to ask you please to take a seat in the lounge and I was to tell them you are here."

"Modern chivalry," said Grace as she sat down.

"Oh, I don't know," said Jane.

The gentlemen appeared and each girl thought how much nicer they looked than any of the other men in what I suppose one will finally have to call the lounge, as it is not the hall, nor the smoking room, nor the Ladies Only room, all these are dead except in our memory. But still we *cannot* say lounge.

A waiter came towards them but was checked by Burden.

"All right, Hoggett," he said. "I'm looking after this party Myself. You can do the commercials down the other end and don't give them the matured whisky, whatever you do. Anything's good enough for people as have been drinking cocktails to my certain knowledge for the last hour. You can charge them for the best. The tips are better that way," and he went on his slow walk (for his feet were always a trouble now) feeling that he had that day lighted a fire in the waiter that would not be put out.

Both young men greeted him warmly. The sisters, to their cavaliers' surprise, hailed him as Uncle and enquired affectionately after his leg.

"Well, Miss Grace," said the old man, "we're getting old together," at which obviously regular repartee the girls laughed and said his legs would be old long before he was, and how was his arthritis. George got up, went over to the bar and came back with two large beers, put one before Mr. Crosse and sat down before the other. Burden was still telling the girls (who were both listening with the kindest appearance of lively interest) how not one of the doctors didn't seem to understand his leg. Dr. Ford wanted to do an X-ray of it, but he didn't hold with being photographed. The only time he'd ever been photographed, he said, was at Brighton the year of King Edward the Seventh's Coronation—the real one, not the one that had to be put off, because it stood to reason if a thing was put off well it was put off. The whole party very sycophantically said once a thing was put off, it was put off; which pleased old Burden, who added the rider that if a thing was put off, well it *was* put off.

George—feeling rather a spoilsport, but he was hungry—
asked Burden what was on the menu.

"Now, Mr. Halliday," said Burden, "you leave it to me. That
cook we've got now he's a foreigner and he can be awkward.
Leave it all to me. There's a small loin of mutton, sir, beautifully
hung it was and nice close meat and lovely fat on it too. AND
kidney—ah, you'll go a long way before you see a kidney like
that. I spoke to the cook about it myself when you rang up about
the dinner, Mr. Halliday, and you can rely on him."

George said that was capital.

"There's only one thing, sir," said Burden. "he's a foreigner,
sir, and a bit touchy. Perhaps you wouldn't mind sending a
message to him to say you liked the dinner, sir. It all makes for
peace and quiet."

George said of course he would.

"And I leave the wine to you, Burden," said George. "Or you
have a talk with Burden, John-Arthur. You know much more
about drink than I do," so Mr. Crosse pretended to discuss
vintages with Burden. And when we say pretended, it was
obvious that he knew a good deal about wine but did not wish to
make a parade of it and he and the old waiter talked as experts,
and decided which wines should be served at which tempera-
tures.

All this might have been a little dull for the guests, left with
one man between them, but they were both nice affectionate
young women and so near of an age that they shared most
things, from their clothes to the young men who crossed their
path. They were talking in a comfortable way about Mrs.
Morland's last Madame Koska thriller when their attention was
distracted by a kind of turmoil near the entrance. George looked
round.

"Lord! it's the Mixo-Lydian Ambassadress!" he said. "She
simply cannot help making a noise wherever she goes. I wonder
what she is doing here? Oh Lord, she's coming at us!" and sure
enough the Ambassadress, of commanding figure, dressed in a

kind of compromise between a tailor-made suit and a sack, a Mixo-Lydian blouse of coarse cotton heavily embroidered in red and blue, and a rather dashing hat or cap of cock's feathers which hung round her face like a lobster's claws, was bearing down on them.

"She was at Granny's party," said Grace to George. "She came after you had gone. She is very—I don't know how to describe it."

George said Powerful, and then they all got up.

"Ha!" said the Ambassadress. "Which joy that I am seeink my old friends. I am still unrecovered of the Receiving which was of highest rank."

"I'm awfully glad Your Excellency liked Granny's party," said Grace Crawley. "But you look quite recovered now. This is George Halliday. He lives at Hatch End. And Mr. Crosse."

George shook hands with a kind of bow which did great credit to his presence of mind. Mr. Crosse suddenly lost his presence of mind and became dumb. Partly because the first impact of the Ambassadress was apt to bowl anyone over at once, partly because her manner of speech had appeared to him worthy of study and he did not wish a moment of her visit to be wasted.

"He is well dressed," said Her Excellency, eying George as if he were on show, "but I shall be telling you he is farouche. In Mixo-Lydia our young men are acquainted of social comfortableness from the mother's breast. Never do you see a young man which is left."

Grace said that must be so restful. All these left young men, she said, absolutely bored one stiff and their hair and their manners so untidy.

"Ah-ha, I over-voice in with you," said Her Excellency. "And you too, do you not, monsieur l'Ours?"

"Rather, your Excellency," said George. "With you, voice I quite and altogether over."

"Ha! see me this Yorge with spiks as a Mixo-Lydian," said

Her Excellency. "We shall spik together of moch, but in English. For these Prodshkina, they do not onderstand my fine language. Bot they will onderstand me when I say they are as Night and Day. The Dark and the Light. The Night and the Day, the Moon and the Sonn. Ah-ha! I know much. I am old Scrzy, what you coll which in your child-tails."

Even George, the most daring of the party, could not deal with the Mixo-Lydian—or for that matter the English—but the honour of England was at stake.

"Whatever your Excellency may call yourself, you can't say you are old," he said "Oh! I see what you meant, you meant that Scroozy, or whatever it is, means a witch in a fairy story."

"Ah! bot that is whay I *say*," said the Ambassadress. "I say you coll witch, we call Scrzy. So now, Zwe Bog—" and she lifted her glass.

Mr. Crosse said most unchivalrously under his breath, "And to you too, with knobs on it," but drank all the same.

—"which is like your expression of Goddam," said the Ambassadress. "For God, we say *Bog*, which is a word of high nobleness. As for *God*, it has no sense at oll," and she crossed herself in what Jane afterwards described as a very upside down kind of way and departed.

"I thought it better to wait, sir, till the lady had gone," said Burden, who had been hovering for the last few moments. "Your dinner will be ready almost at once. If you will follow me, I have kept a nice table for you," so they went into the dining-room. Here the old waiter had kept for them the most coveted of all the tables in a bow window at the far end of the room, where they could look down the High Street, or up it towards the Close, with the most beautiful spire in England faintly rosy in the summer glow.

"Golly! I *do* like that cathedral," said Mr. Crosse fervently, and his friends echoed his praise with variations.

Then did Burden, who had impressed a young man on approval into his service not caring in the least what the other waiters or the other diners might say, serve as good a dinner as the White Hart could supply. And very good it was. Not imaginative, we will leave that to foreigners. But good clear soup (made from real stock), fillets of what looked and tasted like real fish (for the White Hart had a private arrangement with a fishing village on the coast—though how long it will be able to keep that up we do not know) with a sauce obviously made with real butter, and then the lion of mutton. If it was mutton it could barely have left the nursery, so tender it was, and with such flavour.

"Eats like a sweetbread, sir, doesn't it?" said Burden. "Most of the people we get here now, sir, it's no pleasure to serve them. There's not one of them knows good from bad and they'll drink beer with a partridge or a pheasant. And champagne—well, sir, some of these business gents, for gentlemen I cannot call them—they'll think nothing of champagne with sausage and mashed."

George asked if they tipped well.

"Well, sir, they tip highly," said Burden. "I wouldn't say well. Now a gentleman like you, sir, or the other gentleman, you'd look at the bill and you'd think back over the dinner and tip according. Now sir, if I may presume, I'll give *you* a tip." George and Mr. Crosse laughed sycophantically at the joke and said they would be delighted and honoured.

"If you are dining, sir, at a *good* place, I do not mean the Ritz, or other hotels which are quite good class but do get some queer guests, foreigners and that like," said Burden, "but at a place—I will name no names—where the English guest is still studied, I would advise, if I may make so bold, that you should divide the bill roughly by seven. The result, sir, will give you a tip of fifteen per cent. You will, of course, tip the wine waiter separately. That sir, for the provinces, is reasonable and more than a great many gentlemen do who did had ought to have known better. Of course, if I may say so, it pays better, to tip on the high side in a place you often go to. It is Remembered and you will always get attention. If you are not going to a place again, you can tip less. I *could* mention a name, sir, but they say walls have ears and I have My Reputation to consider."

"I could name it too," said Mr. Crosse. "I'll bet five shillings it's—"

"Pardon *me*, sir," said Burden, "but walls *do* have ears."

"Well, they can't read," said Mr. Crosse and he scribbled something on the back of the menu. The old waiter looked at it and his face crumpled with suppressed laughter.

"Oh Lord! sir," he said, "excuse me laughing, but you've hit the nail on the head. And the young 'un's just as bad when he's here."

"Dreadful fellow, with his Chromo-Rotogravure art post-cards, or whatever he calls them," said George Halliday.

"Oh, you mean that ghastly young Hibberd," said Mr. Crosse, taking care however, to lower his voice, "the one that his father is Lord Aberfordbury. Father can't stand him. Nor can anyone else. Well, thank you, Burden."

"Thank *you*, sir," said Burden and went away to attend to one or two chosen guests.

Then they fell, as was almost inevitable, into Close gossip, in quiet voices and hints, or writing a name on paper as before, till both sisters had the giggles most delightfully. When the meal was coming to a much regretted end, after good coffee and best brandy as a liqueur, George asked the party if they would like to go to a film, or do a night tour of the Close. As the evening was warm the girls said Close and George asked for the bill. Burden brought it, ceremoniously on a plate, folded, lest the ladies' eyes should be insulted by the total.

"Whew," said Mr. Crosse, who had unfairly snatched it to look. "Halves."

George said a man who halved a bill would steal sheep.

"Heads or tails then for who pays," said Mr. Crosse, and spun a shilling in the air. George said heads.

"Tails it is," said Mr. Crosse. "Here you are, Burden. It was a delightful dinner and I shall come again soon."

"I hope so indeed, sir. Thank you very much, sir. Good-night, sir. Good-night, Mr. Halliday. And I hope the ladies have enjoyed the dinner."

Both ladies were loud in praise of the food and Burden's care of them.

As the party left the room, Burden stopped Mr. Crosse.

"Excuse me, sir," he said, "if I make a suggestion."

"Fire away," said Mr. Crosse. "You go on to the Close," he said to George and the girls. "I'll catch you up. Now, Burden, what is it?"

"My name is pretty well known, sir, in West Barsetshire and I may say a bit beyond that," said the old man. "If you are ever in any trouble in an hotel within a hundred miles or so of Barchester sir, run short of money or anything, ring me up here, sir. I know most of the men in the hotel-keeping line and they know me. If you've run out of change and want to cash a cheque, it isn't always easy—there's lots of queer people about. That's all, sir. I wouldn't have mentioned it, sir, except that you are a bit new to our side of the county. Thank *you*, sir."

Mr. Crosse thanked the old man, put into his not unwilling hand a further tip and walked up the street, under the grey archway, into the Close. He could not see the others, but he would find them somewhere. Burden. An old headwaiter had given him advice and offered help. Perhaps the old man had been saving all his life and had hundreds of gold sovereigns in a box under his bed, or quite likely in these degenerate days, Government securities which would go on paying interest, one presumed, just so long as there was peace in the world. But a very kind thought and a very kind offer. Where the dickens had the others gone?

He soon found them by their voices and the charming though irreverent laughter of the two sisters before various funerary tablets on the walls of the cloisters, especially one lately put up by the Friends of Barchester Cathedral to the memory of the Reverend Thos. Bohun, D.D., one time Canon of the cathedral, surmounted by a bust of the same with his head in a night-cap, looking, as Jane irreverently said, like someone in the madhouse in *The Rake's Progress*.

"Oliver Marling, the one that married Maria Lufton, wrote a ghastly book about him," said Grace. "He wrote loads of poetry to Mistress Pomphelia Tadstock who was a canon's widow who had been married three times. There's a tablet to her somewhere about and he went to London to see the Plague and died for it."

"Served him right," said Mr. Crosse cheerfully.

"It was more than that," said Grace. "What he *really* wanted to see, was what people looked like when they died of the Plague and if one could really see their souls coming out of their mouths or the top of their heads."

"I never thought of that," said George Halliday.

"Misspent youth, my lad," said Mr. Crosse. "You had all the chances you'll ever want at Vache-en-Foin."

"Chances!" said George indignantly. "When you're expecting to be bombed from above or blown up from below or just run through the stomach with a bayonet, you don't worry about whether whose soul's coming out of what. All you want is to see the other fellow's soul and give it a kick in the pants for luck."

He then apologized, quite needlessly, to the girls.

Jane said she didn't think that people that were killed's souls came out, because it would be so horrid for the souls. And as there was no particular answer to this, nobody made one. Mr. Crosse and Grace walked away to where the river ran close under the cathedral walls and watched a man sitting on a chair in a punt, a rod in his hands and a large stone jug beside him.

"I say, you don't think it was silly of me to say that, do you?" said Jane softly to George.

"Of course not," said George, looking down at her upturned face and her dark hair. "When you've seen people die it doesn't matter what you say about death. There it is and that's that. But if I had to choose I'd rather die between the harvest and the ploughing."

Jane asked why.

George said he didn't know. Just a feeling that if one died when everything was in, one would feel tidier.

"Like the old Scotchwoman who prayed that the Lord would let her die on a Saturday night when the kitchen weel redd up," said Jane, and laughed.

It was such a pretty gay laugh that George laughed too. Jane asked what he was laughing at.

"I don't know," said George. "Partly a good dinner. Mostly you."

"Did I say anything very silly?" said Jane, feeling her face go red and hideous, but George, who only saw a most enchanting pinkness, said of course she didn't.

"I mean you couldn't say silly things," he said. "Everything you say makes sense, but I can't help laughing with happiness about it," with which words she felt she was redder in the face than ever.

"I've known you an awfully long time," said George.

Jane, rather indistinctly, asked How.

"Oh, we used to meet a lot at children's parties when we were very small. Then there was the war. And I've been pretty busy ever since. The working farmer doesn't count on holidays. His men do. I'd almost forgotten about you," said George. "Then, the moment I saw you, I knew I knew you. Oh, dash it, that's as bad as ever. I mean, I can't see anything but you at the moment. I don't know what sort of a fool I made of myself at dinner, because *you* were there."

"Oh, do you mean I made you—I mean that I said something silly—I mean that I was horrid?" said Jane, standing still and looking away.

"IF being the best thing in the world and the thing I love more than anything else or anyone else I've ever seen, or shall see, or want to see," said George, showing a cool courage worthy of all the days at Vache-en-Écurie and elsewhere, "is horrid, then you *are* horrid."

"I don't quite understand," said Jane, whom any impartial observer would have thought uncommonly red in the face.

"That doesn't matter in the least," said George. "I do. And that's all that matters. I fell in love with you the minute I saw you grown-up. I'd have loved you just as much even if you *weren't* keen on pigs. I'd love you even if you were as silly as Edith Graham."

Jane did not answer, but was secretly pleased that Edith Graham was silly. One didn't like silly people and if other people didn't like them either, that was nice too.

There was then an embarrassing silence. George did not want to scare the beautiful strange bird who was sitting on its branch, so near him. Jane waited. George also waited.

"Do you like Browning?" she said suddenly.

George, puzzled, wondering if this was a Test for Lovers, and whether his answer would decide his fate, said he liked the bits he knew.

"So do I," said Jane, looking away from him,

> "'then the silence grows
> To that degree, you half believe
> It must get rid of what it knows
> Its bosom does so heave.'"

"If that is all," said George, speaking very calmly for fear of breaking this strange spell, "it can stop heaving. Jane!" and he put an arm round her. As she stood quite still he put his other arm round her. She tucked her head under his chin and there they stood, the picture of romance, or idiocy, or nature at her eternal task, or any of a million things that are all one.

George relaxed his hold.

"I could hardly breathe," said Jane. "When shall we get married?"

"Do you mean—I mean—oh, dash, do you really—"

"But of *course* I love you," said Jane, rather indistinctly owing to her face being again pressed against George's manly bosom.

"My *Precious* Pig-Fancier!" said George, inspired to poetic heights he had never dreamed of. "Let me look at you!"

He removed his arms, but very gently, lest she might take alarm and vanish.

"It's all right. It's you and you're there," he said. "Will you mind marrying a farmer?"

"Of course not," said Jane. "I'd die if I had to live in London—or even Barchester. We'd better tell Granny. And tomorrow I could ring Mother up. It's no good tonight because she and Father are dining with the Grantlys and it would excite them too much."

"I think," said George, "if we are going to tell Mrs. Crawley we ought to ring your mother up tonight. She'll want to be the first to know. You could quite well ring up the Grantlys and ask to speak to your mother and she can tell them if she likes. I say—DARLING—do you think your mother will like me?"

"Tell me first if yours will like me," said Jane.

"Oh Lord! you are going to wear the trousers from the word Go," said George, rather coarsely. But we think he was fairly correct in his prophecy, for all Crawley descendants were masterful; Octavia Needham, eighth and youngest child of the deanery, being a striking example.

"Do you know the poem abut the Bishopess?" said Jane.

"No, but I'd love to—if *you* say it," said George.

"I don't know the beginning," said Jane. "It's all about how she bullies the Bishop and usurps all his prerogatives. The first verse ends, 'So I took my husband's apron off, And put it on myself,' and each verse ends like that, about his waistcoat and his gaiters and all the things that have two syllables."

"Well, my love, I like the sentiments," said George, "but I'm damned—sorry, angel, but you'll have to get used to an ex-soldier's coarse way of speaking—if I'll take my breeches or anything else off for you to wear."

"But I wouldn't *want* to," said Jane. "Unless you had a very old pair of trousers you didn't want and I could put them over my breeches on very cold winter mornings if there was a pig ill, or anything."

"I believe you would, darling,"said George. "I know Martin Leslie says he can never keep a good pair of corduroy trousers because as soon as he's got the stiffness out of them, Sylvia takes them. She takes his for cows, and you mean to take mine for pigs, so it's all the same. I say, I wonder where your sister and John-Arthur have got to."

Jane said they might go and look; their first journey together, she added, so of course George had to kiss her again and they walked on in what to a dispassionate onlooker might have appeared like two mild drunks going home on a Saturday night, but was really the difficulty of adjusting their steps to their close proximity.

"Perhaps they've gone back into the Close," said George, but even as he spoke the couple appeared, each with an arm round the other's waist and talking nineteen to the dozen.

"Hullo, Jane," said her sister. "We're having a terrific argument about Crosse Hall."

"Do take my side, George," said Mr. Crosse. "This girl says we ought to have oil heating. I was telling her how difficult it is to keep the house warm in winter. There used to be a fire in every room, so all the old retainers tell me, and it was one man's job to bring up the coals. We do have one in what was my mother's sitting-room sometimes. Father and I like sitting there."

"I do wish I'd known your mother," said Grace to Mr. Crosse, "but she was dead before we knew your people. At least before I did. Granny knew her of course and says she was an absolute angel."

"And I wish to goodness she had known you," said Mr.

Crosse. "She always wanted a daughter-in-law, but I couldn't oblige. I feel a perfect beast doing it now when she isn't here."

"But she'll be just as pleased now," said Grace with a calm efficiency that impressed George Halliday, though he was glad his Jane was more yielding. "I'd like to use her room very much, but we must ask your father first—at least we must find out carefully and not frighten him."

"Bless you, my girl," said Mr. Crosse. "You think of everything. I wonder if Mrs. Morland would help."

"Do I know her?" said Grace. "Oh! you mean *the* Mrs. Morland. The one that writes the Madame Koska books."

"The same," said Mr. Crosse. "And might have been my stepmother, I gather, if she could have brought herself to it. I'd rather like a stepmother. Why do stepmothers in fairy stories never have stepsons, only stepdaughters. And if they have stepsons in novels there is always trouble. Dear, dear, what a world."

"Platoon! 'SHUN!!" said George suddenly. Mr. Crosse automatically stiffened to attention, unstiffened and laughed.

"Do I gather," said George Halliday, "that you and Miss Grace Crawley are engaged? If not, forever hold your peace."

"I'm engaged, too," said Jane.

"Dear me, that seems to make three," said Mr. Crosse, "unless—?"

"Of course I'm engaged too, you old fool," said George affectionately. "And what's more, my lad, we'll be brothers-in-law," which seemed so funny to these not so young soldiers of the war that lay behind, that they both laughed consumedly while their future wives looked on as mothers may look at their infants and tell them not to make so much noise, dear.

"I think," said George Halliday, "that we had better take the girls to the deanery and tell Mrs. Crawley. Then we can beat a masterly retreat and leave our betrotheds to hold the fort," which seemed good and sensible advice. So they all went through the twilight and into the deanery where Dr. and Mrs. Crawley were peacefully talking with Canon and Mrs. Joram in the drawing-room overlooking the Close. The Jorams were delighted to see the girls and their cavaliers, who were both known to them.

"How nice of you to bring the girls back, George," said Mrs. Crawley. "And Mr. Crosse too. I am sure the dinner was good. Old Burden always looks after us."

"He's a good old chap," said George. "He gave us grandfatherly advice about not overtipping, so of course we overtipped him."

The Dean said it must have been a very good dinner, to judge by the hour. He had, he said, listened to the nine o'clock news. Trouble in the Near East as usual, or Middle East, one never knew which was which. Drat those small nations, he said, who could not keep their hands from picking and stealing and coveting their neighbour's canal or his pipe line, or anything that was his. Some of those toy nations, he said, could never be happy unless they were coveting their neighbour's ox and his ass. On the other hand, the advice given from heaven to the children of Israel, Exodus 23, appeared expressly to encourage them to take any land they fancied and drive out, massacre, and persecute the owners. But it was not given to us, he said, to understand all these things.

"I know, dear," said Mrs. Crawley kindly. "And now the girls have something to tell us, I think. Will you forgive us, Mrs. Joram?"

Mrs. Joram, who had been perfectly fascinated by the scene and had a strong feeling that something had happened among those young people, said perhaps she and her husband would go home now.

"No don't, dear," said Mrs. Crawley and though she barely gave a shadow of a glance towards her husband, Mrs. Joram took her meaning at once and said of course they would love to stay a little longer. We do not think that Canon Joram felt these Fine Shades, but as his wife wished to stay he was perfectly happy to do so.

"How *did* you know, Granny?" said Grace. "*We* didn't. I mean it just happened."

The Dean asked, rather peevishly, *what* happened?

"We were dining at the White Hart," said Grace, as the elder, "and then we went for a walk by the river, at least Jane and George Halliday did and I went for a walk with Mr. Crosse. The cathedral was looking as lovely as ever."

The Dean said it usually did, which was so unlike his kind manner of speech to his granddaughters that Grace stopped.

"So what did you do then?" said Mrs. Crawley, who could willingly have smitten her husband with his jaw-bone of an ass for being so stupid.

The girls looked at one another, a little alarmed by the Dean's manner, though if they had seen him quelling dissidents at a meeting in the chapter-house, they would have thought him at present as mild as a lamb.

"We all got engaged, grandfather," said Jane, who was perhaps his favourite.

"Got engaged? What do you mean?" said Dr. Crawley.

"But which to whom?" said Mrs. Crawley.

"I am sorry if we are being rather a trouble, Mrs. Crawley," said George Halliday, who was very fond of her. "Of course I've known Jane on and off for ages and I've always liked her awfully—and so did father," he added, perhaps with a slightly mean wish to enlist Mrs. Crawley's sympathy through his father's death. "And this evening I liked her more than ever and I asked her if she would marry me. Of course I'll tell you and the Dean everything you want to know about my affairs and I think I am justified in asking your approval. And before any announcement is made we must ask their parents' permission."

Grace said they were both over twenty-one.

"Never mind about that," said Mr. Crosse to his love. "You do the thing properly, or not at all."

"Jane will marry me in any case," said George calmly, "but if you could both be pleased it would make such a difference. And mother would be so pleased."

"With me," said Mr. Crosse, who had been champing at his bit to have an innings, if we may so express ourselves, "it is just the opposite. I have only met Grace a few times but I think I fell in love the first time only I didn't know it. Today I did. That's all really. If you want any references, sir," he added to the Dean, "perhaps you and my father could meet, and the head of the Bank would, I think, say I was clean, honest, and hard-working."

"Now listen, young men," said Dr. Crawley, almost threatening them with his great shaggy eyebrows. "A step at a time. I can *not* give permission."

The four betrotheds stood silent and rather frightened.

"Although you seem to forget it," said Dr. Crawley, "I am their grandfather and have not the patria potestas," which made both men feel rather silly. "I suggest that you should communicate with their parents. But as their parents are dining with the Grantlys, this is NOT the moment to ring them up."

Black despair descended on the betrothed couples. George, who had dealt with worse situations—though not where his heart was involved—saw the point of the Dean's words and was the first to pull himself together.

"I'm sorry, sir," he said. "I suppose falling in love makes one a bit silly. Jane and I will write to her father and mother. Meanwhile I shall go on being engaged whether Jane likes it or not. But couldn't you, sir, in loco parentis, give a qualified approval? And perhaps we could be married in the cathedral if you and Mrs. Crawley like it. Of course if we could all be married together—I mean both on the same day—it would be marvellous."

We doubt whether even this appeal would have moved the Dean, except for George's final words. If these marriages took place, it should be in the cathedral and he would do the marrying. A double wedding, in his own family, in his cathedral where the Bishop had no jurisdiction. It should be done.

"I think I might," said the Dean with a kind of grim approval. "What do you think, Mrs. Joram?" he said, suddenly noticing his guests who were sitting there, entranced.

"But of *course* you approve," said Mrs. Joram. "It will be perfectly marvellous. The whole cathedral to marry them in and heaps of guests, and the early autumn flowers are so good for decoration they seem to have such long stalks. I mean those great brass jars or whatever they are need tall flowers; the short ones get so bunchy and swallowed up. Oh! I do *hope* the Palace won't send any wedding presents."

Her husband said that if he knew the Palace, it would send one very small present left over from the preceding Christmas wrapped in paper that had obviously been used before, which remark was very well received.

"I rather enjoy his lordship's not very frequent visits," said the Dean. "The episcopal throne is extraordinarily uncomfortable even with a cushion, and if the window above it is left open— there is a bit at the top that can be opened only we mostly don't because birds get in—there is a most disagreeable draught."

"Oh, I *know*," said Mrs. Joram. "It was just the same in the church at Pomfret Madrigal where I used to live. We had to put some wire netting over it. The vicar had a kind of butterfly net on a very long stick, but if he did manage to net a bird it always got its claws so entangled, poor lamb, that he had to cut the net to get it out, and even then he didn't like to hold it too tightly in case he hurt it and usually it escaped and flew up into the roof and started all over again."

"If the Dean felt any impatience at this Scene from Clerical Life, he did not say so, for Mrs. Joram was, as it were, the spoilt child—or rather, indulged, for no one could call her spoilt—of the Close.

"Birds or no birds, the window shall be open," said the Dean.

"Curfew shall *not* ring tonight," said his irreverent grand-daughter Jane.

The Dean looked at her from under his shaggy eyebrows.

"Darling, I didn't mean to interrupt," said Jane, most un-truthfully. "And you *must* look at your eyebrows in the looking glass when you shave because one of them is like that fish that has a kind of long thing like a soft fishing-rod dangling over its mouth to attract smaller fish."

As all those elders present were familiar with pictures of that fish in the Natural History Books of their childhood—in the Dean's case the delightful books of Miss Arabella Buckley, which we should like to see again—they couldn't help laughing. And so pleasant was the atmosphere of this exciting evening that the Dean laughed too.

"Of course," said Dr. Crawley, suddenly remembering to spoil as a grandfather and command as a Dean, "we must remember all this is subject to your parents' consent," to which his grand-daughter Grace irreverently said that she was free, white, and over twenty-one. But seeing that her grandfather did not ap-prove she kissed him very affectionately and said she was sorry. She had just remembered, she added, that she first saw John-Arthur at a children's Christmas party wearing a kilt.

"Not my fault," said Mr. Crosse. "Nannie's. She told mother that her last young gentleman always had a kilt for parties and bullied her into it. Thank God it was only tweed, not a sham tartan."

He then wondered if he should not have said Thank God in front of two clergymen, one his future grandfather-in-law, but thought it better to let the matter rest.

"I have been trying," said Mrs. Joram plaintively, "to go for the last half-hour at least. William, we *must* go. Mrs. Crawley will be very busy."

"All the business I have, Lavinia, is to get these young men off the premises and go to bed," said Mrs. Crawley, though not unkindly.

Her future grandsons-in-law rose as one man, stiffened, saluted, and advanced a pace.

"Good-night, grandmother-in-law," said George Halliday. "Good-night, sir. Thank you most awfully."

Mr. Crosse also thanked the Crawleys for their kindness.

"Now you girls," said Mrs. Crawley, "take these young men down and see them off," which the girls, almost blushing—if our young do blush now—did.

"It reminds me of the evening you proposed to me, Josiah," said Mrs. Crawley. "I think we took three quarters of an hour to say good-night and Mama came down with a flat candlestick because they *would* not have electric light till years after everyone else and frightened you away."

The Dean, apparently rather proud of this amorous interlude, said one could only be young once.

"That," said Dr. Joram getting up, "is a matter of common knowledge to all our generation. Come along, Lavinia. Good-night Mrs. Crawley, and all my sincerest wishes and prayers for the happiness of your children. Good-night, Crawley."

The Dean, who felt not unreasonably that Canon Joram had rather usurped the place of leading man, said good-night, and then repenting said My dear fellow. As this was obviously a preface to one of what his wife irreverently called Mr. Crawley's Curtain Lecture, the Jorams, with thanks for a delightful evening, escaped, both going downstairs rather loudly to warn the lovers, who were discovered in the hall at least an arm's length apart. They were all nice, well-brought up children—for so they remain to us—and said good-bye prettily. George opened the front door for the Jorams, waited till they were safely down the steps, and shut it again.

"And now you two boys must go home," said Mrs. Crawley over the banisters. "Kiss the girls and go along," and such is the power of a future grandmother-in-law (and in the girls' case a loved grandmother) that the young people submitted very pleasantly. The front door banged.

"And now, both go to bed," said Mrs. Crawley. "Off with you," and having watched them go upstairs she followed her husband into his study.

"Well?" she said sitting down.

"Well," said Dr. Crawley firmly. "Extremely well," and we think he was right.

CHAPTER 9

As our reader has doubtless foreseen, everyone was pleased with the news. The Crawleys were of some standing in Barsetshire, connected with the Grantlys and hence slightly with the Omniums, and all their supporters sent presents to both girls. Mr. Crosse had not county roots yet, but his father had made a good beginning and probably his grandchildren would be entirely of the county; though here there was some feeling, for East and West Barsetshire were in sporadic rivalry, felt in the Close and even as far as Allington at one end and Beliers at the other (not to speak of the large new manufacturing suburb of Hogglestock where children who had never been beyond their own streets exchanged good Saxon abuse in bardic verse, such as "Dirty West, Hole in your Vest" and "Silly East, You're a Beast"; only the adjectives were rather stronger); the one rallying as it were to the brides' party, the other to the bridegrooms'. As for George Halliday there was no doubt about his being on the right side. Hallidays had, as we know, been at Hatch End in West Barsetshire for well over two hundred years, compared with which the Crosses were, in the language of the Lake Country, offcomes; tolerated and even liked in East Barsetshire, but still slightly suspect in West. Mr. Crosse's marriage would probably do more to settle the family position than Lord Crosse's quite considerable wealth, or his valuable work in and for the county.

Mr. Crosse, though truly in love, was still able to do his work at the bank (whatever it was) as competently as ever and had an extremely intelligent and progressive grasp of policy, which made his father very happy. It had been decided that none of the persons concerned should say anything till the parents of the girls had been told and given their consent. As Mr. Crosse had pointed out, both girls were over twenty-one and no consent was needed, but they would have been surprised and very unhappy if their parents had not at once agreed. Before the news was made public—though a quite remarkable number of people had come to know of it—Lord Crosse asked his son to bring Grace Crawley to lunch so that she might meet her future father-in-law and see her future home.

So on an appointed day Mr. Crosse took leave from his banking, called for Grace at the deanery, and drove her over to Crosse Hall. It is a very beautiful drive but we doubt whether either of them was cognisant of anything but the fact that they were alone together in Mr. Crosse's very comfortable car.

Peters, the butler, who used to be at Pomfret Towers, opened the door.

"We are very pleased to see you, miss," he said. "Mr. Simnet, the Reverend Joram's butler, passed the remark to me when I was in Barchester yesterday that the Alliance was considered in the Close to be most satisfactory and I beg to offer you my best wishes, miss. His Lordship is in the drawing-room," and he conducted them with some ceremony through the wide corridor, opened the drawing-room door, stood aside to let the couple past and said, "Miss Crawley, my lord and Mr. John."

Grace, a little shy, saw a pleasant not too elderly gentleman sitting with a lady, but as they were near a window with their backs to the light she could not recognize the guest.

"I am very glad to see you here, my dear," said Lord Crosse, taking Grace's hand. "I have always hoped that my son would marry and I see that he has been very wise as well as lucky. My wife would have said the same," and then he kissed Grace, not (as she said afterwards to her sister Jane) lecherously, as one or two of their father's contemporaries did (or so the girls felt it, though nothing would have surprised, nay shocked, any of these very middle-aged gentlemen more than for their salute to be so interpreted), but very nicely and uncle-ishly.

"Thank you, *very* much, Lord Crosse," she said. "I'm most awfully sorry about Lady Crosse. I should have loved to have a mother-in-law. Mother says father's father and mother were much nicer than even her own ones," which made Lord Crosse laugh.

"And now I want you to meet Mrs. Morland," said Lord Crosse.

Mrs. Morland, who was, consciously or unconsciously—and we think the latter—taking in the scene, parts of which would doubtless appear in one of her delightful thrillers, greeted Grace warmly and congratulated Mr. Crosse on having found such a wife.

"It is *most* important to have a good wife," she said. "It makes all the difference."

Mr. Crosse, slightly overawed by Mrs. Morland, who was in one of her more Sibyllic moods, said he was sure it was.

"Your mother, whom I *wish* I had known," said Mrs. Morland, "must have been quite one of the nicest people and I am sure your Grace is. It is an excellent background and it will be so nice for you to have so many new relations. The Crawleys are all delightful. The women are always top dog of course. Not their fault—they are just born that way. After all, women are *far* stronger than men."

Mr. Crosse said he had noticed that.

"I do like people who stand up to me," he added. "It does me good. Mother always stood up to my father—in my remembrance at least."

"Your Grace will stand up to you both," said Mrs. Morland. "And you'll like it. But you must stand up to her. She'll like that too. Women need being stood up to, if that is English. I never was, unfortunately."

"You might have been, perhaps," said Mr. Crosse.

"If you mean your father doing me the honour to ask me to, it would not have done," said Mrs. Morland. "I should always have won. Now a man like Lord Pomfret could do it. He could stand up to anyone or anything."

"Lord Pomfret?" said Mr. Crosse. "I thought he was rather—I mean I thought—"

"Whatever you are trying to say is wrong," said Mrs. Morland, kindly but firmly. "If there is one man in Barsetshire who is just, understanding, and inflexible, it is he. When he is dead, having probably killed himself in work for the county—and in the Lords though London never suited him—people may realize what he was. Or they mayn't."

"I didn't know all that," said Mr. Crosse, impressed rather against his will by Mrs. Morland's words.

"You young men don't," said Mrs. Morland, "nor do some of the older ones. But you will see. And that boy of his is the same. He will be like his father—a fiery soul in a body that isn't up to it. With a good wife he will get through, just as Lord Pomfret has. Now, tell me about yourself and what your and Grace's plans are," and of course Mr. Crosse was delighted to do this till the gong, sounded with more than usual virtuosity by Peters in honour of the occasion, drove them all in to lunch.

"I didn't have champagne, my dear," said Lord Crosse to Grace, "but the Châteuneuf du Pape is very good. I hope you will like it."

"I *love* it," said Grace. "Father is pretty good at wine—he says if a clergyman can afford wine he ought to have a good cellar. I do hope you'll like him, Lord Crosse, and mother too. They really are rather nice."

"After meeting you, my dear," said Lord Crosse, "I am prepared to believe everything that is delightful about your people.

I very much want to know them. We shall probably be meeting before long to settle things."

"Oh, if you mean *settlements*," said Grace, "Jane and I both have some money that father looks after. He'll probably tell his lawyers to get together with yours. I say, I *do* like this house. It's just what a house ought to be like."

Lord Crosse was, to put it mildly, slightly flabbergasted. He had heard of the modern young woman and here she was. He wished—though when was he not wishing—that his wife could be there to help him. But the rest of the talk was very pleasant and easy and he was quietly glad to find that his prospective daughter-in-law had very sound views on the up-keep of an estate and expressed a special wish to see Peters in his pantry after lunch. He said she certainly should and while Peters was clearing away perhaps she would like to see the house.

What woman would not like to see a house. Grace was deeply interested in the rooms, admired what should be admired and even if she thought of possible changes for the better did not speak of them. Not even in the attics, until Lord Crosse raised the subject.

"It's a pity we could never use these for nurseries," said Lord Crosse. "They are too low and then all the stairs."

Grace said why not have the roof raised and put in a lift. "Isn't that what your daughter—I mean Mrs. Carter—did in the Old Manor House at Hatch End?" she added.

Lord Crosse looked at her.

"That is an idea," he said. "Make the attic floor into a sort of flat, as my girl did with hers."

"The rooms at the back will make splendid nurseries," said Grace, "they get most of the sun. If you can't fit a lift in, you will have to build a lift shaft onto the outside. That room at the end of the passage would make a nice nursery pantry with a sink and a gas-ring. And you'll want a speaking tube to the kitchen of course."

"It all sounds very sensible," said Lord Crosse. "And how soon will you want it?"

Grace, who had as usual been happily talking over everything in her plans, looked at her future father-in-law with interest.

"Well, it all depends on when the wedding is," she said. "My grandfather wants to do the service. When would you like it to be? I think soon would be rather nice, only we must see what Jane wants."

"And who is Jane?" said Lord Crosse, vaguely wondering if it was a rich aunt, or a very special dressmaker.

"My sister that's engaged to George Halliday," said Grace. She nearly said Of course, but a second's reflection had told her that there was no valid reason why Lord Crosse should know. "We want to be married on the same day in the cathedral. You will come, won't you?"

"Of course I will," said Lord Crosse. "You know, my dear, I am not so young as I was and can't quite keep up with you. No, I don't want to know now," he went on, seeing that this handsome girl was already preparing to run everything, including her own wedding. "I think we shall get on very well. And I very much want you to know my daughter, Mrs. Carter, at Hatch End. Suppose we go down now and see what Mrs. Morland and John-Arthur are doing."

"I know what I have been doing," said Grace. "I'm being forward. Mother is always trying to cure me. Have I been rather a pest? If I have I'm most awfully sorry. You see, I get over-excited whenever I think of being married and living with your son. I can't help loving him," and the managing young woman was suddenly lost in the girl who had just met an entirely new life face to face.

"Now, don't cry, my dear," said Lord Crosse. "People are often rather silly when they fall in love and are going to be married. I remember trying to fit my feet into the wrong boots for nearly ten minutes when I was first engaged. One loses count of everything."

Somehow the vision of a young Lord Crosse, perhaps the age that John-Arthur was now, madly trying to force a right-hand foot into a left-hand shoe—as another had tried one summer evening long ago a-sitting on a gate—brought a sudden swimming of tears to Grace's eyes.

"I am *very* sorry about your—about John-Arthur's mother," she said.

"Thank you, my dear," said Lord Crosse. He was never good at expressing his deeper feelings and knew it. His wife could have done it for him. He stood looking out of the window onto the garden that he and his wife had planned and made and loved.

"'It *was* the azalea's breath and she *was* dead,'" he said aloud, to himself.

Grace heard the words and felt that under them there was a poignancy beyond her understanding.

Lord Crosse said they would go down now and if she would visit Peters, the old butler would really appreciate it. He took her to the butler's pantry and left her there.

"I suppose Lord Crosse told you all about us, Peters," said Grace, accepting an armchair with a red plush seat, evidently come down in the world.

"Why, miss, in a manner of speaking he *did*," said Peters. "And I may say miss, and also on behalf of the rest of the Staff here, though it is not what I was accustomed to at The Towers of course, that we was all highly delighted to hear of the engagement. Mr. Tozer—whom you may have met, miss, the head of the Catering Establishment in Barchester—said the Close thoroughly approved, being as he knows the Upper Servants all round the Close—except of course at the Palace where they don't even keep a Man and have mostly foreigners from abroad. I understand from him, miss, that there will be two weddings on the same day."

Grace said, oh yes. She and her sister, who was engaged to

Mr. Halliday at Hatch End, meant to be married in the cathedral by their grandfather, the Dean.

"And then, miss, we hope that you and Our Mr. Crosse will be residing here," said Peters. "His lordship is not one to complain, miss, unless it was about the libery windows not locked at night, or a book put back in the wrong place after being dusted; but he is alone too much, miss. I might even say without offence that he mopes. Mrs. Morland, a very nice lady, comes to see him and that cheers him up, but he never got over the loss of her ladyship, miss, nor never will. There *has* been people, miss," said Peters, so far forgetting himself as to sit down, "as has said he ought to marry again. He will not, miss. It was the same with Lord Pomfret—not the present Lord Pomfret who came into the title later, but *my* Lord Pomfret. After the late Lady Pomfret's death he had no pleasure except riding about the place with Mr. Wicklow, the agent, whose sister is the present Lord Pomfret, and he died just before the war."

It was lucky that Grace had been brought up to know something about families and could disentangle these remarks, which would otherwise have seemed almost like a monologue from Mrs. Nickleby. She said That was very sad and she hoped that if she and Mr. Crosse came to live with Lord Crosse he would feel happier.

"Lord Crosse showed me all over the house," said Grace "and I told him one could make a very good nursery flat on the attic floor with some alterations."

"I understand, miss, that the late Lady Crosse had the same idea," said Peters, "but unfortunately her ladyship died before any of the family was married. Probably, miss, you know Mrs. Carter, his lordship's daughter, over at Hatch End. She is a very nice lady and has a nice young family. This house needs some young people, miss."

"Well, Mr. Crosse and I will do our best, Peters," said Grace. "And now I must go. I hope you will be at the wedding."

"Indeed, miss, I should be honoured," said Peters. "Now that, if I may say so, miss, is where a Lady comes in. His Lordship is a most satisfactory employer, miss, but it needs a Lady to give the final touch."

"As you do to the silver, I am sure, Peters. I couldn't help noticing at lunch how beautifully it shone," said Grace.

She could not have given more acceptable praise. If a butler can blush, Peters did. But he was not one to give himself away.

"I may say, miss, I have Studied silver," said Peters. "It's not only the plate powder, nor the methylated, nor anything else, miss; it's the handling of it. I can assure you, miss, I've breathed on the spoons and rubbed them gently round and round in the palm of the hand more than you'd believe, and then give them a finish with the shammy."

"I say, Peters," said Grace, "how often do you wash the shammy? I wash mine that I clean my own bits of jewellery with almost once a fortnight in warm rainwater and the best soap flakes and rinse it two or three times. I often clean mother's best silver too and then I polish it very gently with the shammy, and on the palm of my hand, I mean that fat part at the bottom of one's thumb."

Had Peters ever gone to church on Sunday evenings instead of sitting in the butler's pantry reading the more revolting of the Sunday papers, he might have said "Oh Lord, now lettest Thou Thy Butler depart in peace." Here was a mistress for Crosse Hall who Understood The Silver. The Tradition would continue. How many ladies in these degenerate days would speak of a shammy? Probably they all used those pink cloths with something or other in them, so that they were all covered with black marks off the silver and if you washed them they were just like any other bit of rag. Emotion choked him and Grace said did he ever try Koffo-cure pastilles; they were better than the Kurokoff ones.

But before this question could be answered the boy came in.

On seeing a lady, sitting in Mr. Peters's Own Room, and in His Special Chair, the boy stood astounded, waiting for the sky to fall.

"This is The Boy, miss," said Peters. "He has been under me for some time and he'll be wanting to better himself. If you happen to know of anyone in The Close miss, as wants a boy who has finished his schooling and wants to work in a gentleman's house, I should be glad to know. He's got a long way to go yet," said Peters, lest the boy might be too set up, "but if he goes on the way I learned him he might—I say might—be a butler some day."

"Please, miss," said the boy, "if I can't be a butler I'd like to go in the catering line. Dad knows Mr. Tozer and Mr. Tozer told Dad there was always a chance for a boy who wanted to rise. Scatcherd and Tozer he is, miss, Dinners, Balls, Masonic Meetings and Weddings Attended. It was him as did the wedding at Hatch End, miss, when the Reverend Choyce married Miss Merriman."

Peters, who liked to do all the talking himself and had seldom heard his underling say more than "Yes, Mr. Peters," or "No, Mr. Peters," was astounded, but also rather pleased. It was His teaching that had learned the Boy to speak proper and keep his nails clean and press his trousers. And now that so few people had an establishment suitable for a butler, there was something to be said for the catering trade, and Scatcherd and Tozer were framed for the high-class quality of butler or majordomo that they supplied.

"That's enough," he said, not unkindly. "If Miss Crawley hears of something, perhaps you'll be good enough, miss, to let me know and I will communicate it to the Boy. Thank Miss Crawley and then cut along."

The Boy gave the Scouts' salute, which Grace at once returned. He grinned and went away, shutting the door after him.

There was a silence.

"I am sure, Peters," said Grace, remembering her duties to the staff, "that he will give satisfaction after being under you. Tell him to let me know if he finds something suitable in Barchester and I will do what I can. And by the way, will you be staying on here?"

Peters went red in the face.

"Well, miss," he said, "I was considering whether I would retire, but if you are coming to live here, miss, after the Wedding I mean, I shall be glad to oblige. I know His Lordship's ways. And Mr. Crosse is, if I may say so, a very considerate gentleman. I valet both the gentlemen, miss, at present. At The Towers of course I would never have done such a thing. The gentlemen brought their own gentlemen with them in the hunting season, or if they didn't, one of the footmen valeted them. But times have changed."

"We shall get on together, Peters," said Grace getting up and putting out her hand. "And I look forward to seeing you at the wedding."

The butler shook his head without words and she went away.

In the library she found the father and son and Mrs. Morland, talking nineteen to the dozen.

"And how do you like the ancestral residence?" said Mr. Crosse. "We haven't got a ghost. We aren't old enough."

"Very much," said Grace. "I've been having a long talk with Peters. I gather that nothing will make him leave as long as there's a Crosse in the house," at which the company laughed.

"I have always been afraid of that," said Lord Crosse. "Mrs. Morland says I am keeping him on from cowardice, because I daren't give him notice."

"But, Lord Crosse, you will have to support him in any case," said Grace. "As long as he can work well you'll have to keep him—and you wouldn't get another like him. And when he can't work you will have to let him keep his cottage and add something to his Old Age Pension. Has he a wife?"

"Yes, a very nice woman," said Lord Crosse. "She works here every day. But we hardly ever see her, because she is terrified of the gentry. Peters married her after he came to me. A local woman."

"There you are," said Grace. "You'll have to help to support him because one does and when his wife can't work here any longer you'll have to help to support her too. Old pensioners never die. Mother has an old nurse like that and they all live for ever. Still, one must do it."

"Le respect humain," said Lord Crosse, whose French when he had to speak it was remarkably good. But we do not think he was heard.

"My sweet girl," said Mr. Crosse, "we must go. Gladly would I stay here all night gossiping, but I must get back to work. Being more or less self-employed I can take my time off when I like, but I always make it up. I'll run you back to the deanery first."

Lord Crosse bade Grace a very affectionate good-bye and kissed her. Mrs. Morland said she would send them the Omnibus Book of some of her novels, specially bound, and so they drove away.

"Tired?" said Mr. Crosse as they drove towards Barchester.

"Only nicely tired," said Grace. "I do like your father, John-Arthur. Do you think he really wants us to live with him?"

"The real question," said Mr. Crosse, "is, do *you* want to live with *him*? If you do, I'm your man. If you don't, well, I'm still your man."

"I expect," said Grace, looking out of the window, "your Mother would like us to."

Mr. Crosse pulled up on the grass verge.

"Come here Charlotte and I'll kiss yer," he said and put the same into execution. Grace, who was well educated, laughed and they drove on.

For George Halliday things were not so easy. Much as he would have liked to visit his lovely, quiet, dark-haired Jane, a

busy farmer cannot spend his time in dalliance. And if his Jane
came to see him, time would again be wasted: no, not wasted,
but it would be foolish to let his work grow slack and at this time
of year. With all the harvest in, the roots lifted and stored, there
would be more time—if there is ever time on a farm. So Jane,
who had nothing particular to do at the moment, went home for
a time to tell her parents all about it and then, with their consent,
for they were affectionate and sensible parents, came back to
stay at the deanery and visit Hatch End almost every day. Much
as George loved her, he feared that her visits might disorganize
his work; work that he could not delegate at present. But to his
great pleasure she made friends with the men, did odd jobs
about the place, showed a real knowledge of pigs which impressed everyone, and got on very well with Hubback and old
Mrs. Fothergill.

By a special Providence, or so George felt and blamed himself
for feeling it, Mrs. Halliday, together with her hostess Mrs.
Dunsford, had gone to Mentone; though not to the Pension
Ramsden but to a quiet hotel recommended by friends. Here
Miss Dunsford could come to lunch or tea with them. The
English church was near and there were quite a number of nice
English people and would be more as the colder weather drove
them out of their beloved country. Mrs. Dunsford always remained splendidly immune to Abroad. Mrs. Halliday had already some acquaintances in the town and found to her great
surprise that she now woke up every day feeling happy.

Perhaps Glad Confident Morning is what we most miss as we
get older, if our lives have not been altogether smooth. From
leaping out of bed and hurrying towards the business and
pleasure of the day, we wake wondering who we are. After not
ceasing from mental fight, we do remember and are slightly
depressed by it. We must do today the things we had put off
yesterday, if it isn't too late. We must keep the dull lunch
engagement that we accepted because we were too cowardly to

refuse it. We must—in the case of Mrs. Morland—get on with writing another book exactly like the last because what the Liberty Reader likes is A nice book like the last. We must answer our letters, pay our bills, do our local jobs, go to tea with poor Miss Buss because she is lonely; go and shout to Miss Beale who is deaf; look in on old Mrs. Griffin because she does so enjoy talking about herself—as indeed most of us do if we get the chance. If only we could do these jobs with zest our state would be the most blessed. Still, there are moments when we can recapture the joy of waking to another day and we are glad to say that Mrs. Halliday was now happier than she had been since the time—some two years ago—when her husband's health began visibly to fail and his feet were set on the journey from which no traveller returns.

Much to Mrs. Halliday's surprise—and we may say to her pleasure—she met Lady de Courcy whom she had known slightly at home, was asked to the Villa Thermogène, made fresh friends there and began to enjoy social life. Mrs. Dunsford, whose tastes were more in the clerical line, had made the acquaintance of the family of Mr. Highmore's great-uncle who had been English chaplain and found them agreeable. This was just as well, for if Mrs. Halliday and Mrs. Dunsford had kept themselves to themselves they would have had a dull time and possibly got rather tired of each other. As it was, while they much enjoyed their meals, or walks, or excursions together, each felt free to do as she pleased. And if our reader wishes to know how Miss Dunsford, who after all was the originator of the Riviera plan, liked the incursion of the older generation, we may tell her that Miss Dunsford had found a Slave Friend and for the first time in her life was tasting the sweetness of bullying someone else. We need not be sorry for the Slave Friend, for she was born to be one and like a delicate climbing plant needed a stout pole to twine round. And when we add that Miss Dunsford called the Slave Friend Wendy because her name was Bronwen and the Slave Friend called her Friendy, our reader will see how perfect the arrangement was.

Jane Crawley's almost daily visits to Hatch End naturally interested the village. The Choyces asked her to lunch and both fell in love with her. Hatch End as a whole stood aloof for a while, as if it had done with every fresh wave of invaders from earliest time, but as news filtered down from Hatch House via Panter the carter, Hubback when she came down to shop or to have tea with one of her village friends, and old Mrs. Fothergill's slow, endless Barsetshire talk at the kitchen door with everyone who came into the yard, they began to think well of the affair. And when Jane—not in the least realizing how important this was—first asked Mrs. Panter, whose whole soul was in her washing and ironing, which last she did at her open doorway the better to exchange gossip, whether she would wash and lightly press two jersey-nylon nightgowns, as the Barchester laundry did them so badly, her conquest of Hatch End was complete. Caxton, the old estate carpenter, said she was a lady as *was* a lady; not one of those, he said darkly, as would use a chisel as a screwdriver, or break the tip off a gimlet using it on wood as was too hard, or try to saw through a piece of wood as had a knot in it with his best saw. In fact, he added, for he was old and a past master of his craft, she was a top-sawyer. As few of the younger generation knew what he meant they paid no attention, but the compliment did come to George's ears and gave him deep pleasure.

George, with what we consider very nice feeling, had told Lady Graham about his engagement almost at once. She had of course been deeply interested and made—as her mother Lady Emily Leslie would have done—affectionately searching enquiries about the bride. The Crawleys were friends of long standing, though not intimates, and their granddaughter seemed to Lady Graham a most suitable chatelaine for Hatch House, so she asked George to bring his betrothed to lunch one day and not to bother about clothes. This however was not meant to be taken too literally. George named a day when he would not be cleaning out the farm drain or the pig-sties, or lying under the tractor covered with axle-grease an oil. Jane drove out to Hatch End in her normal clothes, picked him up and drove to Holdings. Lunch was pleasant. Lady Graham admired Jane's looks and was impressed by her knowledge of pigs, as was Sir Robert. George sat eating his lunch with adoring looks at his Jane and longing to get back and see what was wrong with Caxton's electric lathe.

It was not often that Lady Graham was seriously ruffled or discomposed, but her daughter Edith had given her a good deal of trouble of late. Sir Robert Graham may have been a martinet, but he was fond of his wife and had let her have her own delightful, maddening way in most things. The boys he had kept firmly under his own control. They were now all in the Brigade of Guards and well able to run their own lives. His daughters he had left to his wife, having a well-placed confidence in her capacity for handling them. But the youngest of a family is always the most likely to be the spoilt one. Not a deliberate spoiling—that may be left to the grandmothers who cannot do much harm. As one of Lady Graham's nannies had said of Lady Emily Leslie when she had interfered quite outrageously, though with her own charm, in some nursery matter, "Poor lady. She likes it, so I let her." Only Edith remained. And much as we love her, admire and respect Agnes Graham, it must be admitted that she had allowed her youngest child far too much rope.

The hedges and fences that the young desperately need—though when we are young we do not know this—had been levelled before her, yet all—at the moment—was vanity. What availed Edith's trial of estate management, her visit to America, her return with a wardrobe of enchanting clothes, if she had not charity—by which we mean in this case a true consideration for the feelings and the needs of others. Her grandmother, Lady Emily Leslie, had once said that Clarissa was an Undine. Now it fitted Edith. An enchanting creature without a soul—or a soul that had lagged behind the body that hid it. It was all a great nuisance and if someone of sufficient station and means sought her hand, both her parents were ready to approve. Both liked George Halliday whom they had known all his life. He had a home and a background and was of unimpeachable integrity. That he was not rich did not much affect their feelings. Edith would be suitably dowered. They liked and trusted George and he was a good farmer and citizen, rising steadily in county esteem. But had he the strength to bear with or direct their self-willed youngest daughter? They also liked, in a different way, young Mr. Crosse, perhaps not with as much background as George, but a good solid one, his family on the up-grade in East Barsetshire and an excellent position in the banking world. Now each had chosen his bride. And as Mr. Crosse had never shown the faintest sign of being in love with Edith—or no more than many young men and young women feel for one another in neighbourly intercourse—he was not to blame if he fell in love with a young woman of a more suitable age.

Both men had told Lady Graham of the double engagement before it was formally announced. Her ladyship had thought it extremely suitable and said if Jane Crawley wanted to see more of Hatch End she would be delighted to have her at Holdings for a visit as George's mother was away. Jane sent her thanks to Lady Graham but remained quite content to pay her almost daily visits to Hatch End, the better to learn about the farm, returning to the Close after tea.

Now, seeing Jane again with fresh eyes, Lady Graham was struck by her unusual, quiet beauty: the oval face, so rare now, the dark shining hair, the violet eyes and—a great asset in Lady Graham's opinion—the elegant bones, telling of race.

"This is most delightful," she said, folding Jane in her soft scented embrace. "I remember your father so well. I used to dance with him when I was a girl and he wasn't a clergyman yet. I wonder if any of your children will be clergymen," said her ladyship, who often thought aloud just as her mother did; though as none of her thoughts could really hurt anyone it didn't much matter.

"It would rather depend," said Jane. "I mean there are livings and livings. The one father's grandfather had at Hogglestock was awful. I mean about a hundred and sixty pounds a year and he had a family and one girl from the village to help."

"It is extraordinary," said Lady Graham, "how everyone used to have at least one servant even if they were frightfully poor."

Even the Micawbers had one, George said, and her ladyship smiled the kind of understanding smile that one assumes when one doesn't really understand.

"But, Lady Graham," said Jane, "lots of people who are quite well-off don't have one now—or only a daily—because they like the house to themselves. Only one can't run the farm *and* a nursery—at least I don't think I can, especially with more than one."

George said One what?

"One baby of course," said Jane. "Of course I could tie it up in a shawl on my back like peasants—"

"No darling, you couldn't," said George. "Or even if you could, you shan't. When we have a family Hatch House will be like Bolton Abbey in the Olden Time with half the village round the doors wanting to help at half a crown an hour—or probably five shillings by then," but he felt, with a delicacy for which many of his friends would not have given him credit, that he and Jane were not talking Lady Graham's language, so he asked after Edith.

"Oh, I do want to see her again," said Jane. "George says she is delightful," at which George looked rather sheepish, for though he had quite got over thinking he was in love with Edith, the fact of having given her a piece of his mind, almost brutally, had somewhat established for her a kind of claim on him.

"She went to lunch at the Towers," said Lady Graham, "but she promised to be back early to see you. I don't much like her driving alone but there it is."

"Oh, she'll be all right, Lady Graham," said George with the easy optimism we have for the affairs of others. "She's very steady so long as she keeps her temper."

"I do wish she would settle to something though," said Lady Graham. "She is like a hen trying to cross a road," which maternal reflection made the young people laugh. Then Lady Graham put George through a searching examination about the linen at Hatch House and the kitchen equipment, to which Jane listened with great interest.

"I know," said her ladyship, "that your mother has a lot of very beautiful linen. She showed me the linen cupboard—or really it is a linen room—quite beautifully kept, with big rollers to hang the best damask tablecloths on so that they will not crease. You will be able to give delightful dinner-parties—you and Jane," and her ladyship went off into a kind of housekeeper's dream of dinner-parties and festivities, to all of which her guests listened with apparent interest, while really thinking of one another.

"You know Jane is rather a pig expert," said George when he could get a word in edgeways, "and if I may take her round after lunch and find Goble—"

"Oh, I _would_ like that," said Jane.

Lady Graham said they must do whatever they liked and then they had coffee on the terrace in the sun very pleasantly. The sound of a car was heard and round the corner came Edith with her cousin Ludo.

"Dear Ludo, how nice of you to come," said his cousin Agnes. "You have grown again."

Lord Mellings said Only sideways this time and indeed he had put on weight in a most becoming way since the previous year and was filling out in proportion with his height.

"George Halliday you know," said Lady Graham, "and this is Jane Crawley, the Dean's granddaughter who is engaged to George Halliday."

Lord Mellings shook hands in a very friendly way with a kind of slight bow that much impressed Jane.

"Hullo, Edith," said George Halliday.

"Hullo, yourself," said Edith. "I'm delighted to hear of your engagement," which she said with a prim air that amused her elders. "What shall I give you for a wedding present? Two French hens or a Partridge in a Pear Tree?"

"What I really want more than anything is a pair of long-handled shears for nipping off high-up branches," said George. "Tozer and Burden in Barley Street have the best."

"I'll ask Goble to get them next time he's in Barchester," said Edith carelessly. "What's she like? Oh, there she is."

George was for the moment almost stunned by Edith's bad manners—indeed amounting to rudeness and, he thought, deliberate rudeness, though why he could not imagine. He would very much like to have smacked her, but these Petruchio manners do not do at all unless one wants to marry the girl: which he certainly didn't. So he turned away and talked to Lord Mellings about a vixen, well known in Hatch End and popularly supposed to have moved over from the Pomfret Estate when the earths in Hamaker Spinney were stopped.

"Thanks awfully," said Lord Mellings. "I'll tell Uncle Roddy. And Giles. He knows every fox's name and address and telephone number in the county. I wish I did," and his dark eyes filled with melancholy, for though he would have liked to do everything a future landowner should do, he had never been able quite to conquer his boyhood fear of horses and rode passably to hounds from a sense of duty alone, whereas his younger brother could ride anything with four legs.

"Never mind, you know a lot of other things," said George, sorry for the tall young man who, like his father, seemed to be overburdened by the station in life to which he was called by no wish of his own. "What do you think of my Jane?"

"A winner!" said Lord Mellings. "I say, what would you both like for a wedding present? I was thinking—only it's rather dull and you couldn't show it to people—"

"Fire away," said George. "It's a perfect description of pornographic drawings that you have to keep under the bed."

"Ass!" said Lord Mellings. "What I meant was a Life Subscription to the London Library."

"Oh, I *say!*" said George. "Really, Ludo, you can't!"

"But I can," said Lord Mellings. "There's a bit of unexpected cash turned up—a bad investment that suddenly began to pay—that came to me under old uncle Pomfret's will. So shut up."

"I shut," said George. "Jane *will* be pleased. Come and talk to her," and he took Lord Mellings in tow and left him to talk with Jane.

Then he saw Edith standing alone on the terrace and felt sorry for her. She had behaved very badly, but probably she hadn't meant to. So he went up to her.

"I'm sorry," she said. "I wish I was dead."

"Well, don't," said George. "What do you think of my Jane?"

This might have seemed a want of tact after Edith's rudeness, but George had known her since she was born, broadly speaking, and could in years almost have been her father, and was sorry for her. No one's enemy but her own and a sad thing to be.

"She walks in beauty like the night," said Edith. "And I'm terribly sorry I was rude. I'm not always rude. Something makes me be rude when I don't want to. I was rude to John-Arthur once too. Is his wife—I mean the one he's going to marry—as pretty as Jane?"

"Difficult to say," said George. "She and Jane are day and night—sun and moon. Lord! how poetical. I mean Grace is as fair as Jane is dark. I'm awfully glad she is dark."

"Gold and ebony," said Edith. "I'm only ordinary brown."

"You know, you think too much about yourself, my girl," said George. "Your brown is very nice. Just stop thinking about it."

Edith was silent and George supposed he had offended her again. Rum things, girls. But his dark Jane wasn't rum. She was Jane.

A general move was now made by the party towards the farm, except Lord Mellings who stayed behind with his cousin Agnes. Not that he disliked pigs, but the Pomfret side of him turned unconsciously to Pomfret blood and he loved to hear his cousin Agnes talk about her own mother, Lady Emily Leslie, a sister of the old Lord Pomfret.

"Cousin Agnes," he said presently after some family gossip, "may I ask you something?"

Many of us would take alarm at such a question, wondering if our secret sin or vice has been discovered, or if Jones wants to touch us for a fiver, or if Rebecca wants to borrow our fox fur again to wear at a wedding. But Lady Graham had, most luckily for her, no imagination at all. To be practical to one's finger ends, well capable of looking after oneself, but to give the impression of frail beauty that must be cushioned and sheltered; what more could one wish? Beyond her husband and her children and her home—whether conscious of it or not and we rather think not—Lady Graham had never had any immortal longings in her. Now, with three sons doing well in their father's profession and two daughters happily married, what more could she want. Only one thing and that, as we all know, was to see her youngest daughter, her most difficult child, safely and comfortably married and off her hands.

"Of course, Ludo dear," she said.

"What the hell is the matter with Edith—sorry, Cousin Agnes, but it is really like that," said Lord Mellings, going rather red in the face but manfully holding his ground.

"If I knew, Ludo, I would tell you," said Lady Graham. "Of course the beginning is that she is a spoilt child."

"But weren't you and Cousin John and Cousin David spoilt?" said Lord Mellings.

"Dear boy, what an interesting question," said Lady Graham, attracted, as we all are, by the prospect of talking about herself. "I daresay you are right. Darling John wasn't exactly spoilt, because Gay died—his first wife whom we all loved—and he learnt to lean on himself in the hard way, till he met dear Mary and married again. I don't think I was exactly spoilt. Darling Mamma gave me lovely holidays and I had a most delightful London season and then I got married. Your Cousin Robert proposed to me at a ball."

"Yes, darling Cousin Agnes, it is a divine story and I can almost tell it backwards, word for word," said her irreverent young cousin. "Of course Cousin David has terrific charm, but he is bone selfish—except that he can't be selfish to Rose because she is selfish in a stronger way than he is. Women mostly are."

His cousin Agnes did not reply. Lord Mellings half wondered if he had put his foot in it.

"I don't quite know, dear boy," she said with the smile of piercing sweetness that was so like her mother's. "The Pomfret women *are* difficult. Darling Mamma was an angel if ever there was one, but she *would* reorganize one's party, or get all the furniture moved, or there was that time—years ago, at Rushwater—when she took up enamelling and would have her furnace in the serving-room which made it so awkward for the servants when they brought the meals in. It annoyed Papa, but he said nothing and one day he got up from the lunch table and ordered the car to take him to London and went on a cruise to the Northern capitals of Europe," and her ladyship fell silent in a dream of the past. Her cousin was overcome with laughter.

"Dear Ludo, I do like to hear you laugh," said Lady Graham, apparently unconscious of the cause. "Do you know," she added, after looking at him intently, "you are nearly grown up."

Lord Mellings went red in the face in a kind of mixture of pride and shame.

"Which," said her ladyship, "is curious, because as a rule men mature less quickly than women," and she looked at him with a sort of challenge.

"I never knew that, Cousin Agnes," said Lord Mellings. "Edith and I are about the same age, but I should say that I am more grown up than she is. Anyway I hope I'm not so up against things. I do wish I knew what was wrong, then perhaps I could help her."

"Oh, dear, you are so like your father," said Lady Graham. "Dear Gillie, he has always been the same ever since he came to the Towers on approval, oh, twenty years ago it must be. He has always been the pillar that other people lean on, the back that carries the burdens, the person to whom everyone takes their troubles—but he keeps his own troubles to himself and spends himself for the estate and the county—and the country in the House of Lords. He is the bravest as well as the most sensitive person I have ever known. Your mother didn't make him—he had made himself—but she saved him. She has stood behind him in everything, always."

Seldom did Agnes speak so seriously and deeply. Lord Mellings made no reply, no comment and sat thinking. From the farm a sound of voices came, the pig-party returning probably.

"I didn't know, Cousin Agnes," he said.

"Dear boy, one never *does* know about one's parents," said his cousin.

"It must be heaven to have someone behind one," said Lord Mellings, "but perhaps it is better for one to be the one behind and make that one's own heaven. Cousin Agnes, before they come back, I must say Edith has shown some foul tempers at the Towers sometimes. Even father roused himself and told her off. I couldn't help wondering if it was the same at home. I hope I'm not interfering."

"Not in the least, dear Ludo," she said, laying her hand on his.

"But she needs a strong hand. Her brothers don't stand any nonsense when they are here, but their home is the Brigade of Guards. Robert is always very busy and she is a little frightened of him. She does obey me—she has up till now—but I sometimes wonder what might happen if she didn't."

"Then I should come in," said Lord Mellings.

If she had not been sitting on a garden seat, Lady Graham would have sat flat down on the garden path.

"Ludo!" she said.

"I mean it," said Lord Mellings.

"It has been difficult for her," said Lady Graham, weakening.

"I daresay it has," said Lord Mellings. "A lot of things are difficult for all of us. Things have always been difficult for father, but he had mother to stand by him. I think I shall have to stand up to Edith. I can't have her bullying you, and Uncle Robert doesn't seem to notice much. I suppose he wouldn't give her a thrashing if she is rude to you, would he?"

Lady Graham, divided between a desire to laugh and to cry, and even more impressed by her young cousin's manner, said she didn't think so.

"Then I must see about it," said Lord Mellings. "I will not have you unhappy, Cousin Agnes. Aunt Emily, whom I do remember, could not have borne it. It was eight years ago that she died, Cousin Agnes. I was pretty young then, but I do remember her and her eyes—like a very loving hawk, so bright and brooding."

"Dear boy, how you remember," said Lady Graham. "There is some poetry somewhere in the Pomfrets. Darling Mamma had it. I don't think any of mine have—except perhaps Clarissa. You have it. If you *can* do anything about Edith, I won't interfere and I don't think Robert will notice. The boys do snub her occasionally but of course the Brigade keeps them in London and very busy. Do whatever you like. If it is a success I shall thank you forever. If it isn't it won't be your fault. Here they come back from the farm"; and there they all came, full of pig-talk and excitement about the approaching Barsetshire Agricultural.

There was tea in the Saloon, with much noise and cheerfulness. Then the party dispersed to their various homes on foot or in their car or someone else's. Lord Mellings found his cousin Edith and said good-bye.

"Come over again soon," he said. "And try to think of someone besides yourself. Not lots of people. Just one at a time. Your mother for instance. And don't be rude to people. It doesn't pay. And what's more *I* won't stand it. And if you are in difficulties, come to me," and he kissed her in a cousinly way and went off.

Luckily no one was about and Edith was free to behave as badly as she liked. Never in her life had she been spoken to like that! And by Ludo! Ludo, who was her own age or only a little older! Just because he was going to follow his cousins into the Brigade of Guards he thought he could be rude to her. She would jolly well be rude to him. How, she didn't quite know, but she certainly would. No one understood her, especially Ludo. She walked towards the farm, kicking everything she could kick, such as a loose stone on the drive or a fallen twig. All the flowers were a horrible colour, she felt. Reds and yellows, much too autumny. Well, it would be autumn before long and then winter and everyone was getting married and she would have to go to George's and John-Arthur's weddings, she supposed, to those awful deanery girls—though as she barely knew them the adjective was only used to lash herself into further self-pity. So angrily was she walking and talking that she nearly bumped into her father in the peaceful pursuit of eradicating dandelion roots from the grass border with a new gadget given to him by Sir Edmund Pridham who said it was a great help when your lumbago didn't let you stoop. Sir Robert had not got lumbago and had no intention of having it, but he liked the little tool.

"Careful, Edith," he said.

"Oh, sorry, father," said Edith. "I was just walking along and didn't notice."

"If you can't see an elderly retired general with a spud, you need spectacles," said her father. "Where are you off to?"

"Oh, I don't know, father," said Edith. "Just anywhere."

"I'll come with you then," said Sir Robert. "I want to see Goble."

Edith did not particularly want company, especially when her father had just seen her in a temper, but she was a little in awe of him, so she walked by his side to the farm. There was an old mounting-block in the big yard, near the pig-sties, and on this Sir Robert seated himself, so Edith sat down too.

"We'll wait for Goble," said Sir Robert. "He ought to be here soon. Meanwhile I want to know what you mean to do with yourself, Edith. You have been given your choice. You didn't stick to it. You had your American holiday. You are the only one of the family that does nothing. It won't do. I don't interfere with my daughters. That is your mother's affair. But if I find anyone being inconsiderate to *her*, then it is my business."

Never had Edith felt so surprised, hurt, offended, outraged; and what was worse, guilty. She could feel her face getting hotter and redder while her father, having said what he meant to say, sat by: rightfully annoyed but always prepared to be just.

"I don't understand, father," she said, and knew it was a lie. So did her father.

"You understand perfectly well," he said. "This term you will go back to the estate management school and do the whole course. I have accepted a post abroad for six months or more and shall be taking your mother. She needs a change. You can't stay here alone and I will not ask the Pomfrets to have you again. I shall find someone—probably in the Close—that you can live with while we are away. If you get your diploma or whatever it is, you can start real work here. And I may add that I shall be very glad of your help. Old soldiers never die; but they do get older. Understood?"

Edith's world was rocking, but she was a general's daughter and the sister of three professional soldiers.

"All right, father," she said, though in so small a voice that it was more a token than an outright acceptance.

"I daresay Mrs. Crawley will have you as a P.G.," her father said. "The deanery will be rather empty with both granddaughters married. And Mrs. Crawley understands girls. That's all," and he almost added: "Dismiss."

"Very well, father," said Edith. "But I might marry a curate."

At this threat her father laughed heartily. The admonishment had been given: it had been taken in a way he approved and he was not sorry he had spoken. And now his wife would at last have a complete change and a rest.

"Marry anyone you like, my dear," he said, "so long as he's a gentleman. One of the Omniums was a curate—a generation or two ago. He was made a bishop finally and addressing letters to him was the very dickens, what with his ecclesiastical and his civil titles. Someone told me at the County Club that one of the Duke of Towers's sons, Lord William Harcourt, has taken Holy Orders. Not a bad thing. He'll be a bishop all right. He has been ordained and probably it's only a question of time till he gets a living. A very good thing for the Church."

But Edith was not interested in Lord William Harcourt; only in herself.

"If you and mother are abroad, father," she said, "it will be awfully dull in the holidays. Or could I come and stay with you? Where is it?"

"Mixo-Lydia," said her father. "They want some professional help to organize their army. What with the Russians and one thing and another I daresay they are right, except that no small army can stand against a surprise attack. We might have to come back earlier. If there's trouble I shall send your mother home by air, of course."

"You've got your strategy arranged, father," said Edith, "and I hope you won't have to use your tactics," which sounded very grown up and she hoped she had not made a silly mistake. Sir Robert laughed and said they might as well go down to the farm and let Goble talk to them about pigs.

CHAPTER 10

Sir Robert was not one of those who, having put his hand to the plough, drew it back, and his furrow was always dead straight. He talked with his wife about Edith and she agreed with him that it would be an excellent thing for her to catch up with the estate management work and why not ask Mrs. Crawley if they would have her at the deanery. Mrs. Crawley seemed genuinely pleased at the thought of a young girl about the house, which was going to feel sadly empty when her granddaughters would no longer be coming to stay with her as they used.

For Grace Crawley all was going smoothly. Mr. Crosse was, within bounds, his own master and the bank was giving him some extra compassionate leave together with a hideous silver punch bowl chased within an inch of its life with a gilded inside. Two of the Wedding Present Committee wished to have Gwyn a Eur incised on the spot which had been left unchased for an inscription, but as no one else knew any Welsh or had read the work of Thomas Love Peacock, another and more normal inscription was adopted. The honeymoon was to be spent in the Pomfrets' villa at Cap Ferrat, kindly offered by the Earl and Countess.

For Jane all was much the same, except that the presents were less expensive because George Halliday was not as well off as Mr. Crosse—which is a very human and normal procedure. To him who hath remains as true as ever, but the second part has been modified and to him who hath not shall a less expensive present be given. But the sisters had no feelings about it, each, we think, being so blissfully certain that her own choice was in every way the better that no rivalry was possible. Edith was of course to be one of the brides-maids. She managed to persuade Mrs. Crawley to choose for them the kind of dress she wanted for herself and showed great intelligence about the decorations, which were to be of a rather harvest-festival description with great swags of greenery and fruit-laden branches.

The Dean's new chaplain, the Reverend Lord William Harcourt, was also most helpful and caused to be sent on loan from his brother the Duke of Towers's great conservatory a number of bay trees and orange trees in tubs which suited the cathedral better than vases of flowers. Lord William had been at the Dean's old college at Oxford and saw eye to eye with him about the new Master of Lazarus, who called himself a Liberal, thus causing several professed wits in their second year to say that to dislike him was a Liberal education; which sounded very well— though, as Mr. Fanshawe, the Dean of Paul's College, remarked, to tell even a Liberal that he was like the Master of Lazarus would be asking for trouble.

If anyone is wondering why the wedding was to be in Barchester and not at the Crawley girls' own home, there are two answers. The first is that it suited us better. The second, which is true but not convincing, is that their parents had always been in subjection to the deanery. Their father because he was very fond of his parents and wished to please them and their mother because she had for many years been a mild invalid, enjoying poor health like anything and all the advantages that it gives one. Most luckily she had not tried to make slaves of her girls, but sent them off to their grandparents whenever possible, which suited the philoprogenitiveness of the deanery very well. Both girls inherited the quiet self-reliance of their great-grandmother, wife of the poor parson at Hogglestock, and as they were very kind to their parents everyone was content.

George Halliday had of course written to his mother about his engagement. In his letter he said that he and Jane would love to have her at the wedding and hoped she would come back to Hatch House while they took a brief honeymoon, and mustn't feel that it wasn't her home because it always would be if she liked it. The latter part of the letter was of course quite untrue. He and Jane had talked a good deal about it. Jane said after all French families and Italian families all lived together and why shouldn't they, which had made George think she really wanted it, so he had tried to show that he also really wanted it, but made a poor business of it. Jane, who had plenty of common sense, then said he had better write to his mother and say they looked forward to seeing her before long. George said he supposed she would like her own bedroom and he had put that looking-glass into the door of the dress cupboard specially for her.

"Well, now it is specially there for me," said Jane. "We will certainly have your mother, darling, but *not* in the best bedroom with the dressing-room and bathroom all opening out of one another. Anyway write to her and tell her we are looking forward very much to seeing her. It's no use making too many plans ahead."

So George wrote a very nice affectionate letter to his mother, putting everything in as kind and pleasant a light as he could, but with rather a sinking heart, and then as a kind of penance he put it in the letter-box himself.

A few days later when Jane came over as usual, George said he had heard from his mother. And he said it so peculiarly that Jane felt a little frightened in case some kind of family row was brewing. But looking at the outsides of letters does not get one anywhere, so she summoned up her courage to read it. George watched her changing face with some amusement.

"Read it aloud, darling," he said, "then you'll feel better."

"If you like," said Jane and read,

"'Dearest George. Many thanks for your delightful long letter about arrangements. I look forward to seeing your wedding with all my heart' and she stopped.

"Go on, old girl," said George. "Its bark is worse than its bite."

"'—but only as a bird of passage,'" Jane went on. "'I have thought a good deal about Hatch End and feel I can hardly face it without your beloved father. Lady de Courcy wants me to spend the winter with her at Villa Thermogène. I have known her for a long time off and on, but out here we have found many acquaintances and tastes in common. The life and the climate suit me so well that I feel better and younger than I have since your father's long illness began. I do feel rather unkind in making this plan, but I know you will understand. When you have time, will you pack the rest of my clothes in one of the big trunks and send it to Lady de Courcy's town house. One of the family is always coming out and would bring it. Give your dear Jane my love and I want her to have all the jewellery I have at the bank. Nothing very exciting except your grandmother's diamond necklace, which I hardly ever wore and certainly shall never wear again.' "Oh George! I don't know what to think."

"Well, nor do I," said George. "It makes one wonder what next."

"I'm sorry if you're sorry, darling," said Jane. "But not being French does make things difficult."

George, not unreasonably, asked what the dickens she meant.

"I mean French families like to live together and English ones don't." said Jane. "But we'll make the other spare room very nice and put another bathroom in and then if she comes to stay as a guest that won't be so bad."

"Not bad," said George. "But I'll tell *you* one now. That small house next to the Old Manor House in the village belongs to me. If mother seriously wants to come home I'll let her have it. I was going to do it up anyway. Look here, old girl, I *must* go down to the pigs. Are you coming? And I'll write a beautiful

letter to mother about how sorry we are and we quite understand."

"Right, darling," said Jane. "But don't make it *too* sorry. She
might come over all maternal and feel her first duty was to you."

"Little beast!" said George in a loving voice. "*Darling* little
beast. Now come on. That runt of a pigling is doing nicely now,
thank goodness. I've had a fair sickener of handfeeding."

Events, for the time being at any rate, moved on in their usual
way. Sir Robert and Lady Graham flew to Mixo-Lydia where
Lady Graham was of course an enormous social success with the
whole aristocracy (if one could call it that) and had the whole of
the resident Corps Diplomatique at her feet. Mrs. Crawley was
most willing to have Edith as a boarder or paying guest during
the autumn term and in a week or so Edith felt quite like a
child—or rather a grandchild—of the house. She went to her
classes every day and for the first time in her life began to
concentrate on what she was doing and enjoy it, discovering also
for the first time the differences between theoretical and practical work, so well correlated by Mr. Squeers, and the value of
knowing why you did what you did; which we hope is clear.

In the Close the Barsetshire Agricultural made very little
impression. Edith, brought up on a gentleman's farm, was
surprised at the total want of interest in livestock shown by the
Crawleys and their friends and felt tempted to follow in the
footsteps of Miss Fanny Squeers and pity their ignorance and
despise them. But when Holdings Goliath was awarded the
First Prize she was puffed up beyond measure and went over to
Holdings on Saturday afternoon to congratulate Goble. Luckily
she went early in the afternoon, for later in the day Goble,
having seen the great champion comfortably back in his own sty,
went off to the Mellings Arms, there drank beer knee to knee
with his friends, was taken home in a wheelbarrow after closing
time and woke next day feeling as fresh as a daisy but a little

vague as to how he found himself in bed fully clothed except for his boots.

Being the youngest of a large family Edith was used to living among her elders and found the society in the Close much to her taste. The Crawleys were old friends as were Sir Robert Field-ing, Chancellor of the Diocese, and his wife, and to a less degree the Jorams. And here the country-bred girl, used to driving anything from one mile to ten miles to parties, or even further when a really good dance was the goal, discovered the pleasures of a closely-knit society all with different outlooks and interests, but united by common dislike of the Palace and—more agreeably—by a common interest in the Close and the Cathe-dral. There were a good many dinner parties to which Mrs. Crawley would willingly have taken her guest, but Edith's good resolutions were holding firm to do her homework every evening, and Mrs. Crawley, approving this, told her friends that Edith could only go out at the weekends.

It was a pleasant deanery custom to have friends to supper on Sunday evenings. But not to cold meat, which when combined with Sunday can be a potent depresser. In Barchester itself it was luckily not too difficult to get servants and the deanery had always kept a very good table, even through the war. To Edith the idea of a party, even a small one, was very welcome, because if one didn't go to parties one couldn't wear one's American dresses and there was one dress of dusty pink taffeta rather like an ankle-length crinoline which she had never worn since she came back to England. Qualms as to its propriety for a Sunday and at the deanery assailed her, so she very sensibly showed it to Mrs. Crawley and asked her advice. Mrs. Crawley, after a private view, said Edith must certainly wear it as it would make everyone feel envious. If Edith had not already made up her mind to do so, Mrs. Crawley's words would certainly have decided her.

So, on a warm evening with a great harvest moon rising, the

dinner guests began to arrive, the first being the Fieldings, followed almost at once by the Jorams and then Mr. and Mrs. Miller from St. Ewold's. Everyone admired Edith's dress; the women quite whole heartedly as even if they could have had one like it not one of them could have carried it off. Everyone began to talk rather more loudly than usual, which cheers a hostess's heart, but they were still a man short.

"I do hope Lord William won't be too late," said Mrs. Crawley to Lady Fielding. "I always expect to see him brought back to the Close on a shutter. He will drive so fast in that two-seater."

Even as she spoke the quiet of the Close was shattered by the noise of a car, apparently doing its best to explode.

"Lord William, I suppose," said Lady Fielding. "Robert feels that he ought to do something about it, but he doesn't quite know what."

"Sometimes it means that he can't stop it and sometimes that he can't start it," said the Dean. "And he can't afford to buy a new one. The Towers family have been badly hit by death duties—two lots far too close together. Death duties are killing our best families," and this was so true that no one answered. During the lifetime of everyone present, except Edith, the fabric of society had been twice rent and shaken to it foundations and then pillaged. There was no hope that things would become better or easier with the mongrel Middle East stirring and the brutality and lust for power of the Slavs and Tartars breaking loose. Better perhaps to spend what one had and enjoy the passing day. The deep-rooted instinct of the nation of shop-keepers had told them to think always of the generation that was to follow them; but now the morrow itself was overcast and doubtful, as all the lesser breeds without the law, obsessed with a blind obedience to ambitious and power-drunk autocrats without tradition, began to kill and take possession. What thought could one take that would not be overturned by them?

What inheritance could be preserved for the children, the grandchildren and the whole future? The prophets must prophesy woe, as they have always done. Perhaps the only truly happy were those who still defended what God had abandoned. Faith in forlorn hopes might save. It had saved. One did not know.

The butler, who was called Verger though it is difficult to believe, then announced Lord William Harcourt and the last guest came in, with apologies for his delay.

"I am so sorry, Mrs. Crawley," he said. "I went to see my people this afternoon and my brother kept me rather a long time over some business."

Mrs. Crawley said in that case he must certainly need some sherry and asked Edith to bring a glass, which she did on a small tray without slopping it. Mrs. Crawley made the introductions.

The combination of a title and a clerical collar is always interesting. Edith, who had never met it before, was fascinated, but behaved very well. Lord William was amused and rather hoped he might be next to her at dinner. Then she went to refill the glass of the other guests and he talked with his hostess.

Presently Verger, who for such occasions almost assumed the role of Toastmaster, exercised by him at the Club of the Upper Servants in the Close, announced dinner. There was no ceremony on Sundays and guests went down anyhow, mostly continuing the talk they had begun upstairs. As Edith had helped Mrs. Crawley to arrange the table she was able to shepherd some of the guests to their places. When she had shown Lord William his seat he stood waiting.

"Oh, I'm not here," said Edith. "I'm over on the other side. And I see Mr. Miller getting lost" and off she went to rescue the vicar of St. Ewold's and put him safely between Mrs. Crawley and Mrs. Joram where he enjoyed himself immensely. Then Edith went to the other side of the table where her neighbours were Sir Robert Fielding and Canon Joram, both very nice comfortable people if not very exciting to a young lady.

It is most important in dinner parties to get everyone talking in couples, only they must be couples in sequence, if we make ourselves clear. At Mrs. Crawley's end all was well, but the Dean had by a gross oversight continued with Lady Fielding a delightful talk begun upstairs about a complaint made by the Barchester Borough Council's Sanitary Inspector of the state of the dustbins at the Palace; whereas he should have been talking to Mrs. Miller. This threw everything out and Edith on one side of the table and Lord William on the other were left stranded. Edith, one of a large family, used to odd numbers, was quite happy to watch the grown-ups (for so she still thought of them) talking away, but Lord William was not comfortable. Not that he felt neglected, but his parents had brought him up properly and he realized that his hostess was a little put out by her husband's inconsiderate behaviour. However, there was nothing to be done about it, so he went on eating his dinner and looking round the table. Edith was doing the same. Their eyes met for a moment. Both saw the funny side of a dinner party out of control and smiled, Edith with a tiny shrug of her pretty shoulders and then a perfect Victorian blush. Blushing has gone out as far as one knows, but it can be very attractive; or at any rate Lord William thought so. Then at last Mrs. Crawley, by a kind of telepathy, or a raising of the eyebrows, or a wifely look in his direction, made her husband realize his lapse and saying to Lady Fielding that he must apologize for having monopolized her, he turned to Mrs. Miller with whom he always got on extremely well. Mrs. Crawley breathed a hostessish sigh of relief. Lady Fielding asked Lord William if he was doing any more family research.

"You were going to write something about the beautiful Duchess of Towers, weren't you?" she said. "That one who was a Hungarian."

"Oh, Mary Seraskier," he said. "She was Hungarian and Irish and a beauty."

"And the good looks go on in the family, don't they," said

Lady Fielding. "Your sisters are so good-looking," but she did not add, So are you, though it would have been quite true.

"I'm glad you think so," said Lord William, "but alas, no relationship with the beautiful duchess. She did have one child, a boy, but he was a bit queer and died. Just as well perhaps. Her husband must have been a very nasty piece of work. He was in the Diplomatic, frightfully good-looking I believe, but seems to have had no other qualities at all, and when he became Duke of Towers he was simply a mass of bad qualities. He led her a terrible life and the doctors all say that was why the boy was queer. Then she managed to get a separation from him. Not a divorce of course—one didn't then—it wasn't done. I think she went in for good works, after that, you know, committees for the poor—who *were* poor then. My wicked relation died unregretted without an heir and my father's people came in. They are all highly respectable. So am I, as far as I know."

Lady Fielding said she had seen somewhere a photograph of that Duchess and she was certainly very lovely—a pure George du Maurier type. Lord William said his people had the photograph, done in Hungary by a man with a name of ten consonants and only two vowels so that none of them could pronounce it, and he hoped she would come and see it some time. Then they talked very comfortably about the Close and, as was inevitable at any party in the Close, got onto the Palace, where we can happily leave them.

Mrs. Joram and Mr. Miller were well away about the council at Grumper's End, which unsalubrious slum of Pomfret Madrigal had now become a large building estate where the oppressed working class got houses with all mod. con., a nice bit of garden, and one or more large TV aerials on every roof for practically nothing. But as none of the inhabitants noticed the aerials and had the Telly on at full blast from the opening item at three to the closing down late at night, not to speak of the ordinary Home Service from 6:25 A.M. to the bitter end at 11:13 P.M., and if asked by any member of the family to turn it off or down, always said Ow, I didn't notice it was on, we need not feel nor waste sympathy for or on them.

"But when I go to Grumper's End, where I still have a few friends," said Mrs. Joram, much of whose life when she was Mrs. Brandon had been spent near what was then only a country slum, "what really interests me is the way the language has changed."

Mr. Miller begged for a further explanation.

"Well, when I was a little girl, it was a loydy with a boyby, and then it turned into a lydy with a byby," she said. "And now it is a woman with a kid."

Mr. Miller said indeed, indeed such changes in popular speech were most interesting and whereas the clergyman used to be Parson and later, owing to the war-language, Padre, it was now mostly Mister. He had, he said, been addressed as Holy Joe and would very much like to deserve the title except that his Christian name was not Joseph. Then Mrs. Joram asked for news of the present incumbent, Mr. Parkinson, a very good and conscientious vicar, and his nice hard-working wife with three nice children.

"Both being as good as gold and the church is quite three-quarters full on Sundays," said Mr. Miller. "I wish it had been so when I was there, but these things are sent to try us."

"But, my dear Mr. Miller," said Mrs. Joram, "there weren't enough people then. Pomfret Madrigal was only a village with those cottages out at Grumper's End. Now it is almost a small town so of *course* more people go to church," which was a rather specious argument but cheered Mr. Miller a good deal and he said a great many people came out from Barchester to St. Ewold's and he was wondering if to all his blessings a curate might be added. He looked up the table, saw his wife comfortably talking with the Dean and smiled; for she was his chief blessing.

Mrs. Crawley and Sir Robert Fielding were talking West Barsetshire County Council and Edith looked quite happy with

Canon Joram, so Mrs. Crawley stopped being a hostess and allowed herself to enjoy her own dinner party.

After dinner when the ladies were in the drawing-room they were able at last to have a really good talk about he Crawleys' granddaughters and their double wedding. To the Dean's not very well-controlled delight the Bishop would be back from his holiday, so for him would the uncomfortable episcopal throne be prepared; above his head that small open window would—it was hoped—shed down a draught that would bring him as many ills as Prospero sent upon Caliban and shorten up his Lordship's sinews with ague cramps; though this of course was not said in so many words. And, as the Dean explained with a commiseration that did not in the least deceive anyone, the Bishop, being robed, would be all the colder.

Lady Fielding invited Edith to come and sit by her which Edith, on her best behaviour and enjoying it, willingly did. Then, remembering how her mother had told her more than once that people would like much better if one asked them about themselves than if one talked about one's own doings, she asked Lady Fielding how her daughter Anne was, for the Fieldings' only child had married Robin Dale, a cousin of the present Lady Silverbridge, better known to the reading public as Lisa Bedale, the author of a number of very good detective stories. Lady Fielding said Anne was very well and so were the twins and their brother. And then, wishing to reward Edith for her politeness, asked her what she was doing.

Edith, whose mother had also advised her to speak when she was spoken to, very willingly gave a brief account of her own doings during the last year or two, including her visit to America.

Lady Fielding said it sounded very pleasant and what was she doing now.

"Well, I didn't behave very well," said Edith, who felt that Lady Fielding was a person who would see through one if one pretended. "I went to stay at the Towers and go to Barchester every day to the College of Estate Management, because I like pigs and I could help father with the farm, but then Uncle David—do you know him, David Leslie, and Rose, that's his wife—asked me to go to America with them. It was wonderful but when I came back I felt rather awful and mean."

Lady Fielding said she was sorry about the meanness, but probably it would wear off.

"Oh, it has," said Edith, "because father was Severe and then George Halliday and John-Arthur Crosse both got engaged, so I thought I had better work really hard and I am living at the deanery while father and mother are in Mixo-Lydia."

"Oh yes, I know their Ambassadress," said Lady Fielding. "She came to us as a kind of cook-general during the war and took a degree by correspondence course before she went back to Mixo-Lydia. It was very nice to find her as Ambassadress here. She comes to stay with us sometimes. And have you enjoyed the party tonight?"

Edith said very much. But what she was really most looking forward to was the double wedding in the cathedral, partly because she was going to be a bridesmaid and partly because she had never seen a wedding before with so many clergymen helping.

Lady Fielding, amused and a little touched by the mixture in her young friend of grown-upness and the schoolroom, said the Close was delighted about it, on the very reasonable ground that the bishop was known to disapprove.

"May I come and join you, Lady Fielding?" said an agreeable voice and there was Lord William, looking down on them in a friendly way from his considerable height.

"Oh, do," said Lady Fielding. "This is Edith Graham whose father you know of course—Sir Robert Graham."

Lord William said he had seen him several times at the County Club, but being a very new member himself he had been too shy to speak to him.

"Oh, father isn't a *bit* like that really," said Edith. "Of course," she added, having still a lively memory—though entirely without rancour—of her father's plain speaking, "he can be a *little* fierce. I mean," she added, going rather pink in the face, "he nearly always does know better than other people, but he doesn't say so unless they are being nuisances—like Lord Aberfordbury the one that was Sir Ogilvy Hibberd."

"Your words double my admiration for Sir Robert," said Lord William and then he and Lady Fielding plunged into Close-and-County gossip while Edith listened and idly wondered how much Lord William's clerical suit cost. She knew how difficult her three brothers had found it, while they were still growing or broadening, to have civilian clothes up to the standard of the Brigade, and remembered the unfortunate year when, owing to backing the wrong horse for the Oaks, they had only two really good evening suits among them and had to toss for them.

Soon, as was almost inevitable, the double marriage of the deanery granddaughters came up and here Edith was on sure ground for was she not to be a bridesmaid. Lord William, amused and attracted by this pretty, well-mannered girl, so encouraged her that she was getting a little above herself when Lady Fielding gave her, though quite kindly, a Mother's Look. Edith at once subsided, at the same time managing to convey to Lord William an impression that she could, if she were not checked, give him a good deal of the low-down on Close Politics.

"I suppose," said Lord William, "you have heard the latest news about the Palace."

Lady Fielding said Not since the Bishop's wife tried to sell the hideous dress she had worn for every garden party for the last no one knew how many years, but no one would buy it, so she would probably be wearing it for the Crawley wedding—for so everyone called the ceremony, completely disregarding the bridegrooms.

"Well, one oughtn't to repeat gossip about one's spiritual

superior," said Lord William, "but my mother's maid did hear from the mother of the Palace kitchenmaid—who is giving notice—that the Bishopess had insisted on her husband wearing an old pair of woollen combinations in the cathedral because of the draughts getting under his episcopal robes. They were moth-eaten, I understand, and the head housemaid was told to darn them and said they weren't worth the darning. There the matter rests."

Edith couldn't help laughing and a very pretty laugh, Lord William thought; but Lady Fielding, though she had immensely enjoyed this gossip, felt that was enough—as perhaps did Lord William, for he did not enlarge on the words which had made Miss Graham laugh so delightfully.

The date of the double wedding had now for various reasons been finally settled for October, by which date the heating would be on in the Cathedral—though without prejudice to the little window above the Bishop's Throne being inadvertently left open. This gave satisfaction on the whole, as even in summer a cathedral can be chilly and it always took some time to get the furnace going properly. There had been talk of having the whole heating system converted to oil, but the Dean had been against it and to judge by further ominous and uncomfortable occurrences in Egypt and elsewhere it might be that the question of oil would—as the *Barchester Chronicle* said—loom large in our domestic economy; though, as Lord William said to Mrs. Crawley at a small lunch party, it would more probably loom small. The ladies present had smiled but obviously did not know what he meant and he wished Edith with her ready laughter were there; but she always had lunch during the week at her estate management college.

On the following Saturday Edith went to see Madame Tomkins in Barley Street about the bridesmaids' dresses. When she got back she heard voices in the drawing-room and there to her joyful surprise she found her mother with Mrs. Crawley.

"Oh mother! how *lovely*," she said, stifling her own voice in a violent embrace. "I didn't know you were coming."

"Nor did I," said Lady Graham, "but your father thought I had better."

Edith asked why—much to Mrs. Crawley's relief, who was longing to ask the same question herself but felt she might be intruding.

"My husband," said Lady Graham to Mrs. Crawley, "doesn't much like the look of things in Mixo-Lydia. Not that anything is actually wrong there yet, but Robert says he thinks there will be a lot of trouble in Middle Europe soon and as the Slavo-Lydians next door are very Russian in their outlook anything might happen. So he sent me back by plane with a charming man from the French Embassy in London, who turned out to be an old friend, a Monsieur Boulle. His family took the vicarage at Rushwater—my father's mother's place where Martin and Sylvia live now—one summer when Edith was very small and she fell into the pond and Monsieur Boulle went into it in his white flannel trousers because they were all playing tennis and got her out. I have asked him to come down and stay with us."

Mrs. Crawley said how delightful and wouldn't Lady Graham stay to lunch, which she did and the three ladies had a very pleasant time. As there was to be a great trying on of the bridesmaids' dresses that afternoon, Mrs. Crawley asked Lady Graham if she would care to see them, which offer was accepted with pleasure, for Lady Graham had inherited from her mother Lady Emily Leslie a passion for poking, in the kindest possible way, into other people's affairs.

Accordingly after lunch a bevy of charming young ladies turned up, not at all shy and with very pretty manners, followed close upon by Madame Tomkins herself, the dresses having been fetched earlier in the day by one of Mrs. Crawley's staff. There was a suitable amount of mutual admiration and giggling among the girls. We do not know who they were, but they were mostly about Edith's age and had very nice manners. Lady

Graham thought Edith was the prettiest and most elegant among them, but naturally did not say so. When the girls had peacocked and enjoyed themselves and Madame Tomkins had put in a pin or snipped a stitch to let something out everyone changed back into day clothes and went home, as did Madame Tomkins, leaving the dresses to be taken back to her lodgings.

It was a pleasant afternoon so Mrs. Crawley and Edith walked with Lady Graham across the Close. So far Edith had not had any chance to be alone with her mother, but while Mrs. Crawley stopped to talk to a Minor Canon she said she supposed she could come home now her mother was back. Lady Graham, who had talked over this possibility with her husband, said Edith had better stay with Mrs. Crawley, as arranged, for the rest of the term, otherwise everything would be unsettled again.

We regret to have to state—for Edith has been improving a great deal lately—that she behaved very badly. She was enough in fear (though an affectionate fear) of her mother not to stamp, or say anything rude, but her face did not take the faintest trouble to disguise its owner's feelings and Lord William Harcourt, almost running into them round a corner, was perturbed by what he saw. Edith quickly smoothed out her sulky looks and made Lord William known to Lady Graham, who at once remembered having met the Duchess of Towers at the Omniums some years ago and the two fell into families, while Edith, back in the schoolroom or the nursery by now, walked in sulky silence a little behind them.

"I am so glad to have met you again," said Lady Graham. "You must come and dine with us when my husband is back," which Lord William said he would be delighted to do. Then Lady Graham heard the cathedral clock booming three and said she must really be going home as those nice Carters from the Old Manor House were coming to tea at four. She kissed her daughter affectionately, gave her hand in farewell to Lord William, and went away through the Close gate to the White Hart where she had left the car.

Lord William turned to go back to his work and saw Edith, who was busy working herself into a rage. She had not done this for some time now, but one cannot lose a bad habit all in a moment. It was an uncomfortable situation for him. He did not particularly want to force himself upon her in her present mood. Not that he was afraid, for fear was hardly in his nature, but he was not sure if he would do any good by noticing Edith's moods.

Edith however, who had plenty of courage, saved him the trouble by sniffing inelegantly and saying, "Don't look at me, please. I'm in a horrible temper."

"Then," said Lord William, in a very ordinary voice, "let me come with you into the cloisters. I always find them soothing," and he took a step in that direction. Edith followed him and then walked by his side into what we must truthfully call the chill air of the cloisters and the chill of the paving stones which perpetually sweated damp. They walked once round in silence.

"I'm sorry," said Edith in a very small voice.

"Not half so sorry as I am," said Lord William kindly.

"Well, I'd be sorry for myself if anyone was as beastly to them as I've just been," said Edith.

"It depends upon the kind of sorriness, I think," said Lord William. "I'm not sorry for myself. I am so very sorry for you because you are unhappy."

"I don't think I'm exactly unhappy," said Edith, trying hard to disentangle her feeling. "I'm mortified," which word she brought out with some pride.

"Sometimes mortification isn't a bad thing," said Lord William. "There's something or other by Bach about Mortify us by Thy Grace. I've heard it in the cathedral. Now, could you stop being mortified?" which words he said so kindly that Edith felt it would be unkind to disappoint him and said she had quite stopped now.

"I do like your mother so much," said Lord William. "I think she and my mother would get on splendidly. Perhaps Lady Graham would bring you to lunch one day. Mother has a very charming house. We used to live at Harcourt Abbey, a ghastly place, but luckily my father managed to unload it onto a big sporting syndicate before he died. They shoot and fish and have tennis—I mean Royal tennis with a proper court indoors—and golf and fishing and pretty well everything and we live our own lives. My brother and his wife have a very pleasant house too. She was an American and makes a very good duchess and had some money, which was just as well, for we haven't much."

"And where do *you* live?" said Edith.

"Oh, anywhere," said Lord William. "You see, I'm the youngest. I live partly at home with my mother and my two elder sisters and I have lodgings here. But if I get a living of course I'll live in the parsonage. My brother has several livings and he said he would let me have the first vacant one when I got married."

"Oh, I didn't know you were married," said Edith, in a cheerful voice, though she suddenly felt rather low and unhappy.

"You couldn't, because I'm not," said Lord William. "I ought to have said If I got married. But I hadn't thought much about it till lately."

Edith's heart jumped unaccountably and then fell several hundred feet. But she was not a general's daughter for nothing.

"Well, I hope your wife will be nice," she said.

"So do I," said Lord William. "Of course she might be difficult."

"But you could always help a person not to be difficult," said Edith, determined not to show any feeling of any kind.

"I don't know," said Lord William. "Some people are difficult and one might want very much to help them and they wouldn't let you. Perhaps they don't understand—or they don't believe in you."

"If anyone could help me to stop being myself—" said Edith, who was looking at—though with unseeing eyes—the stone in memory of Mistrefs Pomphelia Tadstock, thrice married, widow of a Canon of Barchester. "But they can't."

"No, I suppose not," said Lord William. "But they might help you to tidy yourself up a bit, and to laugh at yourself sometimes."

To his surprise Edith, her face towards the open arches of the cloisters while his back was turned to the light, blushed slowly and deeply.

"If only I *could* laugh at myself I'd be all right," she said. "At least I would feel encouraged."

"If you will let me laugh at you—and with you—you will feel quite encouraged," said Lord William.

"But I don't like being laughed at," said Edith.

"Of course you don't if it's your family," said Lord William. "But an outsider—a friendly outsider of course—is quite different."

"Is it?" said Edith, looking up at his considerable height.

"William!" said a pleasant rather authoritative voice.

The couple almost sprang apart.

"Mother!" said Lord William. "and Gwendolen and Elaine! What luck. This is Edith Graham, mother. Her father is General Sir Robert Graham and her mother is a daughter of old Lady Emily Leslie."

"I remember Lady Emily very well," said the Dowager Duchess of Towers, "and her sister Lady Agnes Foster who had a passion for the clergy and died unmarried. It is very pleasant to know Lady Emily's granddaughter."

To Edith's deep interest, who had only read of such things in books, the Dowager Duchess unhooked a face-à-main from her rather majestic bosom, put it up and looked at Edith.

"Very nice," she said. "Your father would have liked her, William. He used to pinch pretty girls, but he always was twenty years behind the times. These are William's sisters," she added, addressing Edith. "I can't think why they don't marry. Gwendolen has such a passion for celibate clergy that I have given up hope. Very un-English this celibate business—it's only because she hasn't fallen in love yet. Elaine was engaged to a hunting man near us, Dobby Fitzgorman, but he broke his neck."

Edith, rather overwhelmed by these ducal annals, said she was very sorry.

"No need, my dear," said the Duchess. "The Duke wouldn't have allowed her to marry him in any case. He was a Liberal and shot foxes. Do you ride?"

"Oh, we all ride," said Edith. "My three brothers who are in the Brigade all ride to hounds when they get leave, but I only ride for fun and I'm rather frightened of jumping."

"Quite right, my dear," said the Duchess. "Don't think of jumping when you are married till you have started a nursery. I nearly lost Elaine that way, but it wasn't the mare's fault. She shied when that man Hibberd tried to stroke her. Quite right. I'd have shied in her place, but not with myself in an interesting condition riding me. How old are you?"

Edith, by now feeling as if she were in a kaleidoscope, said nearly nineteen.

"A dull age, but one gets through it," said the Duchess. "Do you know the Palace?"

Rightly understanding her Grace to mean the Bishop and Bishopess, Edith said her mother was always polite to them and both her parents dined at the Palace once a year and asked it back when they knew it would be away.

"When I was small," she said, "I made a poem about the bishop, because he took away the bell in the pond that the fish used to ring for their dinner. It ended 'And now the bishop is in hell.'"

The Duchess appeared to take the liveliest pleasure in these words and Lord William thought his beloved and slightly eccentric mamma would slap her thigh, as she did at home when amused, but she didn't; possibly from a feeling that Edith needed to learn the family ways by degrees.

"And do you do anything, my dear?" said the Duchess.

"I am going to the College of Estate Management in

Barchester," said Edith. "That's partly why I am staying with Mrs. Crawley just now. Father and mother were abroad. Mother has come back but father hasn't yet."

"You must let me know when Edith's people are back, William," said the Duchess, "and I will ask them to dinner. Just ourselves. You will like my eldest son, my dear. He does all the right things in the county and sits in the Lords, though what good that does now one really does not know, except that it gets him to London and he can go to meetings of the Royal Society. His wife races. Do you race?"

Edith said she had been to a lot of point-to-points but never to a real race.

"You ought to go to Ascot," said the Duchess. "Of course you have been presented."

Edith said her sister Clarissa had been, but she hadn't yet.

"I shall speak to your mother about it," said the Duchess.

"Put the brake on, mamma," said Lord William. "You always did plunge at your fences. Give Edith time."

"I was called The Plunger when I was a girl," said her Grace with some dignity, "and so I am. If no one plunged, we wouldn't get anywhere. I shall call upon Lady Graham. One of the girls can drive me. Now I must go. Come along, girls," and the ducal party went away.

"Good girl," said Lord William, as he and Edith went back into the Close.

Edith asked why.

"Standing up to mamma, and being nice to Gwendolen and Elaine. They don't have much of a time."

"Well, when I'm married I'll find the two nicest clergymen in Barsetshire and jolly well *make* them marry them," said Edith firmly.

Lord William said Why clergymen. Not, he added, that he had anything against them, being one himself, with every hope of becoming a married one some day.

"I don't know," said Edith. "It just came into my head. But

they must be clergymen with good backgrounds and some money of course," and as they were now at the deanery they parted. Lady Fielding, who was passing at the moment, smiled at them and went on to her own house, where she told her husband that Lord William and Edith Graham were a case. Her husband chided her for the lowness of her speech and they talked of other things.

Two weddings in one book would be one too many, so much as we should like to do so, we will not describe the scene in the cathedral at any length. The dark bride and the fair bride each looked as lovely as the other. Both the best men had the ring ready and each managed to keep his principal fairly calm. The Dean performed the ceremony at the chancel steps with dignity and deep feeling.

All right-thinking people will be glad to hear that the Bishop was in a most unpleasant position, enthroned below the open window, so that by the time he was escorted to the Altar he was cheerless, cold, and cross, did not linger over the Blessing and deliberately did not read the noble Exhortation which follows it. There was a general hope among right-thinking people that a thunderbolt would fall on his Lordship (though not touching anyone else in his neighbourhood), but it did not. It was however understood that he had subsequently one of the worst colds the Palace had known and that his wife had refused to give him the hot rum and water which would probably have nipped it in the bud. But this is only hearsay.

Edith as chief bridesmaid had looked forward to this day and it was even more exciting than she had expected; at least exciting was the word she used when telling her mother about it, but we think that what her young inconstant spirit felt was a peace that passed all understanding, transcending all the ups and downs and excitements of the last year. As she walked down the aisle with the other bridesmaids, behind the brides and their bridesmaids, she saw Lord William and tried not to look at him. He also tried to concentrate on the ceremony, when suddenly, sweetly, strangely, as Lord Tennyson wrote, his eyes were met by hers.

COLOPHON

Angela Thirkell, granddaughter of Pre-Raphaelite artist Edward Burne–Jones, was born in London in 1890. At the age of twenty-eight she moved to Melbourne, Australia but did not begin writing novels until her return to Britain in 1930 after which she produced almost a book a year until her death in 1961.

The text of this book was set in Caslon, a typeface designed by William Caslon I (1692-1766). This face designed in 1725 has gone through many incarnations. It was the mainstay of British printers for over one hundred years and remains very popular today. The version used here is Adobe Caslon. The display faces are Adobe Caslon Outline, Calligraphic 421, and Adobe Caslon.

Composed by Alabama Book Composition, Deatsville, Alabama.

A Double Affair was printed by Data Reproductions, Auburn Hills, Michigan on acid free paper.